Georgi

Betwixt and Between©

By

Sipho Ernest Mahlobo

PHYSICAL ADDRESS:
61422 Motel Road,
Mqedandaba,
Estcourt,
KwaZulu/Natal
South Africa
3330.

Front Cover Image Created by
JialiMediaBooks
Edited by
Liwa Maldina Creative Arts

The problem with the stigma around
mental health is really about the
stories that we tell ourselves as a society
-Matthew Quick-

A writer should cause trouble.
-Henry A Giroux-

CHAPTER 1

Prologue

Hi! I'm Odessa. The story I'm about to share is a cathartic family tale full of secrets. It features a rollercoaster of events wrapped in ill-advised, fatal attractions.

The intelligence intrigue and post-apartheid political paranoia fill the narrative with deception, making every claim from the fickle characters close to us unreliable.

I share these episodes because they help me stay connected to my little sister, with whom I have a symbiotic relationship that goes back to our toddler days.

As you'll see, our closeness is a recipe that pulls us deeper into the devil's abyss.

However, recounting our past, as I do here, will hopefully serve as a restorative retreat.

Odessa has a Little Sister.

Odessa emerges from the Rosedale Subway and strides purposefully through her familiar neighborhood. She is feeling a bit restless this time because she believes her days on Canada's snowy plains and hills are ending. A wave of dread gradually creeps into her thoughts, along with rising misgivings from her parents about her supposed journey. Her favorite Beatles song, 'Here Comes the Sun,' has become her confidence-boosting mantra.

Odessa was a toddler when her parents discovered the icy North American country. They lived briefly in London and moved when Kian, the patriarch, joined the Bank of Montreal. Two decades have passed since then, and the affluent suburb of Rosedale is firmly rooted in their hearts.

Odessa knows Toronto like the back of her hand. It is her only home with any familial roots and memories. She wakes up full of wonder about the strange country at the southernmost tip of Africa and vows to take action regarding it.

Understandably, butterflies keep whirling in her stomach about her make-believe venture: how lonely it will be without her parents, friends, or little sister; or how she will cope, since he cannot speak the languages of her ancestors!

In Toronto, the first snowflakes of early fall have been melting in mid-air. Fitful and hesitant airstreams tease gently, playfully reminding us of the unkind wintry weather ahead. The sun has been growing paler and weaker. Yet, today is one to enjoy before the severe arctic temperatures begin to take hold, picking up pace and gaining control. Human nature's fickle emotions are easy prey for the overpowering caprice of inclement conditions. As she skirts around the silent part of Rosedale-Moore Park, Odessa shouts raucously, 'Well, Ontario, you can keep your freezing weather. '

She inhales the woody scent of century-old decaying tree bark and sun-drenched flowers nudged by frisky swarms of bees. Then she pauses and sighs, "On the other hand, I love fall with its foliage display! I adore this Ken Thomson corner of the world, Africa or not!"

Anyone studying Odessa's demeanor—her calm, self-assured expression, high cheekbones, and almond-shaped eyes gazing stoically—would find no hint of her inner conflict as she hums her sunny tune in her heart. To all appearances, a faithful black ice maiden walks, confident in every step and move. The proud tilt of her head, her lithe stride, and her tall, inviting body all attract recurrent appreciative glances.

The 27-year-old Odessa stumbled upon her frosty feminine world during her teens, when she suddenly became aware of her own body, realizing that for a girl to feel good about herself, she had to conform to the crowd. All the teachers' pets she knew were mostly nice-looking, unintelligent, and having a great time at school. Her self-esteem took a battering one morning when she overheard a bunch of white boys refer to her as 'Professor', an unflattering tag for 'bright but not so cute'.

Even so, it later dawned on her that she could not be herself while following the crowd simultaneously. She thought, 'Nature gave me quality brains plus a great African body. How I look to outsiders is their problem, not mine.' In retrospect, she had found parental motivation, laced though it was with thinly veiled sarcasm, quite compelling; 'Walk tall, girl,' they would each repeat. But even at her age, the secret battle inside continues.

Odessa has a younger sister, an elegant woman who carries herself with confidence wherever she goes. When she was younger, Georgi enjoyed riding bicycles, going swimming, and playing soccer as a goalkeeper. Luca, Odessa's boyfriend, once described Georgi as a wild girl — a volcano erupting unexpectedly and disrupting every situation. The sisters have been inseparable since they were toddlers, surviving on a rollercoaster of a symbiotic relationship due to their different personalities. While she always acts sisterly and cultured toward Georgi outwardly, she secretly harbors deep resentment. Occasionally, their rivalry would break out openly like a furious rush of waves crashing against the Wild Coast rocks, but over time, it would fade away like ripples that only circle beneath the surface.

Monica shrieks like a Cockatoo.

It's been a long while since the siblings have had an open catfight, one that their parents once witnessed. One day, during their silly, juvenile season, the girls got into a little scuffle that left their egos bruised. Odessa had accused Georgi of her sleepwalking habit, which disturbed her peaceful sleep. Georgi's rage turned unpleasant when Odessa poked fun at her over her sleepwalking. Georgi grabbed a pair of scissors and stabbed her sister, whose defensive wounds had to be attended to by Ellen, their long-suffering mother. Georgi sustained a red nose, while Odessa had her yellow miniskirt ripped off her body and tossed out the kitchen window. As Ellen tried to deal with Odessa's injuries, Georgi kept threatening to kill them both.

When their father returned from work, he found Odessa heavily bandaged, while Georgi sat on the porch, immersed in her Vogue magazine. Although Kian was disturbed by what had happened, he instructed Odessa to keep the incident under wraps. After pondering how to de-escalate the potentially volatile situation, he summoned his 'disruptive' Georgi inside for an explanation. But, upon laying her eyes on Odessa, Georgi shouted, to everyone's bewilderment, "What happened to you?"

"What happened? You attacked me, you moron. Where the hell does the red blood on your shirt come from?"

"Why did you stab Odessa?" asked Kian, breathless with alarm.

"Who stabbed Odessa?" Georgi responded irritably.

Kian remained mystified while Ellen felt she was holding a demon with both hands. As for Odessa, she was seething inside, considering the most effective method of avenging herself on the fair-skinned sister she had tolerated for a long time.

After supper, Kian grounded both girls for two weeks, during which time they were not allowed to watch television or entertain their teenage visitors. He had further 'encouraged' them, using more stick than carrot, to memorize the lyrics from the Beatles' tune, *'We can work it out'*, and to recite every evening during the 'sentence'. Ellen secretly took Georgi to a mental clinic for observation while she accused her mother of paranoia.

During a quiet night of punishment, the girls begin to open up and pretend to be friends again. Thinking she is being deep, Odessa says the Europeans will pay for making black lives a living hell.

Georgi says, "How will you make them pay, Odessa?"

"We can begin by pushing them and pulling their hair."

"You know their police will clamp your butt with zip ties for that."

"I can't stand white people."

"Anyone in particular? You can't just go about hating every white person."

"All of them until they prove they are normal human beings. No normal human can be a racist."

"You don't hate Mrs Hitler or Miss Rybakov, do you?"

"Not anymore; not after they fixed Monica's rabble rousers. But white people tolerate us. How should I feel about such people?"

Mrs Hitler was a label given to the principal for being a strict disciplinarian. Monica, a 12-year-old soccer enthusiast, was a trusted goalkeeper on Rosedale's A-team for over eight months. One day, the coach, Miss Rybakov, puts Monica on the bench and replaces her with 12-year-old Georgi. The match is crucial for both competing teams, as they have reached the semifinals. However, as the Scarborough Primary players finalize their tactics in their locker room, the Rosedale players get embroiled in the Monica storm that threatens to scupper the entire match. Led by Monica's mother, several white parents are shouting, accusing Rybakov and the school's sports department of applying

Affirmative Action. The principal suggests that Monica, the white girl, resume her original position. Against all expectations, the coach stands her ground, arguing that neither the principal nor the parents has any knowledge of soccer. When they realize that the Affirmative Action card carries little weight, the white parents start accusing Rybakov of being a communist, whereupon a scuffle ensues between two learners, one white and the other Indian.

To settle the dispute, the principal makes her final decision: Each goalkeeper, that is, Monica and Georgi, will face eleven 'penalty kicks,' taken one after the other by members of each team. The goalkeeper with the most saves will be declared the winner.

Both Monica and Georgi make six saves each out of ten. It is now up to the last two kicks to determine the fate of the goalkeepers. The air is tense when Kian, Ellen, and Odessa appear on the pitch. The nail-biting atmosphere deepens when Monica clears her seventh kick. Should Georgi fail to clear, the game is over.

When Georgi tries to hold on to the ball from one left-handed kicker, it slips from her grip and rolls around the penalty area. The kicker follows up to administer a perfect goal. The ground erupts, but the referee disallows it, invoking her penalty shootout rules.

After a further stand-off, the principal makes her final ruling: "Let's toss a coin to decide who will be the goalkeeper. And this is final."

Georgi triumphs, and Monica shrieks like a cockatoo. Her mother and white supporters stomp out of the sports grounds, leaving a teary Monica reeling in confusion. Georgi's faction, mainly black, rallies behind her, chanting Nina Simone's 'To be young, gifted and black'. After a while, Monica slowly walks up to Georgi, and as they hug, the crowd cheers excitedly.

The embrace goes on forever, and neither wishes to pull away until Monica says, "Do your best, Georgi. Good Luck. Protect our A-Team. We must win."

Many years have passed since those exciting times of soccer games. Georgi lost contact with Monica after she emigrated to New Zealand with her mother. For her part, Georgi has grown into a young lady with hazel eyes and a dazzling smile that melts even the frostiest hearts. She loves poetry and writes 'scraps and knick-knacks', as she calls them. However, she occasionally loses control and shreds to a pulp anything she has written. Ellen, her mother, has expressed frustration at Georgi's bad habit of shredding her writings.

"You will regret the day you lose your God-given talent," she once said; to which Georgi retorted, "If God had seriously needed my poetry, he would not have created all these puffed-up armchair critics with empty portfolios."

"Odessa, you mean?"

"Everybody. Odessa could be encouraging of what I do as my big sister."

Thinking about it carefully, Georgi could hardly remember shredding her work. Whenever she felt miserable, she would march outside and lie spread-eagled on the lawn or, if inside, on the bedroom carpet; a habit Ellen found downright annoying.

Ellen bought Georgi a present: a book of poetry by Diana Ferrus, which she wedged between her pillows. Georgi owns two bookcases: the smaller one is labeled 'Poetry' and the other, 'Miscellaneous'. She pulls out Ferrus' anthology, her gift, and showcases it among 'prominent writers'. Ellen gave Georgi another book, saying, "Read and understand that the indigent and wealthy can only live a full life if they navigate together."

"Oh, that's profound, Mama."

"What's profound is the idea of feeding and clothing the needy without making them feel inferior."

"I love you, Mother, because you appreciate my poetry, that's why."

"Okay, I confess; I stole that line from your secret poem, 'False Faith'.

"You mean the one about feeding the indigent without making them feel inferior? I know Mama."

CHAPTER 2

Nice legs.

Odessa has always felt uneasy about Georgi's appearance, especially her fair skin, which has become more noticeable as the siblings grow taller. While the rest of the family has dark, black hair, Georgi's fluffy, 'candy-floss' hair has never sat well with her keen-eyed, black-haired sister. Naturally, a hint of jealousy sneaks into her thoughts. Light-skinned girls often get first choice, higher grades, and more breaks in Canadian society... and in cultures around the world. Their chances in love tend to be much brighter, Odessa knows from experience. Fair-skinned girls always carry cultural advantages with them, no matter where they are from, and people with narrow minds pay more attention when such girls share their opinions.

While Georgi's hairstyle receives mixed admiration and approval, Odessa's kinky hair sparks political debate or subtle mockery. When she attempts to change it using various Afro hair products, some Left-Wing individuals, primarily men, criticize her for betraying her black heritage.

Odessa once lamented privately to Ellen, her mother, "You know, Mama, Georgi does nothing to her straight tresses all week long; then the guys cheer, 'Oh, how unique that hairdo is. I do the same thing, leave my Diaspora kinky unattended for one day, and it's, 'better start doin' something about that tight coil, Girl'. I hate the Angela Davis armchair fan club."

"Oh Lord," her mother had responded, 'Lead us not into temptation. Amen'.

Odessa once expressed similar feelings of unease about her African looks to Okobi, her platonic boyfriend from Ghana. Okobi said, "But you are pretty for a black girl, Odessa."

"For a black girl...?"

"You know what I mean."

"No. What do you mean?"

"Pedantry will cause you palpitations and heart failure, Odessa."

"Since I am pretty for a black girl, what do you think of Georgi?"

"Georgi?"

"Yes, Georgi."

"She's pretty, too."

"Are you saying I am as pretty as Georgi?"

"Yes."

"You know, Okobi, I was thinking of getting down on my knees to propose."

"Marriage? Me?"

"But I've changed my mind."

"Why?"

"You're not my type."

"Type? Just because of what I said? You know how it is. It was a slip of the tongue. You are pretty, period."

"Yeah, right."

"You always try to put me in a corner. You know I enjoy everything about you…"

"Spare me your vanity."

"Why worry, Odessa? What I see is a wholesome African woman to die for. Besides, the blacker the berry, the sweeter the juice."

"Yeah? I guess you recite the same line to all your dumb African girls."

"No, I'm fond of you. I hope that one day you and I will take our friendship to the next level. We can start our foreplay right now. I learn it takes time for a woman to warm up."

"Where do you want to start?"

"I don't know. Why don't we hug and kiss?"

"Have you ever escalated your friendship with any girl, Okobi?'

"No. Odessa. As a woman of the world, you can show me the ropes,' Okobi chuckled and disappeared.

Ironically, Okobi's hollow wisecrack, 'the blacker the berry the sweeter the juice', did some trick as Odessa began to walk a little taller from then on.

Tonight is the night. Odessa approaches home with a sense of unease. She has memorized the lines she hopes to recite before her family, in the hopes of making a good impression. Her mouth is slightly dry, and her heartbeat bumpy and firm against her breast as she approaches the covered porch. She is about to face her parents with what they might view as earth-shattering discoveries or plain silly. It will not please them, for sure.

Armed with her debating skills, she uses to soften hearts; she pulls open the glossy screen door and inadvertently lets it slam violently behind her.

Luckily, Ellen and Kian are up to their hilarious fun, dancing to the tune of *'Jambalaya'* by Fats Domino like young lovers. Once that is over, they settle down, pretending to be serious.

"Was that the Bill Haley dance, Mom?" Asks Odessa from the serving hatch.

"No, that was the Ellen-Kian Tango," quips Kian.

Ellen has been showing signs of frayed nerves lately, which is why Kian's attempt to revive fading passions is notable.

"Hi, Mom, Dad."

True to form, Ellen shouts, "You're late. Freshen up, sit down, and eat. We have asked the Good Lord to bless the meal even in your absence," she points out.

With a fresh smirk, Odessa pauses near the doorway and surveys her family congregating around the dining room table. She thinks they look like a black television commercial and half smiles at the stray thought.

Ellen is one of the few women Odessa has ever seen wearing an apron and cooking real food from scratch, rather than stocking the refrigerator with takeaways. Her bank-official father, known as Kian, is wearing his pristine white business shirt and a sober necktie, as is expected of his occupation. Behind his back, mother and kids often make unflattering remarks about his dress code being at odds with his large square frame. White streaks are just beginning to thread the dark grizzle of his close-cropped hair. This handsome middle-aged black man is an imposing figure with a disposition most women find enchanting. Flushes of youthful mischief remain visible on his gleaming eyes and over-industrious fingers.

Odessa smiles and nods in response to Ellen's assurance that the Good Lord has blessed the food. She lingers there, bestowing her approval and mentally storing the scene as a cherished memory. Their congenial supper progresses like so many before at this same table, stretching back to her distant childhood.

When they first arrived, people in Canada struggled to pronounce their names. A flash of creativity produced 'Moffet-King', a quantum leap from 'Mofokeng'.

Odessa tries to focus, amidst the chaos of supper; she half-listens to the updates regarding the day's comings and goings at Teddy's school, a few anecdotes about some happenings at her father's bank, and smatterings of neighborhood gossip. Teddy is the 'baby' of the family, and he knows more about which boy has been dumped by which girl than the contents of his books. 'He could use the best orthodontist in town,' Odessa often teases. After Teddy's updates about his day at school, Georgi brings her listless family up to date with the 'latest fashion trends from *Elle Magazine* this season'.

"Anything intelligent going on in your world, Georgi?"

Georgi flaunts a new pair of red ankle-boots and flashes a broad, cynical smile in Odessa's direction.

"Nice legs. Don't you think, Odessa?"

"Narcissist, this girl," Odessa mutters.

Into the lull of dinner, Kian says to Odessa, "Penny for your thoughts!"

"Oh, Papa," she heaves thoughtfully, "Like I hinted, I have something important to tell you guys."

"Planning on going out to buy your boots?" Teddy cackles.

"Shush, Teddy," Ellen shouts out.

The startled pairs of eyes gaze at Odessa, who begins to invoke her powers of memory to recite her lines for the benefit of her clan. After clearing her throat, she starts, "Mama, Papa, I have decided to go home; yes... home, the land of Nelson Mandela, to live among the rainbow people of South Africa."

A bemused silence fills the house, followed by Teddy's playful chortle. Odessa can feel that she has fluffed her lines somewhat. Mother and father are now looking at her with concern. For a few awkward moments, the silence is complete.

Creased up with delayed laughter, Georgi lifts her arms and playfully urges Odessa on, "Go on. Where did you get that humdrum struggle verse from?"

While the rest of the family suppresses their amusement, pretending to be inspired by Odessa's recital, Kian impassively says, "Explain."

"I think she wants to go to Africa, Dad," Teddy explains.

"Yes, I want to go home..."

"Home?" Kian exclaims loudly. "Did you just say 'Home'?"

He is on his feet, employing his significant presence to tower above his family. His chair crashes to the floor, but he continues, "Canada is your home, young lady! We turned our backs on that racist society over twenty years ago; we brought you out of hell to where you enjoy equality and gave you a fine university education. Canada is where your home is."

Everyone is aghast at Kian's 'over the top' reaction, and the lyrical glint of Mandela's rainbow nation has suddenly turned grey.

After a while, Ellen holds Odessa's hand and asks, "Tell us why you want to go to... why ask for the moon while the sun shines, Odessa?"

Following a collective loss of appetite, the family settles down over mugs of cocoa. The Rosedale suburban atmosphere is filled with the colorful rumbling, hissing, and chugging sounds of trains, screeching cars, and roaring motorcycles. Gradually, the noise quiets as night deepens. The family members try to detach their minds from Odessa's 'rainbow nation' dreams. Georgi buries herself inside the latest French edition of Vogue magazine. For her, the preceding and ensuing conversations happening in bits and pieces nearby could be taking place on another planet, for all she cares. Instead, her contribution is limited to a dreamy 'Yes', 'No', 'Fine'.

> Back to the topic at hand, Kian adds reluctantly, "Do you know how your mother suffered in South Africa? She was once mugged on her way home from work, in her crisp uniform..."

Georgi thinks, My debating teacher would call that a red herring.

Odessa is aware that her parents' suffering at the hands of the apartheid regime continues to rankle with them. Still, she senses intense longing for Africa regardless of what they say. The faraway homeland they have vowed never to see again is closer to their hearts than they admit.

In their bedroom, in the quiet of the night, Georgi also struggles with her parents' memories of South Africa, particularly the terrible hardships black people endured under the Christian apartheid regime. Georgi asks, "Odessa, are you crashing yet?"

"Yes, Georgi. Do likewise. I'm drained. Good night."

"Say, what do you think of Dad's performance, all the histrionics about inane incidents... like mother's purse-snatching while she was in her hospital uniform? Do you buy all of that? Everyone is going back to South Africa now that we are free. What's with these two people?"

"Hiding something, maybe."

"They could have been spies that escaped the 'necklace' street justice."

"Oh, shut up, Georgi. I want to sleep."

After a while, Odessa says, "Georgi, are you asleep?"

"No."

"Good. Can I ask you something?"

"Not another 'boyfriend' question, please, I don't have one these days. And I know you don't either. And don't tell me about Luca..."

"Shut up. It's about our poor mother..."

"It's weird, you know? I never regarded Mother as sad, lonely, or bored, but she must sometimes be all that."

"She's too busy to be bored. Besides attending church, she volunteers at Meals on Wheels or soup kitchens, as she calls them. I felt so sorry for her the last time I went with her to one of her soup kitchens. She appreciated my company; she held my hand afterward and then cried."

"Oh! You should have been proud."

"It's like she left her whole crowd behind in South Africa. Did Mother have anyone close over there? I wonder."

"You mean like friends and lovers?"

The girls break into sisterly laughter.

"Don't you think our country will be another basket case, like the rest of Africa?"

"Odessa, you said you want to go there to see the rainbow nation. Why don't you check it out and tell us when you return?"

"My supervisor says Africa is a basket case."

"I'll go tell him myself he's talking BS."

"Be careful, Georgi. They are aware of your mental history."

"What bloody mental history?"

Luca, the 'Toronto Activist'

Odessa developed curiosity in her line of research while writing a college assignment: 'The Great South African Diaspora of the 20th Century'. In the morning, she tells her family that she has recently contacted some informants, former South Africans, to explore the reasons behind their departure from the country of their birth. How do they feel about their new life in Canada? What lifestyle differences do they experience? Do they have any regrets?

Her understanding has grown due to unexpected responses and curious emotional reactions to her study. Her white informants began to portray contradictory images of South Africa, some appealing and others uninteresting. For the most part, the migrants cherished the country they had left behind. Some departed because they saw no alternative on the horizon, witnessing life deteriorate before their eyes. They worried about the risks their children might face in the future. Some appeared bitter, blaming the apartheid government for yielding to communists. Others held the new democratic government accountable for the white man's troubles.

Odessa says, "Many whites feel there is nothing to act contritely for. Mama, you always read us the bible, but nothing about the Edomite Europeans who dominate the world and lie about everything, including wholesale land theft wherever they go."

"Yes, the descendants of Esaw, Jacob's twin brother," says Kian, "That's the only part of the bible I believe in."

"You believe in anything political," responds Ellen.

"White colonialists claim that if they had not gone to Africa, blacks would still be involved in tribal skirmishes and living in caves."

"They will stop their insulting remarks the day we go back to using our country's original names. I am proud of African nations that have restored their dignity or started discussions on the topic of names. The South African leaders must move away from colonial tags and rename our country 'Azania' because that's the name of our country. Imagine how embarrassing it is to talk to colleagues from Tanzania, Zimbabwe, Namibia, Libya, Ghana, and all that, and then tell these people you come from South Africa. Imagine how small it makes us feel! These racist whites who think they own the country and its wealth will start respecting us, they know they are no longer in their apartheid South Africa, but black Azania, just as much as they are proud of their white Europe."

"Subliminal racism is woven into every conversation... in North America. Jim Giles, our white supremacist, has a large following among whites in Africa. Some say that if they had known how effortless the changeover to the new regime would be, they would not have emigrated. An elderly man told me they used the picture of Nelson Mandela for their target practice even after De Klerk had unbanned the ANC."

"Yes, they started with beer cans, then pigeons, and then Mandela or Joe Slovo, whom they call a Jewish sell-out," Kian backs Odessa. "But here, the self-same white exiles expected Canada to be a carbon copy of good ol' South Africa..."

"Only with snow in winter, minus black faces on their subway trains and first-class planes," Georgi sniggers.

"There's something about this country from which I sprang!" Odessa expresses herself with emotion, "and I am now ready to see it myself."

Kian is paging through the Toronto Sun while Ellen is anxious to keep the discussion calm to avoid upsetting him again. Opening a debate about crime and affirmative action would not help the situation. However, the conversation takes a different turn.

"Dad, Mom, I met Luca's mother. She said something funny."

"Yes?" Ellen and Kian murmur in unison, in great anticipation.

Odessa impersonates Luca's mother: "Ask your parents when they last were in Africa. Tell them in two months, I will be there for the unveiling."

"What cheek!" Kian rants.

"And what did you say to her?" demands Ellen.

"I told her to come here and talk to you herself."

"Good show," Kian says excitedly.

"But I told her," Odessa continues, "I'm going there soon... to South Africa, I mean."

Kian puckers his lips and struggles to avoid a scowl on his face.

"Odessa," Ellen murmurs, "What in the world has come over you? That place? We don't call it home anymore. You can't honestly say you are unhappy here," she reasons, her aging face showing.

"Doing research from such a distance isn't good enough, Mom. I can only get valid findings close to the action."

"Action? What jargon...!" Kian strikes clinically.

Ellen asks quietly, "Does Luca know what you are up to lately?"

Kian clears his throat, preparing to lay down the rules. "Luca is probably behind the whole idea. You heard what her conniving mother said. Let's not talk about that boy. I don't want to hear his name again in this house." He folds his paper and flips it open again. "I'm quite disappointed you continue seeing the arrogant idiot, Odessa."

"Papa, we've been here before..."

"All of this pilgrimage to South Africa is his doing. I see his hand in all of it. And let me tell you again, you'll marry into that family over my dead body," Kian puts it, his face as black as thunder.

Georgi suddenly jumps up as if her feet are on fire, "Are they getting married? Why the secrecy, Odessa?"

"Who said anything about marriage, Papa?"

"Please! Please!" Ellen appeals, "Let's be decent about these things. You told me Luca obtained his work permit. Are you leaving with him?"

"I knew it. You raise your child... and then this!" Kian slowly folds his newspaper again, as if in his final stage of despair.

"Not even a hint, Odessa?" Georgi smiles and clowns, "Engagement?"

"Oh, shut up, Georgi," Odessa yells. "Luca's gone already."

Luca and his mother have lived in Canada for over a decade. According to him, they have maintained their 'cultural connection'. Kian and Luca have clashed over cultural issues many times. Things came to a head when he accused Kian of being a traitor to the black course for using only English at his home. Kian had advised Luca to respect his elders, to which Luca had responded, 'All my elders are in Africa, not in some snow-bound concrete jungle where certain people are trying to be white'. Luca was an angry young man. After a mob killed his father in Khayelitsha, he vowed to avenge his death one day. In 1986, amid the confusion regarding President PW Botha's indefinite state of emergency and failure to cross the Rubicon, Luca and the rest of his family took off from Jan Smuts Airport on a one-way exit visa. Luca became a 'Toronto activist', always hinting vaguely at some 'unfinished revolutionary business in South Africa'.

"He is back in South Africa to sort out... something," Odessa tries.

"Understand this: you follow Luca, you are on your own."

No one contradicts Kian while in this mood, and Odessa nods submissively, although she thinks her father is overreacting. The discussion persists into the following days. Kian and Ellen make a formidable team, but any capitulation on her part is definitely out of the question.

"If Luca has gone," says Ellen, "good for him, and nothing more to be said about your relationship."

"Luca is only a small part of this deal. I'm contacting Home Affairs in South Africa to inquire about the possibility of returning as a former exile. After all, Uncle Bekker (or Lenin) has been a... hero of the struggle. While there, I might as well look for him. If he's alive, he must surely be a part..." She pauses in the face of her parents' flinty gaze, "he must be part of the new government structure."

Mimi-Koo

Kian had been born Thlokomela Mofokeng. However, following the old colonial practice of giving black children European names for use in their dealings with white officials and employers, his parents purged 'Thlokomela' from all their interactions with one another and replaced it with 'Bekker.' Their father worked in the gold mines while their mother taught Pedi at an 'enlightened' Saint Henry's, where both sons, Bekker and Daniel, received their education. By the time Bekker had reached the end of his school days, he was a young white gentleman in all but the color of his skin. His friends were white – he spoke English for the most part – and black cynics described his thought processes as being in line with the English culture and language.

Bekker presented himself on the job market with as much aplomb as his peers from St. Henry's. The local employment market in the 1960s was not yet ready for Bekker Mofokeng, as he was unable to participate in the white man's cryptic conversations. Personnel managers, mainly English-speaking white males, found him 'too white by half,' forward, and cheeky. Some secret arrangements, engineered by the parents of Bekker's former schoolmates and other significant connections, proved unsuccessful—the reality of his situation as a black man hit him where it hurt.

Bekker started to lose his self-confidence. A disturbing relapse in his normally cheerful personality had set in. He secured a menial job as a messenger to a stockbroking firm. When he crossed the line by daring to hug the sister of one of his white schoolmates, his spell at the firm ended. At the time, deep-seated racism affected the entire social tapestry. Not only was racism legalized, but its religious tenor also defended stereotypes regarding the perceived inferiority of Africans. Most even believed, without studying biblical texts, that Africans were cursed. This unschooled belief entrenched the culture of entitlement on the part of those who thought that only whites should have unrestricted access to resources and free political expression. Job reservation laws and white privilege had become normal conditions of life. However, Bekker had missed the township coaching to be streetwise in a white man's world, or as they used to say in the townships, to be *'clever.'* African children were taught behind closed doors how to say 'Baas' or 'Missus' convincingly when addressing a white person. The word 'Baas' carried more weight than the *Dompas* identity document. Black boys knew instinctively that kissing a white girl was a risky undertaking. Bekker missed such township education because he hung around with white teenagers whose conversation focused on their last holidays in exotic American and European destinations or the most effective mixture for removing creepy pests from their swimming pools.

The valiant liberal newspaper, 'The Rand Daily Mail,' graphically presented the demon of apartheid in cartoons as a cadaverous Scrooge-like figure dressed in a top hat and funereal black tailcoat – alive and well and stirring up trouble wherever he went. Most white readers in the country missed the irony because the caricature carried no particular emotive weight apart from its comical value.

Overwhelmed by the setbacks, Bekker moped about his Soweto home, sleeping most of the day. He continued sending off job applications, seldom receiving so much as an acknowledgment. One evening, as he listlessly sealed yet another envelope, his father came in from the mine to announce that Bekker was to report to the shaft on Monday morning. His shift boss had agreed to give him a chance as a clerk underground. Their mother burst into tears while Bekker and his sisters stood by helplessly.

"If it's been good enough for us all to live off my labor underground, it is good enough for my son," said the patriarch.

The details of the following few months while Bekker worked underground, deep in the earth's bowels, remained hidden from family and friends. People in Soweto had a particularly negative perception of working underground. It was something reserved for the simple rural folk or foreigners, the general attitude went.

One day, the family received a shocking message: Bekker was in the mine hospital after an 'incident' underground. When he was well enough to return to work, the authorities accused him of insubordination, a charge for which Africans lost their jobs without due process. He went back home, still bearing the marks of fresh injury to both his limb and ego, and walking with a pronounced limp. Bekker rarely spoke, and as the weeks passed, his folk began to limit any conversation with the dejected figure to the bare minimum. Only his younger sister, Kora, managed to elicit a rare smile from him despite her admonitory refrain, 'Stop feeling sorry for yourself.'

Unlike his brother, who was a natural scholar, Daniel was studying for his final examinations, oblivious to anything except the all-important papers that would determine his future.

Then Bekker disappeared, and the name Lenin emerged from somewhere, aided and abetted by the partial media. After that, the family heard only rumors in hushed tones throughout the townships. His assumed tag of 'Lenin' catapulted him into the role of an active freedom fighter across the border. Occasionally, people swore they spotted him here or over there. Screaming headlines echoed across the country: 'Lenin wanted for bank robbery'. The authorities seemingly believed the bank robbery tale because they began to target the Mofokeng household with renewed zeal.

Daniel Mofokeng had learned a bitter lesson from his brother's misfortunes. When his turn came to pursue a career, he landed a clerk's job with Barclays, a bank whose policy of black advancement proved progressive. He worked hard, enrolled to write banking examinations, was selected for special training, and generally did well. The bank later posted him to London for a short management training program. The rumor mill about Bekker, now openly known as Lenin, fizzled when the Special Branch suddenly arrested him in Cape Town. He narrowly escaped the death penalty; the prosecution having failed to prove certain charges beyond a reasonable doubt. Soweto had something to celebrate. Lenin served time on Robben Island with Nelson Mandela and other struggle heroes. His aging mother visited him twice a year. She always returned tight-lipped and full of sorrow. Soon after his release, he vanished into the 'shadowy' world of resistance politics. The townships buzzed with gossip about his daring acts, and his name became synonymous with bombings and attacks on government targets; countless chants were sung in his honor. The serious incident for which Bekker served time involved a landmine blast that killed a teenage girl. She was white. In South Africa, that detail is crucial because it influences media interest, public enthusiasm for the arrest, and the severity of sentencing. Someone planted a bomb in a dusty stretch of road in the small farming town of Cloetesville. Newspapers highlighted it, expressing collective white outrage. Lenin's name was everywhere, and hysteria continued unchecked. A police profile described him as 'Bekker, the terrorist who is armed and dangerous.' According to the original story, the young girl was with her family, traveling after a Sunday service at their conservative Dutch Reformed Church. Named after Mimi Coertse, a South African opera singer, Mimi-Koo was in her usual cheerful spirits, her rusty tenor echoing across the countryside when their car hit the mine. The rest of the family escaped serious injury, but Mimi-Koo spent two months at the Hospital and later died. Mimi had a sister named Sofia, who often had unplanned visits to a mental health clinic for observation. When she visited Mimi, Sofia found her cheerful as always.

"Please, Mimi, I don't want you to die because I love only you."

"Don't worry, Sofi, I won't die. I dream good dreams these days; one day, I'll marry a handsome man, and do you know what I'll call my first baby? Skylar."

"Skylar, your doll?"

"Yes, she will never tell me lies. Ouma says so. I know someday you will also find a man who never lies because you always tell me the truth, even when it hurts me sometimes. Ouma says the truth will set you free."

"Is that why you want to tell the truth about Willem?"

Mimi freezes with a convulsion that causes her to shake uncontrollably. One morning after, Mimi-Koo's ward was eerily still. Only voiceless faces, soaked in tears, told of despondency in the wards and shiny corridors. Mimi-Koo, the cheery little girl with endless energy, had died in her sleep. The Helderberg staff held a memorial service, a first for the hospital. They remembered Mimi-Koo's voice resonating through the wards from dawn to dusk. A few weeks later, Lenin had stepped out of his hiding place into the hands of a phalanx of white intelligence officers who whisked him away to face a catalog of terrorism charges.

CHAPTER 3

A nine-day wonder

Odessa was unaware of the humiliation her parents had endured back in South Africa. For her, only broad outlines of her uncle's story somehow remained buried in her subconscious being. Odessa is also unaware of Kian's true identity, a fact she will discover once she sets foot in South Africa. Today, in a suburban home in another hemisphere, halfway across the world from their beginnings, Ellen goes over it, "I think that security police studied under Adolf Hitler's stormtroopers in Nazi Germany. They always arrived at four o'clock in the morning, just before dawn, when people's energies were at their lowest ebb. The sounds of *casspirs* and *ratels* – great armored vehicles like you have never seen – squaring up against ragged unarmed civilians, revving and grunting in the distance, coming closer, stopping at our door, boots stamping, rifles dismantling, triggers cocked, swear words ringing out, always in Afrikaans..."

"Yes, is it any wonder many blacks resent the Afrikaners!"

"Yet the same blacks adore the Afrikaans language like crazy," crows Ellen, whose eyes are heavy with hidden tears.

"It serves as a status symbol, better than your English by far," Kian shows off to his girls. "But status or not, Afrikaans is an ingeniously crafted language of Africa that has escaped the tag of vernacular..."

Ellen continues, "Sometimes I hear them still. The noise would come closer, shouting, cursing, laughing, and hammering around the house. If we failed to open promptly, they kicked the door open. Some of the white police were not even twenty."

"Was it that bad, Mom?" Odessa asks with misgivings.

"What? It was worse," responds Kian heatedly.

"I wonder where those youngsters are today," Odessa muses.

"Took flight deep into their ancestors' farms at the sight of democracy," Kian says.

The security police used to interrogate Daniel anywhere, anytime, and the bank authorities grew increasingly impatient with the escalating police visits. One day, the security police detained Daniel at John Vorster Square, the most notorious hub in downtown Johannesburg.

"Goes to show just how unintelligent their security machinery had become?" Ellen puts it. "They were evil; that's all I can say."

Ellen avoids her husband's gaze as a long, shuddering sigh escapes her lips. She continues her story, speaking more briskly, anxious to finish, hopeful that it will change her daughters' minds about their planned venture. Tears shimmer, and she blinks fiercely.

Her husband pats her shoulder awkwardly. "Hush," he says, "hush, it's over. You are safe here."

"Perhaps some of them live in Toronto," Ellen quips. "But seriously now, sometimes the officer in charge would be coarse and crude; other times elegant, maybe spoke English…" Her voice trails away as she recollects the bygone days she would rather forget had it not been for her daughter's insistence on returning to South Africa.

"Amen," says Kian, "and never to set foot in Africa again."

"But Papa," Georgi speaks up, "before Nelson Mandela was released, before he became president, before a black government took control in South Africa. Surely you feel differently now?"

"No, Georgi," Kian utters a weary sigh, leaning back in his chair and folding his arms across his broad chest in a defensive gesture. He gazes pensively at each of his girl children and concludes, "We can't go back to Africa. Not ever."

Freak accident?"

Georgi has been conducting her inquiries behind the scenes. Her mission is personal. She is restless, her soul consumed by dark thoughts about her true identity. Like rising damp, the feeling began to creep up on her slowly and insidiously. She remembers how it took more control of her after she read Margaret Walker's poem 'Childhood,' which her father posted on their living room mantelpiece. Lately, the unwritten rule in the household dictates avoiding deep discussions about South Africa, although they often flout it in dark corners. This time, Kian takes it as an opportunity to tell his tales of struggle while Ellen breaks completely out of it. Georgi is wary of expressing her feelings openly, but her morbid nightmares and uncontrolled tantrums are symptomatic of something deep and dark. Yet those who find it hard to put up with her can never live without her.

"Odessa, tell me about Luca. You reckon there's some prospect on the horizon?"

"I don't know, Georgi. I'm pretty pissed off right now. He had the nerve to confront Mom and Dad and call them sell-outs because they left South Africa instead of staying on to fight the struggle."

"What about his parents?"

"No one is spared his vitriol. He'll sing a different tune the day he hears what miserable times parents endured."

"Don't you think Luca is an obsessive zealot, still chasing 'A Luta continua' despite liberation in South Africa being a fait accompli?"

"Yeah, I'm mad at him, and he is mad at me when I call him Lucas. When he corrects me, I giggle, and he says I behave like a white bitch. He says I must stay in America for good, as the African Continent is too dark for me."

"*C'est dommage*! What does his name mean, anyway?"

"I haven't got the foggiest. Something to do with 'the struggle'?"

Many weeks have passed since Odessa seems to have aborted her African expedition. The household is almost done with dinner when piercing telephone peals invade. When nobody attends to the phone, Kian lifts himself with a growl.

"Princess Odessa, it's for you. Please, people, learn to answer the damn phone, will you?"

"Who is it, Dad?"

"If you had answered the phone, you would know it's Luca's auntie," he snarls.

"Aunt?" Odessa cringes.

The rest of the family hears Odessa say, "Hi, Gwendolyn. Have you heard from Luca?"

Odessa's face twists in pain before she cries, "No! No! No! It can't be. Please don't say that."

The suspense is too much for the wide-eyed spectators. Odessa's body is so numb that she can hardly wiggle her toes. The stricken silence lasts forever. She drops the receiver and buries her face in her hands. They watch her keening, bending forward at the waist, rocking her whole body as she exclaims excruciatingly. "It was a freak accident outside a pub in Johannesburg. He's dead. He's gone!"

The story gradually emerges. Luca was in a pub in Johannesburg with some new friends. It is sheer blind chance that he was there. The pub is known to be frequented by blacks, gays, and, sometimes, illegal immigrants. The old right-wing elements do not care much – they suffer from xenophobia, homophobia, anti-Semitism, racism, and whatever else. Any old target will do. Their *modus operandi* works anytime: spot a target, mostly a bar, create a brawl, and *donder* as many blacks as you can in the ensuing commotion and confusion.

"Freak accident?" cries Ellen.

"So, four young men, three South Africans, and a Canadian are in the hospital; not expected to live. Luca died instantly. The police arrested a gang of right-wingers..."

"Cold comfort, indeed!" snarls Kian.

Odessa says she must go to Luca's family. Gwendolyn will need comfort to repair the ravages of grief.

Into the long silence, Georgi poses the question that is foremost in everyone's mind: "Do you think she'll still go to Africa after all this?"

A simultaneous retort goes, "No," says Kian, and "Yes," says Ellen.

Ellen says, "If she's still obsessed about Lenin, then yes, she will. The Lord's will, indeed, be done on earth."

"We want to go to South Africa to discover who we are. I want to know who I am," she lets slip.

After an awkward silence, Ellen says, "You know who you are, Georgi. God knows who you are. Isn't that enough?"

Kian roars, shaking his head in irritated disapproval, "Georgi, Georgi, Georgi, haven't we lost enough? South Africa is a dangerous place. Here's Luca. Have you been there for what... six months? And his young life is no more. Just think of the last time you saw him: cheerful, energetic, optimistic, and alive! Now he's on a slab as an anonymous casualty.

Get real, girl! Let's be grateful for life in a civilized country instead of chasing rainbows on the other side of the globe!"

"Dad, we'll talk some other time, or maybe never," she mutters.

"And you'd better finish college first. How can you secure a decent job without a good education? A few more months, and you are through."

Little realizing how soon it would happen, Luca had joked about his wish that they bury him in his South African homeland. Gwendolyn has granted his wishes. The weeks pass briskly in the cross-Atlantic drama; telephone calls, e-mails, faxes, and documents are exchanged and signed. The authorities return his personal effects to Toronto, where Gwendolyn is still too distressed to wade through them.

Another year passes, and each of the Moffet-Kings pursues activities and dreams without confronting Kian about South Africa. Despite continuing to save for the big venture, Odessa finds that her heart is no longer in it.

'I have seen the light,' she thinks, 'South Africa is too far, too dangerous a place to mess with.'

As she approaches the finals of her college year, Georgi is a prime mover in the scheme, challenging Odessa at every opportunity. She insists that if Odessa has developed cold feet, she will take up the African expedition alone. However, she will keep pushing her before finally dipping her toes into the inviting waters.

Then September 11 pounces upon humanity like an evil cyclone. The New York World Trade Center suffers a devastating and humiliating attack. Apart from the great Twin Towers, America loses government installations and over three thousand lives, and gains insecurity and anxiety. The infamous 9/11 attacks exploded across the world. Sifting through ash and rubble, America brings out bodies and body parts for DNA testing to determine which family can put which loved one to rest. Securing American interests, a metaphor for vengeance, occupies center stage, and the Islamic world is troubled. The sheer horror of the 9/11 act of violence marks a defining moment in world history. American public sentiment turns fervently against Canada for that country's liberal attitudes toward foreigners. Once airports in the West reopen, airline authorities and governments will step up security. There is widespread racial and religious profiling of travelers.

'War on Terror' has taken over from the 'extinct' Cold War paranoia, with propaganda campaigns occupying cyberspace more than ever before. Al-Qaeda, a militant group founded by Osama Bin Laden, as well as the Taliban, another militia group based in Afghanistan, replaced the one-time bogeyman of the West, the USSR (Union of Soviet Socialist Republics). The Mainstream Western media, posing as the beacon of objectivity and accuracy, are embedded with the US and British Coalition and convey messages their governments want citizens to hear. Emboldened by the evil murders of ordinary people, Al-Qaeda is now more motivated than ever before. The West answers by attacking 'terrorist' camps, abducting suspects, and detaining numbers in Guantanamo Bay, the US detention camp in Cuba. The Pamela Geller hysteria gained momentum throughout America.

Bureaucracy renders travel excruciatingly slow and unpleasant. In Africa, al-Qaeda reinvents itself as Al Shabaab. Odessa and Georgi are now terrified of flying, although neither would openly admit it. As for Georgi, she takes her full medication before she flies because her extreme phobia causes her nightmares, and she often throws up days before. She has repeatedly mentioned to Odessa that her greatest fear is that her plane might be struck by lightning.

Kian and Ellen are now completely laid-back, with any mention of Africa done only in passing.

"The girls' favorite pursuit has died a natural death," Kian tells Ellen triumphantly.

"Yes, a nine-day wonder," says Ellen, cackling.

Ellen and Kian are not aware that their daughters' adventurous pursuit is anything but a nine-day wonder. Throughout the anxious period, Georgi keeps returning to the subject. Odessa has been wavering. However, a message from Gwendolyn changes everything. The Truth and Reconciliation Commission (TRC) has freed the Khayelitsha men who killed Luca's father. No family member was aware of the man's application for amnesty until they came to testify. Gwendolyn explains that the case was 'low-profile' and, accordingly, 'of little interest to the media.'

Determined to unearth the truth about Luca's murder, Odessa finally makes up her mind to rejoin Georgi. She likes the advertising work and knows the highly acclaimed South African industry will boost her profile. While she wishes for good fortune in finding a job in the industry, Georgi is pursuing her own agenda. She realizes her sister has her work cut out for her, but she is determined to support her. They secretly lay out all the plans. Then Teddy, in his innocence, gives the game away, "Hey, Mom," he says as Kian comes in, "can I have their room when they leave? I like the view."

"Whose room?"

"My sisters' room, of course, Mama."

Ellen avoids her husband's eyes as he drops his attaché case and stares at her accusingly.

"Yes, Teddy," says Ellen with a weighty heave.

Ellen maintains her feminine silence. She resents Kian's snappy attitude toward her and is about to clearly express her feelings when Kian asks, "What's this about?"

"I know what you are thinking, Kian. I told the girls repeatedly to brief you about their plans."

Kian walks to his usual seat and says to Ellen, "Strong coffee, please."

He angrily raises his newspaper and then lowers it to his lap again.

"And when were you going to break this momentous news to me? New Year's Day, I suppose. Happy New Year, Mr Kian! Your daughters won't be home to see in the next one."

"Leave me out of it, Kian. says Ellen softly. It is their responsibility to tell you, not mine. They are both determined adults." Ellen throws a clumsy grin.

The confrontation comes as soon as the girls both arrive.

"I believe you girls have something to say," begins Kian threateningly.

Georgi, ever more direct, 'Maggie Thatcher' to her acquaintances, meets Kian's challenge, "Yeah, Papa, can you recommend a good hotel in Johannesburg?"

"What hotel?"

The girls make their determination clear, despite their lingering fear that he might withhold his blessing.

"When we get out there, we'll be searching for Bekker or Lenin because I believe it's the same person.

"Yes, Odessa, let's refer to him as Bekker because he is family."

Having silently conceded defeat, the parents will now struggle with the unpleasant repercussions of their daughter's decision to go to Africa. And what repercussions!

Georgi says, "Mom, Dad, wish us a Bon voyage as we prepare for fun at Mapungubwe!"

CHAPTER 4

I got the job

Georgi receives a letter of employment from South Africa.

"Mom, look; I've been hired in Cape Town."

Sprightly Georgi chants. She waltzes into the kitchen, throws her arms around her mother, whirls her around, and then dances off to locate her father.

"What is the job all about?" asks Ellen as she charges behind her, smiling all the while. "How can you have a job in Cape Town? Stand still for a moment and tell us what is going on?"

"Yes, what's the buzz?" Kian puts it.

Georgi pushes Kian's book aside and puts an open letter before him. Georgi had applied for a job through a Vancouver international au pair agency. They placed her with a diplomatic couple in South Africa. The couple spends six months in Cape Town, Pretoria, or Johannesburg while Parliament is in session.

"No kidding?" Kian squeaks.

"There are two little girls and a baby boy. I'll be their 'Mary Poppins.' Jean Mackenzie gave me a brilliant reference, which clinched the deal for me. Mr Taung is on a diplomatic mission, and Mrs Wagner-Taung – another woman mover and shaker, like Jean, no doubt – is a political press attaché. What do you think about that, huh?" she brags.

Kian adds, "Attaché? It's the new South Africa, hum."

"How did we end up with a surname like Mofokeng, anyway? We are supposed to be Xhosa-speaking. Aren't we? That Mofokeng kid from Lesotho we met last year was not a Xhosa. She told us Mofokeng is Sotho."

"Of course, our clan is strong in the Eastern Cape. And we are Xhosas. Our origin, of course, is the Bafokeng Valley, North-West of Pretoria. After forcefully taking the land, the Afrikaners changed the name from Bafokeng to Bechuanaland. Our people are now reclaiming it through the land restitution process."

"I take it they're a black couple? I have never heard of Ms. Wagner-Taung," says Ellen.

"No matter; we'll speak English, anyway," crows Georgi.

Teddy and Odessa come in, attracted by the cheerful clamor in the living room. Georgi looks at the snow over their patio, the blinding light reflecting through their front windows, making her blink uncomfortably.

"Soon, we'll be basking in the sunshine," she sings. "Odessa, I got the job with the Taung kids..." she tosses a smirk at Kian, "They liked my credentials and are prepared to stick me on 'probation,' as the letter says."

"Nice one, Georgi," Odessa puts it hesitantly.

"If the children enjoy my company, the job is mine." Georgi does another pirouette of joy.

"I am baffled by your excitement, Georgi."

"Why?"

"For a woman who excelled in sports in her childhood, I find your sudden interest in being a nanny quite disappointing."

"Oh???"

"I know where I'm going, Odessa. One day I'll be a publisher…"

"Mind your biological clock, Georgi Girl."

"Life is about taking chances, and I'm sure you know that."

"Yes, I know. Take note: as you take your chances, I'll be with you all the way because you are my little sister."

"You mean it?"

Odessa shares more updates with Georgi. Gwendolyn has given her a letter tucked inside Luca's Good Book after his death.

"The Bible? Go figures. He probably meant to hide it till eternity."

"I guess he's been asking questions about Bekker."

Odessa pulls out the letter from a crumpled envelope. She has read it so many times that she can recite its contents from memory. She tells Georgi that Luca seems to have heard so many conflicting stories about Bekker that he can hardly tell what is true and what is just rumor.

"One thing is certain: Bekker made enemies everywhere. In the letter, Luca says Bekker might still be alive, although one woman he met offered to take him to Bekker's grave. And listen to this! At the time of his murder, Luca had plans to have the body exhumed."

"A right royal mess," Georgi squirms as she struggles to negotiate through the salt, snow, and muddy, slushy roads, focusing all her attention on the confusing message in Luca's letter."

"Pray tell, how serious was your affair with Luca?"

"Like trying to aim at a moving target. I felt sorry for him. Because of traumatic experiences, he saw everyone as an enemy. My teacher liked to say, 'Girls must avoid serious relationships with a man under 25."

"Yeah!"

"Men often look for women with positive qualities of their mothers, and many of them never grow up."

"Yeah! I guess some become their daddy's copycats. You like Okobi, don't you?"

"I really find Okobi interesting because he is witty; breaming with jokes and stories from Africa…"

"Why do you always refer to him as your platonic friend, then?"

"I just prefer it that way, Georgi. Love is a complex emotion. Let's talk about Luca's suggestion that Lenin might have been a double agent. Bekker appears in some of the murkiest secret records."

"That's scary. I don't like the sound of this. Luca travels to Johannesburg and starts investigating the Bekker mystery, but some right-wing Afrikaners target him. Too perfect!"

"I don't want to tell Dad. He will be devastated...! What if he tries to stop us from leaving just when he's beginning to accept it? Don't let's tell him, Odessa. Not even Mom. You know she can't keep anything from him. And I'm sure the whole story is not true."

"I know you're right. Luca has entered some names and places in his letter. We can go check them out if you like."

"Yeah, when we move up to Pretoria?"

"Robben Island, too, where Bekker served Time, remember? That's outside Cape Town, a museum today. I understand it's almost a shrine to the activists..."

Odessa focuses on the letter as the car slowly comes to a stop near the internet café. Nothing else matters right now. The girls stay in their seats, lost in deep thought, anxious about their new mission.

"This is going to be more interesting than my first college day. I am such a bundle of nerves."

"Don't fret. We'll be together," says Georgi.

"But Mama and Papa still refuse to go along with this. You're not just doing it for me?"

"No, I'm doing it for me. I'm just worried about Mom. Do you know, the other day, she was crying tears, begging me not to go and asking in biblical language to 'prevail on your sister, my child'? She looked distraught and full of grief. Quite weird."

"What did you say to her?"

"I almost said, 'Pull yourself together,' but she looked at me strangely and then asked an odd question about how I feel about myself. I told her that aside from strange dreams, I felt good. She said dreams are warnings from the spirit world. She also said she prays I'll love her forever."

"How strange."

"Anyhow, here's another incredible piece of news from Luca's letter. Actually, two. Number one, Luca discovered that Bekker had a son. The mother was a Jewish journalist, a foreign correspondent from Berlin, and a photographer for a newspaper. I think we should tell Dad."

"Yeah. Luca mentions something about 'locating the glass.' Something rang a bell when I read that. A few months ago, I found a note Dad had written. It said, Glass, strong leads."

"How silly of you, reading Dad's stuff."

"Georgi Sister Dear, your halo went 'puff' before you reached puberty. The letter mentioned that the Glass was 'safe in the park.' Thoughts?"

"Safe in the park? It's as cryptic as you can get. I think they are talking about the girls' best friend," smiles Georgi.

"Or just a girl, pure and simple."

"Dad must be an undercover agent...," they giggle.

A Glimpse of Cape Town

Finally, the sisters land at Cape Town.

An obese official of Indian extraction feeds his eyes on Odessa's passport and makes a comment in a language she thinks she recognizes as Xhosa. "I'm sorry," she shrugs, "We are Canadian. We speak English and French."

The man pauses and then nods slowly. His public opinion wavers as his searching eyes dart between Georgi and Odessa.

"Well!" he yelps, continuing to nod mechanically.

"Stupid ass," murmurs Georgi to Odessa.

Their luggage clears customs smoothly. A square, unsmiling, silent white woman in a khaki uniform shows no interest in their names, relationships, or languages. Georgi's prospective employer has arranged for a driver to pick her up, and as they step into the arrival hall, she bites her lips in anticipation. Men and women of all shapes and sizes hold up placards with the names of strangers they are to meet. Among the welcoming crew is a tall black man in a pale safari suit whose board reads 'Moffet-King,' printed in large letters.

"That's us," says Georgi, extending a hand in greeting.

"Moffet-King," the man puts it shyly.

"I'm Georgi," she says. "This is my sister, Odessa."

They are soon ensconced in soft, sumptuous leather in an enormous black Mercedes-Benz and onward to a highway that dazzles in brilliant sunshine.

"Sunshine, Georgi..."

"Try brilliant, Odessa."

Living in Shacks

"What are those funny little cabins almost falling onto the road?" asks Georgi. "They look like... kids' drawings of doll houses."

The makeshift structures of tin and plastic homes huddle precariously together, acre after acre, stretching back from the roadway and visible far into the distance. The two Canadians have never heard of the notorious township called Crossroads. Shacks close to the road tilt drunkenly, nearly falling into the ditch that runs alongside. Lines of ragged laundry, strung haphazardly like assorted tawdry banners, create a striking eyesore even to the most indifferent. From that safe distance, what lies behind the scenes reveals the harsh realities of grinding poverty, unemployment, crime, and humiliating survival.

The driver, Gibson Ncai, says he has worked for Mrs. Wagner-Taung and her husband, Sanna, for five years. His job is to drive the Madam and the Master as they instruct. He also takes his employer's children to school or shopping malls.

"What you have just seen is called squatter camps," says Gibson. "Black people, they build those shacks to live in. The government aims to improve housing, but the number of people in need is large, and the funds allocated are limited. Most of them are without jobs. If the state gives them better houses, they cannot pay the rent, so they live in shacks, as you see," he sighs audibly and continues, obviously drained of despondency, clearly implicating himself in the suffering lot. "They struggle to pay for electricity, water, and transportation for their children to school. Even if schooling is free, it is a big problem because the children are alone at home most of the time," he says, shaking his head dolefully.

"Plus ça change, plus c'est la même chose," Georgi shouts.

Gibson answers an avalanche of questions from the naïve Canadians as best he can.

No sooner have they left the squatter shacks behind than they drive past more sturdily constructed homes of reasonable size, set further back from the main roads.

"This is where colored people live," he says, stealing a peek at Georgi from his rear-view mirror. "Their lives are better; they have jobs and get a better education than us. You see houses, not shacks, but not many trees or flowers. Aieeyah! People don't care. They got no pride."

"I don't understand," says Odessa. "Are you saying enforced ethnic separation still exists?"

"Enforced or not, it exists everywhere in this country."

"You said black people live in those awful huts and that here, where the houses are... bricks, they're occupied by a different race of people?"

"You should ask Madam," replies Gibson, trying to wriggle out of the conversation. "It is very complicated. There is no apartheid, but still, people live in groups: white with white, colored with colored, black with black, rich with rich, and poor with poor. Is it not like that in your country?"

"Not really. Our government believes in placing sub-economic houses in the center of middle-class suburbia. Moreover, don't forget that Canada has always been a haven for people fleeing persecution. American slaves used to run away across the Detroit River to Windsor in search of freedom. It was called the 'underground railway,'" says Odessa.

"You speak a tough language. I'm just a regular driver. I don't understand all these issues about the economy and suburbs. All I know is that there's bad blood between people of different colors here. Some folks believe living in a shack was ordained by God."

"Only those who don't live in shacks can think that way," responds Georgi.

"Yeah, Paulo Freire wrote about it long ago," adds Odessa

"That's why they don't fight the white man who put them there in the first place, but they kill each other and steal from their neighbors who look like them," complains Gibson.

"Internalized inferiority," says Georgi.

"They feed on each other, internalized inferiority and internalized superiority," concludes Odessa.

"Where do you originally come from, Mr Gibson?" Georgi asks.

I have a house in Butterworth. My children live there with Gogo, Granny to you. But my wife and I live in a cottage with the Taungs...

"And where is Butterworth? And your children...? Why don't you bring them along? Don't you miss them?"

"It's a long story. Butterworth is hundreds of kilometers from here. My wife's job is doing laundry for the family. Master, he is very fussy about how his shirts and suits get ironed," he beams. "You will see. Lovely place, the Taung house is."

"Odessa, just look how close Table Mountain is now."

The famous landmark looms overhead as they enter the Cape Town city streets. The words' the last remaining flourish of British colonial empire' are ringing in Odessa's head.

"Oh, it's just as inspiring as I thought. Look at the cloud, funneling down through the cleft there."

"Master says I must drive through Cape Town because you have never been here. The street is called Adderley. This museum was 'Slave Lodge' and around the corner, 'Slave Tree,' where they auctioned slaves."

Traffic lights slow their progress as he turns a corner. To their left, he gestures to a squat Gothic church. "This is the famous St. George's Cathedral, which used to be Archbishop Tutu's church. You know Tutu?"

"Yes, he came to our school once in Toronto," says Georgi.

They drive down a long street lined with shady trees on both sides. To the right are buildings, and on their left is an enclosed park.

"These were vegetable gardens for sailors. Ships come here to get fresh water and vegetables. Now, it's a beautiful rose garden! And here, this building—the Museum-Iziko," says Gibson.

After turning another corner, he points toward impressive Corinthian columns that would not disgrace a Roman forum. The building stands at the beginning of a tarred, palm-lined avenue. A man in a white uniform topped with a white safari hat stands at attention at the entrance.

"Mount Nelson Hotel," Gibson says in tones of reverence.

One can catch tantalizing glimpses of a white building behind the foliage from the road. The girls are captivated by everything: the flowers, the trees, the shrubs, and the blue Impressionist sky above.

"I think I died and went to heaven," breathes Georgi.

Gibson turns the car around another corner and speeds down past a spired

~ 29 ~

cathedral.

"St. Mary's," he points out, "Roman Catholic. And look, do you see the policemen on duty? That's the Houses of Parliament, where Madam works. We come here every day."

The face-bricked courtyards, with attractive buildings behind metal railings, remind Georgi of Teddy's toy soldiers and fort structures. Another turn, and they go through tiny streets, slightly more than foot lanes—pedestrians and road traffic jostle for space.

"Now back along Adderley again, then up Strand Street," he pauses while navigating a rising street with palm trees along the center island. Now we are turning onto Long Street, the longest street in Cape Town. If you look back, you can see the ocean at the bottom of the hill."

They do. Odessa dabs at her teary eyes. Her mind suddenly leaps back to her sad loss. Luca's smiling face is always present, and the scenes and scenery they are experiencing fill her with deep emotion. She knows Luca had traveled to that part of the world before his untimely death. If only he had been there with them.

"Are you okay?" asks Georgi.

"I'll be fine."

Flanking both sides of Long Street, they admire charming old buildings featuring pediments, art deco designs, bright pillars, interesting pubs, antique stores, and deep overhead verandas. Later, they will learn that these buildings are from the 18th-century Cape Malay era. Above them, people laugh and chat as they lean over wooden railings enclosing deep, shaded verandas. On both sides of the street, locals, tourists, and filmmakers with their crews fill the busy sidewalks like ants. It's a lively social scene and a memorable first day in Cape Town for the girls. A mosaic of humanity seems to spill over the scene, enjoying the sparkling day.

Curbside tables outside coffee shops, pubs, and bistros create a lively, carnival-like atmosphere. Gibson expertly guides the Luxury Mercedes through the busy street, weaving between parked cars on either side of the one-way road.

"Here, this is an ancient mosque," Gibson points to one overshadowed by tall palms inside a small leafy garden. Georgi loses her sense of direction when she realizes they are passing by Mount Nelson again—Table Mountain rises behind, glowing and purple in the clear light, mysterious and commanding.

Soon, they left the small town and drove past neighborhoods with manicured lawns, well-maintained homes, and gardens. They saw late-model vehicles shining in the morning sun, signaling a rising economic tide. The scenery makes Georgi ask, "Who lives in these suburbs?"

"As if we didn't know," Odessa butts in.

"This is called Bishops Court, and only rich people," responds the driver. "Any color, as long as they got a good job," he laughs. "It's mostly white," he concedes, "But we hear black empowerment people are streaming in with lots of millions. They are well-connected."

"Not all rich black people are well-connected," reproves Odessa.

"Well," says Georgi, "I heard about Bishops Court from a South African girl on a visit to Toronto."

Yeah, Amina; you remember her. She insisted she was Indian and not African. She told us she lived in Bishops Court and added, 'It's much better than any place in Canada.' I guess she was trying to tell me something.

"Yeah, something alright," Georgi says lazily.

"Well, I don't know Canada. I can't say," Gibson shies away from the issue.

"The more things change, the more they stay the same," adds Odessa. "How many empowered blacks do you think make their living here?"

"Difficult to say. Maybe the tourist office or Home Affairs can tell you. You will have to wait for months to get that information unless..."

"Yes?"

"Ask Madam. She will get the numbers for you pronto. The Madam and her husband don't stand in queues like us."

"Snooty!" Georgi whispers.

They remain silent as the vehicle softly moves along well-kept roads, heading toward distant peaks that rise into the sky, pale purple and lavender in the distance. Gibson tells them that this place is Constantia. The girls are overwhelmed with information. They don't ask any more questions until the vehicle leaves the highway and enters the oak-lined avenues bordered by hedges and calming multi-shade green foliage. Lush, brightly colored flowers are everywhere in this Mediterranean paradise.

I'm the au pair you hired

A short while later, they pass between white pillars as a motorized gate opens to welcome them. The car comes to a gentle stop. Then, a well-groomed, attractive couple of indeterminate age walks up to greet them.

"Welcome, welcome," says the woman Gibson addresses as 'Madam.' "The children are so excited; they're just swimming, and the baby is sleeping. But do come in," the queenly woman calls breathlessly, and she takes Odessa's hand.

"And is this your sister?" she politely nods at Georgi. Gibson will show her to the cottage while we talk."

"No," Georgi interrupts," I am Georgi. She is the sister. I'm the au pair you hired." The woman's face contorts with embarrassment. Her husband's hand freezes in mid-gesture.

"But," he says with raised eyebrows, "but... we particularly asked for a... eh... black person."

"Black person!" Georgi and Odessa respond in unison.

Georgi is furious. She shakes with bewilderment. But people back home don't call her Maggie Thatcher for nothing, and she says, "I'm sorry I am not black enough, but you did hire me. Didn't the agency send you a picture?"

Exasperated, she is flushed. Her charm and ethereal beauty come alive.

The woman brushes her long, dark hair to rally her equilibrium, "Come in, come in, please... Georgi," she says with discomfiture, "and Gibson will show your sister to the cottage and take your luggage over. You can join her after we've spoken."

Much later, Odessa and Georgi relax on the patio of a small but spotless two-room cottage that will serve as Georgi's home for the upcoming months. Nestled beneath peaceful oak trees, the lodging has brought Georgi nothing but satisfaction. "Oh, wow," she chirps, "Is that Wagner woman a well-oiled machine or what! Jean Mackenzie could learn a thing or two from her. Her schedule is unpredictable; to make up for it, everyone else must run like clockwork. The kids, sorry, are children in this country. She told me that the children have a strict routine; each staff member has a duty list in the pantry. There are specific days for chores, and I've got my list too," she says, checking it with a touch of elation.

"She didn't order you to refer to her as Madam and Moroka as Master

"Oh No! No! No," laughs Georgi. "I'm to call them Moroka and Marcia, but they are so grand and majestic that I think I will always think of them as 'Master' and 'Madam.'"

"Did they explain their faux pas when we first showed up?"

"Mistaking me for you? Marcia gave me a long story about 'equal opportunity.' She said, 'It's a bit embarrassing for us to be employing a... well, we expected a black, black person if you see what I mean'."

"And you still took the job?"

Well, I reminded her that the most important skill she asked for was the ability to coach the girls in French. I asked her if a black South African would fit the bill. She wouldn't comment on that but added she knew someone from Ivory Coast who would. 'Fine,' I said, 'but could the Côte d'Ivoire candidate speak good English?' She said, 'You know what? I like you,' before disappearing somewhere with her husband. I overheard Moroka muttering about my skin, and she angrily shut him up.

"So, you are prepared to sell your soul to the devil? Why didn't you decline it? These people are setting you up for failure. They don't want you. You're not black enough for their needs. Can't you see?"

Georgi catches a breath and says, "Time will tell. I met the girls, Jamaica and Verona, and they are sweet. They are very shy and soft-spoken, yet bright, I think—two peas in a pod, just a size difference between the two. Marcia says we can use the pool as much as we like, except when they are entertaining. Look, I need the job and the space. This is ideal to acquaint me with my country."

"And to find Luca's Killers," Odessa adds.

"Odessa, wouldn't it be a good idea to focus rather on finding Uncle Bekker's whereabouts?"

"Suit yourself."

"Of course, you know I'm with you, but if we have limited time here, as we do, we'll have to straighten out our priorities."

"Well, my priority is to find Luca's killers."

Odessa's burst of irritation disturbs Georgi. She says, "Can we chat about this later? You need a job and a place to stay. That's our priority."

"With due emphasis on the latter, Odessa snorts. "I must move before 'madam' evicts me."

Georgi is not amused. "She'll do no such thing. She told me you are welcome to stay as long as needed. You can see these people are drooling with Dollars and Euros."

"Lucky for them..." Odessa snaps.

She also gave me a lecture on being security conscious, hijackings, muggings, and, believe it or not, rapes. I will have a mobile phone to use in an emergency. I am not to take the girls to the mall at any time. And I always have a can of mace to store in the auto."

"She thinks you're a moron. I'll have to get a temp job soon," Odessa says with resignation, "Pretoria, preferably."

"I believe the Taungs will be going to Johannesburg, not Pretoria. They have a residence there as well."

"Residence here and everywhere. Was it Allen Drury who referred to them as an extraordinary society?"

"Whoever he was, he sure got that one right!" Georgi sniggers.

"Whoever he was? Drury won the Pulitzer Prize for 'Advice and Consent.' Rather conservative novelist."

"I'll get you Drury someday. Right now, I need a shower, and then we can go explore the fairest Cape tomorrow, Sister Girl. We're here at long last, the land of our forefathers!"

CHAPTER 5

To Robben Island

Georgi is in high spirits as she collects her sister from the 'bed-and-breakfast' spot. They are on their way to Robben Island, where Odessa is looking forward to seeing Robert Sobukwe's cell, where he was confined to solitary confinement away from the rest of the prisoners.

In the meantime, Moroka has offered to 'see what I can do' to expedite the issue of a work permit for Odessa. He might also learn about a job prospect for her at an Advertising Agency in Johannesburg.

Georgi has dreaded saying goodbye, but she is still excited about the prospect of staying close to her sister. Odessa agrees to call Moroka the following week. But for now, 'Robben Island, here we come!' They park in an underground area at the waterfront and soon listen to a pre-boarding talk at the ferry launch site. We arrive by ferry at the flat, arid island. The island depends on water from the mainland. After the lushness and gentle scenery of the Cape Peninsula, Robben Island is unbelievably harsh and forbidding, with the relentless sun reflecting off the icy Atlantic surrounding the historic site. No rolling hills or majestic mountains soften the bleak landscape. Corrugated iron roofs sit atop stark square buildings under the inhospitable sun. The air pulses with heat like a giant outdoor oven. Ultimately, the visit to Robben Island is a mix of sadness and cliché. In some ways, it feels strangely unsettling. In others, it's disappointing because of the guides' quality. Still, Odessa and Georgi remain optimistic that the trip will help solve the Bekker mystery. Marcia had painted a vivid picture of the island. When the Dutch occupied the Cape in the mid-1600s, they used the island for grazing livestock. It was full of shrubs, herbs, and flowers, and streams flowed generously. "Then some foolish Dutchman," Marcia said, "brought a half dozen cute little grey rabbits from Holland, and before long, the place turned into a desert, and the rabbits had to be culled by greyhounds—though not very successfully, since the plants never grew back. Just another example of colonialism's legacy," Marcia added solemnly. The history of Robben Island is rich and diverse. It dates back to pre-colonial days when passing sailors identified it as a strategic spot for defense or attack. Later, there were failed attempts to make it a market garden and a prison. The authorities left lepers there with little regard for their basic needs like medical care, shelter, or food. Odessa remembers a similar fate for a group of lepers, mostly Chinese, dumped on remote islands off the Vancouver coast. On Robben Island, British convicts had begged to be sent back to England, crying out for death rather than being abandoned on this bleak land. The haunting image of desperate prisoners trying to grow vegetables in the barren soil lingers. It's enough to bring tears. Some even tried to swim across the icy Atlantic to reach the mainland, but those efforts usually turned into nightmares before they could reach their freedom. Nowhere else in the world is the phrase, 'so near and yet so far,' more fitting. The girls feel a deep sense of awe as they absorb the scale of the island's history. Later, when they come across more well-known names, they start thinking of Lenin Mofokeng. The shiny surface of the limestone quarry, where the intense, blinding light had blinded many inmates, is eye-opening even to the cautious. The few tourists without dark glasses squint and shield their foreheads as the guide drones on, making the island's powerful history sound dull and flat. Yet, right here in the quarry, giants of the struggle like Mandela, Asmal, and Sobukwe had sweat blood, working beneath the curses and blows of lesser men. The stone bungalow where former governors once lived still stands firm and practical. Resembling Canadian military barracks from colonial times, a cool, wide veranda surrounds three sides of the building. Odessa finds it charming. Nearby, at the water's edge, the remains of a brick barbecue show that the more privileged residents had leisure time, enjoying meat, beer—and freedom. Georgi pauses, thinking about where the detainees' minds might have taken them when the smell of the barbecue wafted through their dry barracks. Did they long for simple food and social pleasures they could no longer enjoy? Or were they only focused on freeing their country from white oppression? She believes that being involved in the struggle doesn't mean ignoring other needs. She feels the closeness to the Cape's shoreline poignantly as she imagines the prisoners listening longingly for the distant sounds of life—music and laughter—drifting across the water on peaceful nights. Perhaps their hearts transported them to home, to shantytowns or rural villages, where their women's bodies radiated with alluring scents, their lips numb with desire, their bodies burning with endless temptation. Each man's mind must have stirred a mixture of yearning and restless nights, dreaming of who was foraging in his Garden of Eden back home. A colony of tame Jackass penguins—so unafraid they risk being hit by the tour bus—keeps visitors snapping photos with their cameras.

"The penguins get star paparazzi treatment," Georgi giggles, sending ripples of laughter running through the touring party.

The Sobukwe Clause

A reverential hush descends when the guide points at the cell that Nelson Mandela occupied. A collective sigh washes through the group. However, the grim-faced guide informs the tourists that they will not go inside.

"Imagine spending decades confined in this tiny, claustrophobic box," someone whispers.

They climb a few metal steps to view a gun emplacement. No one has ever fired the gun in anger. It points across the mouth of Table Bay Harbor. The authorities placed it there in the late 19th century to protect the young colonial outpost from attack from the ocean approach. The guide points to a cottage occupied by Robert Mangaliso Sobukwe of the Pan Africanist Congress of Azania during his incarceration. Only one member of the tour is aware of Sobukwe's situation. A young American woman mentions that she is working on a PhD thesis about Sobukwe and the Pan Africanist Congress of Azania (PAC).

"Do you know the Sobukwe Clause?" she asks the group. The tourists remain stone-faced, and only two shake their heads 'No' out of politeness. No one says anything. Her attempt to persuade the guide to take them to Sobukwe's quarters results in a cold frown. The group is eager to move on to more interesting sites.

Odessa thinks she might learn something about Bekker from the expressionless guide. She asks him if it's possible to get information on an inmate who served time with Mandela, but he shrugs, "I don't think so."

She tells him he is her uncle, hoping to touch something inside the man's cold heart. While the rest of the group seems interested, the tour guide signals otherwise, "Let's get on with it, people. Everybody now claims to have spent time on Robben Island, if not related to someone who did," he says dismissively. "It's the new status symbol. Yes?"

You can't check? Was his name Bekker or Lenin Mofokeng, please?

The guide bursts into laughter before scoffing at the idea in Afrikaans, "Lenin! Oh, bless me! What possible interest would anyone have in that one? I see we have one or two research scholars here today. Please, ladies and gentlemen, time to go."

Georgi confronts the guide, "I take it this is your full name on this tag?"

The man hesitates and asks, "Yes, why?"

Despite the setback, the trip to Robben Island has inspired Odessa to intensify her search for Bekker. Meanwhile, Georgi has nearly given up the hunt. Instead, she sinks further into what Odessa calls 'the bottomless pit of the Taung household brainwashing.'

Parachuting Themselves

Georgi tells Odessa about meeting with Barend van der Watt at the clinic.

Enraged, Odessa rants, "You had to sneak over to the clinic behind my back? Why didn't you alert me? It's me he wanted there, and you had no business to take my place."

"Take your place? Odessa, you are a million miles from here. I thought you'd be pleased. You didn't want to go, remember? I visited him on your behalf, and as you said, you had to be elsewhere on business."

"Well, you went there for yourself, not for me."

"Do you still want to meet with him? He mentioned that the next time we see each other, I need to tell him about the *Jazz Festival d'été de Quebec*."

"You? See each other? How much do you know about jazz, Georgi? Zilch."

"I know poetry. What should I do now? He wants to meet me somewhere. I think he has uncovered something about Bekker."

"Did he tell you where and when you'll meet him?"

"He'll call me in the morning to confirm."

"I don't like it, not a little bit."

"I don't like it any better, but spare me your chameleon behavior... as if you are Queen Margaret."

"Stop projecting. Who keeps denying she stabs people in the back for a living?"

"I'll hear the man out and then report to you. How's that?"

"Something smells fishy to me."

"Like what?"

"Like you, Georgi. What do you know about jazz?"

"Forget about jazz, stupid. How's Johannesburg? Are you getting around?"

"Different culture... poles apart from your lily-white Cape Town. Now I can feel I'm in Africa. Anyway, talk to you tomorrow."

Barend calls and directs Georgi to the spot where they are to meet. It is a newly constructed McDonald's outlet two kilometers outside Mandalay. Georgi is infuriated to find a Four-by-four with a black driver waiting to take her elsewhere.

After several tense exchanges between Barend and Georgi, she finally relents. The driver takes her to Café Mozart on Church Street, where she finds Barend hiding in a non-smoking section.

"You can't be serious, Mr van Dyk, using tricks to drag me here."

"You can call me Barend. The man you refer to as my driver is actually a colleague of mine. Please, let's relax. May I call you Georgi?"

"As you please."

"Your sister is... she's an angry woman. Are you angry too, Georgi?"

"Who isn't?"

"She called me from Johannesburg. How she got my new number is a disturbing mystery to me. Any ideas?"

"Did you ask her?"

"Never mind. The lapse won't happen again?"

"Odessa wants the truth about Bekker and Luca."

"How can you be angry with me when you don't even know me?"

"I know a lot about apartheid."

Now, sitting on the cafe pavement and sipping refreshing cold wine in the late sunshine, her sour mood is easing in the pleasant surroundings among other people having a good time. There are young people of many backgrounds, but only one mixed couple.

"I see these white girls pointing in our direction and giggling."

It's still an issue here. We sent people to the moon decades ago, for God's sake, yet some idiots are giggling over skin color. I sympathize with them. We need to learn to get along with people like you, and it's easier to talk to someone like you – a Canadian, that is. But," he continues, "I swear I have no untoward intentions...

"You are blushing," she crows.

"In my little community, we could not speak openly to females," he says seriously.

Georgi can tell from the man's eyes that something weighs heavily on his soul.

However, as the lid is relaxing, she feels an uncanny force drawing her towards him. But this man belongs to the surviving white apartheid ghost haunting the new order. Her feminine intuition alerts her to what looks like a hidden threat to her and her sister.

She asks cautiously, "So, what are you doing playing secret service cops and robbers in the big city instead of cowboys on the family ranch?"

Responding incoherently, Barend continues, "There's something called 'land redistribution' taking place these days. It's wild sometimes. Some form of land affirmative action, I suppose. Farming for us white guys has become a hazard. There is no family ranch to go to anymore."

"Aren't you people being paranoid, Afrikaners, I mean?"

"A bull in a slaughterhouse is always paranoid."

"Looks like two bulls in a China shop to me. I always wonder how the Africans felt when the whites started expropriating African land without compensation in 1652. I guess the African bulls got paranoid, too, although they had no power to defend their ranches. My sister, who reads a lot of politics, says white people in South Africa have nothing to worry about as they still have their Cape of Good Hope and all the wealth..."

"Yes, but this is still part of Africa, and we are afraid."

"We all have issues, I suppose, but I get the impression that people in Cape Town live in a country separate from Africa. I don't think you've read the book 'The House Next Door to Africa' by Denis Hirson. His father was a Jewish communist who left South Africa for France with his family on a one-way ticket. Like them or not, many Jews tried to shake white conscience on the Continent."

"The truth is, we Afrikaners don't adapt that well on the continent, even though we believe we're as indigenous as the Khoi..."

"Really?"

"You don't think so?"

"You don't believe that either, do you? The Khoi and the San remain as poor as the inhabitants of Haiti or Jamaica. Have you ever been there?"

"I'm just a displaced farm boy."

"What farming does your family do?"

He motions to the waiter for another bottle, and she returns with sterilized glasses. Then, he removes the cork with a satisfying, rapturous pop. Once he pours into both glasses, he responds, "What kind of farming? My pa is a grape grower in the Robertson district—God's country. My older brother is interested in experimental fruit farming. He attended an agricultural college in the Eastern Cape and returned with no interest in viticulture, but a burning passion for fruit. Once he gets going, he can bore you silly, like I'm doing right now," he smiles again.

"Carry on."

"Now, my kid sister, Sofia, has an equally strong passion for becoming a professional winemaker. There aren't many women in that field. And to make it more complicated, my father is a grape grower, not a wine maker."

"I don't understand the difference."

"No doubt you've done the wine route, right?"

"Only slightly."

"Then you haven't seen all the hype: tourists, wine tours, wine tasting, cute little cellars, fancy glasses with logos, carriages that take you around the estate, lectures on the vats, whether wooden or steel, methods of maturation, and how automated the bottling process has become these days. You might meet the winemaker and recognize his name from the publicity. It's a competitive and glamorous world. People have to work hard for recognition."

"I hope Sofia is taking care of it."

"She keeps her thoughts locked inside, like a closed book."

"Sounds like a risky business."

"One year with a poor crop, and you're back at the bottom of the heap unless you have plenty of capital, an alternative cultivar, or an open-minded government. Being Winemaker of the Year, both nationally and internationally, the prices your wines fetch at auction are all incredibly important to stay in the race." Barend takes a thoughtful sip and continues, "My father decided to skip all that frenzy. He grows grapes—so many hectares of red and white. He sells his entire crop to the co-op upfront. Right now, he's talking with one of the big food chains that wants the grapes for their in-house brand in boxes. My sister is furious. She calls it prostitution, but for us, it's not much different from sheep or cattle farming. And we don't have to spend our weekends making small talk with tourists."

"That's interesting. Do you all think your sister is crazy?"

"When Willem, my youngest brother, joined us, she packed her stuff and left for an old granny flat on the farm. But she is not cut out to be a winemaker."

"Oh, why not?"

"She lacks the temperament. Plus, there are other family issues as well. Her explanation for leaving when Willem moved back was that she resented people parachuting into a game they know nothing about."

"You call that family issues?"

"If you want chapter and verse, you won't get anything from me. I'm sure you have family issues you'd rather keep to yourself. Don't you?"

"Uh, yeah, sure, unless things are in the public domain. Princess Diana could hide stuff about her marriage for a long time to pursue her dreams wherever she could find a place for them. The family supports her passion but worries about the practicality of her choices in a volatile industry. Each of them has their paths shaped by their family's history and the uncertainties of the farming world."

Barend's explanation of their different goals reflects a deeper conversation about legacy and survival, especially as they navigate the complexities of their cultural identity amid South Africa's changing landscape. It's a delicate balance between pursuing one's passion and maintaining financial stability, creating a tension that many families in similar situations can relate to.

"If you'd like to discuss this further or need specific details about the context, feel free!"

"It's common knowledge that my other sister died at sixteen. We hit a landmine, and that was that."

"I'm sorry, what was her name?"

"I'd rather we didn't talk about her if you don't mind."

Barend empties his glass and refills it thoughtfully. "Come with me sometime, will you? You could see every farming activity for yourself?"

"You're kidding, right?"

"It will be fun. I can see you're interested. No one else has ever listened to my boring tales like you have, and that means a lot to me."

"Oh, and what would the neighbors say? What will the family say when this nice Afrikaans farm boy brings home a black friend?"

"Not quite black..."

"What the hell is that supposed to mean?"

"Sorry. I didn't mean to be offensive. I have a lot to learn. Apartheid damaged all of us, you know..."

"Yeah, only in South Africa is my skin color such a big deal. But let me assure you, I am a Black woman. And from what my sister says, you can help us find our Black uncle and our family hiding somewhere in the country. My sister has a great influence on me because she throws us curveballs. I can see your sister, Sofia, is just like that."

"Talking about influence, my great-grandmother died when I was eight. She came from French-Huguenot roots and was a big Anglophile. Her family was from Chantilly, a charming rural town near Paris. Grandma, as we called her, used to read to all of us kids from English books—Alice in Wonderland, Noddy, and Cinderella. Our childhood felt like growing up in a nursery. After she died, we lost much of that."

"It must have been a strict upbringing. What were you taught about black people?"

In hindsight, maybe it was just fear. To us, blacks were an unknown, almost alien presence that we were supposed to avoid. They were uncivilized, inherently inferior to us. Society's systems have timelines.

Mother, Ellen, had us memorize Ecclesiastes 1:9: 'What has been will be again; nothing is new under the sun.' It's all about self-preservation. Human beings will never learn from yesterday's lessons.

"Quite!"

CHAPTER 6

Girl in a wheelchair?

The move to Gauteng occurs in stages. First, Moroka leaves earlier than planned to attend a meeting in Pretoria. Marcia and the children fly there during the Easter break. Gibson and Sanna, the nursemaid, all leave by train. Finally, Georgi drives up in her assigned Polo. A housekeeper and gardener stay at the Constantia house.

Georgi loves its sturdy, square, red-brick facade. On one side of the house, a large porch overlooks a swimming pool with crystal blue water, bordered by a flower-filled barbecue area.

Marcia explains that this space is intended for entertaining guests. The grounds are modest, and there are no staff accommodations.

Once, when Odessa visits Georgi, she makes sarcastic remarks about the spacious, airy rooms and comments that the high, ornate ceilings remind her of the colonial era of Cecil John Rhodes. Behind the house are quarters for Gibson and Sanna to sleep.

Odessa is frustrated by this arrangement and says, "This property needs a major overhaul. How can the Taungs have swimming pools and tennis courts while their loyal employees, a married couple, are cramped in a single room with hardly any space for their child?"

Georgi reflects sadly on her sister's words as she shares the bright, sunny nursery with baby Taylor, with Jamaica and Verona in an adjoining room. Odessa's protests about the unfair space-sharing at the estate remind her of Barend's strange invitation to his family farm. She doesn't know how to tell Odessa the hidden feelings she has for Barend, which have been brewing inside her since she first met him. She remembers Ganon's warning to 'beware of the man.'

Early in the morning, Georgi quietly enters the servants' quarters to talk with Sanna, hoping for a woman-to-woman chat that might clarify the warning about 'the man'—referring to Barend. The area has a small kitchen with basic supplies and a bedroom. Sanna seems uneasy, feeling she needs to 'entertain' Georgi. Though her English is limited, she makes up for it with her flawless Xhosa. During their conversation, Georgi notices a passport-sized photo of a girl in a wheelchair taped to the cover of an Xhosa Bible on the table. Sanna knows little about Barend but is eager to find out if Georgi is related to Marcia.

"No, I am employed by the Taungs."

"I work with my husband, too, but I've noticed we're treated differently. Is it because you're from America?"

"Canada. I'm South African. Why do you think we're treated differently?"

"Gibson isn't happy here, and we argue about it. They make him work long hours and pay him little. I see that your bedroom is spacious, equipped with a shower, and features a toilet. How much do you get paid?"

"No, Sanna, that's private."

"Sorry, I shouldn't have asked. Please don't tell Mrs. Marcia I inquired about your pay. She might fire me, and it would be hard to find a new job..."

Georgi feels like a typical sell-out. Although she's curious about how much Marcia pays the couple, she's too afraid to ask directly, so she says, "You work long hours and get paid little?"

It's better than five years ago. When I started here, my wage was R450 a month, and Gibson earned R900. Now, we make double that.

Georgi senses Sanna is probing her soul for an answer regarding her family's situation.

"That picture in the Bible—the girl in a wheelchair—who is she?"

Sanna quickly grabs the Bible from the table and heads to the bedroom. When she returns, she says, "Oh, that girl? She's just a girl... I don't know her."

Georgi isn't pleased with this explanation. There is only one spare bedroom with a bathroom, kept ready for essential guests. Any visitors staying in the other three bedrooms would need to share the shower and toilet down the hall.

"This is our lock-up-and-go house," Marcia explains. "We consider Constantia our home and don't even keep pets at Houghton. A cleaning service prepares the place for us before winter arrives, and we also have a gardening service year-round, though we often forget about it when we're in Cape Town. It's big enough for what we need."

Georgi envies the stunning, secluded estate, which is three times bigger than her home in Canada.

CHAPTER 7

First Day at Work

The girls are in the television lounge, and Taylor is asleep when Moroka arrives. Meanwhile, Marcia and Georgi are in the kitchen. Moroka storms in like a hurricane and ominously drops his briefcase on the floor.

"Marcia, we need to talk," he gestures restlessly.

"I'm listening," smiles his wife, as she vigorously shakes her special salad dressing over which, she swears, she is on top of the game. It is a rare moment of pleasure for her to perform domestic tasks, and she looks relaxed and happy.

Moroka pauses briefly before saying, "I have been posted to Bonn. I have to leave next month."

At first, Marcia seems fine. She places the shaker on the kitchen counter, and their eyes meet uncomfortably.

Just like that? No discussion with your wife? No, 'Hey, guys, I've got family to think about. I have a small baby. I've got daughters in school. I have a wife who works her tail off for this country. Nothing like that?"

"Don't you think I...?"

"You said you wouldn't do this until the baby is older. What are you up to, Moroka?" she whispers, her voice trembling with anger.

Accepting an overseas position is my only chance for a promotion. I need to remain open to any opportunities that arise. You understand this, Marcia. Do you think I'll be stuck as a glorified clerk forever?

Marcia's anger suddenly erupts. Georgi quietly slips away, pretending not to see the chaotic scene behind her.

Moroka, which promotion are you talking about? You probably won't be an ambassador, except maybe somewhere far away! Esteemed embassy positions are for dedicated political 'deployees'. Do you deserve ambassadorship? Absolutely! But it's not realistic. What kind of advancement are you thinking of?

The conversation continues, with Moroka's gentle responses standing out. Her tears, whenever they come, seem to make no difference. Moroka is preparing to travel to Germany and shows signs of exhaustion from playing Mr Wagner, which triggers another emotional reaction from Marcia. They move to the sitting room, where Georgi pretends to be interested in her Elle magazine. The disagreement still lingers.

"Now, on top of everything else," Marcia says, "I have to raise three kids as a single mom! Paying most of the bills in this house isn't enough."

"Hardly on your own," retorts Moroka. "You've got a veritable army of helpers," he sighs deeply. "It's only two years, Marcia, and we can take turns to visit. Let the girls come with me for a year if it is too much for you."

~ 43 ~

"Not a chance! Forget that right now, Moroka. The girls are staying here with me. When you return, the baby won't even recognize his father. And who's going to take care of my so-called army? This one has a sore throat, and that one's son is getting into trouble with the police. Or they disappear for three weeks to attend their grandmother's funeral! And to whom do they turn for help? Me! That's right. Not you, Mr Moroka Taung, but me, Marcia Jayne Wagner. Besides, as my partner, I expect you to help carry the load. I can't do it all by myself."

The two little girls run into the room and plant themselves on either side of their mother.

Moroka departs for Germany despite Marcia's resistance, and the household quickly adjusts to a new routine, shaped by winter and an absent father. Georgi has less free time because Marcia is constantly busy with meetings and work commitments. Marcia often comes home after the girls are already in bed, though she tries to join them for breakfast. Gibson takes the girls to school every day and then returns to drive Marcia to various activities. Georgi picks up the girls from school and their after-school activities each afternoon. There's almost weekly ballet, music, sports, and birthday parties. Georgi wonders how a single working mother usually manages such a busy schedule.

Engaging in small talk and attempting to spark a meaningful conversation with Georgi, Odessa says, "It seems to me nowadays you either have a sneaky husband with half a dozen kids, or you mess up your life chasing a career. There must be another way out of the ordinary..."

"Not in the 21st Century, there isn't."

Look at Dad and Mom: educated, well-informed, intelligent, not to mention civilized... but do you think they are happy? I don't think so. They rarely take a holiday, not even to Africa. I believe they feel trapped in North America, Odessa.

I'm not sure about that. But changing the subject, here's the thing: like you, I received this anonymous note:

> Dear Miss King, I warned Georgina, your sister, about Van der Watt, but I saw them kissing and drinking wine at a restaurant. It's a trap. What's wrong with you people? By the way, your father was seen in Pretoria last week. Do you know where he is? I know everything. If you see him, warn him about the white man called Van der Watt.

Afterward, Georgi says, "Our coming here was, somehow, an escape for me. And I know I can rely on you because I must find myself and where I'm headed. But why do men find me unattractive? Look, I am young, no steady relationships, no flirting, no one-night stands, nothing. Since we arrived, has anyone asked me out? No. There must be something wrong with me."

"Is that why you've resorted to kissing a white man and drinking wine with him? Stop overreacting about men finding you unattractive. Have you become so desperate that you're willing to date an Afrikaner who wants to introduce you, a Black girl, to his farm workers?"

"Don't start now."

"Well, the Taungs aren't any different. The plebs know their place."

Georgi is upset. She says, "We don't know any plebs. Everyone is treated equally here."

"And you don't know any ordinary people? Take my advice; don't let the white man fool you into thinking you're like an honorary white. His Black workers know who they are; they belong to the working class because that's where they've been for hundreds of years."

Georgi finds herself in an awkward position after her sister's reprimand. She says, "So, tell me about your experience at work. How do they treat you?"

Odessa swears she can create complete literary works about the happenings at Trentraders. She reflects on her experiences and her first day at work, saying, "I won't bore you with minutiae, but let me tell you about my initiation and life. With school, you leave behind the traumas of control and the humiliating dramas of submission. Once you head off into the world, you quickly come to your senses; school was not such a bad place. One can drive around the bend on the first day of one's first job. It's both exciting and daunting. You want to start taking control of your life, yet something sinister begins to take control of your soul. This corporate world is a unique political system with a distinctive brand of democracy. Many smiling faces of executive-looking yuppies in fancy cars represent a false exterior. The corporate world is full of duplicity and insincerity. To survive, one must play by the rules, but to succeed, one must use one's own rules.

"Is that an opening for your research abstract?"

"It's a direct appeal to my sister, trying to appeal to her sense of respect for me as her older sister and to motivate her to respect herself. Let me continue. You should listen because life needs a plan. If you thought the top high-fliers of the corporate ladder got there by being decent human beings," Odessa begins, "you know nothing about self-preservation."

"Get to the point. This isn't a lecture room."

"Focus, Georgi. I am trying to tell you about my work experience in South Africa."

Odessa's first day raises tricky questions. She tries five different outfits: a dress, pants, jeans, and a pantsuit. Ultimately, she looks in the mirror again and feels 'dressed up to the nines,' her mom's favorite expression. No, I'll wear a dress. It is cool, flattering, and feminine. Or is it too sexy?

She takes a shower before slipping into her usual outfit. 'Picture perfect,' she decides; a neat, respectable, and proper dress is essential on her first day at work. Pushing down a panic attack, she squares her shoulders and heads down Rivonia Road to the high-walled complex housing the advertising department. In the Highveld, the hands of the climate clock have slowed almost to a halt, and it still hints of summer—brilliant bougainvillea and a riot of color over stark white walls. The sun is already beating down in the early morning, intensifying the chaotic traffic: cars, scooters, trucks, buses, and pedestrians all jostling for space. Later in the afternoon, clouds and showers, accompanied by lightning and thunder, will cause all traffic lights to malfunction, further worsening the traffic.

"So nervous I couldn't decide. I was doing the whole butterfly thing; you have no idea..."

"Whatever," says Georgi, a little bored, while Odessa appears eager to tell her sister more.

"Well, let me tell you about my first day at Trentraders Incorporated. This is Advertising 101. Trentraders is a private company with four directors and a staff of twelve."

At the reception desk, a smiling red-haired girl shakes her head.

"Sorry, Mr Finian Trent isn't in today. Someone else will help you?"

"I'm Odessa Moffet-King, starting work here today."

"Oh. Hi. I'm Reeva Trent, Fin's sister. I missed your interview. Call me 'Reeva'. I'm running scuttlebutt for now."

"Scuttlebutt?"

Odessa feels abandoned and slightly resentful. What a welcome!

Reeva pulls a face, "Maid of all work—tea girl, eh... tea person, receptionist, or gofer. I'll get you coffee and show you to your desk. Right along here, if you follow me."

Reeva has a perfect body, an elegant walk to match, and striking green eyes that sometimes highlight her genuine red hair. Her smile is constant, the kind you have to interpret from one moment to the next: is she 'chuffed' or 'edgy' or 'fuming'? The office is spacious and features a bright, open floor plan. Large windows to the north and east overlook neat lawns and gardens surrounded by the usual security fencing. Five desks fit easily; one is next to a drawing board, all equipped with computers and screensavers, each displaying an image or text, possibly hinting at the user. Reeva points to the desk furthest from the windows. The computer screensaver reads, 'Please help me. I am new here.

"Me too," murmurs Odessa fervently as she stashes her purse in an empty bottom drawer. The desk is clear of clutter. Reeva returns with two mugs and hands one to Odessa.

"It's good, strong North American coffee."

Odessa nods appreciatively. The coffee is quite sweet. After taking a sip, Odessa places the mug on the desk. There's an overflowing entrée. Odessa reaches for it.

"Oh no, you don't," Reeva shunts the tray out of her reach. First, you have to undergo 'Induction and Orientation'. Only if you survive can you start on that lot. Finish your coffee, and I'll introduce you to Leslie—that's the other ugly sister." She flashes her rich smile to tease.

When she starts the interview, Leslie's forehead furrows with irritation upon discovering that Odessa does not know any African languages. Leslie stands up and walks away toward Reeva's office. There, she expresses her utter disbelief that Odessa can only speak English, Dutch, and French. Reeva ignores her.

Upon returning, Leslie asks Odessa, "But didn't Finian ask about your language skills? They assured me of your bilingual status."

"Status? I am bilingual."

"I mean English and vernacular."

"And what is that?"

"Vernacular? I mean an African language."

"Well, I am not bilingual in any other languages besides the two I mentioned earlier.

"Oh, Finian! Finian! We wanted someone to appeal to the Black market, forgive the expression."

"Finian asked if I was Sotho-speaking, and I told him I was Canadian. My parents spoke Tswana, but I've been in Ontario since I was knee-high. He didn't give any indication that speaking an African language might be necessary."

Leslie throws up her arms, looks at the ceiling, and then comes back down to say, "You mean you can't string a sentence in any of the vernacular languages?"

"Look, Leslie, Finian met my sister, Georgi who speaks both English and French. Mr Taung introduced me to Finian, who invited me here. But to answer your question, I can't put together a sentence in any of your vernacular."

"No need to be prickly. I'm doing my best here. But we definitely need someone like you to energize the agency. Did you study art in college?"

"I took art classes at the university, but it wasn't one of my majors. I majored in English and Economic History, with marketing as a minor, as you will see from my résumé right in front of you," Odessa throws her brusque response, and Leslie looks upset.

"I'm sorry, Odessa, but you need to understand that Finian has thrown us under the bus here. Typical of him. He goes off on his own tangent, does his own thing, makes decisions unilaterally, and changes plans we've all agreed on. He never bothers to fill us in, then leaves us to clean up after him. He didn't brief me about your appointment. Of course, Reeva, is rubbing her hands with glee as we speak. As for Finian..."

"He must be something," says Odessa, taut with irritation.

"Brilliant and creative, of course. He gets away with anything. Nobody told me he would not be in the office today. Some weeks ago, he talked about hiring a..." she gasps for politically correct jargon, "...a new person who might fill our quota needs," she finishes lamely.

"Quota?"

"Something like that."

"Yeah?" says Odessa. "I know all about quotas... widely held in the US."

"Not in Canada?" Leslie thinks she has cornered her.

"Canada is a democracy, and both the economy and the government understand the importance of redress. We don't need quotas."

Reeva walks in. She looks at Odessa's mug and observes that she hasn't used her good, strong North American coffee.

"You should have told me you don't take coffee," Reeva snaps.

"I do take coffee, but not sugar."

"But most... uh, people take sugar. You should have told me..."

"You should have asked."

Reeva grabs the mug furiously and heads for the kitchen sink.

Leslie has had enough of the interview. She opens the door to a long hallway and mutters, "Follow me. I'll introduce you to Kris."

Odessa obeys and follows Leslie, who rushes down the corridor. After recounting her career's unpromising start, she yawns tiredly.

"Rules of engagement in Africa," Georgi sighs. "A long way to go, I see. Back home, race isn't such a hot issue at the workplace, or is it?"

"At Trentraders, the generally bad-tempered atmosphere is worrisome. Egos are flying around, each trying to outmaneuver the others. I used to have a patronizing view of South Africans before we left home."

"After all, it's the dark continent of Africa, right?"

"But skin color and hair texture... still the main gauge here. Imagine hiring me to care for what they call 'your people' and 'appeal to the Black Market.' What rubbish!"

"And where's that black market? Squatter camps? Do we still have this homogenous thing called 'the black market'?"

"I asked Fin and Leslie. They told me about the 'lack of market densities,' that 'the African client base is scattered and unprofitable,' and that 'the resources it requires are expensive to roll out...' People use jargon to sound important, allowing them to keep milking the system and earn huge salaries. Over there, they use fancy terms like 'gender equity,' 'paradigm shift,' 'downward trajectory,' and 'consolidating neighborhood marketability.' We are drowning in gobbledygook. The old staff members nod their heads like sheep. Ask them what it all means, and they refer to some manual before they quickly take off."

CHAPTER 8

Our Aunt Kora

The letting agent describes Odessa's bed-sitter as a 'studio apartment.' Georgi realizes how lucky she is to live in a warm, welcoming family home. Meanwhile, Odessa's rented place is empty and uninviting, situated above a struggling bakery on a busy street. The unit itself lacks charm. The open-concept kitchen is dingy and unattractive, and the bathroom is dirty despite daily cleaning. Windows with dull curtains overlook a parking lot, flanked by a dull-looking building that blocks the light, leaving the room with a gloomy, rundown appearance. The furnishings are sparse and uninspiring, creating an atmosphere of mediocrity. Georgi knows she wouldn't want to live here. She hopes Odessa can move out soon.

"And I'll bring transport to help with your bags, okay?"

"Bags! Is that all I'm worth?" Odessa snuffles.

"Sorry, personal effects."

"Ah! I feel much better."

Reeva's elderly parents live on a farm adjoining the Van der Wats' in Robertson.

"The rich folk hang together," remarks Odessa. "And the older sister, Leslie, has been okay to me since our first bumpy encounter.

Odessa remains fixated on the Luca case: "Georgi, when is your next weekend off? I want to go looking for Aunt Kora. She's the one who told Luca she knows where they buried Bekker. I'm cautious about our chances with her, but she is Dad's sister, and we should locate her…"

"Oh, I forgot to tell you. Marcia used her office to locate Aunt Kora. I have her contact details."

"And when did you come by those details?"

"Weeks ago."

"You know, Georgi, if you carry on this way, I'll stop talking to you… forever."

"We can take a drive and look for her this weekend."

"My patience with you is reaching breaking point, believe me."

"Well, here's another thing, Odessa; I can't return home. Maybe for a vacation, but never back to Canada to settle there."

"What are you saying? You promised. You'll break Dad's heart. What's your problem?"

"I can't imagine living that lifestyle anymore…"

"Georgi, that's not the life you're trying to live here. It's Marcia's. This glamorous lifestyle isn't real. They're just acting out. It's the catwalk side of politics that hides the reality of squalor in South Africa from view. Surely, you can't be charmed by such idolatry."

"Please stop. You're beginning to sound like Mother."

"Mom was right. This is not for us. Our parents taught us the virtues of moderation, and I intend to live by their example."

"It's like... Ah, forget it, Odessa. You won't understand!"

"Try me."

"I feel as if I've come home. There's something about this land that speaks to me. It says, 'Your blood has been spilled into this earth, your people labored under the yoke of servitude, and because of that, you are now free to stand tall and speak your mind.'"

"All sounds like tacky poetry to me," she laughs. "Believe me, Georgi, I understand, that's not the point. Our real home is Toronto, good old Rosedale – not some fancy corner at the top of the hill – but down there, below the middle-class bottom of the hill. Our family is waiting for us over there. Unless you've finally found a nice white guy who wants to take you to the wine estate and up Table Mountain for your honeymoon. Look at yourself and then study the real black communities far from the mainstream of the good life."

Is it really black? On the other hand, I feel a clash among cultures here that makes me think maybe God has deserted the damn place. What can I do? I want to be here to face the challenge. Isn't it time for Africans to pull their weight? I noticed Africans in the Cape are somehow bashful. They won't even look you in the eye when they speak to you.

"Bottled up resentment."

That explains the violence. But there's something peculiarly strange about the way different types of blacks connect. It's so bizarre. And you? What do you think of the colored people? Tell the truth, now. Do you like the coloreds?

"Different types of blacks? One day, Monica, that white racist goalkeeper – remember her – said, "No, Georgi, you're not black, you're different.""

"Monica was no racist. Mother Ellen called her a child of God. Do you have any idea what a racist looks like?"

"So, you go along with Monica and say that you're a different type of black?"

The girls head for Hammanskraal, north of Pretoria. Using a basic rule of thumb for detective work, they locate a Mofokeng family member there. Mrs. Kora Mofokeng-Tladi is their father's sister. They find her at Hammanskraal High School, where she is attending a conference on Outcomes-Based Education. The girls can't help but notice the squalid condition of the school. The area is dry and unwelcoming. Georgi recalls one of Gibson's quips from their first trip to Cape Town: 'Any color, as long as they are rich.' She thinks, 'No one would bother searching for rich folks in this high school precinct.' Kora, a large, somber woman in a plain dark suit, is expecting them. Her hair is short, and her dark eyes assess them behind stark, unadorned spectacles. Georgi feels that Kora's demeanor would be less intimidating if only her glasses were more feminine. Odessa notes that Kora's forehead and bulky nose bear an uncanny resemblance to Teddy's.

Kora offers them a cold, hesitant handshake. Odessa feels anxious that her fears are coming true. She has a nagging suspicion that their aunt might still hold some resentment because her brother turned his back on his homeland and family. Still, Odessa smiles, trying to create a warmer atmosphere. Georgi remains grim-faced. Odessa holds her aunt's hand and brightens her eyes at her mysterious face.

"I am Odessa, and this is Georgi, my baby sister."

"She is pretty," she sneers at Georgi, her incongruous gaze lingering steadfastly across Odessa's face and bosom.

They find a suitable wooden bench beneath a mature Marula tree. The tree's massive trunk tells a story of its past; many souls have rested under its generous shade, countless rumors have been spread, cultural disputes have been expressed, and solutions have been found under its watch. In this part of the world, the Marula has a variety of medicinal uses, ranging from promises of fertility to the brewing of its alcoholic beverages. The Marula is impressive in its sheer grandeur. People compose poems in praise, while malevolent forces hold back prayers. During spring, the captivating red Marula flower begins attracting the black-headed oriole from across the seas, while its mature nuts do great good for the starving children of Hammanskraal.

Kora is gasping for air. She looks uncomfortable, as if she's holding back with fierce energy, like a volcano inside her chest. Odessa starts a conversation, "Aunt Kora, Luca said he spoke to you last year. Did you know a bomb blast killed him?"

"I heard in the news that he had died, but I am happy to meet you," says Kora without a flicker of emotion.

Kora shares details about her husband, Sabelo Tladi, and their three girls. She takes off her dark glasses, showing her apparent displeasure about her siblings' issues. She enjoys talking about her children because she gets into the details.

"They are in good health," she adds, "and I hope one day they can go overseas and get a good education. Are you girls educated?" she asks and moves on, indifferent to any answer. "Many of your MK and APLA soldiers went into exile and returned here with nothing. All they do is complain about the government as if they are more entitled than the rest of us who stay in the country. In the 80s, we gave bread to the young comrades fighting against Afrikaans..."

"We are also pleased to meet you, Aunt Kora," rushes Georgi, "and we look forward to meeting other family members."

Kora takes no notice of Georgi's gesture. She tells them that she is an assistant to the Registrar at the University of the North-West. The conference is close to her heart because she wants to specialize in outcomes-based education. She then stresses that she is a sister to Bekker and Daniel, while both brothers took their grandfather's name.

"There was another sister, Precious, who died last year," she adds.

Odessa remarks, "So, only three of you are still alive."

Kora responds dejectedly, "No, Bekker is dead. Ellen buried him. I can take you to his graveside. Did your mother not tell you?"

"Mother knows nothing of what you are saying. And I don't understand, Aunt Kora," says Odessa, "why mother would have buried him? Surely, that was his parents', his sisters', and his brother Daniel's responsibility. Everything I've learned about your culture tells me it was not my mother's place to bury her husband's brother. My mother and father have no idea what happened to Uncle Bekker."

It's your culture, too, although I don't know about the girl you call your sister here. You are right, of course, that it was not your mother's place to bury our brother," Kora says. "I don't understand the rights and wrongs, whose place it was, or what terrible things happened. I can only tell you what I know. Ellen buried Bekker in the stealth of night so that no one would know about it. But under the Marula, among the thicket of bushes and shrubs, I saw her. I did, with my own two eyes, because my ancestors gave me a signal in my dreams. In the hours of darkness, if you take cover behind nature's foliage and brush, no one can see you. That was me. Ellen thought she had gotten away with murder."

Losing her composure, Georgi says, "Aunt Kora, why don't you tell us exactly what happened? You are speaking in tongues. You say it all happened in the stealth of night, but where? How come we don't know these things?"

"Remember, both sides were howling for his head," Kora responds, her demeanor fixed on Odessa.

"Both sides?" asks Georgi.

Kora heaves impatiently and slides back her glasses to cover her face. The enigmatic face returns, and the girls remain in obedient silence as she prepares to give them a long tirade. "I see you are just like those Model C children; all you know is your European history. When Bekker died, nobody could say who had killed him. The South African police were looking to kill him. Our people, those in the struggle, and some elements in the townships all wanted him dead. They were wrong, of course, to want to kill a human being because of gossip. They branded Bekker a traitor. Whether he was a traitor or not, I do not know. Who can look into the soul of another person? The police told me Daniel was under interrogation. I hear you call Daniel with a different name, Kian, in Canada. When people want to keep secrets, they change their identity. For me, as a sister, my brain does not align with the picture painted of Bekker, which suggests that he was a traitor. My father was dead, and my mother was too sick to lift her head to the light of day because her firstborn had broken her weak heart. You can ask: Who was there to give Bekker a Christian burial? Well, I could have done it, or my sister Precious could have, not to mention our mother, who brought him to this world. But no! Ellen stole the honors, acting on behalf of her husband, Daniel. How did Bekker come to be at Daniel's house?" She puts it with contempt. "Ask your mother. How did he die? Was I angry that Ellen did this? Yes, and I still am. My two brothers obtained an education, while we girls were just ordinary African women in the eyes of all concerned. Precious and I had to work as domestics. I was a nursemaid in Cape Town when I met Sabelo. With my limited education, I consider myself lucky. It is a blessing to have this job at North-West. My night-school certificates? That wouldn't have been possible under the old regime. I know some people are hostile to affirmative action," she says, her gaze drifting toward Georgi, "but enough of that," she adds, focusing on Odessa. "Do you want to see Bekker's grave?"

"Yes," says Odessa.

"No," shouts Georgi, "we don't want to see the grave. If it is true that my mother buried your brother, then it's clear that she was the only one brave enough to defy the South African government and give her dead brother-in-law a proper resting place. I know she and my father loved your brother; despite all the negative stories you've been spreading. The family owes her a debt of gratitude for taking on that responsibility."

Kora crosses her arms over her ample chest. Her sharp gaze meets Georgi's piercing eyes with disdain. She asks, "And then? Who are you?" Odessa notices the striking resemblance between Kora and their father, even more noticeable with Teddy's generous nose.

"Me? I'm Georgi. I'm Kian's second daughter, born just before the family left South Africa."

"What nonsense is this you speak? Daniel and Ellen had no other children. There was only Odessa. You don't even look like a Mofokeng with your skin," she says, shaking her head without removing the expression of resentment on her face. "Odessa, she looks just like us, like her mother. And you, whatever your name is..."

"Georgi! My name is Georgi!" she raises her voice a decibel.

"Whatever. It doesn't matter whether you think Ellen was right to bury Bekker. You, whoever you are, may believe that, but..." She raises a solemn index finger to emphasize her words, "Many questions remain unanswered. Is it true that Bekker lies in that grave? If so, we will leave him buried in the land of his ancestors. Even now, people are negotiating to have their ancestral farms in that district returned to our tribe. If it is my brother, Thlokomela Bekker, in that lonely grave, let him rest in peace. There is nothing more to say of Thlokomela Mofokeng."

Kora removes her glasses again, takes Odessa's hand, and places it in her bosom. Her face begins to drip with tears.

"I am the only surviving sibling of your father," she says. "Ask him to come back to his country, just once. I want to see him with my own eyes once more—only him and I, the last Mofokengs of our bloodline. My name is no longer Mofokeng. I am a Tladi, as you know. But I am a man when discussing issues of the Mofokeng family. I have been a man for over twenty years."

"Aunt Kora," says Odessa, "we have a younger brother, Teddy. He is sixteen, the last of the Mofokengs. It's me, Georgi, and Teddy."

Kora is no longer angry, as if someone suddenly lifts a heavy burden from her shoulders. She begins to dab at her sorrowful eyes. Odessa holds her hand and wipes her face.

Kora exclaims, "Aieeeya! How I would love to see this young lion called Teddy. I have three daughters. After the second, I prayed that the next would be a boy. But, alas!

Do you have photographs of this boy, who is my nephew, no, my son? He must come. Soon, he will be the man of our house. We must introduce him to our ancestors. He is our only hope."

"You too, my child," she says to Odessa, turning her attention away, gazing far into the mysterious distance. "Our long-departed ancestors must look upon you for the sake of your children. You must come to our land so they can place their protective hand on your shoulder.

Meanwhile, Georgi is nervously flailing around like a flag, unable to sit still. Kora asks Odessa, her eyes fixed on Georgi, "Does this sister of yours take drugs?" Without waiting for a reply, she continues, "Never mind. Long ago, when King Shaka led his imperialist campaigns, our Mofokeng clan resided in the Bafokeng Valley—an independent community with mountain springs and a thriving life centered on farming, culture, and commerce. King Shaka's attempt to weaken the Bafokeng was met with strong resistance. Our king sent elders to scout, while young men and women moved in to trap the enemy," she emphasizes. "We defeated them. But the same strategy failed against the Boers. When fighting the Zulus, we were united, but during the Boer attack, some warriors betrayed us for money. That's how Africans are defeated—by some of us worshiping whiteness. Our ancestors, with their wives and children, became outcasts in the Eastern Cape; our land, mountains, and rivers became known as Beesfontein. Yet now," she smiles contentedly, "with our freedom, some land has been reclaimed. Soon, we will hold our first traditional wedding there since reclaiming Beesfontein, a celebration for the whole community. Teddy, the young lion, must come from Canada to experience his ancestors' valley. Come, let's eat—there's a coffee bar here for delegates and staff. We need to talk more," she concludes.

Georgi is upset with Kora over her insinuation that she uses drugs. On their way to the bar, she whispers to Odessa, "This woman!"

"She is our aunt," Odessa whispers back. "Learn to be civil for once and stop expecting everyone to think you are Princess Diana. Our Aunt is more important than Marcia, your boss. Aunt Kora is our aunt. She's no woman to you."

A strange note

Georgi and Odessa are in the lounge, partly watching a video and partly reflecting on their lack of progress on the Bekker case. Georgi checks on Taylor, who sleeps soundly.

"You said you discovered something about the German photographer."

"Yeah, the name 'Puri' keeps popping up. A few weeks ago, I received a strange note, 'Leave Bekker alone.' I didn't know what to make of it."

"Where did it come from?"

"Mr April. I picked it up after enquiring about the photographer at the library. I threw it in the bin and forgot about it."

"Very clever. Now we have no evidence."

"My search revealed a lot about Puri, along with some snippets about her connections with the comrades in Angola. Puri probably isn't a common name. How many people named Puri could have been foreign war photographers in Africa in 1980?"

"And how many Moffet-Kings have you found in your research?"

Marcia calls Gibson to inform him she is returning home. He is supposed to meet her at the airport in the morning. She asks Georgi to accompany Gibson at the airport.

"Bring Taylor too. Don't take your eyes off my baby until I get there."

Some disturbance had happened in the area, and Marcia became paranoid.

Reeva invites Odessa and Georgi to meet at a nearby coffee shop. The three women settle in comfortably, unaware that Barend is hiding in the corner, watching them.

Odessa lifts her eyes and notices Barend pretending to be reading a newspaper. Without saying a word, Reeva walks over to Barend's table, sits in front of him, and after a minute, she walks back to her table.

That's your Barend, Georgi.

"He denies he is shadowing us. He warned me about April and Wolter."Dr Wolter, is an apartheid operative who manufactured drugs to kill apartheid enemies. He employed a man called Bekker at one of the state laboratories. Their job was to experiment, produce, and promote chemical and biological warfare – mind-bending drugs, addictive substances – and test them in black townships and African countries like Angola and Mozambique.

"Bekker? Are you sure, Reeva?" asks Odessa.

"It seems that Bekker went to Tanzania or Kenya and disappeared for some years. If you try to follow his tail, you'll walk until you hit a mirage — if you're lucky enough to survive. Leave Bekker alone…"

"Right, Reeva. It's time we let sleeping dogs lie."

As they walk out, Georgi says, "You make me sick, Odessa."

The sisters linger around a spot diagonally opposite the café. The verbal assaults start again.

"I always make you sick, so what's new?"

"Odessa, stop involving Reeva in this. The Bekker case is a family matter, and Reeva isn't part of the family. I'm done with Bekker Mofokeng. I believe Dad knows something about this. He warned us over and over. This is the end. I don't want to use that name again!"

"Why are you so bothered?"

The spectator's interest increases. What began as a trickle grows into a small crowd. The gloves come off, and the spat escalates into name-calling.

"Aren't you curious about the truth? You're disgusting."

"I'm disgusting? You repeat that, and I'll kill you. You keep chopping and changing. What makes you think Reeva can be trusted?"

"Aren't you scared to hear someone wants to strangle our relative?"

Odessa looks around at the smiling faces of Africa. She curses the day she ever thought of leaving Canada. All her dreams have turned into a nightmare. Georgi stomps toward the car, with Odessa right behind her.

"Just drop me off at the office. I don't have transport. And remember Donald's barbecue invitation. After all, it's only your pretty face that those whites are hankering after. Just drop me anywhere I can use the internet. I'll take a taxi afterward. But we must hear what that man has to say about strangling Lenin."

"Forget it," Georgi retorts as the car rolls away.

CHAPTER 9

As in Lesbian?

Georgi has returned to the spacious Houghton Estate, her heart a jumble of excitement and unease. Meanwhile, Odessa stays up quite late, which is a mistake since she has to leave early Monday morning. She is fixated on the dark possibility that Georgi might be harboring deep romantic feelings for Barend. She plans to warn their father about the looming trouble threatening the family. In the morning, she pours out her heart to Reeva, sharing how conflicted she feels about her life choices. From the beginning, her mother had opposed her leaving Canada for Africa. Now she feels her life flashing before her eyes and questions what she is doing on earth.

"You have Georgi. Spend time with her and wait for the right moment for the situation to resolve itself.

Odessa can only shrug while trying to keep Reeva in the dark about her troubled relationship with her sister."

"Unless, of course... if you can't tell Georgi everything about yourself. Can you? I know about the sibling game, Odessa."

"Yes, Ree. It's been like that all our lives," Odessa begins to share with a confident, "poor me, always the 'hunter' slash 'gatherer'. I show up with my friends, and before long, they fritter away and gather around the eternal main attraction, Georgi. She's never had to lift a finger for people to be drawn to her. And worse, she pretends she doesn't revel and wallow in the attention."

"You have a situation with your sister?"

"Yeah, forever butting heads and causing each other little headaches..."

Don't you think it's time to hit the reset button while you're in Africa? Visit the Kruger; see how a pack of elephants functions as a family unit.

"I don't know, Reeva... but I wonder more and more about me," Odessa cackles. "Men! All that they say to me is, 'I admire your intellectual faculty'. Reeva! I mean, I am a woman, for Helen Reddy's sake. Sometimes a girl wants more; a genuine compliment, something flattering, as a woman. 'Intellectual?"

"Men are real pigs, selfish," says Reeva, feeling snowed under by Odessa's grumpiness. "Don't tell me you harbor jealousy over Georgi and Barend. Do you? I've heard rumors, you know. Interracial affairs are problematic, especially in this neck of the woods."

"Except if it's Barend hanging around with Georgi, of Course? You don't have to answer. Racial prejudice is a worldwide phenomenon, and life seems to get friendlier the fairer one's skin. Interracial? It's not an international UN problem. I have experienced it in my own family. Georgi will do no wrong. I don't know what family means, and I can tell you now, those Kruger elephants would be wasting their tuition on us."

"Do you sometimes have good moments with Georgi?"

Odessa briefly reflects and says, "Yes, after we sing the song 'We can work it out'. There's something spiritual and redemptive about that song. No matter how low we sink into loathing each other, which happens every time we are together, once we get back to it, the anger vanishes like smoke in the air."

"Maybe I should try it with my mother..."

"I think Kathy Clayton finally saw the light. As for me, I need a genuine hug to calm my itchy nerves, to raise my spirits a little. I am more than cerebral material. My body burns because I also have other needs as a girl... Oh gosh! Sorry, Reeva."

"Your mother?"

Reeva looks disappointed. She says, "You don't think much of feminism?"

"We all have needs, Odessa. How do you feel about... other women?"

"As in lesbian?" Odessa giggles awkwardly, while Reeva's face remains straight as an arrow. "Well, I was smitten once with a French girl called Sapphira from a rural town of Montpellier. Her English was atrocious, but who cares when you have a replica of Sofia Loren right in your face?" "So, what became of the French Sapphira?"

"She went back home after a year, and I simply gravitated toward the male species."

"Nothing after that? No magnetism towards women?"

"Not quite the same. But Reeva, at the risk of sounding facile, you ask as if something is bubbling beneath the surface. Is there?"

"I'm a lost sheep roaming the desert; confused, you might say, and I don't know who I am."

"But Reeva! I never suspected you were..."

"Gay? 'Suspected'? Nice turn of phrase, Odessa. After repeatedly dodging the issue, I finally talked to my mother. I must have been seventeen. I'd known her as a very liberated woman, member of the Black Sash and all the rest; completely a liberal. When I brought up the subject, she snarled like a wounded Rottweiler. Dazed, I went back to my room with my tail between my legs, never to come out again, so to speak. I almost ruined my life after that, self-medicating with alcohol and sometimes dagga. Then one day I woke up and said, 'Reeva girl, stand up and start walking'.

"Good for you."

"Yes, but it's the ticking biological clock that's about to run out that scares us women into action, you might say. I don't want to wake up one morning only to discover I've made the wrong choices. I know I need to commit my life to something, sooner rather than later."

"Life's a gamble, Reeva. But why do you think you're a lost sheep?"

"My entire family has never looked me in the eye since the day I met with that unexpected rebuff from my mother. I guess they later ran long sessions in my absence and then came out with 'certain recommendations,'" Reeva hoots piercingly.

"Recommendations? Like what...?"

"Who knows? I can only guess they followed the line of, 'let's agree to disagree but keep everything under wraps.' Their attitudes toward me changed, but I could easily tell who was on my side and who was undecided."

"But you are still family, and you still do stuff together?"

"Yes, 'polite', 'double-talk' or 'hooey'."

"It hasn't been easy with my mother. Whenever we need to talk about something, we connect through Fin. He's been an unofficial intermediary for years; the only one who calms other people's fires," she laughs sweetly."

"You don't think you should try to hit the reset button and start all over with your mom?"

"I tried before. But it takes one family member to hit that default key again, and we're back to Square One."

Odessa's exploration of the internet for Villiers Wolter yields more pages with little substance. Barend's simple facts summarize the situation; nowhere does the name Bekker Mofokeng appear. Odessa concludes that he was a minor player in the murky world of international chemical warfare. Still, he might be able to incriminate Wolter, who had slipped easily through the cracks of the justice system.

Mercy, Leslie's typist, is at the reception desk.

"Briefing... Conference room," she greets Odessa, "They're all in there. You'd better move it, on the double!" she whispers.

"Well? Hi to you, too!" Odessa mutters as she hurries to the venue. She's determined not to be anyone's lackey. This is her first time attending a meeting in this room, but she refuses to let her eyes wander around the unfamiliar setting. They've decorated the meeting space beautifully, creating a welcoming atmosphere to impress the guests. She slowly takes a seat.

Perched in the top corner is their state-of-the-art digital imaging projector, connected via remote control to a laptop. This setup feels less overwhelming than other boardrooms she has seen, with muted colors highlighted by vivid images and African bowls displayed on a shiny wood sideboard. Everyone on the creative team is present, including Reeva. Finian wants Odessa to sit next to Reeva. Reeva holds a small remote-control device, which she hands to Finian. He seems to enjoy the power it gives him, twisting it as he begins to speak and then pressing the button, causing his body to shake in sync. The message on the wall reads the letters 'SAPDC'.

"Right troops," he says, "battle stations, cancel your private lives for the foreseeable future. We'll be eating, sleeping, drinking, and making love to only one entity until further notice. And that's what we're going to talk about now." He pauses to look searchingly at each person in the room. They all gaze expectantly back at him.

"At the same time," Finian continues, "we will not slack off on our existing workload. So, don't use this project as an excuse to fall behind on other work. There will be big rewards for success, but a trash can if we fail." He presses his toy and reveals the letters CHA-CHA on the wall. "For the uninitiated, and I hope there aren't any in this room right now, this is the logo of one of our biggest rivals, Chaitowitz and Chambers. Word on the Gauteng streets is that they've blown it with their biggest client. And that is who, Kris?"

Kris smirks and says laconically, "SAPDC."

Finian clicks to reveal a purple-on-orange logo with the letters SAPDC. Odessa, definitely one of the 'uninitiated', notes that they stand for South African Platinum, Diamonds, and Copper. She has never heard of them.

"But wait," Finian holds up a palm and flips another digital page, revealing, in sequence, "Namibian Platinum, Diamonds and Copper, and Royal Canadian Platinum, Diamonds and Copper. Keep these giants in mind as we explore what Cha-Cha has planned for their client.

He presses the remote control, and the presentation begins. They watch a five-minute video showing blue skies and tall mountains, where the voice-over states that platinum and diamonds are mined. The video then shows images of the mining and refining process, with employees wearing SAPDC logos. It emphasizes what a fantastic company it is to work for. Next, shots of magazine ads appear, featuring headlines that praise the company's environmental awards. Finally, a sultry-looking, scantily dressed model explains thoughtfully how SAPDC plans to merge with a Namibian group and a Canadian one to form the most important and influential group in this sector. Finian playfully cuts the image and sits at the table as the blue sky over the mountains reappears.

"We're not going to do a post-mortem on the corpse, but anyone here who doesn't know why that ad is a bummer should seriously consider switching to a different career," he crows. Finian is too energized to sit still. He jumps back up, looks around at his team, and says, "This is the plan: two weeks from today, fourteen working days, we will show SAPDC how it's done. I want to leave that pitch with all their business. Henri, you and I will handle the presentation, with Kris as backup. Odessa, you'll come with us, but I don't want you to speak unless to smile," he flexes his arm muscles as if he's stiff.

Odessa is itching to respond to Finian's disparaging attitude, that she roll over, lie on her back, and smile. Reeva quickly hands her a note, 'Keep mum.' Odessa recalls Moroka's words, 'you're on your own in this country if you're black'.

"But to reach that point, we've got work to do, guys!" Finian continues. "Marina, your team will do research; that is, you, Reeva, and Odessa. You need to find every visual and audio ad that Cha-Cha has created for SAPDC over the last five years since they received the contract. They must have done good work at some stage. We don't want to duplicate their stuff; we want to make ours different and better! If you can't get hard copies, make sketches. You may even try to Google it if you're that inclined."

Finian asks Kris and Henri to analyze the strategy, determine what the images they saw communicated, and identify the target market to which it was intended.

"Ha! Ha! If we want the job, we'll have to guess right," jokes Doreen.

Reeva whispers to Odessa, "This is Fin's wife, Doreen."

"I have an important job for you, Doreen. We need a bio on all of Cha-Cha's big clients. You're familiar with how this industry operates. When SAPDC fires Cha-Cha, their other clients will escape like rats deserting a sinking ship. We can decide which ones to pitch for, and we'd better do some homework on them."

"We could probably use another copywriter," says Henri.

Whereupon Finian bestows a dazzling smile on Reeva, "For starters, I want Reeva in that empty desk, Henri. You can move into the Factory today, Reeva. Tell Leslie her girl can stay at the reception desk. Get a temp." Reeva is delighted. She nods, smiles her thanks.

"Before we start, everyone, remember: what we talked about stays in this room. Cha-Cha hasn't been officially let go yet. This insider information gives us an advantage. In this industry, building relationships with government officials and politicians is a wise investment. By the time our competitors realize what's happening and begin their scramble, we'll be celebrating our new client and attracting several others. Please make sure you sign the confidentiality forms in front of you. I'm sure you've all heard of the Scorpions. Speak out, and you're out of the Western World. As I mentioned, we have connections in influential positions. Right, Odessa? Any questions?"

Odessa poses a question about foreign companies. The boardroom falls silent until Finian speaks up, saying, "Oh, yes, Odessa. I've been receiving some unusual prank calls about you lately. Is there anything you want to declare to me... to us, I mean; something that may compromise the running of Trentraders?"

Odessa freezes. Reeva challenges, "Crank calls?"

"Well," says Finian, "rumors about Odessa's uncle named 'Lenin'; no, not Vladimir, the founder of that failed ideology we used to call communism..."

"Get on with it, Fin," shouts Reeva.

"Yes, rumor has it the lesser-known Bekker, the South African version I mean, worked for Dr Wolter... Know anyone by that name, Odessa?"

"What's that got to do with my work here?"

"So, you know him, then?"

Odessa cannot hide her irritation and, raising her voice, she says, "Mr Finian, I don't know where this whole conversation is taking us, but you can continue without me," she says, picking up her handbag and marching out of the boardroom. "I see Margaret Thatcher has her following in Africa," Finian says. "Tell Odessa, the Iron Lady's hand-bagging theories don't work in this country."

A heated discussion follows. The matter is finally resolved when Finian promises to stop hounding Odessa. When she finally agrees to come back, Finian says, "I have been instructed to cut the drivel. So, let's forget about the unscheduled commercial and carry on, right?"

However, Odessa refuses to cooperate. Finian acts contrite. He formally apologizes for poking fun at her, and the meeting resumes.

"To answer your question about the Canadian companies," says Finian, "Canada had to shuck their South African subsidiary after your American man, so-called Reverend Sullivan, made it too hot for North American groups to be in bed with the apartheid companies. The Namibian one used to belong to SAPDC before independence. Now, hey presto! South Africa is the month's favorite, and everyone wants to be friends with us. Any further comments or questions? Please, let's stick to relevant inputs."

Odessa feels so low that she cringes at how she handled herself during the 'Finian Show'. If only Georgi were here, she thinks; the very same Finian would have been salivating, 'What perfume are you wearing, Georgi?' instead of sticking his nose in the Lenin/Bekker affair.

Odessa says to herself, 'I won't stay in South Africa. The country is too much for me.

CHAPTER 10

Nathaniel

Jamaica and Verona are flying back from Bonn this morning. Reacting to the vibes, Taylor becomes restless and overly demanding. The Taung house is warm, with gas fires and anthracite heating keeping the sharp bite of the Highveld winter at bay. Georgi had not expected below-zero temperatures in this sub-tropical paradise. Nor had she bargained on how bare and stripped the Gauteng landscape turns out to be in winter; trees are skeletal, lawns and shrubbery brown and sere, Icy gales swagger their way through frosty mornings and toss dry leaves and branches to the hard, chilled ground. She can appreciate why people pray for the spring rains to bring their world back to life, which will be soon.

Jamaica and Verona pass through customs, but flight attendants do not accompany them as expected. Instead, their father is there with them.

At the same time, a young man from Germany on a temporary visa arrives in Johannesburg incognito. Odessa receives an email from April informing her about a strange man named Nathaniel from Germany who has been inquiring about Bekker's files in Pretoria. In the meantime, Barend has taken a keen interest in the goings-on at the Moffet-King household across the oceans since he met Odessa. Like April, he discovers Nathaniel's activities and dispatches his secret officials to put the mysterious German under strict surveillance. Barend is not aware that he is also a victim of the 'Spy vs Spy' culture characteristic of states that have just emerged from tyranny. The intelligence industry is divided into factions along the lines of political maneuvering.

Nathaniel spends time at Vorna Valley in Midrand and pays daily visits to the Rissik Street Main Library in Johannesburg, where he immerses himself in old newspapers. One day, while poring over archives and dailies, he notices something frightening: the spy shadowing him. Nathaniel disappears and immediately relocates from Midrand to Centurion, South of Pretoria. He joins a couple of tourist trips to black townships: Alexandra, Mamelodi, Sharpeville, and Soweto. In Sharpeville, he visits the seventy graves of the victims of the 1960 massacre. He spends quality time at the Hector Peterson Memorial in Soweto and, for the next two nights, stays at Nambitha bed and breakfast, a few meters from the old Mandela residence on Vilakazi Street.

Barend's secret agents later see Nathaniel appear outside Archbishop Tutu's home in Soweto. He finds a party of Japanese tourists a spectacle and watches them from the stoep. Then, a red flag: an unmarked black BMW with tinted windows is lurking about. Nathaniel disappears, outmaneuvering Barend's professional agents.

Barend panics, concerned that the strange man might be Georgi's secret lover. 'Come to think of it,' he says to himself, 'I know little about this mysterious girl except I find her attractive.'

Barend is aware that to keep Georgi in his grasp, he must know more about the identity and intentions of the strange German guy. He considers calling Odessa to sound her out about the man, but thinks better of the direct approach. Instead, he does the roundabout way, challenging Odessa about her wanderings in 'the crime capital city',

"What?"

"Hillbrow! We spotted you and Reeva in old-fashioned hot pants, getting into expensive BMWs,"

"No. No! It's not what you think," Odessa refutes the insinuation. We were not soliciting, I swear. Reeva came up with the idea because these girls know many high-flying officials in the black economic empowerment companies and government, as well as their clients, who may be able to assist us. Something about Bekker."

"No need to explain anything. It's your life," he says, hanging up.

Barend's call leaves Odessa mortified. "What cheek, this man. Reeva, you're the one who came up with this silly idea," she starts. "And look now, this dog will tell Georgi, and she won't even wait for the morning to call Mother and start blabbering away about Hillbrow. Maybe I should ring her first and tell her the truth. Do we look like whores?"

"What do whores look like? Relax. You call her, and then she'll put two and two together. Take it easy, will you?"

With Barend's half-hearted help, Odessa and Reeva trace Nathaniel to an apartment in Centurion. Nathaniel assures them he is in South Africa for an interview. He works for the South African foreign mission in Bonn and has asked for a transfer to South Africa. The women do not believe him.

"So, why have you been on our tail all these days? Does your interview involve stalking people around?"

Nathaniel looks uncomfortable. He stands up and produces an interview letter to demonstrate his bona fides. Odessa gets to the point. "Why are you investigating the Mofokeng family? What possible interest does that bear on your interview?"

Nathaniel claims he has no idea what they are talking about. However, after a little while, he admits, "My father was a South African. I'm trying to find out what happened to him."

"Wow! I mean, really?" says Reeva as she notices Odessa's dismayed glance.

He tells them that Lieber is his adoptive name and that his mother is a German photographer. They live in Zurich.

"Did you take pictures of us in Hillbrow?" asks Odessa.

"Ja, I take snaps of suspicious characters who stalk me. I found Jardine's Beauty Salon to be an interesting venue. Do you know what happens there?"

"What?"

"Behind the scenes, it is a satellite for Nazi hunters. South Africa is a fascinating country," he giggles. "Nazi hunters know everything that happens around them."

Odessa and Reeva take an anxious drive to Hillbrow. They park outside Jardine's Beauty Salon and try the steel gate that stands slightly ajar.

"Sorry, girls. We are closed for the day," says a skinny white brunette with a silky voice. She tries to press the door shut, but Reeva sticks her foot forward and jams it.

"What about that woman inside?" asks Reeva.

"Last patron for the day."

Jardine's answer fails to convince them, and Reeva tells her they smell racism.

"We're not racists, please understand; we just can't handle ethnic hair."

The phrase reminds Odessa of what Kian once called the world's 'colorism phenomenon,' and she whispers, "Ethnic hair?"

"We're not here to do ethnic hair," snaps Reeva. "Tell us what happened across the street a year ago, remember? You told the police you saw two black men racing off in a BMW. But the papers think you lied to the police."

"Oh, Luca?' Jardine heaves as she relents. "Come in; five minutes."

The white client gawks at Odessa. Jardine leads the two to her private office.

"I told the police everything."

"Listen, Jardine," says Odessa, "that was my friend they killed. I need to know the truth."

"Very well, let's talk. I'm not a racist; I don't feel comfortable with this rainbow nation. Since 1994, most blacks, I mean South African blacks, have developed huge chips on their shoulders."

"How so?"

"They think they can boss me around. This is my business. Why should I hire a black?"

"Who's forcing you to hire a black?" asks Reeva.

"Ag, you know how it is. This Affirmative Action is full of amateur inspectors who come here to boss me around. They even threatened to set my place alight if I didn't do black hair and hire Africans. I tell them my great-grandfather survived Auschwitz. I don't scare easily?"

"Auschwitz? We're familiar with your hair salon. But tell us about the BMW," Reeva says.

"He was a good man, that Luca guy; a little naughty, but he paid me in dollars. I hid him here for a couple of days. He told me he was on to something big. A gentleman, he was. When I asked him about his accent, he told me he was Jamaican. Trust me, I don't waste my energy helping a local black."

"And the two men you saw running away, could you identify them?"

"You're joking. Like I told the cops, it was early evening. How could I see faces?"

"We know you are very good at reading faces. Your salon has done its bit for International Nazi hunters. So, say something about the black faces you did not see."

"This is a private salon. What we do here is strictly confidential and potentially hazardous. Here's a name for you..." Jardine jots down the name and hands the piece of paper to Reeva. "That's your man. But another man was waiting inside their getaway."

"Did you tell the police about him?" Odessa asks.

"Whose fault is it if the police don't ask?"

"Jardine, Dear," says Reeva, "Here's my card. I work for an Ad agency. We name and shame all salons that don't like ethnic hair."

"You don't scare me. I told the police I am the direct descendant of King David..."

"So, you know Bathsheba?" Reeva teases.

Corner Table at Portofino's

Odessa connects with Georgi. Odessa has the rest of the afternoon off and suggests Georgi join her for dinner.

"There's a fabulous Italian place, and Reeva will book us a table if you can make it," she says with some urgency.

Odessa tells Georgi about Nathaniel, "And after our little visit to his flat in Centurion, I called him. I thought it would be a good idea to ask him to join us. He seems to have interesting stories to tell, and there's something familiar about him. But be warned; he is a pig-headed son of a bitch."

Georgi rolls her eyes but affably agrees. They head out to Odessa's apartment, and Reeva joins them for an Italian meal. They go up the road to meet Nathaniel. The women are wearing colorful pants and sweaters. Reeva compliments Georgi on her sea-green silk pantsuit, which she describes as 'dangerous.'

"Where I come from, we say 'dressed to kill'. Any target in mind, Georgi?"

Georgi raises an eyebrow in Nathaniel's direction.

"Target? Victim is more like it," says Odessa.

"It's only a cast-off of Madam Marcia. I thought I'd better air it," says Georgi.

As they drive off to Rivonia Road, Nathaniel tells them that he feels like a grilled hostage about to have his head chopped off. "I don't know where you're taking me, but I hope it's not the bowels of Diepsloot."

The night air is freezing, and few people walk out at night, even in upscale Rivonia.

"And where is Diepsloot?" asks Georgi.

"It's a long story," says Reeva.

What an absolute pleasure to be at the table at Portofino's, where a massive wood fire is burning, and the decibel level in the restaurant is already rising to gregarious. After the usual formalities, they sit around chatting. The background music is 'Tunnel of Love' by Bruce Springsteen. Then, the mood changes to 'modern classical.' Reeva's taste runs to Shostakovich, and it complements the mainly Art Deco furniture, touches of stainless steel, and black and white posters on bare walls; stark, functional, and very 'liveable,' thinks Georgi. They continue with small talk, each trying to figure out how to break the ice.

Nathaniel hands Georgi a glass of wine and says, "I see you are also verso, Georgi."

"What do you mean?"

"Left-handed, 'Southpaw' as the Yanks say.

Portofino and Reeva are familiar with each other. He greets her warmly and says he will pick his 'best red' for her table. She informs him that Nathaniel Lieber arrived recently from Germany. Portofino is pleased to see him, telling Nathaniel he will find no better dining spot in Africa.

"Do come again," he says. "Come often! For you, for any friend of the beautiful Reeva, and also for her filthy rich brother, Finian," he smiles cheerfully, "I will always find a table, even if it is in the kitchen!" He winks at Reeva and adds conspiratorially, "And, for Leslie, always in the kitchen!"

"Are you sure it's the kitchen, not some dingy little room downstairs?" Nathaniel taunts.

They all laugh, but Nathaniel remains grim-faced. Georgi thinks the German guy is too pompous for her liking.

The waiter's name is Mario. He suggests oysters to start. Reeva says, "What! Three girls on the loose? Not a chance. We'll all have a bowl of your delicious minestrone."

Mario says, "Nathaniel, you are a man after my heart; young, virile enough to handle all three sexy girls... and you're not as Italian as me?"

"Neither are you as Italian as anything, Alec," says Reeva. "I could easily recognize you from high school days, you know? You're as South African as 'Madam and Eve' and this 'Mario' thing... quite ingenious."

"Shush, lady. I'll lose my business..."

"I'll try the oysters," says Nathaniel, cutting off the 'Mario thing' punch line.

"Bravo," Mario encourages Nathaniel.

Georgi plumps for hearts of palm vinaigrette, and Odessa goes with the minestrone. Mario disappears.

"So, this Italian accent is just a put-on?" asks Nathaniel.

"Some of these Restaurants hire actors who can swing between Italian and German accents at will. They hoodwink tourists into believing genuine Europeans are serving them."

"Exotic atmosphere, hey? Yeah, free enterprise does not belong in heaven," says Nathaniel. "Karl Marx and Adam Smith are debating where they are."

"Capitalism and Communism are dead. Long live common 'sensism!'" Reeva shouts.

"Anyway, this place is 'Wunderbar,' Reeva, not quite as Wunderbar as a German bierstube, but also not that loud. We can talk easily. I love the red-checked tablecloth," Nathaniel says.

"It is pretty good, and Portofino is an angel; he works his butt off, never too busy or too tired to give you a Wunderbar welcome," says Reeva. "But now, Nathaniel, let's get to the real issue. What brings you to Johannesburg?"

"And kindly spare us your fiction," adds Odessa.

"Your interest is touching. But you must know that I am here with you right now because I checked you ladies out and found you wanting," he snipes.

"Wanting? What's that supposed to mean?" Odessa thunders.

Georgi's laugh is so loud that she starts to cough excruciatingly. Odessa directs her anger at Georgi, "Your sense of humor is inspiring, Georgi?"

Nathaniel continues, "After you ruffled me up the other day, I spoke with my boss back home. Please stick to your professions, whatever they may be. Hey, let's enjoy ourselves," Nathaniel says. "We seem to be on the same side. Are we not, Georgi?"

"What?" Georgi mumbles absent-mindedly.

"Are you in the spy business, Nathaniel?" Odessa asks.

"I wouldn't call it business; more like art, something to do with the genes."

Reeva rants, "Do you put people down like that where you come from?"

After a while, once everyone had calmed down, Nathaniel explained that he works for the embassy in Bonn and may or may not be a spy. He is trying to transfer to South Africa. After a few helpings, Nathaniel becomes more talkative. He tells the girls he earned his Master's degree at twenty-two and realized he was getting nowhere as a goalkeeper for a local club. After a lengthy explanation, he said that his boss had advised him to contact Moroka if he needed help. Georgi nearly falls off her seat.

"Moroka is your boss, not so Georgi?" Reeva asks rhetorically.

"Does Moroka know you are here?"

"Maybe you should ask him, Georgi."

"Have you contacted him?" Georgi presses on.

"Well, it depends on whether I need his help or not. I am going back to Germany next Sunday. If there is a job here for me, Wunderbar!"

"Why do you want to work in South Africa?" asks Georgi.

"I would ask you the same question, Georgi. What brought you and Odessa to these sunny shores?"

The sisters exchange looks, but neither answers. Then Reeva says, "Oh, it's a very romantic story. Odessa and Georgi…" She pauses when Georgi brusquely kicks her heel under the table, interrupting her.

Nathaniel says, "I came to Africa to trace my roots, folks, of my long-departed father. He died when I was an infant, and my mother took me back to Germany. It's probably a familiar story. Many Africans fought across the border, and many died during the struggle. Also, there were many more who died in South African prisons at the hands of the police and the army. I'm sure you're familiar with all of that. I've known for years that my father was one of them, but I didn't care. But things do change."

"What changed?" asks Georgi.

"My stepfather, Dr Caleb Lieber, encouraged me to come here. He brought me up as his own. I could not have chosen a better father. But I need to have some closure, as they say. I watched the TRC proceedings very closely. Everyone wants to see the pain behind them," he heaves. "Unfortunately, I keep receiving threatening calls and messages from one mysterious GA ordering me to stop and go back home. I don't suppose you have anything to do with those activities, people?"

"Sies! What do you take us for?" Reeva protests.

"One never knows. You took the trouble to locate me in Centurion, and God knows what you want from me unless you are just pawns on a chessboard of treachery. I've hardly been here a month, and someone monitors my breathing rate. It's absurd. Anyway, when I learned that I had a colored father, I wanted to find my other colored folk. That is all. But one learns quickly that being colored in South Africa carries with it many loaded meanings and consequences."

"You bet," shouts Georgi.

"What meanings and consequences have you discovered?" Reeva asks.

"Some people think I'm related to Saartjie Baartman, while others just say, 'Your face looks familiar.' I hate small talk."

"Come to think of it, your face does look familiar," jokes Reeva.

Nathaniel looks around the restaurant. "May I smoke in here?"

"Sorry, you'll have to park your ass outside for that," Reeva says.

"Civilization has come to this African country," he chuckles and walks out.

"This guy is nuts," says Georgi, "but why tell such secrets about his father?"

"He is too smart. You heard him; he got his Master's at 22," says Odessa. I think he is leading us on."

"Please, people, let's keep our big traps tight," whispers Georgi.

Odessa is concerned, "But his letters from GA? Sounds like Ganon April."

"Oh, yes! You're brilliant, Odessa," jumps Georgi. "If it is Ganon, then..."

"April! April! Ganon April!" shouts Reeva.

"Yeah, if it's him, then we are pawns. You've given me an idea. I think I'll go to Soweto. Bekker and they lived there when they were toddlers, didn't they? It's time for us to make our move. The attack is the best form of defense," Georgi chants.

"And I think it's time I went to the bathroom," says Reeva, "but we must continue this fascinating conversation with Nathaniel!"

Georgi and Odessa are alone. Georgi murmurs, "Don't even think of disclosing to Nathaniel what we are doing here or what we know about Bekker. We don't know this man. I don't want to lose my job. You heard what Barend said about Marcia and Moroka being embarrassed if the 'truth' were to come out. Let's keep mum. I don't know how much Reeva knows, but she'd better keep things to herself, too!" Georgi states, her voice growing more intense. "You, too, stop gossiping about this matter with her since she has become your confidante."

"Don't patronize me," Odessa retorts. "I'm nobody's dumb wallflower. Stop getting upset over nothing."

"You're mad again. You've been like this since we got to Africa; quick-tempered, everything I say irritates you."

"Shut up!" Odessa snaps, quite incensed. "You're getting on my nerves."

When the other two return, a tense silence fills the room. More red wine arrives, and Nathaniel declares it as good as any German wine. He grows more expansive by the minute as the effects of the alcohol take hold. They present the Fettuccine-à-la-

Portofino with flair, smelling and looking irresistible. The group's enjoyment dips noticeably. Reeva and Odessa discuss advertising while Nathaniel and Georgi share their private conversation. Georgi answers each question with three of her own, and the tension rises with every exchange.

"What about you, Georgi?"

Georgi relocates away from Nathaniel and shouts, "Tell us; who are you...?"

"Please, you two! You behave as if you were cut from the same cloth."

A lull in conversation gives Reeva a chance to challenge Nathaniel: "Right, Nathaniel, while we finish this luscious food and even more luscious vino, I see this bottle is from Italy. Tell us the story of your life!"

"As I said, I struggle to find my father."

Odessa says, "We all have struggled to find our relatives..."

Georgi gently but determinedly kicks Odessa to her toes, trying to shut her up. Still, she ignores her and continues, "We're also looking for our uncle, a veteran of the struggle."

"Yes? Tell me about it."

Odessa answers, "Let me tell you..."

Georgi leaps up in a huff, grabs her handbag, and breezes out to the bathroom, leaving a tense moment before Odessa asks Nathaniel, "And your name... Lieber? You do know your real father's name, don't you?"

"Of course. My Mom? She is cool, man. A cool lady. She was this award-winning photographer, Puri Gerhardt. I am proud of her. I am following another promising lead; there appears to be a Canadian connection somewhere and a somewhat unusual Jewish link from my mother's side. Who knows, I might be related to good old Abraham, the one who heard voices telling him to bump off his son, Isaac," he giggles.

"Your mother is Jewish?"

"If she's Jewish, that's her problem. Their situation with the Palestinians is too hot for me. For now, mine is to find my father. I think we ought to stop here for the day. My head is in a haze."

Despite his confrontational disposition, Nathaniel appears charmed by Georgi. He leaves the table to look out for her. When he finds her, he says, "We must get together sometime, away from this maddening crowd. I think you feel the same about me, don't you?"

Georgi ignores Nathaniel's suggestions and walks away.

CHAPTER 11

Makeba's Soweto Home

The atmosphere has become tense. Georgi grows paranoid, suspecting that Marcia and Moroka are lying to her by staying silent about Nathaniel's adventures. When Georgi calls Odessa a few days later, she asks, "Odessa, remember the day Reeva asked Nathaniel what he found out in Soweto?"

"Yes?"

"And he suddenly remembered he needed to go out and pee?"

"Your point being?"

"My point is, let's go to Soweto on Saturday. We'll use one of the tour guides; we need to find out more before we do."

I don't think it's a good idea. I've heard stories. It's not a safe place. Dad and Mom won't be happy to hear we've gone there.

"Well, I'll have to do it alone, then."

"Georgi, don't. See you next weekend. Don't do anything stupid, now."

Georgi ignores Odessa's advice. Instead, she finds her way to Soweto. Her eyes are red because she did not sleep well due to anxiety. Within the circles she has orbited since she arrived in South Africa, Soweto is a foggy, dangerous place where murders and rapes take place in broad daylight.

However, contrary to numerous warnings, Soweto is not shrouded in smog and coal smoke, and there isn't even a hint of armed gangs fighting for territory. She does not witness exciting incidents of hijackings on every block. The tour operator is helpful; he takes her to areas of interest, such as Freedom Square in Kliptown, where the African National Congress (ANC) held its meeting that produced the Freedom Charter. The driver hustles her to Orlando West, through Vilakazi Street, past Arch Desmond Tutu's house, and then the old Mandela residence. They proceed to the Hector Peterson Museum, which Georgi later describes as a 'desperately lonely place.'

The guide drops Georgi off at Wandie's place in Dube, promising to return after three hours, "Once beaten, twice shy," the man said. "If I come back and your boyfriend has picked you up, that's your indaba."

Georgi has her map for her secret excursion written on paper. With trepidation, she walks toward Mofolo Village. After crossing the bridge over a smelly stream, she turns right and asks for directions. Soweto is the most historic African township in South Africa. However, the younger generation knows little about its true icons and idols. To Georgi, it is infuriating to discover that even her neighbors have no clue where Miriam Makeba once lived. Some have a vague idea about her, like her flying to America to sing. Only the older generation knows that Makeba was forced into involuntary exile by the apartheid regime. The jumble of directions she receives from the residents of Mofolo goes from confusing to hilarious.

Despite its age, Soweto continues to have its share of shantytowns, a hodgepodge of single-roomed dwellings made of corrugated tin and scraps of various kinds. The dominant conventional wisdom among successive white regimes was that Africans were temporary sojourners in 'European' areas such as Johannesburg, Durban, or Cape Town. For that reason, they put up low-cost, barely habitable quarters, which lacked such basic amenities as interior toilets, bathrooms, running water, and decency for an ordinary black family. 'It's a long and winding road for Africans in Africa,' Georgi thinks as she recalls Gibson's words, 'Black people, they build those shacks to live in. The government aims to improve housing, but the number of people in need is substantial, and the allocated funds are limited.

Thankfully, the Sowetans do not see Georgi as a central curiosity. In African townships, there remains a sprinkling of people of color who resemble her despite strict apartheid social engineering policies. After some unsettling moments, she finally locates Miriam Makeba's old Soweto home just a few meters from Vukayibambe Primary School. She has now arrived at the tiny four-room home of the internationally renowned icon. Georgi can hardly hold back her tears, imagining Makeba as a little girl fetching water from a tap connected to a toilet outside.

The house now belongs to Mr KK Mkonza, who served time on Robben Island. KK knew Bekker well, as they belonged to the same ANC cell. Sadly, KK has Alzheimer's disease, and so, his conversation is erratic. Richard, his son, is seated on the stoep, barely participating in the conversation. However, he responds with interest when Georgi requests directions to the old Mofokeng home.

Richard flashes a sly smile as he apologizes for his father's condition. He says, "I can tell you're one of the tourists who pass by for fun and then disappear. Well, as you can see, the Boers were good at panel-beating people, and they damaged my father's brain when they shoved him into solitary confinement for six months. American tourists like you take pictures of him and his Makeba house like an animal in a zoo."

"I am sorry..."

"I'll show you the old Mofokeng place, where a man called Bekker grew up. Why are you interested in him, anyway? Many tourists from abroad come here to write stories about our heroes. When they leave, they forget about us. I spent two weeks with a German female professor who said she was writing a book about the Bafokeng tribe."

"Bafokeng? What was her name?"

"She is Puree. She said I must call her Puree. I don't know her surname. People here still admire Bekker. You will see. The community has painted the house to make it look respectable. They think the tenants are Bekker's relatives."

"Do you know them?"

"I know them, but they are not Bekker's relatives."

Georgi and Richard stride briskly across the busy Kwezi railway bridge to 'Pola.' It is a long walk, and Georgi feels the dampness developing around her body. The pot-holed and dusty streets of this old township testify to the level of calculated neglect by the apartheid government. Pola has very little going for it despite the advent of democracy. Factions of unemployable young men bunch together hopelessly on street corners, their mouths and faces painted in distress while their eyes rage with suspicion and hate. It is difficult to distance such faces from the spectra of violent crime besetting the country. If they are not train-surfing, they are drinking beer or sniffing drugs. Some gamble and put their pocket knives to good use from time to time. Others commute to Bree and Jeppe Streets in downtown Johannesburg to engage in pickpocketing. All of these young people crave the life they see on street billboards or television sets; young black men like them in exotic surroundings, accompanied by glamorous black women, amid dazzling colors. Young women here have sex before the age of sixteen and, in the process, pick up HIV or become pregnant or both. 'Pola' is a Nguni phrase with a promising meaning: a quiet, peaceful hole for relaxation.' However, this is a wretched part of the world, offering neither peace nor rest for its inhabitants.

Richard suddenly stops and looks at Georgi. He points at a house in front of them, where 'Comrade Bekker' grew up. Georgi gazes at the desolate Mofokeng house with a mix of awe and disappointment. No tears are rolling down her face, but unimaginable incredulity over the dullness of her origin. Three African children are playing diketo, oblivious of the historical import of the dusty ground on which they have laid their game.

"My father visited this house frequently in his younger days," says Richard. "As activists, Bekker and my father operated secretly around this area and over there in Meadowlands," he points toward a township adjacent to a railway line, where the apartheid government dumped many Africans from Sofiatown in the 1950s.

The backyard is as bare as a desolate desert tract. A small, corrugated-iron shack stands detached from the main house. As they approach, a highly pregnant young woman emerges. Her name is Dombolo. She is wearing light-green knickerbockers, a fraying 'Release Mandela' T-shirt, and a broad smile as she greets Georgi. Her lips are large and wet, and she fixes Georgi with her intense, searching stare.

"Why, Richard? You didn't tell me you were coming."

"She's my girl," Richard reveals proudly. "We'll get married once she is through with this," he boasts, pointing at Dombolo's belly.

Dombolo tells Georgi that her mother had known of the Mofokengs since a young age. "And the local ANC branch members often paint the house with ANC colors to spruce it up. They run workshops and explain politics. The people who now occupy the main house are the Mazibukos. People believe that the Mofokengs are all dead. Are you writing a book, like all those Chinese and Americans?"

"No. I'm looking for my relatives..."

Dombolo tells Georgi about a recent meeting in which internal wrangling derailed the motion to name the branch after Bekker Mofokeng. Ten minutes before the scheduled secret ballot, the branch received a message from the ANC's regional office to halt the voting.

"Everyone was cagey."

Georgi bends over to enter Dombolo's shack. She has crammed her belongings into the tiny space: the double bed, a wardrobe, a television set, a refrigerator, and suitcases in the corner. Dombolo has left her television on, and it is showing The Muppets. A big picture of Dombolo's certificate hangs majestically on the wall. She is a Pretoria University graduate. Like many young black women, Dombolo lives in a dull little room with hardly anything to affirm her dignity as a woman. She wonders what it would take for Dombolo to get her education working for her.

"We have not cooked. Richard did not tell us you were coming."

"Not to worry. I had something to eat at Wandie's. I see you are a Pretoria graduate."

"Yes, but what's the use? I have been looking for a job for eighteen months without success. So, I spent time typing stuff for cash. My mother is heartbroken."

"Where's your mother now?"

"We parted ways when she decided to get married. Imagine seeing your mother, over fifty, hooked up with a stranger. She visits me occasionally, and each time she cries tears," she says with a giggle. "She had many stories about the Mofokengs, how the wayward Bekker and his sister tore the family apart, trying to scare me into line."

"Did she know them all?"

"Yes. My mother grew up here, two streets away. One of Bekker's sisters was called Kora, and she was my mother's close friend. She talks about her quite often lately. This haunted house reminds her of the people who once lived here. But I take everything she says with a pinch of salt. One moment, she tells me Kora was a nice angel. The very next, she describes her as a wicked Jezebel."

"How can I meet her... your mother?"

"I'll give you her address, but you don't know me, right? You got her address from... the police or something. Her name is Edna."

"Tell me, Dolombo... what do you think of mothers?"

"I am Dombolo. Mothers? I'm not sure what you mean. I feel sorry for my mother. It's difficult for them when they are lonely. But the secrets they keep weaken their hearts, and then they die. Right now, I don't even know where she got me from. Maybe that's why I'm suffering; my ancestors are angry."

Get your Skates on

The number of chanting children outside the shack has risen to six. She bends over again to squeeze herself out of the shack. Georgi basks proudly in the unexpected excitement. The impromptu performance is done with the expectation of receiving a reward from tourists, such as coins or paper money, if their day is going well. Georgi believes there must be other ways for struggling youth to survive. Then, a black BMW with tinted windows slowly approaches the spontaneous celebration. A colored woman swaggers like a model toward the crowd. She is wearing tight black jeans, sunglasses, and a menacing grin. Ignoring the rest of the party, she stops dead in front of Georgi.

"Come on. Get your skates on; it's time to go."

Georgi lacks the strength to argue. She thanks Richard and Dombolo for the hospitality before she grudgingly slides into the back of the black luxury car with no registration number. There is a passenger in front.

"I'm Lieutenant Morrison. We're taking you back home."

Richard bends against the window and whispers, "You'd better do something; there's no free dance in Soweto."

"What does this song mean, 'Bekker miles away'?" Georgi asks.

"Clip in your safety harness, Miss King. I drive fast."

"They should have harnessed you and your sister in a Canadian cage before you launched your little African expedition," the male officer says before his contrived chuckle. T

The car pulls off at high speed. The officer says, "So, you are Georgi? Nice name."

Georgi says, "And who are you two? Police?"

"Lieutenant Morrison to you. And this is Inspector Mbatha."

The car heads toward Dobsonville at neck-breaking speed. They weave through traffic like a runaway Soweto taxi. Georgi sits quietly, listening to the two talking about her in Afrikaans. They cruise along Main-Reef Road onto the Highway. Georgi can tell they are entering the white suburban area. Here, the roads are wider and smoother, the environment is much greener, and the cars are more upscale. The car screeches to a stop, and the officers switch roles.

Morrison says, "I am looking you in the eye because I want to memorize your face. Next time you stray into dangerous territory...?" She stops, but the message is clear.

"Yes, next time, we'll keep you on a tight leash until someone higher up schedules your flight back to Canada," Mbatha chortles. Georgi is not amused.

Connect the dots

When Georgi and Odessa speak again, Nathaniel is already in Bonn. They have no idea how far he has succeeded in establishing contact with any of the Mofokeng relations.

Georgi has been waiting to approach Marcia about something that has been bothering her.

"Marcia," she says, "I have something to tell you. "Dear me! It sounds serious. "Do you remember I spoke of my so-called uncle Bekker?" Georgi hesitated, wishing she didn't have to do this.

"Georgi, get to the point. I have a million things to do."

"Sorry," Georgi tries again, "it seems that Bekker is dead, shot in 1980, crossing the Swazi border."

"Oh, I am sorry," says Marcia.

"No, that's not the issue. If he were only dead, it wouldn't matter. I mean…" Marcia raises an eyebrow as Georgi continues, "Anyway, Marcia, he was a traitor. Up to a certain point, he was in the struggle, but then he lost his way somewhere along the line, and he started working with Wolter, a figure associated with those dreadful state laboratories. It seems that my uncle helped to manufacture biological weapons and hallucinogenic drugs. He also got involved in a litany of dirty tricks by the regime."

"And you know this for a fact?"

"We've tried with Odessa to work out the puzzle, but there's no other explanation. Now, Nathaniel Lieber comes up with another tale about his father, Mofokeng, crossing illegally into Swaziland, a baby in his arms, and both getting shot by whoever. I'm unsure what to make of it. I'm afraid it will have to come out, and I know you will have to fire me."

Marcia Laughs and says, "Georgi, Georgi. Sit down. Don't be ridiculous. When this uncle, whatever his name was…"

"Bekker or Lenin."

"Lenin? What a name! What kind of crazy African mother would give his baby such a name, anyway? It's like Hitler, Idi Amin, or Somoza. What do you expect from such names? I see you got another job. No use lying?"

"Ahhh, Marcia. Nothing of the sort. I wouldn't even know where to go if you fired me."

"Are you the only soul with skeletons rattling in your cupboard? Take it from me, the sordid details of Bekker pale into insignificance as compared to those of the apartheid regime. Hello! Wakey and smell the Gousblomme! One of these days, you will learn to keep your mouth shut about your secrets. That's what we all do in this country. I know quite a bit about your father, between you and me. No one told me about it. I just put one and one together from Moroka's cell phone and papers. Now get on with your work, and let me get on with mine."

"You are full of surprises." Georgi smiles and continues, "Tell me, Marcia, since you know a bit about my father, how much of this whole Bekker affair did you know, truly?"

"You know what it's like. A rumor is like a kite; if you yank it a bit, it starts to fly independently."

"Just a rumor? What about Moroka? What does he know?"

"He wouldn't breathe a word to you even if he knew. I stopped discussing his real occupation long ago. I wouldn't be at all surprised if he knew something or everything. We hardly compare notes on such issues. However, I discovered that he had been calling a number in Canada long before you arrived. You can connect the dots if you wish."

"And Marcia, something has been bothering me since I got here: this obsession with race. May I ask you a personal question?"

"Not about Bekker, I hope."

"No, about color and culture. Are you colored?"

"Me? Yes, well, technically speaking, in the old apartheid sense, yes."

"This is complicated. And Taylor? Is Taylor, your child, also colored?"

"This is awkward, I must admit. The colored story belongs in the past, Georgi. Just get a move on. I am black; that's all you need to know about me," Marcia snaps unexpectedly.

Odessa worries that Georgi is becoming more involved in her life as a nanny. The sisters are at Reeva's apartment, where Georgi excitedly shares their plans for the New Year's Eve celebration in Cape Town.

Odessa catches her breath before dipping at Georgi, "When did you decide to be a career nanny? You've been there a year and a half now, and you seem to have lost all your sense of ambition."

"They treat me like family," she shouts.

"Like Loli and Kazi, the domestic women, their madams think they are part of the family as long as they pay them peanuts. There are other professions in this world, you know. The Taungs are not your family. For a college graduate, you're disappointing. Are you planning to work as a domestic for the rest of your life?"

"I'm no bloody domestic. I'm an au pair," she retorts, quite stricken.

"Just a glorified domestic. Tell me this: what's the difference? Just because you speak English with an accent!"

"I don't have a bloody accent. Stop that rubbish."

"Here in Africa, you do, believe me."

"Odessa is right, Georgi," Reeva says. You should look around for something better before your work permit expires."

"Hello! My renewal is already underway. Why would I want to work somewhere else for a pittance and live in a pokey apartment like the one Odessa had before she moved in with you? Frankly, a nine-to-five doesn't do it for me, and it's my life. Mine."

"Take this business of Bekker and Nathaniel. Barend said our association with Bekker would be embarrassing for the Taungs. When you tell Marcia about it, she brushes it aside as trivial. Remember how she wouldn't have hired you if she'd known you couldn't pass for black on our arrival in Cape Town? Frankly, the two of you are way beyond an employer-employee relationship. It's not healthy."

"What the hell are you saying? Are you suggesting we are into lesbianism? In any case, I didn't expect you to stoop that low."

"It's more like you're her indentured slave, like our foremothers."

"Your jealousy has got the better of you."

"And then there is Van der Watt? One of the herrenvolk!" Reeva adds.

"And what's that supposed to mean, Reeva?"

"You know the Afrikaners...? Until recently, they thought they were a chosen race in Africa, in the same league as the biblical Jews. They even made a covenant to build a church in honor of God, provided He could help them through the Battle of Blood River

~ 77 ~

in 1838. But they did not allow blacks and coloreds to enter that church."

"What about you? I know all about the English-speaking liberals, always snooping around in the shadows, exploiting poor Afrikaners by using them as a front to do their dirty job on behalf of European civilization."

"You got it all wrong. The English and Afrikaners aren't on good terms. We have the same divisions as between the French and English-speaking Canadians," Reeva explains patiently.

"Pull the other one. That doesn't wash with me."

"It does with me because we English-speaking folk have never oppressed blacks."

"Oh, how we owe an ode to our cultured English liberals! Shame on the bad Boers."

"That aside, funny, my parents bought a farm in the Western Cape. They have racist neighbors on the next farm by the name of Van der Watt."

"And where is that?" asks Odessa.

"Outside Robertson. The man I saw Odessa approach in the café is Barend; I know him, and that's where he belongs. Now I can disclose..."

Odessa and Reeva are amused.

CHAPTER 12

The African Way

Kora invites Odessa to a wedding at Beesfontein. She makes it clear that her invitation does not include Georgi's name. Odessa is disturbed. She tells Kora that she cannot go without Georgi, as she relies on her for transportation. Kora finally relents after spitting the words, "She doesn't belong with us; she is with her white skin and strange manners...! But," she heaves, "I thought you would enjoy being part of the celebration of your tradition with your family. We must pass down our culture, just as our ancestors did. You will enjoy it."

Odessa sighs, "I will, Aunt Kora, and so will Georgi. She's my only sister, your brother's child, your niece. She'll enjoy the culture..."

"She won't fit in. You know these people. They can't stand it if you speak to them in an African language. It's as if you're insulting them. But bring her if you need her to drive you. That's all. Can you come to my house on Friday so we can drive to Beesfontein early Saturday morning?"

Kora tells Odessa that the couple is 'very traditional,' even though the groom works for the SABC television and the bride is a hairdresser in Pretoria.

"He even paid lobola, a real herd of cattle," Kora shouts. "No paper cattle as they do these days. You can expect the ceremony to continue until Sunday morning. There will be television people there. We may even see Felicia Mabuza-Suttle. Do you know her?"

Odessa says she knows of her. But when she turns in, she wishes she could be more like Georgi: 'Oh, help me, Lord Jesus, to be more like Georgi'; Georgi would have retorted to Aunt Kora's question, 'Felicia? Never heard of the bitch.' She covers her head with the wet pillow and thinks, 'I wonder if Georgi will accompany me to the wedding. We need to see the community that has regained its land from the white farmers. Please come, Georgi, I can't go without you; I don't have a ride. And I need a crutch to face the intimidating Auntie Kora.' Odessa falls asleep.

"Odessa," Georgi levels her sister with an uncompromising gaze, "I hope never in my life to set my eyes on our so-called Auntie Kora or any of her brood again."

Trying her luck, Odessa tells Georgi that she is very excited about the prospect of a family gathering, yearning to be a significant part of this special celebration, and looks forward to meeting the Beesfontein community. "Please, Georgi, you have to see Aunt Kora again. She is our aunt, one of our few African blood relatives."

Georgi is wearing her hair in a ponytail, knotted high on the crown of her head. She flings the strands over her shoulder to underline her words, "Frankly, I am sick of being treated like a pariah. I never had any trouble back home, and it pisses me off to have people question my integrity when I tell them I am an African. So, I'm not a Mofokeng, South African, or African. Imagine that wedding! They'll be introducing you as Odessa

Mofokeng. Then, when you say I am your sister, they'll all stare at me with their dry mouths wide open as if a Martian had recently landed, like 'Duh! Who are you kidding?' I have no problems with the Taungs. When I meet people, Marcia says, 'This is Georgi,' and she may mention that I'm from Canada. From now on, I am Georgi King from Toronto. Don't ask me again to go to your aunt's African cultural traditional ethnic wedding because the answer is gonna be a 'NO!' I am not going. Get Reeva to help you if you need a ride; after all, she's become something of your Afro-echo, and you seem to thrive with each other's dubious interracial company."

Odessa chuckles and tries to hold Georgi's hand, but she snubs her, flips open her magazine, and closes the subject. Odessa lets a long moment pass before she says, "You're not an African, you say?"

"No."

"So, you can't go with me to the wedding?"

"No."

"Shall I introduce you as my Canadian friend, then, 'Georgi' from Toronto?"

Georgi scoffs at Odessa's idea. After a few seconds, she says, "Georgi from Toronto? I'll have to think about it."

"Georgi, don't you think this place, this Continent, is full of demons? Don't you think we should go back home and be sisters again? What happened?"

"Wanna know what happened?" Georgi screams and throws her magazine on the floor, "YOU happened, that's what! You, Odessa. Period. Everything I do, you go through with a fine-tooth comb. Nothing escapes your academic analysis. I've never known you to be this mean and niggling. It's YOU, Odessa."

"Me, Georgi? I miss Father. Remember when he made us recite the Lennon and McCartney tune, 'Try to see it my way'?"

"What? It was Nothing of the sort," shouts Georgi even louder. "You're just trying the easy way out. The song was 'We Can Work It Out'. That's what..."

"It's the same song, Georgi. Please think about the trip and stop being such a wet blanket."

Odessa is persuasive, and Georgi agrees, saying, "But I am not spending Friday night with the Tladis. Imagine sharing a bunk bed with one of her kids. I must be mad to drive to Beesfontein again the next day. I really can't stand Kora. I am sure her family will be equally insufferable. Tell her we will leave early on Saturday morning and meet them on the road. Then we can follow their lead?"

"Don't be such a snob, Georgi. Bunk-bed? I'm sure they don't live in a shack. Uncle Sabelo is a university professor. Living with the Taungs has turned you smug."

"It isn't the housing I object to. I can put up in a shack with a smile any time. It's their attitude I find repulsive. I've been to Nikita's place on steep mountain slopes. People there are more decent than your professors and their wives riding high horses."

On the Saturday of the wedding, Odessa and Reeva are up at dawn. Reeva says, "By the way, I forgot something. I received a call from Jardine..."

"Of the 'ethnic hair' fame?"

"She wants me to meet her at Mike's Kitchen in Parktown, 'without the black lady from Canada.'"

"What?"

"'It will attract unnecessary attention,' she reckons. I asked Fin to go there with me if she was up to some monkey business."

"Finian! What the hell for?"

"Listen, Odessa, I know about the hard feelings between you two, but Fin is an audacious genius; he always gets his way. I know him. He's my brother. In case you're not aware, he worked for the SABC as a crime reporter and has extensive knowledge of the shady side of Johannesburg. He has a sack full of contacts in the South African police."

"What's he supposed to say to Jardine?"

"Jardine is now singing like a chorister since Fin took the matter up with the law, and there's progress at last with the Luca case."

"You don't say!"

Georgi immediately confronts Reeva: "I see you have invited yourself along for the wedding. Do you have any security clearance with the Kora Bureau of Multiracial Affairs?"

"I am so excited," says Reeva, "I've always heard how fab African tribal weddings are, and this one's extra special; out in the country, all those people traveling from all over the country to join the happy up-market couple. Isn't it a glorious morning, you guys?"

"You, too, are into Odessa's ethnic thing?"

Reeva ducks the question to avoid what she knows is Georgi's storm brewing. Odessa once advised Reeva, 'Sometimes you have to play possum when you deal with Georgi.'

However, Odessa has a bone to pick with Georgi. She says, "I learned you went to Soweto, and you kept quiet about it."

"Your sudden interest in the subject is touching. Is this the same Odessa who, not so long ago, told me how dangerous the black township was and how our poor daddy and our poor mommy would be upset to learn their tiny little civilized girls ventured out into the black township alone?"

"But you went there without taking me into your confidence."

"Your sudden interest in Soweto is touching, Odessa. I went there thrice and met Dolombo's mother twice. Her name is Edna. She tells me sibling rivalry dominated the Mofokeng family, leading to their parents' demise. I just thought, "What's new? Your aunt, Kora, was the prime township troublemaker, and nobody escaped her caustic tongue. Edna says grocery shops nearby refused to serve Kora because she habitually returned purchases and had a history of arguing with the shopkeepers and their assistants. On one occasion, after they arrested Bekker, she threw stones at the police van, breaking the windshield. When the male police officers came to arrest her, she paraded naked in front of them, and they left her alone. 'She was a wayward girl with a mind of her own,' Edna told me. Soon after she shattered the windshield, she disappeared from home. Edna later received a phone call from her, asking for some cash. She was stranded in Cape Town, looking for a job."

"Did she return Edna's money?" Odessa asks as if absent-minded.

"Money? Odessa, why don't you find out for yourself in Soweto?"

"About Bekker, does Edna have anything to say?"

"She says Bekker was too clever to get himself killed at the Swazi border. She believes he is still alive, perhaps lives in Tanzania."

"Did she say why he gained such a bad reputation?" asks Reeva.

"Dolombo says Bekker was planted into various organizations to siphon off information for the outlawed ANC. Every year, since liberation, their militant branch in Ward 45 holds a vigil in honor of Bekker."

"Do they run a dagga plantation in Ward 45?" shouts Reeva. "Please come on, guys, let's lay off the heavy stuff and enjoy the morning; the kind of morning that makes the dead want to rise and share the human joy of it."

I was a Nanny

The three women meet with the Tladi family at a roadside stop outside Pretoria. They look forward to a drive through the fresh, grassy countryside. However, Kora insists that Georgi leave her car in the covered parking and that the three girls travel with her family. Georgi wants to argue, but after one look at Kora's unwelcoming stare, she decides against it.

Sabelo Tladi drives a comfortable 8-seater with all the 'mod cons': air conditioning, power steering, and a CD player.

They climb into the car's middle row, introducing Odessa to her uncle and three girl cousins who sit in the back. They form a relaxed and friendly group. Kora seems happy and at ease, which Georgi finds more unsettling than her usual, sharp attitude. Her notable glasses stay in place. The car drives away, leaving Pretoria farther behind. The scenery becomes less lush; short bushes line the road, and scraggly undergrowth, devoid of flowers, darkens the landscape. The recent rain is the only gentle touch, despite the annoying muddy pools scattered along the edges. They pass small villages where thatched huts nearly meet the paved road. Occasionally, a stray farm animal, usually a goat or cow, wanders peacefully in front of the vehicle. Sabelo drives carefully and skillfully to avoid dangers. Then the paved road ends, and they start to travel on gravel side roads. Purple mountain ranges, hazy from heat and distance, dominate the horizon, creating a vast, dry, and timeless landscape.

The Tladi daughters are Notemba, Sibongile, and Mosidi, and they range in age from twelve to sixteen. To spark conversation in the thick atmosphere, Georgi says, "Our brother, Teddy, is the same age as you, Notemba. He turned sixteen last month. He thinks he's a big deal because now he can get his driver's license."

Notemba's fascination is limitless. "Does he live in Canada? Here, we can only drive when we're eighteen, but we take lessons at school. Papa says I can't drive the Volkswagen. He says he'll have to go without bread for many months to buy me a small car, and then I can do errands for the family. My mother doesn't drive, hey, Mom?"

"No, I do not," responds Kora with irritation. "Why should I do this when your father is such a good driver?" She turns to Odessa. "And Ellen, does she drive?"

When Odessa responds negatively, Kora breathes an air of satisfaction before she says. "That is strange. Always, Ellen was the sophisticated one. As a high-flying lady, I thought she would drive her German car in that rich American country."

Georgi wants to say something nasty, but Reeva brusquely pinches her thigh.

"My mother prefers the subway," Odessa says quietly, "and the stores are nearby."

"Georgi, you seem surprisingly distracted all of a sudden. Don't you have anything to say about your mother?"

"What would you have me say?"

"Since you don't want to talk about your mother, tell us about your employers. I hear you work for Marcia Wagner, now Mrs Taung," Kora says flatly.

Georgi curls her lips defiantly and says, "Yes, I am the family au pair."

"We call them nannies here. They had to import an exotic maid from First World Canada. Classic Marcia! House cleaners with light skin from Western countries call au pairs and pay them in dollars! She proudly parades you in front of her high-flying friends when she throws her bashes. Does she? Typical of the lady! Nannies are two a penny in this country."

"Why do you say that?" Georgi retorts, feeling drenched.

"When I was young, I served as a nanny for the Wagner family. There were four boys, with Marcia being the baby and the only girl. Back then, nannies were called girls, neither to be seen nor heard. They went about their errands, sweating and silently shedding tears on their bunk beds."

Kora takes her time telling the story of the Wagner family.

"When Marcia began school at the convent in Wynberg, my family no longer needed me at home. Luckily, Marcia's father, Dr. Wagner, arranged a job for me in his office. The wealthy can create and dismiss at will."

The Wagners lived in Athlone, and the doctor worked in a nearby house. The makeshift hall was always crowded with men, women, and children sitting on long benches, maintaining respectful silence. He cared for people and often took in runaways and stray individuals into his home. Many of them suffered from illnesses caused by poverty. Gangsters with knife or bullet wounds hid in his clinic because they knew he didn't like the police very much. Others came for different reasons; they had petitions for him to sign or write because they couldn't read or write. The community called him 'The Mayor of Athlone,' believing he would someday lead the colored people out of poverty into a better life.

Robert Sobukwe, leader of the Pan Africanist Congress, visited him occasionally. The regime had banished Sobukwe to Galeshewe Township in Kimberley, and I think the authorities disregarded some of his movements. He was there for no more than five minutes each time. A garden bench sat outside under an old Oak tree in the shade. Every time Sobukwe came, he greeted us with 'Izwe Lethu Ma Afrika,' and the two men walked to the shade of the tree. When Sobukwe arrived, his entourage waited outside on the street, and everything else had to wait. Whatever happened between the two men must have been top secret because Dr. Wagner never spoke to anyone. One day, Sobukwe came, and they sat under the Oak for more than an hour. That was the last time I saw the PAC leader. A few months later, in February 1978, I heard he had died of cancer. I entered the changing room and said, 'Sorry, Baba Sobukwe. I never even offered you a cup of coffee."

"Tell them about Marcia," Sabelo says.

"Dr Wagner wanted to go to Sobukwe's funeral," Kora continues, "but the police stopped him at the gate of his property and made him go back inside."

"Tell them about Marcia," Sabelo repeats.

"Marcia! Aaliyah!" screeches Kora.

"She used to sing, didn't she?"

"A voice like an angel and a cackle like a witch," her mother often said. Does she still cackle when she laughs? Spoiled like a Hollywood cat! Her father could never see anything wrong with Marcia. Anything she craved, she must have. He even paid school fees for her boyfriend. Imagine! Her brothers went to school in Athlone. That wasn't good enough for Marcia. He insisted she go to the convent in Wynberg. Later, she went to England to get more education. Huh! That Marcia!"

Kora pauses for a few seconds, contemplating the past. Then she continues in a subdued voice, "God was good to me when he sent me to the Wagners. I was lucky. Without Dr. Wagner, I would never have advanced beyond being a maid. Mainly, I was a Xhosa-speaking woman in Cape Town, where job reservation was the norm. The system favored people based on the colonial hierarchy: whites at the top, then coloreds, and Africans at the very bottom..."

Georgi noticed a disturbing divide between 'Africans' and 'coloreds' from the moment they set foot on the country's shores. It has been difficult for her to understand this phenomenon. This is not just an academic issue for her, as Odessa often suggests, but she feels directly involved in the complicated situation.

Odessa can sense that tension is gradually increasing and that Georgi is spoiling for a confrontation with Kora. She pinches her sister's bottom again, sending a clear message to keep her mouth firmly shut.

"What, Odessa?" Georgi shouts. "I'm a colored, ain't I? I'm to blame for all the ills of the African nation," she shouts.

Unyielding, Kora continues, "Nothing much with this new rainbow nation. All we see is people who benefited in the apartheid past getting hot under the collar when we tell the truth."

"What truth? Stop the car," cries Georgi.

"What?" Reeva and Sabelo shout in unison.

"You heard me. Stop the damn car. I wanna get off."

"Are you out of your mind?" Odessa screams. "You don't know a soul here. What do you want to see happen to you? Get raped?"

Sabelo finds a good spot between Bapong and Modikwe and brings the car to a stop beside a pine hedge.

"I see you lack discipline," he says. "You're used to doing things your way up in North America. Down here, you do things the African way..."

"Why don't you discipline your wife and show us the African way? Isn't that what African men are supposed to do: discipline their wives? You sit there and say nothing while she hurls all those insults," Georgi shrieks. She slams the door shut and rushes out, standing still under the horse-chestnut trees. Odessa and Reeva try to understand her, but she ignores them. At this point, Odessa hopes that Georgi remembered to take her daily dose of medication; otherwise, the situation might become dangerous.

"Do you have a death wish?" Sabelo tries again. "This place is swarming with venomous Moroccan puff adders and boomslangs..."

"Better than those venomous snakes in the car," Georgi shouts for all to hear.

"Nothing has changed since the days of the Tricameral Parliament," says Sabelo, "when the white minority deceived the coloreds and Indians into believing they were superior to Africans."

"No remorse, Papa. They now feel a closer connection to Europeans than ever before..."

After a long standoff, Kora urges Sabelo to drive on, "Let us go, Papa," she says. "We can't be held to ransom by a spoiled little brat from America. Let us leave her here; she will catch a minibus taxi back. Those taxi drivers will teach her a thing or two when she fails to explain what she is doing in an African area."

Notemba opens the door and confidently walks over to Georgi, gently holding her hand. Georgi responds, and her body trembles as she absentmindedly touches Notemba's braided hair with her palm. The two cousins share tender smiles, and Notemba runs her fingers through Georgi's hair before quietly leading her back to her seat.

The luxury vehicle glides along for miles. The tense occupants keep their thoughts to themselves as Georgi's mind drifts from Kelly Ellsworth, a Canadian boyfriend she dumped for no reason, to her newly found family, whom she can hardly stand.

Sabelo finally breaks the long silence: "I got a phone call from Germany the other day: a young man named Nathaniel Lieber. He claims Kora is his father's sister. Do you know anything about it, Odessa?"

"No family all these years," Kora breaks in, "and suddenly an avalanche, relations of all hues from all over the world. What did you tell him, Papa?"

"He is coming to work in Pretoria. I told him to contact me again, and we could meet. You can invite him to the house, Mama."

"How old is this young man?"

"He is 23. Born in Angola... or did he say Tanzania? Whatever. His mother is German. He said your brother, Bekker, died in Swaziland. That's news to us."

Kora says, "You'd better watch the road, Papa. The turnoff to Beesfontein isn't far. Oh, this road is terrible. Thank God your tires are good. Sabelo, you will miss the turn. Slow down!"

After a rough ride over bumpy roads, they quickly realize that Sabelo has taken the wrong turn. The tense outing, which began with high hopes, has turned into a risky adventure. To make matters worse, the weather forecast warns of more heavy rains. The passengers, meanwhile, would rather be anywhere else.

Eventually, Sabelo finds the right path, and what happens next is like a fairy tale. Without warning, the calm of the veld is broken by sounds of excited ululating and chanting up ahead, hooters blaring, and drums pounding in the background. They join a line of traffic slowly moving into a large, muddy field designated for parking. Big puddles of mud and sprays of weeds stare gloomily at the newcomers. Georgi feels the breeze on her face, and her hair is tangled. A stronger force quickly follows, threatening to sweep her petite body over.

"What's wrong, Georgi? Don't you have rain and mud-covered paths in America?" Kora asks again.

"I wouldn't know. I'm not from America."

"Here in Africa, we enjoy thick, dark clouds, heavy rains, and mud puddles for children to build tiny dams and bridges. You learn a lot from playing in muddy puddles."

A large field filled with single-stemmed eucalyptus trees and beautiful crowns contains big thatched lapas. To one side, a flurry of busy women emerges from small mud huts that serve various purposes. As they slog up the muddy lane, they realize that this entertainment area isn't in the middle of nowhere. Peering through the foliage, visitors see a large farmhouse built by the Dutch in the 18th century. The noise from the revelers, who arrive in waves and trickles, is rising to deafening levels.

The farmhouse remains untouched, out of bounds. Under the shade, tables groan beneath heaps of food; snacks are laid out before the ceremony, as they learn. Several bars are present, at least two in each lapa, with efficient and attentive bartenders in control, serving only fruit juice and reserving anything more substantial for later. The largest lapa holds plastic chairs, adorned with flounced white skirts and pastel ribbons. A woven carpet runs through the center of the space, dividing it into two sections. At the far end of the rug is an altar with a distinct design. The bamboo shoots form a backdrop to the draped altar. Hanging from this is a large wooden cross bearing a carved figure of a black Christ. Stained glass on either side causes the sun's rays to highlight the outline of the dying Savior with a gold and red halo.

The Tladi clan—each holding glasses of orange juice—greets the bride's family before finding seats in the chapel. Georgi glances around quickly and estimates the lapa can hold about 300 people. It's filling up fast. Adults lift small children onto their lapas, and older kids stand to make room for the never-ending crowd of guests. It starts to get hot, even beneath the cool thatch.

There is a surge at the back of the lap, and spectators turn to watch dancers gathering near the entrance. To the rhythm of drumming, maidens dressed in traditional clothes make their way, swaying and clicking, up the woven carpet, splitting into two groups before the altar, then moving outside the lapa, circling it, clapping and stomping to the beat of the drums.

"The bride's attendants," Kora comments for Odessa's benefit, "they wear brightly colored smocks over long woven skirts."

Sixteen young girls, each with their male partner, dance and gyrate to Sipho Hotstix Mabuse's 'Burnout.' The boys' movements are stronger, more physical, and almost warlike, while the traditionally attired girls arouse the most devout priest around.

"Now the bridegroom's attendants," Kora continues, commentating.

The young men wear bracelets around their arms, ankles, and necks, and only animal-skin loincloths around their hips. They sport feathers in various colors on their tops, swaying gently as they twirl their heads. A mixed group of boys and girls, pre-adolescents, follow the men, mimicking the older dancers. They, too, are dressed in traditional skins, with painted faces and feathered headdresses.

The dance ends, and the dancers move to the front, standing still on either side of the altar. Then, a trumpet-like blast from a long spiral kudu horn signals that something else is about to happen.

"Here come the parents," reports Kora, "his family, then the bride's."

The parents take their seats in the front rows, accompanied by elderly guests, grandparents, and great-grandparents. The bride's mother holds a small boy dressed in a white satin shirt, shorts, socks, and shoes.

That's Mikey, child of Oscar and Dinkie," Kora whispers.

"Who are they?" asks Reeva.

"The bridal couple, Shhhh, here they come."

Next, the Trumpet Volunteer sounds its triumphant anthem. The crowd remains mesmerized. The bride and groom appear at the entrance as the music fades away. The excited guests all stand, leaning forward to catch a glimpse of the beautiful newlyweds. He wears a Nehru jacket with ivory silk trousers; his shiny black hair is braided into countless cornrows.

The bride must be wilting inside the ornately beaded smock and skirt, soaked in stunning shades of deep crimson and peacock green. Gold slippers encase her feet like an Egyptian princess. Through her veil, one can see glimpses of a golden turban. An earthy beadwork covers her head.

The couple makes a slow, deliberate walk down the center aisle, stopping at nearly every row of decorated chairs to greet, clasp hands, and share laughs with their friends.

Upon reaching the altar, a suitably noble-looking priest in white and red vestments meets them. Aside from an occasional whisper of explanation from Kora, the rest of the ceremony confuses Odessa, Georgi, and Reeva. The exchanges take place entirely in Setswana.

The heat becomes nearly unbearable and drowsy, mixed with a strong scent of herbs and sweat without the softening touch of deodorant. Beneath it all is the smell of manure, cattle, sheep, and freshly cut grass.

Mikey rolls over, head on the cushion, thumb firmly in his mouth, and falls blissfully asleep. The service carries on. Georgi thinks she would love to join Mikey on his cushion and may even snooze without it. She pinches her arm to keep awake.

The Beads Come to Rest

Then, the wedding erupts in cheers, singing, clapping, and laughing. Kora tells Odessa that the religious part of the service is now over. The dancing, blazing horns, and trumpets resume as the bridal pair, their families, and finally, the guests cascade into the refreshment area. There, they discard their jackets. Drinks of anything cold, including champagne, circulate for the toasts.

Oscar and Dinkie have vanished. The heat gives way to the storm's fierce rule. From afar, flashes of lightning and peals of thunder signal a tropical downpour. Bright flashes, becoming more intense and menacing, draw near, followed by angry crashes in the sky and then a quick but fierce tropical shower.

Many people in the Lowveld suffer through thunderstorms in silent terror. Occasionally, a tornado outbreak, accompanied by lightning displays, causes chaos in its wake, destroying forests, taking lives, and wiping out the wilds with reckless abandon. When that happens, it is time for the affected community to go on a witch hunt. Like consumerism, witchcraft is a life-threatening cancer, slowly destroying the fabric of African society. It is mostly older women who are driven out of their small homes and paraded naked along grassy paths in front of ululating adults, with a duped audience of young children witnessing.

This time, no destruction happens. "Our ancestors are appeased and happy. They are telling us through the loud outburst that this wedding is truly blessed," says Kora, who looks windswept as she comes in from the refreshing shower from heaven.

Then, the couple makes another triumphal, heralded appearance, transformed into light-hearted entertainment to flaunt new fabrics. It is a form of catwalk where local designers make their mark. He has a gauzy open-necked shirt over his silk trousers. Sleeves rolled up, shirtfront open for coolness, Oscar looks swept away with exhilaration. Dinkie is now in her soft shift, spaghetti straps revealing her well-formed décolletage. She holds her husband's hand, and they cannot take their eyes off each other. There are speeches in English, toasts, and copious amounts of food and drinks.

They open new assortments of presents, and the audience whoops with delight. As shadows begin to fall gently, many of the guests start to leave. Georgi, dying to be elsewhere, looks at Odessa, who shakes her head unflinchingly.

"They invite close friends and family to stay on for dinner and dancing," she points out to the impatient Georgi, "And you will enjoy it."

About fifty people remain. The catering team sets up a long table on the stone floor in one of the lapas. Musicians soon take seats in a corner. Notemba holds Georgi's hand and says, "Come on, Georgi; let's see if you've inherited any of the Mofokeng rhythms."

As they gyrate on the dance floor, Georgi can think only of that wonderful dance with Kelly Ellsworth; at least the stresses and strains of carnal desires are absent tonight. They watch Sabelo and Kora do their boogie, and someone shouts, "Wow, can they dance? What?"

"That's how they met," laughs Notemba. "Mother tells me that when they were young, they did competitive ballroom dancing. I think they wanted to turn professional and then run a studio. But my dad's family insisted he study to be a teacher. He did his post-graduate studies at the University of South Africa. So, no more time for dancing."

Georgi whirls away with a good-looking man who says his name is Lunga Koselo, Dinkie's cousin. She is too busy following his lead to think about anything else. Although his mother is South African, he knows little about his father.

After telling her that his mother once struggled in Gondwana, an African country, he says, "Georgi, darling, you are the most beautiful woman I have seen in a long time."

Lunga feels disappointed when his attempt to charm Georgi fails. While Lunga is disappointed with Georgi's rejection, he charms Odessa to the ends of the earth.

These people are in danger

It has been several days since Marcia and Georgi last spoke. The house buzzes with activity as they prepare for the trip to the Cape. Georgi oversees the housekeeping. Sanna will pack valuable and fragile items that Marcia wants locked away in the storeroom.

Amid all the chaos and clutter, Georgi receives an anonymous call. The man has a strong Afrikaans accent, she thinks. "There's an old couple just touched down at Johannesburg International. They are from Germany. Check them out."

"And who are you?"

"Check Nathaniel Lieber's Centurion flat. You go there. These people are in danger. Stop them," he hangs up.

"What is this?" Georgi mutters.

"Are you alright, Georgi?"

Georgi contacts Odessa, who says she knows nothing about the couple but mentions that the caller might be April. He has called her multiple times, leaving cryptic messages and calling her 'my darling.'

"It's him. Him, Odessa. And when were you planning on telling me about April's calls?"

"I didn't take him seriously. Sounds like a crank caller."

Georgi is furious. She feels Odessa is sidelining her in favor of Reeva. Otherwise, why would she take April as a crank caller when his name has been top of their 'to-do' list since their touchdown?

"Don't worry," Odessa says, "The couple April is referring to is probably Nathaniel's mother and father. Reeva here has figured it out."

"Reeva? What's your story with Reeva?"

Georgi rents a car and speeds to Centurion, arriving at early drive time. As she moves down Koch Street, she senses a disturbance up ahead. The couple has escaped a bomb blast. "We are lucky to be alive," the woman says. "I'm glad we took him seriously. Someone called my husband and alerted us to the situation. As we rushed down the stairs, we heard a loud thud that pushed us forward, and we ended up in the middle of the street."

Her name is Puri, she smiles demurely. She looks elegant, if slightly frail.

"We learn your husband is still under observation."

"Yes, he took a bit of a blow," she laughs out loud, "but remember, Jews survived the holocaust."

Marcia learns from her informant in the President's office that the Commissioner of Police has dispatched an official vehicle from Pretoria, complete with eight officers. After five minutes, the informant tells Marcia that the President's office has instructed the Liebers to be flown by helicopter to an undisclosed location in Cape Town.

Georgi starts to notice a flashing red flag about Marcia and Moroka in her mind. She asks, "Do you know which residence these people will be taken to?"

"According to the Minister, the media is restricted, and we can't speak to the press either."

"So, you have no idea about the residence in question?"

"No," says Marcia

Georgi has confirmed to herself that Marcia is feeding her fibs. She thinks Moroka and Marcia know more about the Lieber affair than they are letting on.

"Can you tell me more about what's happening, Marcia?"

"Okay, I'll tell you what I know. If you didn't realize, you and Odessa have had secret bodyguards since you arrived in South Africa."

"It's the government's National Intelligence Agency. They know everything about you two girls. "

"Curiouser and curiouser! I should have told you this; when I went to Soweto, a female Lieutenant with bodyguards drove me out of there, I tell you. Are these NIA people always parked outside?"

Georgi tells herself she should have stopped believing anything Marcia said from the first day she met her.

Odessa calls to ask Georgi if she remembers one of the men she danced with at the Beesfontein wedding. Georgi tells Odessa that the man she remembers is the one with pink spiked hair who moved like a darter through the crowded dance floor.

"Spare me your poetry, Georgi. His name is Lunga. He's called three times, asking for a date, and we're going out next Sunday, his best night because he doesn't have to work on Mondays. I reminded him that I do."

Georgi feels a twinge of contemplation about their imminent parting. She has a strange foreboding, a dreamlike intuition, that Odessa is about to nosedive to earth without a parachute.

"He drives a four-by-four Merc, does he?"

"How did you know?"

"Just a hunch," Georgi shrugs impatiently.

"We'll be in for early supper and then slow down for a movie."

Odessa reminds Georgi about their parents' expectations for Christmas. However, Georgi is flying home later this year.

The move to Cape Town is smooth, and Georgi accepts the task of looking after the Liebers like she did in her doomsday fate. She hopes the weather will not discourage Puri Lieber and her husband from spending time sightseeing. A wave of debilitating thoughts keeps flooding her mind, telling her that she should be satisfied with her lot in life. Although the officers tasked with babysitting the couple fail to turn up, Georgi knows they are prowling somewhere nearby. Marcia is at work and then with the girls at school. Taylor has started a playgroup.

After showing them to their room, Georgi offers the visitors beverages. The windows on two sides of the room overlook vines, a profusion of shrubs, and flowers against the nearby mountain peaks. French doors open onto a patio, luxuriously shaded by foliage. Georgi later directs them to the poolside.

"I can show you around the property if you wish," she offers.

Tall and athletic, with an unhealthy pallor, Caleb Lieber is enthusiastic and appreciative of Georgi's hospitality.

"I believe you became friendly with my son when he came to Pretoria, yes?" Caleb asks Georgi.

"A group of us went out to dinner one night."

"Right, and afterward, he started writing letters, and he thinks you are intelligent, yes?" Asks Puri.

Georgi is puzzled over which way the wind is blowing. She asks, "Would you like more drinks, Mrs Lieber?"

Georgi confirms her visit to the farm with Barend but deliberately omits mentioning the names of the Liebers. Marcia arranges with her government officials, who dispatch a helicopter. After the high temperatures in Johannesburg, wading into the wintry-wet Cape of Good Hope is a pleasure. Then, the erratic weather begins to pall. One day, it is raining with descending high-ceilinged cloudbanks, dark and menacing; the next, it might be a scorcher, with a stiff South-Easter sweeping everything movable in its wake. The persistent, unpredictable wind eventually becomes quite disagreeable, making the children, even the sweet-tempered Taylor, fractious and demanding. The dams are low, and Capetonians pray for the rain to save the wheat, fill the dams, and restore good humor. At last, the winter rains arrive, too late and too little, but welcome.

Smudges of snow are visible on the mountains while the northwesterly wind carries a chill that the fitful beams of sunshine cannot overcome. Jamaica and Verona are gleefully watching for occasional snow as the helicopter sweeps toward Robertson. Thankfully, the wind dies down, and the sunlight feels cheerful and warm. At the Van der Watt homestead, they are greeted by Lyndon, Barend's brother, regally astride a magnificent black gelding. Georgi will soon learn that Barend has had to fly to Namibia— their escort follows along the driveway to a large, comfortable farmhouse in 'Cape Dutch' style.

As soon as they meet Gert, Barend's father, and Sofia, they spread Trencherman's tea on the large kitchen table, and everyone enjoys homemade scones, *melktert, and koeksisters*. Sofia is Barend's younger sister. Georgi notices that her eyes and those of the Van der Watts never meet. The center of the hosts' attention is Mrs and Dr Lieber, while the rest of them seem to be elsewhere.

It is Georgi's first real introduction to the Afrikaners of the Cape. She finds their hospitality towards the Liebers overwhelming. There is no language barrier since Puri is fluent in Afrikaans, and besides, most people in the Western Cape are bilingual. Lyndon offers to show them around the farm, and Sofia, whose smile seems contrived, lends Georgi a pair of stout boots. Fortunately, they have all brought sun hats.

The day passes agreeably and all too quickly. They say their goodbyes as Georgi appreciates the beautiful Western Cape sunset. She impulsively invites Sofia to Marcia's party, but she politely declines.

"You had a good time, then?" asks Marcia.

"The family is fine, although I thought Sofia had a lasting sorrow visible in her eyes. Our host decided to go AWOL."

"What happened?"

"He went to Namibia. Funny, the patriarch and Barend's two siblings could not even look me in the eye. The kids enjoyed the rabbits, though."

Georgi cannot help but feel that the whole trip has been cunningly choreographed at certain government levels. When Odessa calls Georgi, she sounds frighteningly upbeat about her imminent date with Lunga.

CHAPTER 13

Hava Nagila?

Puri's inquisitiveness towards Georgi has been noticeable. However, after the outing, it takes on an unexpected depth, something Georgi sees as an invasion of her space. She asks Georgi to drive her to Cape Point, where she wants to take photos.

Dressed casually in her jeans and sporting a maroon Jewish headscarf, Puri says, "My husband is having one of his bad days. Luckily, when we received the mysterious call to vacate the damaged flat, he took it seriously. Usually, when he gets himself that sulky, you can't persuade him to scratch his itching knuckles."

Georgi and Puri spend a pleasant time at a famous spot, the symbolic meeting point of two mighty oceans. Georgi observes that the Atlantic and Indian oceans meet at the continent's southernmost point, higher up the coast at Cape Agulhas.

"But all the Capetonians I know fantasize over the two oceans colliding right here; forget Agulhas," Puri says.

Puri is hard at work while Georgi focuses intently on her face. To Georgi, Puri is more attractive than when she first encountered her after the Centurion incident. Her demeanor is now free of any trace of middle age, and her hair looks soft and streaked with attractive grey. Today, she is dressed more credibly in trainers, bush trousers, and the all-pervading garb of the professional photographer: a sleeveless khaki jacket with dozens of pockets, perhaps holding film, light meters, band-aids, aspirin, digestive biscuits – and cigarettes, of course!

Puri expresses satisfaction with the lighting for her shooting. She even trains her lens on Georgi as she leans against the parapet, her glossy hair blowing around her face in the gentle breeze. The holiday atmosphere relaxes, and she becomes companionable.

"That will make a lovely portrait; you are the picture of youthful health today. Your face and body can doll up the entire European magazine world. I'll let you have a copy. It is to say thank you," Puri says as she exposes her vulnerable side.

"Thank you, Mrs Lieber. Thank you. How did you become a photographer? You seem devoted."

"Perhaps one day I'll sit down with you in a more peaceful atmosphere. Then I'll tell you all about it. When I look at you, in the bloom of beauty and health," she confides, "I am reminded of my vivacious youth. I was about your age when I met Nathaniel's father. Where I grew up, a little white girl living in the colonies, it would have been unheard of for one to start a friendship, let alone a love affair, with a black man. Of course, it was also against the laws of South Africa. I met him across the border. Back then, South Africa was considered a European outpost, with the black population an irritation to successive white governments. While the system socializing us was too overwhelming, love had the power to blow away one's bigotry. You'll soon learn that when you're

~ 93 ~

young, wild, and head in the clouds, you sometimes take a quantum leap into the dark. Whatever people say, all you see is their lips moving, nothing more. It's called love, total surrender. Ol' Blue Eyes once crooned, 'If it's love, no in-betweens.' He was the most sexually attractive man I had ever come across, Nat's father, I mean. Never mind love. I've always said I loved him, but in reality, carnal passion prevailed over all else, pure physical attraction."

"Some people are still hypersensitive about Sex across the color line. I think people must treat individual preferences as private and respect them."

Puri gazes at Georgi across the shimmer of the air at midday and says, "I thought I was going to shock you, but for a young woman, you seem to have kept your head when all about you are losing theirs..."

"Rudyard Kipling...?"

"Oh! I'm impressed. No word on a page has ever been responsible for killing anyone. Just looking into your eyes, I can see you are still an innocent girl, yes... a virgin? Am I slightly off the mark?" She chuckles and suppresses a cough, evidently enjoying a good laugh and great companionship she has not had for a long time. Georgi feels an amazing affinity towards her.

They relocate again, but she carries on with some sense of melancholy, "Nowadays it is something to be ashamed of... to be a virgin, I mean. How the galaxy has revolved!"

Georgi does not react, uneasy that Puri, a stranger, would try to scan her soul.

Puri's tone becomes brisk again. Giving Georgi a mischievous smile, she says, "All the same, Caleb has been a good husband and father to Nathaniel."

Following a fruitful conversation, Puri motions her closer, and she demonstrates how to assemble her kit. Then she unpacks it and says, "Now you do it. I want to ensure it is safe when sending you errands."

Georgi jumps like a filly and examines the sophisticated equipment. Puri's vote of confidence in her ability touches her.

The equipment looks heavy from a distance, and she says, "It will take me forever to learn how to use this."

"Everything is controlled by the heart. You can start by using it on something you like. What drives you? You can tell me."

"I like children... and poetry, too."

"There you go..."

"I've just noticed. We can make a documentary about your life as a young poet who loves children, exploring the trials and tribulations that come with it. Many people have a low opinion of poets, which worsens if the poet thinks children are important."

"You must have been a fly on my wall. Trials and tribulations? Tell me about it."

Georgi hands back the delicate equipment while Puri examines the young woman's face as if preparing for a major shoot.

Georgi says, "You said something about errands?"

"You'll never know where your heart is until you walk your index finger on your bosom—photography and poetry are two sides of the same coin. If you love poetry, you'll adore photography. That, I guarantee. Errands? Next time I do something for one of the magazines, I want you by my side."

After shooting dozens around the coastline, they stow the cameras away in the trunk and take a slow drive back.

"That was a delightful experience," Puri says, "and thank you for taking me out. Where else in the civilized world, I wonder, will you find such stretches of unspoiled beach and ocean? I grew up in Swakopmund, Namibia, South-West Africa, and then attended a convent school. For some reason, I never truly toured the Cape. Then, I worked in Windhoek for a while, before Angola, Tanzania, and Kenya, as a freelancer to cover the Bush war."

"Must have been scary," Georgi slows down, trying to maneuver around a gaping pothole.

"Conflict is always scary. But that low-intensity warfare launched by the system against the Northern African countries suspected of harboring guerrillas was a test of the white man's parched conscience. To think that the racist apartheid government swore they weren't fighting anywhere in Africa! They informed white voters, to their tacit approval, that their 'boys on the border' protected their white privilege from communism."

"Yeah, right."

"They had a powerful ideological apparatus, the South African Broadcasting Corporation, aided by one ubiquitous Cliff Saunders, an expert apartheid spin doctor."

"They needed spin doctors, of course..."

"All tyrants crave spin-doctors like the air they breathe, such as Eschel Rhoodie, a consummate apartheid apologist from the 'Muldergate' scandal era..."

"Nathaniel tells me he was born in Tanzania, a camp where the South African Defense Force attacked freedom fighters daily."

"Yes, he and his twin sister, the daughter I lost. Her given name was Esther. She was Esther," she puts it more strongly, all the while searching for validating hints from Georgi.

"This music playing?"

Puri draws a pack of President Cigarettes from her pouch and heaves, "Do you mind?"

"Sorry, but this car is virgin territory," Georgi gestures to a dash decal showing a cigarette with a red slash across it. We'll soon get there."

"I respect that. Never smoke in front of Caleb, either; It's his *bête-noir*. Besides, it's bad for his chest. I've prayed to God to give me the strength and will to stop. Alas! No answer."

"My mother says it is better to pray to do something rather than stop something. I'm still trying to get my head around that."

Puri's face wrinkles, and she returns the pack to its place, holding her cigarette restlessly between her fingers for the rest of the journey.

"Nice music."

"That's Abdullah Ibrahim, our piano player par excellence. The track is from 'The Call'."

"Sorry, I stopped you puffing your cigarette."

"It's my character defect, smoking. I started at thirteen, thanks to my aunt, who lived in Muizenberg. My mother died when I was an infant, but Aunt Pnina spoiled me to bits. She used to say, 'You may smoke, but not more than one a day, and always keep in mind, you're Jewish.'"

As they approach the Taung house, Puri says, "Georgi, I was intrigued to learn from Nathaniel that your name is 'Mofokeng.'"

"Yes, but I use my Canadian name, Moffet-King, or King. My father and mother changed our name in Canada."

The car squeals to a stop at the end of the driveway, and as they walk toward the house, Puri says excitedly, "You must know Hava Nagila, the traditional Hebrew song we sing at such Jewish celebrations as a bat mitzvah, a coming-of-age ritual for girls. We still follow all of that…"

Puri begins to sing and dance. She motions for Georgi to join her, and the two women dance and sing together joyfully in the driveway. When they finally hold each other with satisfaction, Puri takes her long-awaited break to smoke.

Georgi says, "I must see to Taylor, but before that, I'd like to ask you a question, if I may."

Georgi's sudden, staid face worries Puri.

"Of course, you can ask me anything…"

"When were you last in South Africa before this latest trip?"

"Why? Long ago, of course."

"Five years, ten, twenty?"

"Why the grilling now, Darling? I told you it's many years…"

"Do you know a man called Richard of Mofolo… in Soweto?"

Puri halts under the Kosi palm tree and puffs out smoke from her lungs. She sighs and starts fiddling with the smoldering tip of her cigarette before she grins as if caught with her fingers in the cookie jar.

"Please, Georgi," Puri whispers, "Caleb must never find out about this. I was desperate. Caleb and I have been struggling because he thinks looking for Esther is like chasing a mirage. We've not been intimate in recent times because of this headache."

"You mean you have not… had sex for ions?"

Puri slowly sticks her cigarette between her quivering lips and takes three quick puffs before she says, "Sex is not the only requirement for intimate connection. One day, when you've found your man, you will learn something: intimacy wobbles if your daily agendas are mismatched. Right now, the only item on my agenda is to find my baby girl."

"In Soweto… did you find what you were looking for?"

"Soweto? Suspicion is the tapestry of life there…"

"Apart from poverty, you mean?"

"Yes, but once you start talking about Bekker or Lenin, people suddenly remember they have laundry or shopping to do. I found it frustrating. The young man, Richard, was helpful. He can't stand politics; perhaps he looks at his father, KK, and says to himself, 'See what the struggle has done to my folk?' Otherwise, I came back empty-handed."

"What about Nathaniel? When he went to Soweto, did he come back empty-handed, too?"

"Did he go to Soweto?"

"I don't know, Mrs Lieber. What did you tell Dr Lieber before you went to Soweto?"

"Please call me Puri. I went to Russia; that's what he knows, so let's keep it that way."

"Some distance from Soweto, Russia is! You travel a lot?"

She stubs out her cigarette on the dry bark of the palm and says, "My black man taught me long ago how to fix myself a passport… any country. I used and discarded them over and over."

They then relax over drinks on the veranda.

"I see you smoke a lot. One of my friends in Canada told me she smokes to kill off shaky nerves."

"I was diagnosed with stage one cancer a while back. Three years ago, my doctor advised me that I had complete remission from the disease. She gave me a clean bill of health but told me to stop smoking," she laughs. "Bad habits are too hard to break. What defined Winston Churchill was his smoking habit? He won the war against elements of fascism but could hardly kick his habit of puffing on the Cuban Romeo."

"So, you don't have cancer anymore?"

"Cancer is like rising damp; sometimes the only time you know it has grown on you is when it has reached terminal stage four; that's when it is too late. You were saying about your family…?"

"Well, here's the thing," continues Georgi, savoring the delicious aroma of honey-sweetened golden Rooibos, "we think my father and Bekker were brothers."

"We? Meaning…?"

"My sister and I. You'll see her sometime soon. Her name is Odessa."

"Yes, I know."

"What else do you know?"

"Right under my nose! What else can you tell?"

"There isn't much more to tell. According to the sister, Kora, Bekker was dead. Who got shot dead in Swaziland?"

"I told Nathaniel the tale to create closure. I have no idea if the Swaziland story is true; I never got around to checking it out."

"You mean you lied to Nathaniel?"

"Not entirely. All sorts of rumors were flying around. Caleb encouraged me to sweep everything under the carpet, hoping it would disappear. But go away; it could not because Nathaniel grew taller and insufferably impatient. That prompted us to begin making inquiries, and our troubles started with an anonymous pest called GA regarding the suspected sightings of two Mofokeng girls from Canada. My name is April

Odessa is still anxious to know what, if anything, Puri made of her discussion with Kora. Puri tells Georgi that she saw the unmarked grave under the Marula tree. However, Kora knows nothing about a child. She is adamant that Ellen concocted the elaborate plan to bury Nathaniel's father.

"I don't want to stir the big pot," Puri says, "but I must call Ellen. I can hardly sleep for anxiety over what might have happened to Nathaniel's twin sister. Why would Kora lie about Bekker? Perhaps it is time to exhume the body and let the forensic specialists determine who lies in that grave. What do you think?"

"Mother Ellen reckons Kora is talking nonsense. She would be embarrassed if you, a stranger, called and started asking her such weird questions. She says Kora never liked her as a sister-in-law in the first place, and I can believe that. When we attended a wedding in Beesfontein, she kept taking little gratuitous digs at Mother Ellen."

"If I get the chance, I will be as non-intrusive as possible... or perhaps, call your father instead?"

Following Georgi's persistent nagging, she provides Puri with her father's cell phone number, after which she feels like Mrs Judas Iscariot.

Suddenly, spine-chilling peals of the telephone pierced the night. Georgi and Marcia eye each other with foreboding. Georgi recoils conveniently. Marcia has no choice. After a moment, she leans on the side table and tells Georgi of a strange caller. He asked if Georgi was in the house. When she asked who it was, he said, "I'll call again after sixty seconds, and it better be Georgi answering."

The caller was prompt. Georgi puts on her gown as if denying him consent to view her semi-naked body.

"My name is April," the stranger with a brassy voice says, getting straight to the point. "I know who killed Luca. Let's meet at Bester Restaurant, next to the Sex Shop, opposite Parliament – 6 pm on the note..."

"He hung up, Marcia. The same man who called about Nathaniel's parents is coming to the country in April. He'll tell me about Luca's murder at Bester Restaurant near the sex shop."

"You don't want to go there alone, girl. We should never trust a man who knows sex shop locations. The man may be a killer. We've been aware of him for months."

In the morning, Georgi says she has a confession to make, "Nightmare is my middle name. I've had nightmares since I was a toddler. I have suffered from sleep apnea... and then sleepwalking."

"We do not know where our souls travel while we sleep. Some people are responsive to the language of spiritual beings. I think your soul is restless. Do you believe in reincarnation?"

"I don't know what to believe these days, Marcia. My mother is highly spiritual, but she looks unhappy and desperately lonely. Odessa has changed since we left home. It's as if I'm dealing with a total stranger."

"She's hurting, I think."

My First Trimester

Georgi receives a late-night call from Odessa. Seemingly distracted, she makes a few false starts before she says, "Georgi, you'll have to go home alone if you decide to go at all."

"What's happened to you...?"

"I changed my mind. My doctor doesn't want me to travel in my first trimester."

There is silence on the line as Georgi processes the implications of the statement. She gasps and suddenly says, "Don't say you're expectant, Odessa! Abort, Sister Girl. Terminate and get rid of that man. Do the right thing..."

While enjoying her rare afternoon of luxury, relaxing on the patio, Georgi receives an indignant call from Uncle Sabelo, who seems to have difficulty getting past the introductory remarks. He squeezes in a soft line, expressing how he enjoyed her company on the day of Oscar's wedding. She is sure this is not the purpose of the call. She makes some polite rejoinders, telling him how fantastic she found the wedding, all the while thinking, 'What is this call really about?'

A moment of tense silence leads Sabelo to clench his throat and say, "You know Lunga, Dinkie's cousin, the one with a Gondwana father and a Pedi mother? He's the chap we met at Dinkie's wedding. He looks like a bouncer?"

"Yes...?"

"Odessa has been dating him?" he asks, uttering the word 'dating' as though it were demanding on his tongue. I hope she knows about this guy, that he is married?" Sabelo blurts out. "His wife lives in Gondwana. They met here while she was doing a diploma course in architecture with Wits Technikon in Doornfontein. Lunga lost interest in her when she was expecting their second child. After completing his MBA, he secured a cushy job with an Empowerment company in Midrand. The first thing such yuppies get rid of is their offspring's mothers."

"How awful. Odessa doesn't know all that stuff, Uncle."

"Yes, I know. Talk about planting a tree with its roots up in the air."

"She was sniffy about my suggestion to ditch the fool. So, I left her alone. What are we going to do, Uncle?"

Sabelo snorts in disgust, "I thought Canadian girls would have more sense than our teenagers here. As for you, your Auntie said of you, 'Georgi can survive the sweltering heat of the new South Africa any day'."

"I'll take that as a compliment even though it comes from her."

CHAPTER 14

Dozey Crafts

Reeva rushes to tell Odessa that Kris is looking for her urgently. When Odessa arrives, Kris has Sonja O'Barrity in his office. He hands her a presentation folder across the desk. Sonja has a similar one in front of her.

"Good news," says Kris. "We have a new client. They've agreed to study our campaign. If they like it, we're in. I want you and Sonja to front this one."

Sonja has previously told Odessa that she is 'pissed off because people treat her like a backroom girl' and that she had far more autonomy at Cha-Cha. Odessa, who cannot stand Sonja, can sense the temperature rising.

"By 'front,' you mean Odessa, and I will be the talking heads while the creative work remains at the coal face?"

"No, Sonja. I want you two to run with this. Share the work between yourselves any way you like. Call for assistance if needed, but you two are Trentraders for this project."

Kris points at the folders each of them holds. The company in question is Dozey Crafts, located outside Durban. Three very enterprising women started the company as an NGO. Their mission is to empower local women to design, produce, and market their creations. They began with items like pashminas, those woven poncho-type stoles, and expanded to skirts, gilets, turbans, baskets, and sheepskin boots.

"You pair me up with Odessa... you know very well she is sick."

Odessa jumps up and prepares to insult Sonja.

Kris says, "I'll ignore that remark. As for you, Odessa, sit down. Now, back to Dozey. They produce lovely items of excellent quality, with nothing shoddy about their work. Dozey, as you'll see from the folder, stands for Durban Zulu, but the three directors are Deirdre, Una, and Zinzi. It's a lovely acronym. What do you think, Odessa?"

"I'm thrilled. It sounds like a terrific company and a great project."

Sonja replies, "So we get it because it's a woman's thing?"

Kris looks irritated. "If you don't want to be involved, Sonja, just say so. As the more experienced operative, we would like you to lead the project. But get this: Turn down this project; I don't see a future for you at Trentraders."

Sonja changes her tone, "No, that's not what I'm saying. I'm sorry if you misunderstood me. I'd love to do it. Where do you want us to start?"

"And you, Sonja," what do you bloody mean I'm sick? Just because I'm pregnant? Does that make me bloody sick?"

"Right! Good! Looks like you two will get on like a house on fire," Kris clowns and continues, "Just so we know where we stand, read those folders, memorize them, look at everything they've got; ask as many questions as you need to become au fait with their processes, the work they produce, any ideas they have about advertising and marketing, not just the three top honchos, but the workers as well. When you get back, we can have a brainstorming session," he heaves, smiles, nods, and then, "Any questions? Go, Team, go!"

Odessa tidies up a few pressing administration items on her desk. She leaves early, clutching the Dozey file to 'read and digest' at home. She relays her exciting news, "I am delighted at the idea of being a small part of it, Georgi. It also makes you realize the scope within the country to create jobs for people in need via NGO's. I can't tell you how this has grabbed my imagination."

Her enthusiasm is infectious. While most of it is over Georgi's head, she is pleased to hear her sister sound jovial.

Puri calls Georgi in the middle of the night to ask if she will go home.

"Where are you calling from? It's midnight here in South Africa," Georgi says with agitation.

"Oh, we are back in Pretoria... about a week now. I should have called you, but I got busy with an assignment. The Council of Provinces invited me to take portraits of all their Premiers and senior staff."

"A week!" shouts Georgi.

"We are going back soon. Would you like to spend some days with us in Switzerland? Of course, I'll foot the bill... your fare and everything."

"That's cool of you, Mrs Lieber, but the idea would not fly with my dad. And remember, I'm already coming to Sabi-Sabi with you in June. But thanks for the offer."

"You know, we are all very fond of you. After all, you are my one and only... friend. And Odessa, of course..."

There is silence on the line, and when Puri speaks again, she seems hesitant, "I want to ask you something... and please excuse my being rather... intrusive, I suppose... I don't know..."

"What is it, Mrs Lieber?"

"You probably think this is crazy, but bear with me. Would you be prepared to take a maternal blood test? I mean, what they call a Mitochondria DNA test?'

"What? Whatever for, Puri... I mean, Mrs Lieber?"

"Forgive me, but I can't shake this feeling we may be somehow... related."

"Related? You and me?"

"I lack the guts to look you in the eye and say what I am saying right now. That's why I'm on the other side of the line at night. I've been struggling to sleep and think properly lately. Caleb says I'm round the bend. But I must say something to you for my sake and probably yours. You may be my daughter, Nathaniel's twin sister, if you would do me the favor of having the test done so that I can close all my accounts. I have been getting sucked deeper into the mire of depression since I first met you."

"Look, Puri, this is awkward. My mother would surely recognize me. This is serious stuff! Can we end this conversation?"

"Please don't hang up, Esther..."

"Esther?"

"I promise. If the Mitochondria tests prove negative, I won't bother you again."

"Mitochondria?"

"Yes, I know I am right. You cannot look in the mirror and not wonder why you're... so much lighter-skinned than...? Please, give me a chance."

"I'll have to think about it," Georgi catches herself repeating the line.

Satisfied that Georgi has not declined her request out of hand, Puri hangs up.

'This woman is bonkers,' Georgi murmurs. 'Esther!' However, Georgi reflects ever more on Puri's call, agonizing over her disturbing rhetorical question, 'You cannot look in the mirror and not wonder why you are so much...!' Put obliquely that way, Puri's point has thrown Georgi off balance and touched an uneasy nerve.

Odessa returns from Durban pleased with herself after a successful stint networking with the Dozey team. Sadly, Lunga has worked himself into a state of agitation.

"I want you to quit your job and move in with me at my place until the kid is born. You can stay with my mother until then," he says. "That's a much better place for my child here in Johannesburg. You've got no one to look after you."

"Says who?"

"I know. While you are living with Reeva, I am unable to talk privately with you. Fathers have rights, too, and I want my child properly looked after."

Odessa is furious. She retorts, "What you are demanding will not happen. I'm not sure if you understand what 'father's rights' mean. But women, too, have careers, not just jobs."

"How can you work and take care of a kid at the same time? And don't listen to your aunt and uncle. They hate me because I am from Gondwana. Everyone in this country hates foreigners. But my mother is a full-blooded South African. They don't care about that! And your sister, Georgi, what does she know about our African culture?"

A few days later, Kora drives to see Odessa. She says, "Sabelo has warned Lunga three times, saying if he doesn't tell you the truth, he'll have to do it himself to protect you..."

"Who said I needed protection, Aunt Kora?"

"You do. You're still a child to me. My brother's child is my child. That's how they raised us. You wouldn't know about such things because you call them culture. Anything that comes from Africa is culture, something primitive to sneer at. But Hollywood is not culture; it's chic for the civilized. Did your boyfriend brief you about his marital status?"

"Marital...? No, we haven't discussed such things."

"Your naiveté is a pain in my big behind," Kora heaves heavily, looking away into the distance. "I see you never exchanged your portfolios. I learned that present-day X and Y generations demand certificates of good health signed by a reputable doctor. Any boy worth his salt demands a certificate of intelligence from a girl. That's what Sabelo did. He subjected me to what he later told me was a litmus test. When he first took me out on a date, he bought me two mangoes, and we got into a taxi. I panicked because mangoes were my staple food. My grandma had encouraged me to eat loads of it to help with anemia. I immediately suspected Sabelo had researched me, so I told him the truth. I also told him I could not eat the thing until we reached home. When we exited the taxi, he immediately said, 'Kora, will you marry me?' I nearly wet myself."

"That was sweet, Aunt Kora."

"Yes, and I said, 'Yes, you can marry me if you must'. He said, 'Yes, I must. I have offered a mango to several of my dates, and you are the only one to put it away instead of peeling it, tearing it apart, and making a mess of it in someone's taxi. That is a sign of intelligence and orderliness. I must marry you,' he said. He is a man of integrity, which is more than can be said about that boy called Lunga. Tell me, did Lunga not demand a certificate of orderliness?"

"No, Aunt Kora..."

"Did you ask him about his HIV status?"

"He told me he's negative, and I trust him."

"What a long walk to self-destruction. Lunga tells you he is HIV-negative, and you fornicate with him because you trust him? You must trust him then if he tells you he's a married man with a young wife tucked away in some Gondwana village; two babies, to be sure, one of whom may not be his."

Odessa trembles. Even so, Kora continues to express her displeasure: "Sorry, my child. We know all of this because his mother is Sabelo's cousin. Tell the truth, now. Are you pregnant with that fool's fetus?"

She looks searchingly at her niece. The pregnancy is not apparent, but Odessa keeps silent, and Kora shouts a catalog of invectives directed at Lunga. Odessa lays her weight on her aunt's shoulder and cries, Oh! Auntie! "The man has no shame, and the woman has no orderliness! Oh, Auntie! What a mess!" she cries.

"Why don't you go back to Canada? You need your mother at a time like this. According to culture, you go home for your first baby."

Hoping to avoid confronting her parents permanently, Odessa makes what she knows are ridiculous excuses to Kora.

CHAPTER 15

Ryan's Touch

Georgi and Marcia are seated at the kitchen table following Marcia's return from another long day at the 'salt mines,' as she puts it. She tells Marcia about Puri's request for a blood test.

"It's utterly weird, this whole soapy. She's persistently on my case about taking this test," Georgi grumbles.

Marcia wants to know how Georgi personally feels about it.

"I feel quite negative. I don't want to upset my mom and Dad, and I know if I discuss it with them first, it will be as bad as telling them that I believe Puri's story. But I also can't have it done without telling them."

"Then let me ask you this: if you turn out to be Puri's long-lost daughter, how will it enhance your life?"

"It won't. If anything, it would take a lot away from me. My parents, brother, and sister are very close-knit, and I couldn't bear the thought of losing them. It's crazy even to contemplate."

"You've answered your question. Say 'No' to Puri and mean it. But," she studies Georgi, "if you are Puri's child, your mother and father already know that. That would mean they have been hiding it from you from the beginning. These things happen even to the best of us."

"Indeed, they do, Marcia. But I hate it when someone tells me the right thing to do!"

Marcia smiles ruefully, "Sorry, that's my big failing: always playing the devil's advocate."

The 'Ides of Christmas' have gone, and it is New Year's Eve. In Constantia, a vociferous dawn chorus heralds the last day of the New Year. Georgi is up before six, pleased to welcome one of those glorious Cape days that bode well for the night's revelry. Her sense of expectancy makes her smile at herself as she stands underneath the shower with the spray turned to a fierce stinging onslaught. She recalls her same keen anticipation of the year 2000, how thrilled she was to be one of the millions alive to witness the birth of the new millennium. Another thousand years would have to pass before a living soul saw the year 3000. The 21st century and the third millennium are now several years old. She hopes never to lose this awareness and exultation of life and living. More importantly, she feels a frisson of pleasure in knowing that she will also see Barend that same evening. She is somewhat disappointed and irritated that Odessa has opted out of the Cape Town vacation to stay in Johannesburg. Odessa has yet to admit to Lunga's deception openly.

Georgi is determined not to let the disappointment spoil her day. From the shower,

Georgi towel-dries her hair and pulls on shorts and a loose T-shirt. Working gear is always the best when the day is hectic. Although a high-spirited group of caterers will provide the 'ample spread' planned for the party tonight, Marcia will want to oversee every aspect for 'quality control,' as she calls it. Georgi thinks Marcia is a benevolent dictator. The decoration of the grounds will also come under her competent scrutiny, with the entertainment zone featuring lanterns in the trees and along the driveway, as well as decorated lights marking the area around the pool. Apart from celebrating the New Year, this party also serves as a welcome home for Moroka.

He pours flutes for himself, his wife, and Georgi. Into two wine-tasting glasses, he pours a half-shot of the Champagne for the girls and a splash into Taylor's Tupperware mug. Solemnly, he stands tall and raises his glass.

"I propose a toast," he says, "to my beloved family, including our newest member, Georgi. Here's to the New Year."

The girls all drink, wrinkling their noses at the new sensation of bubbles. Taylor kisses Georgi and says, "Thank you," for the first time in his life, giving rise to more fussing and telling him he's a clever boy.

By eight, they are all in their finery. The musical ensemble performs a medley of oldies, 'Knights in White Satin,' 'Mack the Knife,' 'Fly Me to the Moon,' and many others that Georgi does not recognize. The early arrivals are gracefully on the dance floor. Georgi thinks, 'This will be the lot that leaves at midnight! From the looks of things, the party will be composed of only the elite... the crème de la crème of the South African public service. Sabelo and Kora could show this crowd a thing or two about dancing.'

When a young, tall black man asks her for a dance, Georgi says, "Sorry. I've promised this partner all the dances until 9 o'clock."

The man smiles and says he will come back at nine. Georgi curses herself because she feels drawn to him. 'What the heck did I say 9 o'clock for? What if he comes back? Oh God,' she murmurs to herself, 'help me. I am so weak.

She thinks she has seen him somewhere before, although she can hardly place him. Then she picks Taylor up in her arms and continues dancing. All the while, at the back of her mind is the handsome black man whose identity she cannot quite remember.

By nine, Taylor's head drooped on her shoulder, his eyelids fluttering and closing. Jamaica and Verona still dance together, looking happy in their matching, flowered, ankle-length dresses. Waving to them, Georgi reflects that soon they will want to wear clothes that show off their belly buttons and midriffs. For tonight, they are still little girls.

Returning to the party, the band is now getting into its stride, with jazzy pop music making the floor thump and the dancers liven up. The tall black man with a tender smile returns to fulfill Georgi's promise. He smiles again, and Georgi is overwhelmed. Georgi smiles back and says, "You want a dance?"

The two occupy their space and dance like John Travolta and Olivia Newton-John. Still wearing his enchanting smile, the man says, "I know you don't know me, but I've heard lots about you. My name is Ryan Taung."

"Taung?"

"Uncle Moroka and my father are brothers."

"Oh! How fascinating. How come I never heard of you?"

"I always fly under the radar," he laughs.

"At least you continue to fly, "she laughs; "Sorry, one of my sister's silly wisecracks. You are Mr Taung?"

"My father and Uncle Moroka have had this family thing for years. That's why you'll never hear about me from them."

"Yes? And is Marcia also caught up in your family thing?"

Ryan smiles again and holds Georgi by the hand. Georgi senses a deep scar behind his cheerful demeanor. She knows the meaning of 'family thing' only too well. Still, she has also detected that South Africans have developed a special physical dialect to express hidden thoughts they would rather keep to themselves. Georgi feels her immune system wilt to Ryan's touch. She motions him to a dim spot, and he readily steps along.

"Your father and Moroka are not talking to each other?"

"Only when they have to discuss family bereavements," he sniggers.

"Moroka and Marcia... they invited you; that's a start, at least."

"Not quite. As you know, the Taungs are high-fliers who celebrate everything, from the waxing moon to the sighting of their child's first tooth. We get to hear about their bashes from the grapevine. Luckily, they always have enough rations for everyone, including gate-crashers like me."

"Surely, you can't be a gate-crasher at your uncle's party."

"I don't live far from here; I work at UCT as a lecturer, and I only come here to have a good time with my friends."

"Does your extended family know you're here tonight?"

"Marcia saw me, and I suppose my presence is ruining the work. But tonight, I'm anxious to have a word with Uncle. My father is gravely ill in a clinic in Lenasia. He was diagnosed with cancer. Unfortunately, he drank heavily during his heyday, which didn't help his situation. I want Uncle to visit Lenasia and make peace with my father."

"I guess that's what your father wants at this time of his life."

"Life? Well, not quite. I saw him two days ago and told him I would bring Uncle Moroka. And he said, 'Let me die first before I see that man.'"

"What about Moroka? Is he prepared to go to Lenasia?"

"After years of throwing missiles at each other? Your guess is better than mine. I haven't hinted it yet."

Barend comes clattering down the steps, his eyes on Georgi's handsome black companion. He looks cool in a soft pastel shirt open at the neck and nocturnal pale trousers. Georgi can feel her heart beating like thunder in her throat. It is starting all over again! She apologizes to Ryan and walks straight to Barend.

"I'm glad to see you," says Barend, "I don't know another soul here. You look wonderful.

"Thank you," she says, returning the smile and doing a pirouette to invite his admiration. "You look beautiful yourself."

"So, who are all these people?" He takes a flute from a passing server and hands it to Georgi.

"These are guests. I don't know any of them."

"And that guy you seemed engrossed with?"

Georgi says, "I just met him. We were having a chat."

She can sense misgivings in his looks. So, she tries to neutralize his lack of enthusiasm by questioning him about his trip to Namibia.

"I had to fulfill my duties."

"So, you let your sister stand in for you?"

"Who, Sofia?"

"How many sisters have you got?"

"Well, I had no idea Sofia was home…"

However, the icy tension soon melts away when they move agreeably together, chatting sporadically, parting temporarily when Barend walks to converse with Moroka and Marcia. With variations in music genres, he returns to reclaim Georgi, holding her close and whispering flattering words into her hair about how exquisite she looks. Georgi is glad he is there because her limbs feel like liquid. Ryan keeps popping up and disappearing like a small-town neon sign.

It is midnight, and everyone is counting down the New Year, kissing, yelling, and singing, 'Should auld acquaintance be forgotten…?' Georgi's peripheral vision has been scouring the surroundings for the sight of Ryan. When she cannot locate him, she concludes that he may have left out of dejection. Barend's kiss is firm, but he does not take liberties. It leaves her craving for more. She tries to regain her composure as a fantastic burst of color, reminiscent of a digital 'paintbrush' gone mad against a black screen, lights up the Southern sky, arcing into the heavens. Everyone watches the unexpected kaleidoscope, pointing out outstandingly brilliant, dramatic displays.

Hugging Moroka and then Marcia, Georgi offers to escort the girls to bed after the pageant. Marcia chirps, "Don't delay. We'll have dinner soon."

Once Jamaica and Verona are in bed, Georgi calls Odessa to wish her well for the New Year and immediately tries Canada. Although it's hours before midnight, they are pleased to hear from her. Because Ellen sounds distraught, Georgi does not prolong the call. Instead, she returns to Marcia's party feeling disconnected.

A Dark, Deep Voice

The second-round act, Crackpot, plays heavy metal underground, and they are impressive. Marcia has to tell them to tone it down until dinner.

"Knowing the price of lobster would make competition pointless. Just keep playing background boogie until I signal you to showcase your talent," she directs.

Barend pulls out a chair for Georgi as she approaches the table. Their conversation is scattered as the servers serve various courses.

"As of next month, February," Barend says, "I'm no longer on the force."

"Yeah? What's your next move?"

"I have two enticing offers that are both difficult to turn down. One role is for a security chief at a financial firm, offering an attractive salary, but I'm uncertain about the potential for job satisfaction. The other option is as a farm manager," he smiles. "You can likely guess which farm."

"Good on you. Which one will you take?"

"My third offer. May I have the pleasure of this dance?"

Georgi struggles to throw off her homesickness. They finish their Baked Alaska when a mysterious bearded man in a bowler hat stops beside Georgi's chair.

"I believe you are Georgi Mofokeng?" he states in a dark, deep voice.

She nods, noticing Barend standing up from his chair and looming beside her. He fixates on the stranger, his hand placed on the chair behind Georgi's back. This instinctive pose serves as a protective measure against any potential threat.

"I knew your father," the man says. "How is he enjoying Toronto?"

Georgi rises, her height surpassing that of the stranger, granting her a sense of control, if only partially. She responds, "Good, thanks. And who are you?"

He touches the brim of his hat as if drawing an answer from it. "Your father will know me," he says, lowering the register of his voice.

"Did you work with him at the bank?"

He laughs mirthlessly. "No. Goodness no," the stranger says, stroking his hat with an air of sarcasm. "He worked for me at Broederstroom. Please extend my regards to him when you speak with him. Tell him...," he pauses, "tell him, he is a wise man. Canada is a healthier climate than Africa, any day. Also, tell him he has a ravishing daughter. Happy New Year to you," he adds tentatively, as if he has something more important to say. However, he slips into the dark, spinning Georgi's head.

"I wonder who he is; he didn't hesitate in calling me by name," she shrugs.

"I notice you don't recognize him. It's best if you don't," Barend says, feeling uneasy.

"So, you do recognize him."

"To paraphrase Macbeth, 'Be innocent of the knowledge dearest Georgi'..."

It's three o'clock. Although the crowd has thinned, some die-hard fans continue to party vigorously, relishing the Crackpot's eclectic musical lineup, which includes jazz, hip-hop, and funk-rock. Barend criticizes the Crackpot's dismal performance and longs for the pre-midnight band to return, favoring music that allows him to embrace Georgi instead of just 'strap-hanging' to the tunes. As the clock strikes four, the band announces the 'last dance,' prompting someone to yell, "Ladies and gentlemen, let's go swimming!"

Barend says, "I'm game if you are."

He casually wraps one arm around her waist. A subtle scent of aftershave lingers in the air. She yearns to be alone with him.

"Wait," says Georgi, "I'll get the towels."

In the cottage, she slips into her bikini beneath her sea-green silk, smoothing the lovely, soft fabric as she puts it back on and enjoying the *susurrus* that only silk can provide. Soon, they are drifting in a convoy to the beach. The sun dazzles on the blue-green ocean. They park alongside the Muizenberg play area, cross beneath the promenade to walk on the white sands, and contemplate the lazy blue waves breaking on the shore. Someone shouts "Vrystaat!" and everyone runs headlong into the sea. It is cold, invigorating, and wonderful. The water feels like silk as Georgi turns her back and lets the breakers engulf her. She is the only one in a swimsuit. Others are in their underwear, while a few hardy souls have stripped down to their birthday suits. She is relieved to see Barend looking good in a scarlet bikini brief, even though it fits him like a Speedo. She remembers Odessa commenting favorably on his physique and wonders about other thoughts she might be hiding inside her 'intellectual' head. She notices Jack cavorting with an attractive woman with a cropped head, sleek as a seal. They are naked and confident. They walk away from prying eyes and hide behind the wall of sand, surrendering to each other's vulnerable craving. Their cool bodies melt with the heat of passion, but Barend breaks away, and they lie beside each other, facing the sky.

Barend and Georgi are driving home. It's nearly eight o'clock, and they plan breakfast with Taylor. Meanwhile, the others are still lounging in bed. As Barend gets ready to leave, he tells Georgi, "That was the best day of my life. I enjoyed it even more than seeing in the New Year at Trafalgar Square," he reflects.

"What, in particular, did you enjoy?"

You and I expose our vulnerability to the fading stars; you rest on the beach, near my heart...

Odessa's wise saying, 'Never give away all of your heart to a man,' rings loud and clear in her ear.

"Do you love me, Barend?"

"Why do you ask?"

Just so you're aware, I have reservations about a man who responds to a straightforward question with uncertainty.

After the evening's chaos, Georgi feels unsettled as she reclines half-dressed on her duvet. Numerous questions begin to surface in her mind. Growing increasingly anxious about her mother's deteriorating health, her dizzy thoughts drift to the mysterious bearded intruder. 'Who invited him? How did he know my name? Who is he? Why did I feel threatened by him? Is Barend concealing something?' She suspects that Barend and the bearded man might even know each other. 'Who is Barend, anyway?' As she drifts off, Puri's words crash back into her consciousness: 'Would you be willing to undergo a maternal blood DNA test?' Georgi reflects on her situation. When Ryan Taung's face crosses her mind, she swallows a mix of tablets and drifts into a deep sleep.

Oh, Odessa! What have I done?

Georgi's first thoughts upon waking are filled with unsettling images. She takes a shower. As she washes, her body's craving for Barend's touch grows stronger by the moment. She enjoys the calming spray, but suddenly Ryan's face appears in her mind again, like a sudden flash of lightning, temporarily wiping out all other thoughts.

She puts on her favorite cool shorts and continues to reflect on her situation. She flips through the latest newspapers and finds an article about Pedro. The man who once raped her is now in South Africa as an envoy for the Canadian Diplomatic Mission. Georgi is furious but knows she can do nothing to stop him without exposing herself to the media. She has kept her abuse to herself. Georgi feels so uneasy that she decides to fly to Johannesburg to be in Odessa's company. Upon arrival, she learns that Odessa and Reeva plan to have lunch at Fin's home.

"It's a staff barbecue," Odessa tells Georgi. "It will carry on all afternoon and end early evening."

"I'm going back in a few hours. If you'd come to Cape Town, you could enjoy a vacation like me!"

"Sounds romantic. Did Barend have any more to tell you about Bekker?"

"No, I think that subject has fallen off the cliff," says Georgi. "And Lunga? Is he invited to the barbecue?"

"Georgi," Odessa sighs, forcing an awkward smile, "I'm not quite sure how to say this, but Lunga is no longer relevant. He missed an important detail in his profile: he has a wife and two daughters living in Gondwana. He views this as trivial because their marriage followed tribal customs instead of Western law."

"What a snake! I'm sorry, Odessa. What a horrid predicament for you. What are you going to do?"

"Could be worse; I might have married him."

Odessa has now been offered a job with Dozey Crafts in Pietermaritzburg.

"You left Simon's company?"

"You'd better believe it. Una called me at midnight to tell me the good news. She said, 'Happy New Year and happy new job'. How do you like it?" Odessa sounds bubbly.

Georgi suspects Odessa isn't revealing everything about her departure from Trentraders. Why would she risk so much for a small paycheck? Additionally, the Dozey Crafts Odessa mentioned is located roughly fifty kilometers outside Pietermaritzburg in a secluded area. Georgi tries to press her further, but Odessa evades the questions. Eventually, Odessa admits that Finian's comment about her and Georgi being the 'K' and 'H' sisters was the last straw. "I heard all this from Nikita. She told me Finian once asked if we thought we were sisters, and then he started laughing and rambling. If I decide to give birth at the office, they should be cautious, especially since HIV is spreading among our community," she said.

"Oh, Yeah?"

"I'm lonely, Georgi. Let's stick together as sisters."

"Yes, like George and Lennie... Steinbeck's 'Of Mice and Men', you mean?"

"Please, Georgi, I mean it."

"And who is Lennie here? Did Nikita say what 'K' and 'H' meant?"

"Kaffirs and Hotnots. Do you know what 'Hotnots' stands for?"

"That's as offensive as using 'Kaffir'. Don't South Africans have other hobbies besides throwing mud at each other? I guess Hotnots stands for Hottentots. It might have some good aspects, though. Ever heard of the 'Hottentot Venus'?"

"Yea, Sarah Baartman. I got a sneak preview of your poetry collection."

"What sneak preview! You barely read a line of my books, let alone poetry."

"I do read some, occasionally."

"What does that even mean? You've dared to criticize my writing without bothering to read it first. I've never received any praise from you."

"Let's not go there, Georgi, please. If you expect critical acclaim from me your sister, perhaps you shouldn't be pursuing a career in creative writing."

"To be honest with you, Odessa, I wish you could encourage me. I value your opinion more than anything in this world. I love writing and need someone close to me to mention something they like about it."

Let me educate you for once, Sister Girl. Your poem 'Hottentot Venus...?"

"What about it?"

"It's an insult to the indigenous Africans. First, that woman is not Khoisan. That's demeaning language used by European supremacists who don't regard African names as meaningful. They insulted the Khwe Xam woman by naming her Saartjie Baartman, removing from history her real name of Sehura..."

"Oh, Odessa. What must I do now? My collection is being printed."

"If you respect African culture, then you'll remove that poem from your collection and refer to her correctly. She is Sehura."

Georgi falls silent as she considers Odessa's harsh, critical words about her writing. Finally, she says, "It never occurred to me that you cared that much about my writings."

"I care more than you do about my job."

"Acting victim again, are we?"

"Anyway, let me update you on my resignation. Should I go on?"

"Reeva must have been thrilled. How did she take your desertion?"

"I feel like a turncoat. Reeva's not too impressed; she likened me to her onetime lesbian friend who moved in with an older man, a wealthy company director, a day after promising her paradise on Earth.

"Ouch! So, is this Dozey thing just a charade? Perhaps it's time. Let's go home."

"I don't think it will serve any purpose, swapping horses while crossing the ford. Oh, Georgi! What am I doing, pregnant and half a world away from home?"

It's early evening in Constantia, a few weeks into the New Year. The scent of late-blooming roses blends with the aroma of parsley, basil, lavender, and thyme as the irrigation system helps the herbs and flowers quench their thirst in the lingering heat. The Taung children are sound asleep after all the fun.

"By the way, Marcia, who was that older man with the grayish beard and thick glasses? I've never seen him here before. He came and said 'hello' to me," Georgi says.

"As if there weren't at least twelve fitting that description," Marcia replies. "But wait a moment while I talk to Moroka. You mentioned something intriguing. You said your traveling days are over. What does that imply?"

Moroka takes a thoughtful sip from his wine glass and says, "I thought we could discuss this some other time, Marcia. Can you please pass me more mince pies?"

Georgi starts to rise from her chair. "Shall I...?"

"No, no, stay," says Marcia. "Come now, Moroka, you've opened a can of worms, and we might as well digest them!"

"It's not straightforward, Marcia, but I want to discuss my request to transfer back to South Africa if there's a position available. I'm willing to take on the role of a simple clerk, just an ordinary Mister Wagner, if it means being with my family."

Without warning, Marcia throws her glass into the hydrangeas and shouts, "I hate it when you sell yourself short like that, Moroka. There's nothing Mister Wagner about you!"

Marcia discreetly hides her pleasure after achieving her goal regarding Moroka's posting. She turns to Georgi and changes the subject in her unique way: "That man you asked about, Georgi," she says, "The less you know, the better for your health."

"I'll drink to that," echoes Moroka. He pauses, then adds reflectively, "If my wife lets me stay home as a house-husband, that's the story I'd like to brag about."

Georgi clears her throat as if about to say something profound. Their eyes stay fixed on Georgi as they wait. Georgi says, "Moroka and Marcia, do you mind if I ask you something private and personal?"

"Shoot," says Marcia.

"I want to talk about Ryan."

The universe goes dead silent. Moroka says, "Where did you meet Ryan?"

Marcia slowly clears her throat and says, "He was here the night of the party..."

"And what was he doing here?"

"He came to the party, I guess," responds Marcia with a tinge of sarcasm.

"And you didn't even tell me Ryan is here."

"What were you going to do, serve him champagne or smash his forehead?"

The patio space is as silent as the Tsitsikama woods. Marcia says, "Carry on, Georgi; tell us about Ryan."

"Well, I was wondering if we could all visit his father, considering his poor health. Ryan told me he's in a clinic in Lenasia."

"Georgi, do you know how far Lenasia is from here?" Shouts Moroka.

Marcia storms up in a huff. She grabs the nearly full bottle of wine and angrily hurls it at the stone wall. The glass shatters into pieces, and wine sprays everywhere on the veranda, leaving no one dry.

She shouts, "Moroka, you haven't spoken to your brother for twenty years, and all you complain about is the distance to his house. If we don't go to Lenasia in the next twenty-four hours – I mean all of us – you'll see my true colors."

Georgi wonders what other true colors Marcia might still be hiding in her palette.

Kora has informed Ellen about Odessa's pregnancy. When she can't reach her daughters on their cell phones, she tries calling Marcia. Moroka becomes the first victim of her 'rich peace of mind.' The ringing phone sounds—shrill and persistent—interrupting the quiet of the night. Moroka walks through the French doors to answer it. The rest of the house can hear Moroka on the phone, and all he can say is, "I see. Yes Ma'am. No Ma'am. Of course. Yes, I see…"

"Good Lord," says Marcia. "Who on Earth could that be? Sounds like Moroka is talking to Queen Mother."

Then Moroka returns, gives Georgi a solemn look, and says, "Georgi, it's a call for you. Your mother… Canada."

Ellen proceeds to give Georgi the royal dressing-down she believes the girls deserve. Laying down the law, she tells Georgi they should return to Toronto before the month ends, not a day later. Otherwise, she will fly over to drag them home by the scruff of their worthless necks! This is a mother Georgi has not encountered since she set foot on Earth. Like Moroka, she is choking and stammering.

"That was Mother," Georgi needs to fill in Marcia. "She is a bit upset about Odessa's condition, and it's all rubbing off on poor me."

"Damn, Odessa," Marcia says, feeling the telephone ring again. "I'd better answer it," says Georgi. "It's probably my father this time!"

It's Barend. He asks Georgi if she can join him at the farm for the weekend. He wants to pick her up first thing the next morning. He notices the agitation in her voice when she answers. She tells him she will call him back the next day with an answer. Georgi walks to the bathroom to fix the day's wear and tear.

The year moves quickly, and the memory of the Taung party is fading. Georgi is on her way, and the whole Taung family accompanies her to Cape Town Airport to see her off on her internal flight to Johannesburg. From there, she and Odessa will fly overnight on the first part of their return trip to Toronto.

"I can't believe this is happening," Georgi complains quietly to Marcia. "I'm not the one who got pregnant. Why am I being sent home in disgrace?"

"Relax, Georgi," Marcia counsels. You'll be back before Easter. I think it's proper that you support Odessa. Traveling when you're pregnant is no joke, believe me."

Barend meets the group at the airport. The three children swarm him. They tell him they visited an alpaca farm and now want an alpaca as a pet.

"Ha. You'll have to go to Chile for one of those," says Barend.

"No, no, no," Jamaica says, "just to Paarl. The farm is located in Paarl, a bus ride away. They're much better than dogs or penguins. Even Daddy agrees."

"We could get one from Australia," adds Verona. "That's where the ones in Paarl came from."

The farewells dissolve into the usual jumble of airport goodbyes, and before Georgi knows it, she's on a South African Airbus. She feels a little light-headed from Barend's final kiss when he holds her close and whispers, "Please come back. I'll be waiting for you. You should know how I feel about you. Don't make me come over to fetch you!"

Georgi rips open Barend's parting gift as the seatbelt lights turn off. It's a hardcover copy of the South African writer J.M. Coetzee's 'Disgrace.' The inscription reads, 'To the love of my life. I mean it, Georgi. Please come back soon.'

Georgi thinks about the book's title, 'Disgrace.' What a fitting description of her situation as she heads back home! She lets the book rest precariously on her thin lap, leans back, and nods off. When she opens her eyes, her mind drifts everywhere. She tries to make sense of the past year in South Africa, but her feelings about Barend remain unclear, despite her heart sending a different message. Was the looming separation prompting Barend to share his intimate feelings? She wonders about the reality of making her life in South Africa. Her head tilts toward the window, and she sees farms and smallholdings down there, all of which look like tiny spots on the back of her hand. The raging river winding through the valleys of a towering mountain landscape is a small, seemingly meaningless spill. She feels vulnerable flying so high above all living things below. 'Nonetheless,' she thinks, 'one must always take a chance and fly to reach one's dreams; mine are on the Drakensberg and Orange River.' As the flight attendant offers drinks in the cabin and places a tray on her lap, Georgi thinks, 'I am at a crossroads. Which way will I go on this checkerboard of days and nights?'

Then Ryan floods her drained mind like a host of tormenting demons. While doing so, Georgi notices a 'colored' man sitting across the aisle next to her, dressed in a well-cut grey suit and a red shirt. She thinks he is a snappy dresser with a colorful sense of style. He is tall, unkindly lean, and old enough to be her father's younger brother. She had never seen him before; otherwise, she would have remembered the face riddled with unsightly scars, revealing hidden stories of struggles and hardship.

The man suddenly rises from his seat and leans over to her. She feels uneasy.

"My name is April," he whispers. "You did not come to the restaurant. I waited for you. You mistreat me, Georgina. It's not the Boers who killed Luca. People from Khayelitsha killed him. I know them. The newspapers report a lie. He goes to investigate some murders that happened in his family. They shadow him and bump him off in Hillbrow because he is getting too close to the truth about his family."

"You're April?"

"Listen, your life is in danger, my darling. There's revenge against you, people. Go back to Canada. And when you get there, tell your father that three men escaped the Kuito ambush."

"My father? How do you know my father?"

"Tell him April says, 'Uhuru.' Tell him three men escaped Kuito."

The man slips away like an apparition, reclaiming his seat near the cockpit. April's words weigh heavily on Georgi's troubled mind. She closes her eyes and tries to nap. After a minute, she gently turns to sneak a quick look toward the front of the plane. An uneasy feeling of foreboding washes over her when she sees the strange fellow's eyes fixed directly on her face. 'I'm going home to see my mama and papa,' she thinks. Several minutes pass, and she can't get April's face out of her mind. She leaps to her feet and walks toward April. A white man sits next to him. From here, she can see the center console with its trim-tab control.

She whispers, "If I must trust you, give me the contact number of the man in Pretoria, Van der Watt's contact."

At first, April raises his eyebrows in a sneering manner. However, when he notices Georgi's determined stare, he stands and guides her to two empty seats a bit further back.

"What do you want from that man in Pretoria?"

"So, you don't know him then?"

"Oh, ye of little faith. There's nothing I don't know. It's 'Globetrot'. Go back to your seat right now."

"Globetrot? What kind of number is that?"

"If you know there's a man in Pretoria, you can't be asking such a stupid question," April motions back to her seat.

"OK, I'll go, but tell me, what is 'Uhuru'?"

"Your father will tell you, or you can ask your employer when you return," he responds tetchily.

"You know my employer?"

"It's a good job. Make sure you don't disappoint their nephew. I learn he likes you."

"And who's that?"

"Ryan, of course. Pity about his sister."

"Tell me."

"Oh, nobody told you. It seems you know little about nothing. Let's keep it that way. Family secrets are family secrets; nothing to do with me."

Georgi's sixth sense urges her to return to her seat as many curious eyes watch her every move. Sitting back, she observes a heavy cloud enveloping the wing and fuselage, which then flickers and clears, revealing a variety of beautiful landscapes below. The airplane suddenly hits wake turbulence, startling all the passengers. April turns to look at Georgi. Though his smile is more unsettling than the storm, Georgi feels a sense of connection with him, as if he's an angel sent to protect her from the storm within her soul.

After a while, the natural turbulence subsides, and they cruise calmly. Georgi is weighed down by April's cryptic words about Ryan's sister, whom she has never heard of. Additionally, she starts to suspect that April and his faceless associates might be leading her on a wild goose chase. The thought that someone else might have been watching and taking pictures of her while engaging in quick conversations with April worries her.

Odessa waits at OR Tambo. She notices Georgi has only a small piece of hand luggage and one checked bag. "You're traveling light," she says.

Puri and Nathaniel find them in the lineup to book a flight to Toronto. They settle into a busy Airport Café booth, and Nathaniel takes their order. Before he finishes, Sabelo and Notemba arrive. Notemba is beaming as always and hugs everyone, showing off her plane ticket.

Puri takes Georgi's hand. "You're coming back, I hope," she begs. Georgi smiles and nods.

"When you come back, will you take that test?"

Odessa gives the pair a tense, suspicious look. Georgi shrugs.

"We can talk about it here," Puri says uncomfortably. Changing the subject, Puri tells Odessa and Georgi, "I've brought you a present you will love. With this card, you can access the Business Class Lounge at Heathrow. You can shower there, relax in comfort, read... and Odessa, you can even put your feet up. Enjoy it, my dear girls. Nathaniel and I must leave now. I look forward to seeing you when you return."

A little later, Odessa confronts Georgi and asks, "Test? What was that about, Georgi?"

Georgi gives a slight shake of her head, trying to hide her discomfort.

"All so soggy, this Puri lady is," remarks Odessa. "I thought you said she didn't like you? She was positively doting over you. Now it's blood tests?"

"Don't act the fool, Odessa."

"Who's acting here? I hate this charade. Remember when I talked to you about Lunga, the show you put on, pretending you knew nothing? The way you treat me like a child... It's sickening sometimes."

"I missed you, too, Odessa," Georgi says with a wry smile, and they embrace.

The awkward moment passes, and when Georgi opens her eyes, there he is—Ryan, watching the sisters hug. He's wearing cotton Bermuda shorts and a yellow baseball cap as part of his casual golfer's outfit. Georgi's heart starts pounding hard, and her knees threaten to give way.

"Oh, Odessa, this is Ryan, Mr Moroka's nephew. Ryan, this is my sister, Odessa."

Odessa smiles wickedly.

"I had to come all the way to see you off," says Ryan, "to thank you for what you did."

"What did I do?"

"My father. Lenasia?"

"Oh, your father, in Lenasia!"

Ryan's smile is gradually tearing Georgi apart. Odessa senses a familiarity that goes well beyond casual affection. She walks away, whispering to herself, 'This girl! Not a bloody word about this black hunk...!'

"I'm sorry I couldn't join Moroka and Marcia. How is your father?"

"Cancer is cancer. He's wasting away and waiting for the inevitable. But thanks to you, my uncle visited Father, and they shook hands afterward, a spectacle to behold."

"I'm glad it's been resolved."

"Yes. Georgi, there's something we need to resolve between us."

"Yes? And what is that?"

"You've been on my mind since I first spoke to you that night. Please promise... when you get back, we'll zoom together to Kruger, where we can watch birds in the morning, drive slowly during the day, and compare notes on the nature around."

Georgi is trembling. She says vaguely, "Oh, I don't know, Ryan..."

"Please stop hedging around and think about it, then."

"Right, I'll think about it."

Ryan thanks Georgi and walks away. Georgi thinks to herself, 'Think about it. Please, God, make me a strong woman. I must stop reciting such stupid lines.' She runs after Ryan, catches him at the revolving sliding-door exit, and says, "Ryan, I am sorry. Going with you to the Kruger won't be possible because I'm seeing someone else right now."

"Thanks for opening up. That shows you're a woman of integrity. So it's a date then... when you return from Canada?"

"OK, it's a date."

Georgi heaves heavily as she enters the WC. She looks at herself in the mirror and cries. Odessa stands outside the partition and shouts for Georgi to come out. When she finally opens the door, Odessa says, "And then? What's with the red eyes?"

"Oh, Odessa, what have I done?"

Only in the morning do the sisters use Puri's gift voucher. Odessa reveals for the first time that she didn't apply for maternity leave; instead, she resigned from her job. She realized that raising a kid in South Africa without any support would be too difficult. In Canada, she will receive the 'Single-Mom' benefits.

"Well, I can see that," agrees Georgi. However, it sounds like you aren't planning to return to Africa. What about Dozey Crafts?"

"I haven't cut my links with them."

"But you have cut them with Lunga!"

"Dad would never have accepted him in the first place."

"Wanna bet? Lunga has an education, holds a cushy job, and puts his sleek tongue to effective use, let alone his four-by-four... perfect credentials in the eyes of our bank official father."

"Tell me about Ryan, your new knight in shining armor who makes you cry your eyes out inside the airport's W.C. Tell me about Ryan, Mrs Taung. My sweet champagne is ready for the day you dump your white man, who most definitely has a white concubine in Namibia, for the perfect black man who paints your eyes crimson."

"Oh! Odessa."

CHAPTER 16

Homeward Bound

Back in Toronto, the spotlight follows Odessa and her bundle. Ellen is thrilled that her daughters are back home. Humming softly from morning to night, she eagerly looks forward to cuddling her first grandchild.

Teddy spends quality time with Notemba, taking her to interesting places around Toronto. Georgi and Odessa relax in the lounge, enjoying a friendly chat.

"Tell me. Now that we are not returning, don't you think you will let Marcia down?"

"Odessa, I don't want us to be at cross purposes here. I'm not finished with South Africa and don't plan to stay home for long. Of course, I'm going back. South Africa is our country, after all."

"I see you're charmed with Ryan. Or is it the Boer guy you're infatuated with?"

"Do you mean Barend? Smitten is more like it. And please stop referring to him as the Boer guy. Yes, I like him a lot."

"Sounds serious! This man? I don't trust him, Georgi," growles Odessa. "First, he treats me like a doormat. Next time, I'm Princess Grace of Monaco—his eyes... like a white mamba. I could see how he was seducing me with his smooth tongue and piercing blue eyes, as if biding his time to strike. I know he wants you to unlock your thighs for him so he can find out secrets about our family. Therefore, he invited me to that hotel before you took my place. The Secret Service is crafty."

Georgi is disturbed. She recalls Barend's words, 'A bull in a slaughterhouse is always paranoid.'

Odessa continues, "I fear he might strike with deadly precision, and I don't want to be there when that happens. Remember, there are white groups in South Africa who feel emasculated by the new order. Surely, you can't take him seriously after Lieber's gas accident. Don't you think he was responsible? Just a few hours before the explosion that nearly killed the elderly couple, Silvia, with two 'i's, called me from her home to warn me against your white boyfriend. With a sweet voice, this girl told me there was a meeting at the National Intelligence Headquarters between Barend and a dozen white men she had not seen before. When she offered them drinks, Barend ordered her to go home. Barely twelve hours later, the Liebers were in the hospital. How do you feel about him?"

"Like James Brown, I feel good. And I'm going back, come hell or high water."

"Marcia calls me. She expresses her concern that the man invites you to his farm, and when you get there with her children and the Liebers, you discover he has gone to Namibia. Something is going on with your white man. Wake up, Georgi."

"He explained."

Georgi is seriously unsure where the lilies will lead her, although she has been pretending otherwise in front of her sister.

"Can I say something, Odessa? I wonder where this will lead. Miriam Makeba must have felt the way I do right now. What do you think?"

Odessa begins to chant Miriam Makeba's 'Where Does It Lead?'

> *Where does it lead?*
> *This strange young love of mine;*
> *Only heaven and the lilies know;*

"Where does it lead? "I'm hurting, Odessa."

Odessa is equally distressed. She moans, "I feel sorry for you, Georgi. The two men splitting your heart are each from completely different backgrounds. Your white man is from a troubled Edomite bloodline, marked by wars and conquests. Your other man, who painted your sclera, blood red in the airport bathroom, can trace his heritage to the Jacob family. As a black woman, I wish all black women could lean toward the side of the Jacob lineage..."

"Where do you get all that from, Odessa?

"You know I studied black culture. But seriously, I wish I'd never come up with this silly idea of going to South Africa, chasing after spooks like Bekker Mofokeng. Blame it on me, Georgi, my sister. I realized the seriousness of this whole thing when you cried more tears than I'd ever seen you shed before. All because of Ryan? Now, it is making you even crazier and tearing our family apart. Next thing, Teddy will also want to go South looking for his roots."

Silently, Georgi agrees with Odessa because she cannot erase her sister's strange images of Barend from her mind or wish away her intense feelings of love for Ryan.

Ellen picks up Miriam's tune, humming quietly from another room into the lounge where Georgi and Notemba are sitting. Georgi can see that the topic of the baby will never bore either the mother or the grandmother-to-be. Ellen proudly tells the girls about their father's promotion to the Economic division of the Canadian bank's head office, "At last, he can use his brain to its full capacity. He says banking at the branch level is just glorified clerking," she smiles.

When Kian comes back, a small celebration takes place. Notemba treats them to braai pap and boerewors. She tells them, "Back home, everyone is a Boer. We all do Braai."

Later, Georgi has a quiet conversation with Kian. "When we left for Africa," she says, "I believed we would come back home clothed in glory. I was even dreaming of the day we placed a Red Bull onto the podium," she titters, "great reception and all the cheering in Rosedale. Perhaps there's a silver lining; I never expected you and Mom to welcome an illegitimate baby into this house."

"Shhhh," says Kian. "The only thing illegitimate is what Odessa and that Lunga boy did, not the child. What has happened has happened."

"Too true."

The patriarch changes the subject, "The man called Van der Watt. What does he mean to you?"

"Barend? I like him very much, Papa. I don't know him well. There's no commitment you need to get excited about here; you needn't worry."

"I'm glad to hear that. Here's good advice from your loving father: stay away from anyone with the name 'Van der Watt' or any man who benefited from apartheid."

Georgi is stunned. She is silent for a while and then says, "What? Papa, why?"

"I know these people. They are full of bitterness and rancor."

"What do you mean by 'these people' exactly? Do you know anything about him and his family?"

"Let me be open to you; I don't want to see you hurt. You are young and very naive about white people in South Africa. It will be many generations before they change, if at all. I don't like the Boers."

Georgi looks at her father with astonishment. She says, "I've never heard you generalize like that about people. Don't you remember what you told Luca before he left, that he learned to respect people as individuals?"

"Remember what I've just said; never mind what I told Luca. Luca is not my daughter," Kian says with deadly finality.

Georgi is alone, contemplating her father's strange advice that she should avoid anyone named 'Van der Watt.' After many days of worry, she decides to go back and talk to him.

"I see you've not given up," Kian says.

"I want to get to the bottom of this, Daddy. Have you ever heard of a man called Ganon April?"

"Funny name. No, why?"

"Not just April, but also people in high places. They all want to keep Bekker's identity and his involvement hidden. Luca probably upset some people when he went to South Africa."

"How does April come into it?"

"Ubiquitous, Mr April," shouts Odessa as she walks in. "And what are you two talking about, Dad? April...?"

"Van der Watt," interjects Kian. "I am telling Georgi here to be careful because men only want one thing from women."

"And what would that one thing be, Daddy? asks Odessa."

"I'm being serious..."

"Before we discuss what men want from women, Odessa, who the hell nominated you to tell Papa and to fly your kite at my expense?"

"Georgi!" shouts Kian.

"I tell you something in confidence, and you take that as a license to become my Facebook and Twitter ghostwriter."

Odessa stays quiet as Georgi continues, "Dad, I asked April to give me a contact number for his secret service guy in Pretoria... the one who seems to know a lot about

Bekker. He brushes me off and says, 'Globetrot.' I've been thinking about 'Globetrot.' Isn't it some code?"

Odessa scoffs and says, "And you weren't planning to tell me about 'Globetrot,' were you, Georgi? Instead, you bombard me with your boyfriend's nonsense. And when did April tell you the code?"

"On the plane. On our way from Cape Town."

You know, Dad, Georgi's attitude is crazy; there's no difference between her and that self-centered Nathaniel from Germany. She knows we've been working together to crack the Bekker riddle, but she plays her cards so close to her chest that even she can't read them.

"Odessa," says Kian, "I know it's a difficult time for you and Lunga..."

"And did you tell your parents about your new black boyfriend who looks like me?" Odessa continues. "Just so you know, Daddy, his name is Ryan, and his father and Moroka Taung are blood brothers..."

Georgi counters, "What affair? Dad, take no notice of Odessa's irritating whoppers."

"She is in love with the black boy, Papa. She even locked herself in the toilet when the guy left the airport, and she later cried on my shoulder."

"Aunt Kora thinks Georgi has become a new member of the elite family for whom she nannies. And she is right. We know our princess; she's a favorite in this house and wherever she goes. Don't we know?"

"That's rather callous, Odessa," says Kian.

"Well!" snaps Odessa.

Puri calls, and Kian answers. They all hear his terse responses before he snaps into the phone, "I'm sorry, you're way out of line here."

Sporting a troubled frown, Kian shrugs, slips into his Siberia jacket, and marches out without another word. Through the window, Georgi can see him shoveling the thinning snow on the sidewalk, his grim facial expression unchanged.

Under different circumstances, she would be teasing her father and shouting, 'Katorga.' She wonders if Puri mentioned anything to her father about the DNA test she wants her to take.

Georgi turns to Odessa and asks, "Did you have to be so spiteful to Dad? What did you mean by 'we know who the favorite princess is'? That's harsh talk to your father."

"He must start acting like my father instead of sugar-coating everything." She lumbers to her feet and leaves the room.

Georgi follows her out and says, "And that thing about Pedro? Perish the thought. Go back and tell the authorities you are withdrawing the stupid statements you made."

"Try stopping me. I'll do what I have to do because Pedro raped my sister. And when a person rapes my loved one, I take it personally..."

Georgi is silent for a second, then she says, "Your loved one? I've never heard you refer to me as your loved one. Do you mean it?"

"Don't push it."

Odessa has spent most of the day in bed. She believes she has to ignore her nausea to deal with it. Georgi sits on Odessa's bed, and the siblings have little to say to each other. However, they both avoid the Pedro issue.

"Odessa," Georgi says, "I didn't mention 'Globetrot' to you because I know you have too much acid in your bowl. April mentioned Luca, saying that he knows something about the killers. Have you heard anything?"

"I'm hearing stories, Georgi. Please leave me alone to think. I don't need you here right now…"

What a Circus

Everyone has gone out, except the parents, who spend most of their time behind closed doors in the main bedroom. Odessa sneaks into the lounge, looking for Georgi to apologize for her earlier nasty comments. She wants to explain that her pregnancy has brought a whole seesaw of emotions and that she is not always rational. She wants to say she loves her sister and will make it up to her once the baby arrives.

'This endless waiting is driving me crazy,' she says, 'and surely they can empathize.' Then she hears muffled voices coming from the main bedroom. She moves toward the door to eavesdrop and stops short as she overhears Ellen's anguished pitch.

"We can't keep lying to Puri," Ellen whispers loudly. It's been over twenty years, and she still can't let it go. We have no right to hide these secrets from her, from both of them. It's immoral; that's what it is. She did no wrong; she only tried to save her child. God will have his revenge.",

Odessa hears her father say gruffly, "That's all we did, too; try to save her child and mine, don't forget that."

Odessa pushes the door open abruptly and stops in the middle of her parents' bedroom. They look exhausted, and Odessa can tell they haven't slept for many hours. Her heart pounds, but the nausea has faded. They look back at her silently.

"I knew all along there was something wrong with this family," she says slowly. Ellen looks wrecked, but Odessa keeps going, "What is it? What have you been hiding from Puri for two decades, Mom, Dad?"

Ellen slowly rises and prays, "Out of the depths have I cried unto thee, O Lord; hear my voice. Let thine ears be attentive to the voice of my supplications."

"What's happening here, Daddy?"

"Let's go get some tea. I can't handle this migraine," Ellen sighs.

Ellen's face shows lines that Odessa has never observed before. Her mother seems to have become a great-grandmother ahead of her time, she thought. Kian looks hard at Odessa, but her dismissive gaze stays fixed on her mother's face. They slowly move to the kitchen, where Odessa prepares coffee. Ellen sinks heavily onto the kitchen chair. Kian places a hand on Ellen's trembling forearm, but she pulls away from his touch.

"No," Ellen says, "it is time."

Ellen can barely control her shivers. Her voice cracks as she begins to explain to Odessa what happened that night, over twenty years ago: She leaves her biological toddler, Odessa, at her mother's house because she fears what might happen if the police come back. Daniel, Odessa's biological father and Kian's brother, has been in detention for a week while she stays inside, too scared to go out. Daniel's employers have attempted to obtain information from the police regarding his whereabouts, but without success. They only learn that the police want Daniel to tell them where to find his brother, Bekker. Daniel doesn't know, and he can't tell them. No one knows.

"I believed it was only a matter of time before they came to force Daniel to tell them what he knew. We had not seen Bekker since his release from Robben Island. In the neighborhood, nobody talked about him. It was as if even the children were warned by their parents that the sky would fall on their heads if they so much as mentioned his name," says Ellen.

She gazes inward with unseeing eyes, reliving a past that never stops haunting her dreams. No one interrupts. On the sixth day, she thinks she heard Daniel's voice outside her window at midnight. It sounds like the wind rattling the glass. She carefully opens the door, and Daniel falls into her arms like a heavy bag. He looks as awkward as a hog, his clothes torn and his face bruised and bloody. Her medical training takes over, and she tends to him as best she can. Ellen knows he will die if she doesn't take him to the hospital. However, that option is full of uncertainties.

Then, like an answer to her prayer, Ellen hears a soft tap at the door, and a stranger stands there. It is Bekker, the feared Bekker himself. His voice is jerky and gruff. He clutches a bundle to his chest—it's a baby. He tries to hand the baby to Ellen, but she ignores it, whispering for Bekker's help to save his brother's life. He silently enters the house, and they both stand on either side of Daniel's seemingly lifeless body. Ellen and Bekker watch as Daniel opens his eyes. He gasps and tries to speak, but he cannot. Ellen checks his pulse and signals death to Bekker.

Then, into the silence, the 'bundle' in Bekker's arms draws breath and gives a thin cry of fright and hunger.

"Without a word, I sit on the floor beside my dead husband, holding the unknown baby just dumped in my arms by my husband's brother. When I ask him about the baby, he tells me she is Georgi, and she is ten days old."

"Georgi?" the incredulous Odessa yells as she drops the teapot. "Did you say, 'Georgi'? Where did she come from? Whose child was she?"

"She was mine; she is mine," answers Kian, the man Odessa has always believed to be her father. "I am Bekker. I am Lenin. I took your father's place; the only way I could to protect you." His shoulders slump, his pulse beating visibly at his temple. He continues, "With all your mindless digging up inside South Africa's mines of secrets, things have swelled up..."

"Mindless digging?" Odessa stutters angrily.

He drops his head wearily into his arms. "I am not your father, even though you are a firstborn child to me. You are my brother's child, and therefore, you are my child as well. But I could not be Bekker Thlokomela Mofokeng. I fled that life and became Kian Moffet-King. I took it as a supernatural gift from my ancestors," he says, as his mouth draws down in bitter reflection, "What a circle."

"'What a circus' is more like it," cries Odessa.

"You have found Bekker Lenin and lost your father. Thanks to your African expedition."

"The ways of the Lord are strange and beyond our understanding," hums Ellen.

The sun is setting, but nobody has bothered to prepare dinner. When Odessa opens her eyes, Ellen has barely moved. Odessa says, "My heart is full of pain, Mama."

Kian invites everyone to the living room, including Notemba and Teddy. They sit quietly, like a typical township community during a wake. Ellen is sobbing softly, her palms muffling the desperate sounds. Odessa sits motionless, watching Kian justify his tall tale. Her head spins with the enormity of what this devil incarnate reveals about his past. Something deep inside her had instinctively sensed deception ever since Barend Van der Watt told her that Bekker likely fled to Canada in the 1980s. Even in her school days, she could feel that her mother and father were hiding behind a large mask of civility. She wonders how much is still hidden beneath the surface. Odessa remembers one of the poems Georgi wrote, which she liked and secretly memorized.

> When the subconscious deep space
> Tries to store matters toxic to the heart,
> The inner spirit instinctively wipes them out,
> For without the inner spirit's intervention,
> Humankind would perish.

Odessa finds the poem very moving.

When Kian opens his mouth, his dry, large black lips trembling, he says, "Georgi will join us soon, I hope. We are family," he continues softly, as if a chief settling cattle disputes. "Now that the truth is out, you must understand something as family. We buried Daniel on a hillside facing the morning sun, on the contested terrain not far from the valley where they buried our mother's umbilical cord. Before we left, we marked it with a small wooden cross with the inscription, 'Bekker Mofokeng, Rest in Peace.' Some relatives buried my brother there, but I was not around to witness the sad occasion. Having my name engraved on a grave that did not belong to me caused me endless nightmares and humiliating mental blocks. The grave of an African flowering shrub bears my name, yet I am living it up, searching for peace under the Canadian snow.

"Yes, the truth shall set us free," says Ellen. "Each year on the anniversary of his death, your father and I place a wreath at our church here in his memory. We never forget..." She pauses vacantly.

Odessa rises and cries, "Flowers? How generous! How Christian, bloody, charitable of you. My father is dead and buried under some so-called contested field, and all you can tell me is your donation of carnations in his memory!"

Odessa kneels on the floor to mourn the loss of her biological father.

Kian's shoulders slump even more, and he exhales as if he's out of breath. The memory of dark episodes from his past pierces his soul like thorns. While confessing has brought relief, it has also caused discord and uncertainty in the family. Now that it's out, Kian barely notices that he keeps repeating himself and overdoing his act of remorse.

Despite worrying lines of distress deeply etched on Ellen's face, Odessa feels anything but sympathy for her.

Oblivious to the heavy, dark cloud that has formed inside her household, Georgi quietly enters through the kitchen door and overhears Odessa's cries of distress, "How could you keep such secrets from us, Mama...?"

Odessa straightens and clears her throat as she meets Georgi's disbelieving gaze. A flush of panic crosses her face. The more Odessa observes the chaos in her home, the more she descends into open loathing for the strangers around her.

"What's happening in here? Mama, is something wrong?"

No one answers. Georgi turns to Odessa, "What's got into you, Sister?"

"One look in the mirror should tell you we're not sisters," Odessa growls, "and, by the way, she's not your mama, either."

Ellen remonstrates with her daughter, "Don't you take out your fury on Georgi. She's the most innocent and most injured in all of this."

"Oh, yes! Princess Georgi. When Barend Van der Watt told us what a rotten egg Lenin Bekker was, all that Georgi wanted to do was pretend Lenin didn't even exist."

Georgi is mystified. She tries to draw someone in, but Kian quickly says, "Odessa wouldn't rest until she opened this Pandora's Box, and now it's only fair you learn the real family history too, Georgi."

Odessa tastes the bitterness in Kian's voice and accepts that she has no father and can neither forgive nor trust him again.

"What about you, Georgi?" Odessa mocks. "Tell us about your skeletons rattling in your little cupboard. Everyone seems to have suddenly developed a twinge of conscience. Anything to declare?"

"Mom, forgive her. It's the pregnancy. She's been like this ever since we arrived in South Africa. I told her, Papa. It's the demons in that African country. They're everywhere. People are constantly angry; road rage, murders, even rapes! Did you tell Odessa? Tell them. They rape babies. Men say it cures HIV..."

"What's that got to do with your real mother? She wouldn't be that Caucasian lady who insisted you take an HIV test, would she, Georgi?" Odessa sneers.

"Mom, what's going on? Has everybody gone stark raving mad?"

Ellen says, "O God, who can ever heal the brokenness in this house?"

Odessa stalks petulantly out of the room. Georgi sits down as Kian and Ellen try to relate their bizarre story to her. While Ellen gently helps Georgi digest what she's hearing, Kian is less tactful: "I am your true biological father, but your mother here is not your biological mother."

Ellen quietly slides in and explains in detail how the situation happened, hoping Georgi might be less judgmental than Odessa.

"Let me get this straight, Dad and Mom," Georgi says. You, Papa, are my real father, but Mom isn't my real mother, and you, Mama, are Odessa's biological mother, but Papa here isn't her biological father."

"Yes, Georgi, my child," Ellen puts it sluggishly.

Georgi walks out and stands on the veranda. Her head spins. She rushes to the garden, picks up half a brick, and breaks the windshield of her father's car. She throws herself onto the lawn and lies spread-eagled. When all the pieces of the puzzle have settled on the canvas, she asks, 'Puri, is my mother? And Nathaniel, that pompous idiot, my twin brother?' She rushes to the bathroom to be sick. Ellen comes to her aid. After she cleans up, she searches for some reassurance.

"Is this for real, Mama?"

Ellen says, "Please, Georgi, forgive us."

"Forgive...?"

Georgi is back out on the porch again. Kian and Ellen stay numb as snails. When she walks back, Georgi heaves and says, "What the hell happened to the car's windshield? Did you see that, Papa?"

Ellen cries louder than before, piercing their curious neighbors' picket fences. She prays, "O God, you have taken account of our wanderings; put our tears in your bottle..."

Georgi leans on Ellen's elbows and notices Odessa coming in. Odessa suddenly convulses, amniotic fluid pooling on the floor between her legs, her body bent forward as she cradles her large belly with her palms.

"It's started!" she gasps, "The baby's coming!"

Odessa refuses Kian's offer to take her to the hospital. Everything has fallen apart; Georgi reflects on the classic example of a dysfunctional family. She gives herself a mental shake; Odessa, who is no longer her sister but her cousin, needs attention now. Eight hours have passed, with Georgi passing the time flipping through piles of old magazines in the hospital waiting room. She feels sluggish, as if her mind has been in a tumble dryer. Occasionally, she dozes off, and when she opens her eyes, she staggers to the vending machine for more coffee, which she thinks tastes like plastic. She processes the events of the past few hours in waves that fade as her thoughts drift back to the activity in the labor ward.

Back home, Notemba is helping prepare soup. She takes pride in her cooking skills and promises to bake scones for the family when Odessa returns with the baby. Teddy tries to impress everyone with his ability to slice bread rolls.

Kian is happy to see Georgi. The kitchen table is set for five, but Georgi says, "Mom will ring when news arrives about the baby. I'd also like to rest, but next time Puri calls, I'll have to disclose what I now know."

"I have already done so," says Kian.

"Oh! How did she take it?"

"She's wound up. I am everyone's dog right now."

"I am troubled, Papa, but I don't feel hate. The past years must have been a living hell for you and Mother. There's a feeling of betrayal and emptiness in me, not hatred. It's like someone has died. I think all of us need time to deal with the bereavement."

"Yes, quite!"

The Bekker saga is one of the best-kept secrets of the resistance era. Judging from Georgi's experiences, powerful forces want to keep it that way. She is now aware of how influential her father appears to be in the South African scene. When she returns to the kitchen, Notemba leans her tall, lean body close and says, "Don't worry; you're still my cousin, Georgi. We now even have an aunt who is white," she chuckles. The reason for the shattered windshield remains a mystery to everyone in the household, except Emily.

A Swallow, trying to make a Summer.

The ringing phone awakens Georgi from a deep sleep. It continues to blare. Georgi covers her head with a pillow. The ringing persists, and she realizes it might be the hospital. She drags herself back to the phone and says, "Yes?"

Puri feels affronted, but Georgi apologizes and explains that they have had a rough night waiting for news from the hospital.

"Yes, your father told me. Shall I call back later?"

"Yes, that might be a good idea," says Georgi uneasily.

"No, Esther. That's not such a good idea. We need to talk right now..."

"Puri, Mrs Lieber, can we get something straight between us? This is Georgi. That's my name. I'm not Esther..."

"No, you can't be Georgi. You are Esther because you save lives, and you are my myrtle flower."

"And what is that?"

"Please read the book of Esther in your bible. You are Hadassah. People can call you Esther."

"I don't have a bible."

"Okay, after Haman, the Agagites— that evil man... after he plotted to exterminate us, Esther saved us. That's all you need to know about who you are. Georgi is a name with no meaning to us... to you..."

"How can you bloody say that? That's my name!"

"I can't explain what it means to me to have found you. We need to make up for lost time together. I am not willing to lose any part of your life again. Please arrange a trip back to South Africa as soon as possible. Caleb and I will be there briefly. This year, I want you and Nathaniel to celebrate your birthdays together. He was born on March 21, 1980, and you arrived just after midnight on March 22. I know Bekker and Ellen changed your birth date to April 25, but I assure you it was in March."

"Mrs Lieber, please call me later… in three months or next year."

"How can you say that? Unless… it seems, I would have to accuse Lenin and Ellen of kidnapping."

"Why would you even think of such a thing?"

"No, I shouldn't do that, but I haven't stopped hoping since that day at Cape Point, Esther. I can't wait any longer. Please hurry back. I am going to be your full-time mother from now on."

Serious charges of infanticide.

Odessa was supposed to have twins. But it wasn't until after the first one was born that they realized there was still another. The smaller one was already turning blue at birth. If they had known, it could have had a chance.

Ellen says, lifting her tear-streaked face, "That's why they came early. I don't know how that could have happened, but it wasn't until after the first one was born that they discovered there was still another. The smaller one was already turning blue at birth. If they had known, it would have had a chance."

"How is this possible in a first-world country?" A disappointed Georgi puts it.

"When I tried to commiserate with Odessa, your father kept harping on your new name… and he says he's proud of you. What is this about?"

"There won't be a new name."

"Why? Aren't you creating problems with Puri?"

"No, Mama. Do you know what Puri says? She names me 'Esther' because that's the name of a woman who always saves the Jews from genocide."

"Yes, that's Esther, a Jewish queen of Persia."

"That's not me. I'm Georgi. I don't care how they cooked up the name."

"How does she feel?"

"Agitated, I guess. She wants me to go back to South Africa so we can talk about the issue; it makes everything sound like it's on the UN Security Council agenda.

"It is an important issue for a mother."

"Well, for me it isn't. But I have to fly back to Cape Town for other reasons."

"Please stay for a while. You and Odessa must make peace."

"She won't have anything to do with me."

"She seems to think your mission in life has always centered on intercepting anything her radar detects…"

"Oh, please, Mom! Like what? She's wrong."

"You came between her and Barend van der something or other? She says there was something between you and Luca, too. She had promised to take Barend to a jazz festival in Quebec before you materialized and ruined everything."

"That's ridiculous, Mom, and she knows it."

"Try to patch things up with her? She needs your support, you know. She's vulnerable. You are different. Always headstrong."

Odessa has been caring for the baby at home for three days, during which the household has waited for her to reveal his name. Kian stays silent, pretending not to care.

"Please, Odessa, the suspense is killing us. You said after an hour. It's two hours now. Please?" Teddy pleads.

Odessa laughs. "Alright, ready everyone? As you know, a name is a meaningful blessing a parent gives a baby. That name is a spiritual gift linking the baby with the Almighty. Without any further ado, the name is Daniel Junior King – Dan for short."

They all stand up to enthusiastically applaud.

"I named him after his grandfather, Daniel," she smiles at Kian, who naturally feels uncomfortable.

"That's cool," says Teddy, "We can call him Dan King."

"Maybe, but Daniel is a highly regarded name from the bible. Thoughts, Mama?"

Ellen chokes up with tears. Odessa shifts her focus to Teddy.

In the meantime, Georgi has developed a negative opinion of Odessa's religious tone regarding her baby's naming. She whispers disapprovingly, 'Has this girl become the Dalai Lama of Rosedale?'

Georgi walks through the quiet park, trying to consider her options, which seem few. She resolutely vows to improve her skills because she doesn't want to be an au pair forever. Feeling isolated from her family's activities and small talk, she quietly turns away from the doorway and heads to her bedroom. She sits on the bed as Ellen waddles into her dark room.

"I thought I heard you on the stairs, Georgi," she says. "Supper is ready. Will you come down?"

"No, Mom. I'm sure you can go ahead without me. Why should anyone need me?"

"That's not fair, Georgi." Ellen sits on the bed beside her and continues, "I know it's hard for you, but please try to help Odessa deal with all these emotions sweeping through her like wildfire."

"I won't, Mom. I have come to the end of my tether. There is nothing to salvage, and nothing to help resolve this ridiculous situation."

The atmosphere in the house is tense. Georgi finds herself walking on eggshells to avoid upsetting Odessa, who is kind to everyone but her. Then, a lifesaver appears in the form of an unexpected visitor who offers Georgi an escape. Jean McKenzie, the woman whose children Georgi cared for two years earlier, has a week-long conference to attend. When she hears that Georgi might be available, she shows up at the door to ask her to join her and her girls for a conference at Niagara-on-the-Lake. She mentions that the children have fond memories of Georgi and speak highly of her. She urges Georgi to help out since the resident au pair has chicken pox. Georgi quickly agrees. The extra money will also mean she doesn't have to ask her father to pay for her flight back to South Africa.

"Fluff up your tail feathers, and let's fly right now, Hummingbird!" Jean giggles. "I need to be at Niagara first thing in the morning, and that'll save me from having to fetch you. Could we do that?"

"On one condition," Georgi bargains, "I have a cousin from South Africa. Would you mind if she came along?"

"Absolute pleasure," Jean replies gleefully.

As Georgi and Notemba prepare to leave, Ellen says, "Georgi, please promise that when you get back, you'll sit down with Odessa and sort out this thing between you two. It is gnawing at my very soul."

"I can't promise to do that, Mom; I'm sorry."

Jean can't believe her eyes at how much Notemba resembles Odessa. "They could be twins," she says to Georgi.

She promises to take Notemba to the sights of interest before returning to Africa. Niagara is a restorative break, and Notemba has a great time. Georgi has always loved the powerful waterfall and is happy to enjoy the company of the McKenzie children, joining in on various tourist activities. She helps with schoolwork, reads to them, and encourages them to read aloud to her. Jean McKenzie is pleased with the week away and gives Georgi a generous bonus before she heads back home.

As Jean drops them off, Georgi feels a faint sense of apprehension about dealing with Odessa. Everyone is sitting at the dining room table except Odessa. They all admire Georgi's looks and tell her she has gained weight—a rave review to her ears.

Notemba showcases her dress and lifts the pair of shoes that Jean bought for her. Then, they head to the table. No one dares to whisper the name 'Odessa' as lingering hurt feelings weigh heavily on the family.

Odessa appears unexpectedly. She is wearing a broad smile as she rests her arms on her hips. She looks Georgi in the eye and chants, "Hi Negro!"

Amid the thickening atmosphere, Georgi leaps forward like a springbok in the Karoo and races toward Odessa, stretching her slender arms and affectionately embracing her sister. The two remain cuddled as the downpour of tears communicates their feelings.

Ellen and Kian move cautiously to help, followed by Notemba. Only Teddy stays seated, nervously scanning each family member and wondering what all the fuss is about.

"Come with me," Odessa says to Georgi and Notemba. They follow Odessa to the bedroom, where she hands Daniel Junior to Georgi. She says, "The auntie godmother better hold Little Godson. That's what good aunties do."

Georgi proudly rocks Odessa's bundle, showing it off to everyone. Ellen's eyes are wet with relief. For a little while, both sisters keep their inner thoughts to themselves.

A nagging feeling haunts Georgi; peaceful moments are fleeting until the next conflict arises. She senses that Barend will remain a sore spot between her and Odessa. Now that she has confirmed that even her father has negative feelings about the relationship, she needs to keep Ellen in her corner.

Ellen's developed sixth sense prompts her to ask, "Georgi, you have not said much about your friend, Van der Merwe…"

"His name is Barend, Mama; Barend Van der Watt."

Kian clears his throat as if he's about to say something, but then he walks out of the house.

"Tell me, Mama, what do you think of the name 'Van der Watt'?"

"I don't know anyone by that name."

"Mama," responds Georgi, "I feel like a lonesome swallow, trying to make a summer. If I keep going, will that cause the heavens to fall?"

"Tell us about him."

"We haven't had much time to be friends yet, let alone make decisions about the rest of our lives. But if…; no, when I go back to South Africa, I want to get to know him better—his family, shared values, and goals—all of that."

"Wishful thinking, Girl," Odessa counters sarcastically. You'll be coming back home, trust me. As for the Afrikaner fellow? Papa is right to be concerned. My expectations are described in two words: Ryan Taung.

"Georgi snaps, "Stop butterflying…"

Odessa responds by first rescuing her baby from Georgi before she says, "Mama, Georgi knows absolutely nothing about the white man. Blacks and whites still live separate lives in that country. Even political parties are racially divided. They even have a colored party, isn't that so, Georgi? Tell Mama about Kazi and Loli. The common values and goals Georgi is talking about are dreams of a moonstruck, naïve, Rosedale girl."

"Home is where your heart is," says Georgi. "But Mama, I feel Odessa isn't sure what she wants to do with her life. She seems to have let other people determine her battles for her."

"Don't start, now, you stupid girl."

"I will decide my future with or without anyone's blessing… and we shall see which girl is stupid, Georgi or Odessa."

"You know we love you, and you have our blessing…" Ellen pleads.

"Not mine, she doesn't," Odessa retorts. "Not Dad's either. Black blessings aren't that cheap."

"Really? Who needs your blessings anyway? You should be preparing to head back to Africa with baby Daniel…"

Odessa leans in close to Georgi's face and softly but assertively asks, "Which name are you settling for, the white woman's make-believe Esther or Georgi, your other fake name?"

Georgi rushes forward, aggressively threatening to beat up Odessa, shouting, "I'll kill you, Odessa," as Ellen rushes to defend her home from serious charges of infanticide.

CHAPTER 17

The Dutch Reformed Church

Georgi receives a call from Moroka, who briefs her about an attack on one of the Van der Watt properties. After hours of tears and waiting, Georgi learns that the attack took place at a family property occupied by Willem, Barend's younger brother.

Georgi stifles a scream of anguish, and Moroka continues, "They took him to Somerset West, but I'm afraid he died on arrival. I had to inform you as soon as I heard the news."

Georgi struggles to find her voice and gasps her thanks, "I'll be back as soon as I can."

Kian arranges a return flight to Cape Town at daybreak for Georgi and Notemba.

Ellen finally confesses her feelings: "I will miss you, Georgi. I've always been proud to call you 'my daughter' because you are a wonderful person. I am deeply sorry to hear that you are returning to South Africa. I will be praying for you.

I look forward to when you come home for good. I love you very much, Georgi."

Georgi gets up. She walks behind Ellen's chair and hugs her tightly, pressing her damp cheek against hers. "I could never have wished for a better mother, Mom. Did I tell you I couldn't stand her when I first met Puri?"

Ellen's face creases with confusion.

"It's true, Mama," chimes Odessa. "Georgi described Puri to me as a 'miserable, frumpy hausfrau, not a bit like an investigative journalist and professional photographer,' she expected! Didn't you, Georgi?"

Ellen knows that Odessa is whipping up a riptide. So, she says, "It's time. Why don't you sum up your parting shot?"

"Seems like there isn't much we haven't shared for the past two decades," says Odessa, looking Georgi in the eye. "That's all going to change now. I guess that's what growing up is all about. I believe this is the right place for Daniel Junior and me. We are fortunate to have such wonderful parents who are willing to help and offer support. Thanks, Mom and Dad," she raises her glass to Kian and Ellen, who beam their thanks. Then Odessa turns to Georgi, "But this speech is about you. First, I want to thank you for putting up with my tantrums and the good times we had in South Africa. It was an incredible experience. But I'm happy to be home in the real world. I think it's good that you're going back. It's only proper that you return to finish your year with Marcia. It'll give you another year to sort yourself out. When you get there, you'll discover that Barend Van der Watt is not the man for you. Let's face it, you two have nothing in common. And, just as I didn't know Lunga, your situation with the white man is much worse, you'll see. No way are you ready to settle down as a South African housewife, even in such a beautiful place as Robertson. If you finally decide to marry someone, make sure it is the best man, and there is no better man than the one who drove you to lock yourself in the changing room with floods of tears washing down your face." Odessa lifts her glass, "To you, Georgi, my sweet little sister, and your safe return home. We'll be waiting with great expectations."

As Georgi looks around the table, she tries to decipher the faces turned to her. She shrugs and responds, "I will always try to remember my responsibilities to Daniel, my godson, and his grandparents wherever I may be. I've always tried to avoid stumbling along in life. I will continue to struggle, tour the Kruger National Park, or stop by Robertson. But in the end, I shall make choices for which I shall take all the credit and all the blame."

"Nice speech, girl," Odessa says, "but the proof is in the pudding, and what I saw at the airport bathroom tells me the pudding is a tall and dark hunk, more appealing than anything I'd seen before and since..."

Ellen says, "God set my feet like the feet of a deer. He will make you strong, Georgi."

Upon arriving in Cape Town, one of Notemba's relatives whisks her away to her mother's family in the Transkei. Georgi feels sad to part with her loving cousin. However, she is relieved to be in Barend's company. While waiting with him at the barrier, Sofia exudes a sense of despondency and appears uncomfortable. The two women exchange polite greetings, but they stay apart.

Georgi recalls the day of their visit with the Liebers when Sofia kindly lent her a pair of sturdy boots, but the others could hardly look her in the eye. This time, Sofia is stony-faced—ashen with grief over something beyond the current bereavement—and very brisk. Georgi can hardly manage to squeeze in a word of sympathy for the siblings after noticing the aloofness between them. The scene appears puzzling to her.

Georgi has never met Willem, but Barend wants to use the funeral as an opportunity to ensure that Sofia and her family accept her as part of the family. Georgi calls Marcia to tell her she will return within the next few days. While Marcia is unhappy, she does not want to appear as one trying to wreck Georgi's moment of fascination.

The long drive through the mountainous landscape is mostly silent and awkward. Barend occasionally points out a landmark of interest for Georgi's benefit. Then, a muted conversation follows between Barend and Sofia, which Georgi can barely follow. This allows her to admire historic and majestic mountain ranges, as well as vineyards drooping with grapes and wineries—the toast of connoisseurs worldwide.

Just before they enter Robertson, Sofia sits up straight to tidy up her hair and pat fragranced powder onto her face. Then she tries to make small talk: "Barry will have to bring you to see the nature reserve near here. It has the finest collection of cactus plants anywhere in the world. As I am sure you know, they are indigenous to Arizona—your part of the world."

Georgi wryly considers the distance between Arizona and Ontario but decides to let it pass. Sofia is quiet again as they approach the church.

Sofia remarks, "Jan van Riebeeck arrived at the Cape 352 years ago today. For 352 years, he was celebrated as a hero; now, he's viewed as a despised colonial settler. Back then, many decades later, someone would have been penalized immediately for my kid sister's murder. By God!" she exclaims rather loudly.

The glaring omission of her brother in her lamentation over her murdered sister makes Georgi wonder about Barend's family.

Barend says tersely, "That won't bring anyone back, Sofia."

A sea of vehicles surrounds the Robertson Dutch Reformed Church. Mourners slowly enter. Barend directs Georgi to sit between him and Retief, his friend. The service is far more daunting than Georgi could have imagined—endless and conducted in a foreign language. If she is to survive in this crowd, she thinks, she will need to acquire more than just a smattering of Afrikaans and learn the other nuances of body language communicated with intense respect. Amid the pain and sorrow, lingers the unbidden question: Does she want to be an intimate part of the Van der Watts?

There are hardly any tears in the packed church. Men stand with stony faces, filled with grief and anger. Sofia's eyes remain as dry as when she threw her Jan van Riebeeck bomb at Georgi. Only her large, funereal black hat creates a picture of mourning—Barend's frail grandmother clings to Gert, sitting very erect and holding herself in check. The mourners also include family members, young Willem's friends, and former schoolmates. A group from the local farming community sits conspicuously in the back pews. Almost everyone is dressed in black, while some men wear suits that are distinctly rusty with age. Georgi feels uneasy in the casual trouser suit she chose for the journey from Canada, but she reassures herself that the bottle-green jacket is, somehow, of an acceptable shade. 'I might have worn pink,' she thinks! She feels even more uneasy upon realizing that no blacks, not even Dolly, are allowed inside the racist Reformed Church.

Georgi feels relieved when the burial episode ends, but then realizes that the ordeal is not over. The mourning crowds gather around a large, well-built farmhouse surrounded by tall corn stretching out over the plains and slopes as far as the eye can see. In between, there is a well-constructed canal that irrigates the dynasty's acres of land and serves as a key water source for Black workers on the neighboring farms.

On the side are a reservoir and two barns where three colored females and one black man, who were not part of the service, are hard at work.

Georgi is the object of stares and intimidating ogles for the rest of the day. Once they learn that she cannot understand Afrikaans, she notices a heightened interest and curiosity. Someone must have whispered that Georgi is a Canadian. In South Africa, anyone from 'overseas' is treated with courtesy and politeness. The female mourners slow down hesitantly in front of her, smiling delicately as if dissecting her entire being.

Lady Cecilia Trent

A sturdy middle-aged woman beckons Georgi into a quiet corner of the veranda. Georgi doesn't recognize her. The woman's jet-black hair, gracefully fading to gray in spots, is pulled back into a neat bun at her nape. Her sharp features are losing some definition, but she still retains the unmistakable beauty of her youth. She's dressed in a well-fitted dark gray suit with matching pumps, her legs looking good in dark nylon. A black maid named Dolly stands ready to serve them well-chilled wine.

"Robertson's, girl," she responds to Dolly before turning to Georgi. "It's not ours, but a good vintage nonetheless. I'm Cecilia Trent."

Georgi is relieved to have escaped from the crowded living room.

"Have we met?" she asks.

"Aren't you Georgi, au pair to the Taungs?"

Georgi nods mutely.

"I'm Reeva's Mother. I guess you know Finian and Leslie. My husband and I live next door, if you call it that."

The penny drops, "Of course!" says Georgi, "I do know Reeva well, and I've met Fin and his wife, Doreen, but not your other daughter."

"Exactly. I saw the matchmakers and gossipmongers of the district devouring you. And thought I'd better come to your rescue before they brought out the hatchets. I suppose you've committed the unforgivable transgression... getting involved with a man of Barend's ilk, that's what."

Georgi understands that 'ilk' is anything but flattering. She repeats, "Ilk?"

"Sorry, I meant a position in society and this community in particular."

"Position? As in occupation? What does he do? Do you know?"

"Should I take it you've not yet compared notes on your material pursuits?"

"Not quite, but a second opinion does not harm."

"Way to go, girl! You can't be too careful in this patriarchal society. Between you and me, chances are, he's with the NIA," she whispers.

Then Barend's strange words at Café Mozart suddenly hit her: 'Our branch, our area of work, is even more precarious.' She thinks, 'How can it be that the whole world knows Barend is a secret agent when I am without a clue?'

Cecilia continues, "But Barend's idea of bringing you to this funeral is revealing; far from the character I'm used to in this small community."

"You must know him well, then?"

"They are highly regarded here. Barend is an enigma, though, very analytical and aloof. It's part of his training, I guess. His sister is the real strange one..."

"Sofia, you mean?"

"She knows everything in the area because she is everywhere, snooping, listening, and ferreting. One day, she spoke out in the church about the images of a fake white Jesus, whereupon the elders flushed her out. But she later committed a cardinal sin for which excommunication is final..."

"Yes?"

"No, I think I've overstepped the mark. Let's talk about your man. I have never known him to be even remotely interested in any serious relationship. You must mean an awful lot to him..."

"What about casual relationships?"

"Let's not go there, girl."

"You said his bringing me here is revealing. Pray, shed more light..."

"Something is going on here. He planned to make a point to the folk, to blow up a bomb spectacularly and transmit thunderous sounds to reach all corners of Robertson."

"Does it make you uncomfortable... the spectacular bomb?"

"Oh, no, no! We come from a very liberal background; both my husband and I do. That's what we inculcate in our family. Our friends cut across all colors and religions..."

Disrupting her train of thought, Georgi asks, "What about Reeva? Is Reeva your friend?"

Cecilia's smile disappears. She whispers, "Reeva? She's my daughter."

Her under-eye puffiness becomes pronounced, a tell-tale sign of her struggles with her daughter.

"How liberal have you been towards her views and lifestyle?"

"I don't know what you mean. What are you trying to say?"

"I'm sorry, Mrs Trent..."

"Please call me Cecilia," she says, quite unsettled.

"Thanks, Cecilia. I didn't mean to upset you. I'm just curious. Parents must be honest with their children instead of making them believe fairy tales about their identity. You were telling me about Barend...?"

Cecilia is dumbstruck. Georgi does nothing to scoop her out of the awkward pit. Cecilia heaves, trying hard to get a grip somewhere. She finally says, "Yes, I was saying something about him. I think his bringing you here is like announcing your engagement in the Argus Newspaper," she smiles, "and a funeral has a habit of opening up old wounds; its saving grace being, well, at least the family could rally round and protect you from the wolves."

Puzzled, Georgi returns the smile, "I think they've outflanked Barend, and I'm sure the others are too absorbed in their grief to worry about me. The strain on the family at a time like this must be unbearable. My sister lost a newborn recently. It never even drew breath, and we are in shock and numb with grief, still."

Cecilia murmurs, "Odessa lost her baby? I'm sorry. No one told me."

"What a peculiar thing for a first-world hospital to miss a set of twins like that. Anyway, thanks for rescuing me from the maddening crowd and for the drink. I was beginning to feel spaced out with jet lag and lack of sleep from the time we heard about the family attack."

"Well," says Cecilia comfortably, "is there any truth in the rumor that you found your long-lost parents?"

"Oh!"

"Please, if you don't feel comfortable talking about it…"

"In good time, Cecilia."

"Now is as good a time as any. Family is important to me, as I am Jewish. Has Barend shared any niceties about her great-grandmother?"

"Yes, he has."

"Is that a fact? What did he say exactly?"

"He told me he had a great-grandmother who was of French extraction. Do you know anything else of interest?"

"Tell me more about Reeva. You asked if she is my friend."

"And you'll tell me more about the French grandmother?"

"Warts and all. Well, apart from the family's well-kept secret that Avigail escaped the Nazis, nothing much."

"Avigail? I didn't know that. What was she doing, escaping the Nazis?"

"A few Jews survived the Holocaust… millions perished. Avigail's parents and siblings got wiped out, but she lived to tell the tale."

Georgi is paralyzed with incredulity.

"Family is important to us, and so is hiding skeletons. God punished King Hezekiah after he received the Iraqi spies and showed them everything in his treasure houses." Says Cecilia with seriousness.

"Yeah, Samson had sex with Delilah in exchange for his long hair."

"What? Where did you hear that?'

"My boyfriend back home told me. He was an avid bible reader."

"Georgi, I am talking real secrets here. Barend could never volunteer such skeletons because when Avigail married into the Van de Watt dynasty, the two families failed to come to dinner to celebrate."

"Poor girl! It sounds serious. Are you sure of all this, Cecilia?"

"Don't breathe a word of it. It's a stigma some Van Der Watt descendants have had to contend with in silence. Come, you can give me all the latest gossip from Toronto, my favorite city."

It is a gloomy afternoon by the time most mourners have all left. Lyndon, the eldest son, walks out without a word and returns to Stellenbosch. The kitchen veranda is sparsely populated with white faces. Sofia has laid out leftovers on the large wooden table, but no one finds it appealing. Dolly, a lone black female worker, remains seated in the shadows after a long day, waiting for orders. Retief is speaking in low tones to Barend, who nods his approval. Georgi and Gert are seated uneasily on either side of the table. Trying to strike up a conversation, she says, "Mr Van der Watt, I never met your son, Willem, but…"

Gert, his arm in a sling, shakes his head dejectedly, "Thank you, my Dear, but I can't take any more condolences. I'm sorry. Please bear with me. Tell jokes, sing, do what you will, but please don't let anyone talk any more about Willem now."

The air grows thicker as silence hangs much heavier, like an imminent cloudburst. Dolly hesitantly approaches Georgi and offers her drinks. Only too happy to engage herself in something, Georgi appreciates the icy cold ginger ale and small talk.

"Thanks, Dolly. I sat next to Mr Retief inside the church. He pointed at an elderly lady and said she was Barend's grandmother. I was hoping to see her here. Where is she? Where did she go?"

Dolly takes a few moments before she says, "Ouma? She stays in her cottage. She is not allowed to come here."

"How do you know she is not allowed?"

"She told me. She made things worse by allowing Sofia to stay with her when she quarreled with her brothers."

"But Ouma attended the service. I saw her."

"Yes, Sofia and I fetched her secretly, and I pushed her wheelchair into the church very early before the service started. But, please, I don't want to lose my job. I am telling you because you are colored. Don't ask anyone about Ouma. Barend will be upset."

On the other side of the ample space, Sofia leans against the door next to Barend, who is seated and finishing his meal. Addressing him, she says, "Barry, I need to talk to you. Can we go inside?"

Barend's tone is brusque: "I have guests here. We can talk next week."

Sofia has two spots of color on her cheeks. Her mournful face betrays deeper scars inside. She says with composure, "It's important."

He sticks his toothpicks on the napkin, "I said NO, Sofia. Let it go."

"You must come with me," Sofia says more softly, albeit with a firm urgency too hard for Barend to ignore.

He gets stiffly to his feet. Georgi observes with keen interest yet another tense moment between the siblings. Gert walks out when Barend and Sofia disappear into the deep side of the mansion.

When Dolly notices Georgi dozing off, she guides her to one of the visitors' bedrooms to rest, whispering, "I am doing this because they just told me you are Barend's girlfriend from overseas. Only white people use these rooms."

"Thank you, Dolly. I'll remember you."

"Maybe you will."

"I promise. Could you give me your number? I want to talk to you later."

"Secretly, Okay? How did you become his girlfriend? These people here...?" Dolly dips her volume to confide, "Barend will never have a serious relationship with anyone who came from outside the local farming stock. I am surprised to see them treat you differently." Dolly writes her number on a piece of paper as she continues, "These people... they don't like Africans. Even coloreds from around here treat them with hatred. Ask Sofia. You are different because you speak English. I hold a diploma in catering, but am paid like an illiterate."

Georgi interprets Dolly's inappropriate words as a serious wake-up call about her career. As Barend walks in, Dolly hands Georgi the paper with her particulars.

"What is that, Dolly?"

Georgi rushes, "It's her telephone number. She tells me she wants to study further, and I want to connect her with Puri for a bursary."

Dolly walks out. Georgi says, "Does anyone mind if I go to bed now?"

Barend looks at her blankly, "It's not even ten, Georgi."

Sofia enters as Georgi says, "I couldn't sleep on the plane and have had little sleep since. I feel flattened." tired

Sofia offers Georgi better bedding. Barend looks uneasy, and his eyes meet Georgi's as if asking for an explanation. Sofia seems reluctant to leave the room despite murmuring her goodbyes. She walks out briefly but quickly returns to continue her long farewells. Georgi senses a deep conflict in Sofia's heart that she wants to share with both Barend and herself.

Barend wraps his arms around Georgi's waist and pulls her closer while Sofia's gaze stays fixed on Georgi. He kisses her forehead and says, "Thank you for being here today. I don't know how I would have managed without you."

Shaking her head, Sofia's heave is heavy and unambiguously smug. She finally saunters down the passage.

Elsewhere, Cecilia Trent hesitates several times. Finally, she clicks the buttons. Reeva answers and asks how her mother got her private number.

"Please, Reeva, I want us to talk."

"Mom, we exhausted everything there was to talk about years ago."

"Can we meet anywhere, your place... here at Robertson, anywhere?"

"Why, Mommy? Are you finally dying? If you are, I'll be like Jimmy Kruger; remember what he said after his police murdered Steve Beeko?"

"Reeva, I'm not dying. We need to talk."

Reeva disconnects.

CHAPTER 18

Whose baby is this?

Freshly showered, Georgi stretches out, vaguely watching the curtains move eerily in the night breeze. As she reviews the day, she thinks, 'This isn't going to work for me. I wasn't myself all day long, struggling to make a good impression. They weighed me up to determine my suitability for the clan's lifestyle. Is that what they were doing? Why is Sofia so hot and cold at the same time? Is she protective of his brother, or am I being an irrational bitch...?'

Sleep descends like an African night, yet before she realizes it, a tray hovers above her head.

"Tea, Madam," greets Toto, a petite Black teenager. Her English is limited, but she is fluent in Xhosa and Afrikaans. Georgi feels uneasy about the 'over the top' celebrity treatment she is receiving.

After disappearing to the Taung residence for a few weeks, Georgi responds to a formal invitation to spend a night with Barend at the farm. However, Georgi discovers Barend will not be present when she arrives. At his prompting by telephone, Sofia is on hand to help sort out Georgi's sleeping arrangement. Georgi is fuming, but fear begins to take over. Soon after Sofia walks out, she relocates to the couch to listen to footsteps and night whispers, hoping to take appropriate action as the need might arise.

In the morning, Toto serves her a strong, freshly brewed ground coffee. Georgi thinks, 'Perhaps this is a coded message.' As soon as Toto leaves, a loud knock signals the arrival of Barend. He is wearing a yellow T-shirt and white shorts. Georgi thinks he looks like John McEnroe.

"I'm not coming over to that bed to kiss you. Good morning, you look sexy," he teases. He crosses over to sit on the bed and says, "Sorry, I was on call."

"And what call was that?"

"We're always on call in my line of work. I had to..."

"You invite me to your home where you know your people aren't particularly thrilled to see me, and then you go off on some call without arranging it with me? What kind of work do you do?"

"I'll explain this later."

"What did you tell Sofia about me? I learn it's difficult for people like me."

Barend latches the door, and they are both on the bed, scanning each other's eyes and exploring, but hesitantly. Georgi's mouth begins to water, and she can feel a build-up of anticipation in her body. She wonders if Barend will repeat the unwelcome stunt he once pulled on the beach. Each move is instinctive, and every little touch is a prologue to an expedition full of discoveries and surprises. Slowly, Barend nudges closer so that their skins blend, and his skin absorbs her developing sweat like a sponge. Georgi feels the chill between her thighs. She makes her decisive maneuvers until they enfold thigh to thigh. Georgi is shaking with anxiety and deep desire, and she can feel an incongruous release of tears suddenly streaming down her face. Barend's kiss becomes tentative again as if seeking approval. The yearning to touch like this has been secretly lurking inside her bosom from the first moment she saw Barend at Southern Tip, where he played Solitaire. Georgi responds more assertively to Barend's uneasy prompting, her journey of discovery making her body whirl like a brewing storm. Her head is giddy, and she answers to the artillery barrage by stretching her ravenous limbs to claim and enfold him.

"You look great, Barend. Just gazing at you across the room that day was like listening to a Liszt piano concert that turns my bones to water, oh!"

He throws back his head to laugh delightedly.

"I hope you're not just being a big teaser. Will you marry me?"

"Don't you dare!" she detaches from him, "save it for when you can arrange a romantic background, preferably with mood music like 'Stardust' and the grumbling background thunder and the sea breaking on the shoreline. And the moonlight, of course. Don't forget the full moon."

"I prefer the rusty moon, cut in half during an incomplete eclipse. That's been the story of my life; the dark half with the other half missing – and then came you, Georgi."

"Let's settle for the full moon and no rhymes of your ill-omened eclipse. Spare me your limericks, please."

Georgi lies across Barend's lap. Barend's hands are massaging Georgi's shoulders when Sofia clears her throat, pulls the curtain, and speaks from outside through the window that has been wide open all the time. Georgi instantly pulls the duvet to protect her naked body.

"Oh, here you are, Barry. Can I give you a shopping list... to bring from Town?"

Barend's frustration with her sister permeates the bedroom. Georgi is certain that Sofia has been nearby, listening in from the beginning. After a quick exchange, Barend exclaims, "Can't the shopping wait?"

Sofia gapes at the slightly open curtain, her curious eyes scanning the bed area, particularly around Georgi's veiled body, while her fingers fiddle with the lace curtain. Barend shuffles to the door and walks out. Georgi hears the angry tones of Sofia's fragmented voices and Barend's heated replies. Once again, Georgi feels as if half of her being, or her soul, has been detached. She jumps out of bed, shivering. Later in the day, Barend arrives at the family lodge, Northgate, on the hillside overlooking the city, with Georgi in tow. Barend's brother, Willem, occupied the property before his untimely death. Barend plans to return to Robertson the next day, while Marcia expects Georgi on the same day.

"I'm leaving most of my brother's stuff right here," he tells her. "There are just a few personal belongings I need to collect. I'd offer you tea, but I don't suppose the milk is fresh."

Only a battered sofa, a built-in fitment that holds a few trifles, photographs, a clock, and a hi-fi set against the wall remain in the deserted living room.

"That's okay. Black tea will do just fine."

Barend has been looking unsettled since his confrontation with Sofia. Her heart is beating in her throat. This is the first time the two have been 'hidden away alone together.' He picks up a framed photograph, and his face turns grim, obviously still struggling with his grief. It is a photo of an achingly young Willem in his Rugby gear. Barend drops his tired body on the couch and covers his troubled face with a scarf while she silently scours the property, checking out the unlatched rooms. After a long while, Barend is on his feet, and his grim features suddenly make him look elderly.

"Did you see anything in your inquisitive prying?"

"No. Nothing. Is there anything you wanted me to see in my inquisitive prying?"

"Every empty house looks empty, but it is never empty. Each room has secrets. Rookie investigators are trained to tell the story of each abandoned house. You'll be amazed at what they come up with."

"That's scary..."

"Let me ask you a question: have you ever been intimate with another man?"

"What do you mean, Barry?"

"I mean, how many men have you been intimate with?"

"If you are asking me about my sex life, I'll tell you right now; it's none of your business."

"Well, if we're planning a future together, we must be open with each other."

"Barend, I am no rookie, and I don't know what future you're talking about, but where I come from, relationships are based on mutual respect, not control. What you did with your body before I met you is of little concern to me, except the truth about your HIV status."

Caught off guard, Barend retorts, "I'm not HIV positive if you wish to know."

"Don't you think it was foolish of you to have sex with me without a condom when you knew nothing about my status?"

Barend smiles. She smiles back and says, "Perhaps we should give it a little break to give you time to mourn the passing of your brother. Besides, I think certain things need sorting out between you and your sister without my intrusion."

"Sofia? You needn't worry about her. I know she was not pleasant to you..."

"What is your attitude towards her?"

Barend ignores the question and moves around, rummaging and collecting documents and files. Georgi feels there must be plenty of stuff that Barend will not tell her soon. Sofia is shrouded in mysterious serenity. Georgi thinks she is a time bomb waiting to explode. As she reflects deeper on Sofia, a chill passes through her veins. Her mind quickly drifts back to her experiences at home in Canada when Pedro, her brief boyfriend, invites her to his luxurious house. She is fifteen, and he is twenty-three. Pedro tells Georgi's mother that he will take her home after they have dinner with Professor Oliveira. No one can guess the kind of depravity that awaits her there. Pedro's plan is for her to spend an uninterrupted night with him. Not only is there no dinner, but his mother, a clinical psychologist, is away giving a conference paper in Honolulu on patriarchy and gender violence. Georgi escapes but doesn't tell anyone. However, through her contacts, Professor Oliveira learns that Georgi broke her windows before fleeing. Neither Pedro nor Georgi admits to the allegations. Georgi has grown increasingly suspicious that Sofia might be hiding secrets of a similar nature. For a girl, the effects of abuse can linger and deepen much longer than most realize. Barend starts unpacking Willem's boxes, removing stuff, sorting, and repacking. Georgi notices a framed picture of a baby girl among the staff.

"Whose baby is this?"

Barend takes one look and says, "This is nothing."

"You say the child in the picture is nothing? Who is she?"

"Nothing to concern you, Georgi."

Barend and Georgi spend an awkward night at the lodge. He wants them to share a bed, but she insists on the couch. Her sleep is constantly disturbed by fears that Willem might haunt the house and chase them to the other side of the moon. In the morning, while Georgi is in the bathroom, Barend opens the front door to a neighbor, a middle-aged man who has come to report a break-in attempt. He shows Barend where the criminals broke through the wall on the day of Willem's funeral. Barend goes outside with the man. Seizing the moment, Georgi quickly searches through the boxes, finds pictures of the mysterious child, and locates a folder labeled 'Van der Watt.' She stuffs the items into her duffel bag and walks off to think about breakfast. However, they decide to go to Padstaal for the meal. Georgi heads to the bathroom to develop the photos and documents she stole from Northgate. She begins to prepare herself for more surprises about Barend and his family. "I have been hearing something about your sister, who was a teenager when she died. What happened to her?"

"First, tell me about your family; Puri, for starters?"

"Forget it, I'm done. This is no way to sustain a civilized conversation."

CHAPTER 19

Betwixt and Between

Georgi is silently reading an email from Puri. Marcia says, "So things are moving on with you and 'Lover-boy'? I got the impression you spurned his going down on his knees. Or was it in jest, for my eyes only?"

"I'm not ready to deal with the Van der Watt clan yet. I feel uneasy clinging to a man who wants to make me part of his family. Plus, I'm a little strung up over his blowing hot and cold all at once."

"No point getting into a tizzy. I know many things, Georgi, and you are in love."

"Anyway, let me tell you what Puri says in her note. She wants me to spend Christmas with them in Germany to 'discuss our future.' There's also a little matter of my name. Puri insists I'm Esther. Just imagine that, Marcia..."

"Esther! It's a cute little Hebrew name. She's got a point, you know. After all, 'Georgi' is not the name she gave you. Where does Barend fit into all of this? How does he feel about discovering your father's true identity?"

"I don't know, but I think he has been privy to skeletons about us for God knows how long. He asked me to tell him something about Puri. When I asked him about his upbringing, he waffled and blabbered about his grandmother, who used to read Alice in Wonderland and Cinderella for the children."

"I bet the granny also read Alice in Wonderland for Sofia. Many children who spend their formative years immersed in Cinderella or Romeo and Juliet often become intellectually stunted adults. Has Barend told you anything about his brothers and sisters and his authoritarian father?"

"I asked him about Sofia because that girl exudes an aura of rejection, but he managed to evade the issue. I should take more time to get to know Barend. It's a serious concern."

"One needs the luck to become a balanced human being after being raised in a household full of skeletons."

Marcia relates a disturbing story that Georgi had never heard before. Sofia once went to the Robertson police station to open a case against Willem, her now deceased brother, after he molested 17-year-old Leandra, a colored student who did part-time work after school. Sofia first alerted the family, after which the Patriarch summoned Willem for an admonitory session that achieved nothing. However, the father reserved his religious incantations for Sofia, whom he accused of bringing the family's name into disrepute. When she later took it upon herself to report the crime, the entire family descended on her, and the father threatened to disown her.

"The case fizzled. However, Leandra's brothers exacted revenge on Willem, just as Absalom did on Tamar. But don't quote me; I'll deny it."

"How do you know all that?"

"I work for the government, Georgi; that's the bottom line."

"Wow! There was fire in the smoke, after all. What caused the case to fizzle?"

"The Van der Watts are a distinguished dynasty in the Cape, and what the patriarch says goes."

"How scary... I learn she's squatting at her granny's flat, Sofia. Has she been on Sofia's side in all of this?"

"I know nothing about that. However, I think Barend cares deeply for you. Don't lead him on if you aren't sincere. It can be hard on you down the line..."

"Yes, something bugs me. I don't think you're aware of this, Marcia; Ryan has been making advances, and what I feel towards him is more than infatuation. I'm confused..."

"As well you should be. Ryan? Our Ryan?"

"Yes, Marcia, your Ryan."

"Shoooo, Girl! Betwixt and between is an awkward place for any girl to be in. Ryan is a nice young man; big-headed, yes, but he has great ancestry and professional parents. His mother is an Indian if that's important to you."

"Yeah?"

"South Africans of Indian descent are more PC. What makes you think you have feelings for him?"

"A lump in my throat the moment I first saw him; more tears on my pillow than Kylie Minogue's 'Butterflies in my Stomach.'"

"My Grandmother once said, 'Girls must never follow windblown lilies even if they have a cotton candy aroma and dance like angels. She said that in front of the third boyfriend, I was introducing her to him. I never saw him again. I'm not the unbiased party to discuss your Ryan matter with. What does your family say? Odessa...?"

"Odessa? Why Odessa?"

"She's your sister."

"Odessa's particular pet hate is the sight of white people; that much I know. She thinks Ryan is the best thing since Nelson Mandela's Ticker-Tape Parade in New York."

"So, she's biased. Aren't we all? Take your time. What you need right now is a few weeks off the humdrum slope. We leave next week for Johannesburg. I think you'll get to like Esther when you discover you're much closer to your famous German mother than you realize."

"It'll take some doing. But this heavy load... I can't get Ryan off my mind."

"Don't abandon yourself to fear. The future is always a difficult place to locate. I know all about it. And may the force be with you!"

"All about it? I see a genuine twinkle of nostalgia in your eye. Does my mess remind you of someone?"

"Between you and me and these four walls? He was a fine chap, the first I ever introduced to my authoritarian father. My parents had gotten wind of our dating escapades from some loudmouthed teacher. Father ordered me to bring him home so he could examine him."

"That was heavy. Did he pass?"

"With flying colors. The father offered to pay his school fees promptly. 'He must be an advocate. He's clever, my father said to me. But he was a cheating delinquent, hardly a man to be trusted. As I expected, he was soon in and out of police holding cells and became increasingly involved in crime."

"Unfinished business... with Codi, then?"

"Just falling into a reverie occasionally, wondering how my existence would have looked had he made it as an advocate. I quite enjoyed his company. He had a thing about a poem by Henry Reed."

"Reed? 'Naming of Parts' by any chance? Quite profound; not about flowers for sure."

"You bet. It always sounded wonderful, even though I struggled to grasp it."

Georgi cannot help but wonder why the name of Ryan's sister, who used a wheelchair, hardly features in Marcia's chatter. She has no reason to doubt April's sincerity, even though he drops cryptic lines for her to puzzle. While framing the question to ask Marcia about this, Marcia answers the landline and hands the receiver to her. Odessa is so frantic that Georgi can hardly make out what she is saying. Georgi speaks in monosyllables and then returns quietly to sit across from Marcia.

"My father has taken an extended leave. He left a note and disappeared."

"No doubt he has a lot to sort out after the trauma of the past few months. Give him some space. He'll be back, ready to resume life."

"I wonder. After telling him what April said, 'Uhuru,' 'Globetrot,' and things, he concealed his obvious embarrassment behind his broad smile. Odessa thinks he's gone to see Nathaniel and Puri. Perhaps he fears someone might blow the whistle and that he may be booted out of Canada. I hope he is not out on a vengeance spree."

Georgi walks across the courtyard to the cottage, feeling deeply lonely for the first time in months. Under the moonlit sky, she can see the tall Cape Fold Mountains looming behind the estate. The soft darkness is dotted with shimmering stars, along with a reddish outline of clouds at twilight's edge. Somewhere, the Southern Cross dominates the dazzling sky, and she is thrilled to see a Cape Eagle Owl silently swoop across the face of the moon and vanish into the fields. Owls are carnivorous birds of prey. Moments later, she hears a faint squeak that sounds like a squirrel, as if the unlucky creature is about to become the owl's dinner. Keeping the dim lights on, she opens the French doors and steps out onto the patio, smelling the rain-washed stillness. All alone on a starry African night, Georgi feels a deep connection to her roots, surrounded by her African ancestors. 'Yes,' she says with a hint of tears, 'I can build a life here.' The divine silver moon smiles, and she is mesmerized. When she smiles back, the moonlight seems to intensify, and the night becomes as clear as a spring day. She stretches like a contented Hollywood cat, raises both arms above her head, and sighs, 'I've come home. This is Africa. I'm home,'

CHAPTER 20

My Mysterious Guest - Room 607

Barend disappears, and Georgi grows frantic. 'Two men in my life cannot just vanish without explanation,' she thinks. Seven stressful days pass. Desperate, she calls April and asks to meet him at Hillcrest Café.

"You managed to come this time. I was beginning to think bad thoughts about you, Miss King."

"What bad thought?"

"Don't you think bad thoughts about white people or black people?"

"No."

"I was thinking: if I were a white man, you would have jumped to find me."

"Sorry, but I don't know you. I can't just stretch my legs at your say-so."

"Stretch your legs? Nice line. How did you get my number?"

"Tell me about the 'Globetrot' story."

Mr April cackles, "This is nothing; I knew you would take it seriously. I was sending you on a wild goose chase, that's all." He looks around in all directions and says, "As you can see, no one is staring at us because I look like you. We are coloreds, and we look identical," he chortles. "When you are with that Van der Watt, white man, everyone stares at you as if you are from Venus. Do you notice...?"

"Mr April, you said you had something to tell me."

"You work for Moroka and Marcia. Do they treat you well?"

"What's that got to do with you...?"

"You are impatient because I am a non-white person like you. We need our Steve Biko, who will teach us about colored consciousness. Have you observed that when a colored girl talks to a colored man, she is always stressed out and quick-tempered? The same girl will show a white man her wall-to-wall smile even if he is a lowlife she doesn't even know. Note this, Darling; we must look after each other in this affirmative democracy. Nobody wants you. The country is a *gemors*. Do you know what *gemors* is?"

"Sounds like something awful."

"It's worse than awful, Georgina. Democracy is the worst form of oppression. If someone sits on your neck today, you can't complain; it's uncivilized to raise your head and gasp for breath. They say you are uncultured. With apartheid, even Margaret Thatcher, that woman who called Nelson Mandela a terrorist, heard us when we told her the Boers were sitting hard on our necks. It was *skop, skiet en donder*. Ask yourself, Georgina..."

"Georgi."

"Yes, who wants to listen to the coloreds today?"

"Mr April..."

"My name is Ganon," he says. "I was in the trenches of the struggle. I suffered. I served time on Robben Island. My uncle, Mr April, rest his soul... he raised me after my parents died, and he warned me when he saw us throw stones at police vans all those years ago. He said, 'Forget about the struggle, my nephew. The day the Black Liberation Army takes over, they will ask, 'Who are you?' And, as true as Vlakplaas, what has happened after 1994... Sorry, I ordered wine," he says to the waitron. "We the coloreds, we like wine, don't we, Georgina?" April says, bursting out again as the waiter puts a bottle of dry wine on the table.

His demeanor suddenly turns somber, and he mutters, "I should never have gotten involved in all of this."

"Yeah? The struggle, you mean? I get the feeling my folks are in the same boat. You've finally seen the light. Even the best of us notice after the event that the bait can be more alluring than the fish?"

"Nicely put, Georgina. I wish I could run an NGO and help youngsters in my neighborhood. There's too much poverty and HIV where I come from."

April takes time to tell Georgi about his upbringing. Georgi listens with great empathy. As an afterthought, April reveals that Georgi's father is in the country.

"What is he doing here?"

"The struggle has sold out, Georgina. That man, Lenin, sacrificed his life for freedom, just like me. But today, we have become a pariah. Nobody wants to know us. They plant us worldwide with fancy titles to ensure we are out of the gravy action. In his case, they know he will stir the pot, and many comrades will have to face the music. He refused to return after they promised him a top post in Russia and its satellites."

Georgi is on her feet and shouting, "Mr April, where's my father?"

"Your father... three days ago, he was nearly killed by two ex-MK soldiers who survived the Kuito attack in the eighties. Many young soldiers died there. Your father is bold but silly. He came here to meet the men. You know why?"

"To report them to the police?"

"No, in the interest of truth and reconciliation. He wanted to explain what happened in Kuito. I know those men, Darling. Their kind of reconciliation is to see your father in a shallow grave in the middle of Bush 17. He came into the country incognito. Our intelligence failed to spot someone else looking to cut your father's throat and gouge his eyes out. The sister of that man died long ago after your father planted a bomb next to a church. Her name was Mimi-Koo."

"Mimi-Koo? Oh my God! Where's my Daddy now?"

"He is safe because that man, Lenin, your father, can sell heaters in Congo!"

"What about 'Uhuru'?"

"Between you and me? Lenin located one of the comrades, and after threatening to drown his ass in the Vaal Dam, he sang like a canary. Lenin got possession of 'Uhuru' and made a settlement with the killers of one Mtunzi Radebe."

"I don't suppose you know the men he settled with... the killers."

"I know everything, Miss King. I even know your new name, 'Queen Esther.'"

"What?"

"Those comrades are high-ranking government officials now."

After taking a hot shower, she relaxes through breathing exercises, trying hard to make sense of the enigma called Ganon April. Georgi's mind flashes back to each of the boyfriends she collected and dumped in Canada since she was fifteen. She remembers the blotchy face of Miles, the trumpeter who committed suicide at the age of seventeen. All he ever wanted was to become a firefighter, but his mother insisted he train to become a professional musician. Georgi is now crying over Miles. Deep down, she knows the truth about Miles' suicide. After unrequited romantic advances, he blurted out that he would shoot himself, something Georgi never took seriously until it happened. The suicide so affected her that she could not easily break up with any man for fear of nightmares or setting off another suicide. She wonders what she did wrong, driving Kelly Ellsworth into the Catholic priesthood. Then there was Pedro, who magnetized girls of every hue. Georgi has not forgiven him for abusing her and sticking foreign objects between her thighs. Following the death of Miles, Ellen took Georgi to a psychiatrist, where she was an outpatient for over a year.

Something jolts her from her reverie, and she remembers 'Globetrot.' She has been trying to decipher the code since April, when she first stumbled upon it inadvertently in a moment of drunken stupor. She tries the number again, using both Cape Town and Pretoria codes. The latter succeeds.

"Code?" the man answers.

Georgi is lost for words. She cuts off and immediately calls April, "Now, cut the crap, April. I just called Globetrot, and he wants the code. What is it?"

"You what? Sorry, wrong number..." The line goes dead.

Georgi realizes that April's antics are getting her nowhere. She spends the next hours playing guessing games until she finally settles for 'Lenin' as the code. Georgi's breathing exercises are no longer voluntary. She tries the number again.

Predictably, the man answers, "Code?"

"Lenin," Georgi says.

"*Dies ist* 'Globetrot'. Why is Lenin a woman today?"

Georgi's hair stands on end. She can hear clearly, and the voice of 'Globetrot' is distinct. After a brief pause, she says, "Nathaniel, this is Georgi."

The line goes dead. Georgi shakes at the thought that she is not wrong. Her stomach churns, and after taking a glass of milk, she tries Nathaniel's cell number. Nathaniel sounds unsettled.

"Nathaniel, this is Georgi..."

"I know this is Georgi. I've got Georgi's number here."

"South Africa has done little to eliminate those German chips on your shoulders. Tell me this: why did you cut me off just now?"

"How did you get that number? It's not for cousins and extended family."

"Don't be silly. What the hell is 'Globetrot'?"

"I have no idea what you're talking about."

"Nathaniel Lieber... whatever your name is, I have had it up to here with all the pork pies and treachery you've been feeding me up to now. Just tell me in plain language: who are you?"

"You know I'm Nathaniel. *Du bist meine einzige Schwester*. I was planning a get-together: Mother, Caleb, and you, of course."

"Count me out," she whispers. Is this man for real? The names April and Lenin; are you all working together, by any chance?"

"The struggle continues..."

"What struggle is that?"

"To defend our democracy. Even you can understand that. It's good we finally discovered Lenin was no traitor but a hero. You and I must raise our heads high and walk tall. We belong to a stock of heroes and heroines..."

"Speak for yourself, Nathaniel. Who else is a spy? Puri? Caleb?"

"You must go now. But let me tell you, when I first saw you over at Portofino's that night, there was a powerful force pulling me towards you: amazing sexual attraction. I told Reeva about it. I am not a sensual person, but I find the thoughts and dreams, being with you... intensely desirable."

"You told Reeva? What did she say?"

"She said something I can't repeat, Georgi. Do you feel the same magnetism that I do?"

Georgi is crawling out of her skin. She gathers some strength and says, "Nathaniel, you are supposed to be my twin brother. But no! I do not harbor such lewd feelings."

"Jane Austen thinks highly of sibling relationships. Read 'Pride and Prejudice'."

"I've read the book."

"No need to brag. I know of your literary orientation. Even though I have an intellectual predisposition, I read fiction when I have nothing else important to do. You cannot honestly say you don't entertain hidden feelings towards me. I saw how you gawked at me that night at Portofino's, kept walking out in a sweat, and came back to gaze at me. I have this premonition that we will one day satisfy our mutual desire for a deep, penetrating encounter. We both need fireworks to help us deal with the psychological disadvantage caused by a long spell of separation..."

"Nathaniel Lieber, have you ever heard of the word 'incest'? I've had enough of your tedious subject. Let's end it right here."

"Alright, call me again tomorrow, and please, use the family number; no more dramatic calls."

Georgi suffers a recurrence of nightmares; she is with the same boy who is screaming at her while she tries in vain to run away. In another, she sees Jesus on his second coming, accompanied by his hawk-looking angels, who attack her. The bad dream about Miles, her friend who committed suicide, keeps haunting her and making her desperate. One night, while sleepwalking, she finds herself outside, knocking at the cottage door used by Sanna and Gibson. She decides to go for a matinee to see old South African movies. Halfway through 'Mapantsula,' she has to leave when she receives a puzzling, anonymous message. She makes her way to the Garden City Holiday Inn. The stated name of the mysterious guest in Room 607 is unfamiliar to her. She wonders why anyone lodging in such a classy suite would be interested in seeing her. She drops her name at the desk and asks them to call Odessa in an emergency. There is no response when she knocks, but after a few seconds' hesitation, she tries the door.

Her father, wearing earphones in his morning gown, shuffles around in his old, puffy slippers. He swivels around in his chair, instantly closing his diary and shoving everything on the dressing table to one side, apparently making sure she sees nothing.

Georgi burst into tears, "Daddy, what's happening? When did you get to the country...?"

Contrary to her fears, her father looks healthy and strong. He gives her a tight hug, and her tirade subsides. He sags into his chair and explains that he owes Georgi some explanation about her past and wants to turn over a new page.

"Oh, Papa, you're beginning to sound like George W. Bush, after the gullible Americans discovered the story of the 'weapons of mass destruction' had been a Whitehouse invention all along. I hate it when you go all damp and insincere. Back home, you swore you told us all we needed to know about your sordid past, right, Papa?"

"Every canvas is painted in broad strokes, but minutiae are often hidden away."

"Let's start with these minutiae. I heard a rumor that you set up my job with Marcia and Moroka before Odessa and I left home. Is that true?"

"South Africa is not a safe place, Georgi..."

"Talk about pulling the wool over one's eyes."

"I had to protect you, girls. But it was my contacts that got the job. I didn't know Moroka or Marcia from a bar of soap."

"But you knew them from the struggle days, right?"

"Marcia's family? Vaguely, yes. Her father was a Pan-Africanist. Of course, you know I was with the ANC."

"I see. Anyway, is there any other old page of minutiae that you want me to read, unedited, Like Luca's death? Odessa believes you had something to do with it because he was about to spill the beans about your past."

"I would never stoop that low, Georgi. Luca was just an angry young man who played a game of Russian roulette. We have a good idea what happened to the rabble-rouser."

"'We'? Meaning you and the government?"

"I'll say no more after this. Let me start here: Three weeks after April contacted me, I began working at Villiers Wolter's laboratory as a trainee, back in the dark days of apartheid. I did not like what I was doing, but being a double agent had some alluring features in those days. April and another man, highly placed in the Agency today, kept assuring me through coded messages that those on the higher echelons of our organizations were happy with what I was doing."

The timbre of Kian's voice has changed. It has become harder, rougher, and more African in expression. He pushes on, "My main function was to try out the experimental weapons, including bombs and Chinese technology stolen by apartheid agents."

Kian adds something that seems to confirm April's disturbing story. Something happened in the past that made Kian feel he was destined for hell. Their bomb, called 'pinhead,' allegedly killed a 15-year-old girl in the Western Cape. The handlers higher up did not take kindly to the fact that the missions had hit the wrong target.

Kian was later told, "There's going to be much fallout because a white girl was hit, Afrikaans speaking, to boot. You know how it is."

Georgi is swarming with questions and shaking all over. She quietly asks, "Father, did you do something they normally hang people for?"

"Since I came back, questions have surfaced about the actual explosion that killed the child. I believe you know the story of a bomb the Americans dropped on Nagasaki, Japan."

"Vaguely."

"Read about it. Whenever massive explosions occur, opportunistic killings in villages spike; pardon the pun. Fifty years after Nagasaki, a 90-year-old former Japanese detective uncovered the double murder of a couple about to marry. He also presented irrefutable evidence in court that led to the conviction of the culprit. She was a jilted lover, twenty years old at the time...Yes. Wars do kill, but accompanying opportunistic murders take their toll."

"So, it's not your bomb that killed that girl?"

"There's more to the saga than meets the eye."

The dark circles under Kian's eyes enlarge, and his face droops when he laments, "It made me sick to my stomach. The victim was a child."

He sidesteps details but relates his leaving the country and being in charge of a group of young Soweto comrades from the 1976 generation. "I was like a rat, trapped in a hole. But in all this, I believed somewhere higher up, someone knew who I was and what was going on. I did not know that the 'higher up' I always thought existed was a world fraught with deceit and self-interest. The military camps had become killing fields, and many of our comrades lost their lives because traitors created paranoia, continually cooking up fairy tales about apartheid spies inside our camps."

Kian puts his hand on her shoulder and smiles. Georgi is mesmerized by his extended, sparkly glare. He grabs her wrist as if checking her pulse and says, "It is a blessing to have a daughter like you."

He discloses to her that amidst the turmoil in Southern Africa, something extraordinary occurred. He met a woman in Angola. She was a German national working on their side. Her job was to share alternative stories overlooked by mainstream media with the world. She was an undercover agent, a foreign reporter, transmitting back to Europe.

"Puri, right?"

"What else do you want to know, Georgi?"

"You are about to tell me more about Puri and your African adventures. Please, no more broad strokes."

"Our organization held Puri in high esteem. After striking a friendship with her, we used contacts to help us sneak in and out of neighboring countries for our rendezvous, and we spent two weeks together between Tanzania and Kenya…"

"Together? As in romantic together…?"

"She was a workaholic and a passionate artist, keen on nature and life. We enjoyed the last few days in a cabin tent on the shores of the Lake. Did you know Tarangire is the world's largest permanent desert lake?"

"Keep going, Dad. What were you doing sneaking in and out of all those countries with a white woman?"

"Okay, let's talk about Puri. She's no white woman to you but your mother. I was committed to her work and the liberation struggle. She described everything she saw wherever she went inside those African states in quaint words I could not repeat. Like the many dreams at Mona Lisa's doorstep, her manuscripts lay there, and they died there. Puri's writings were not about daisies and romance. One publisher after another turned her down, and she finally gave up. Publishing is located in ideology. Mainstream book publishers are not just there for the love of art, but also to weaponize the art form as part of social control; they are pushing their viewpoints and a mainstream agenda. Remember, publishers are interested in the truth that they can sell to their economically powerful readers. What Puri told was the truth about how the English and the Americans coached the Afrikaners on how to dehumanize black people. Her truth was a hot potato that the two-faced white publishing industry could not handle. Anyway, some months following our fling, she sent a courier message saying she was in an ANC training camp in Kuito. She needed to go home because she was pregnant. However, she had no choice but to spend time in the heavily guarded Mission hospital nearby."

"Mother goose picked an awkward place to nest!"

"Yes, it was. She tried her best under the circumstances, and the chicks finally landed safely in my stressed-out arms."

Kian tells how he sneaked out of the camp to meet Belle Aire. The young soldier had successfully whisked a baby girl from Puri, both of whom were in danger. Kian did not know then that Puri had given birth to twins. Belle Aire relayed the message to Kian that the baby girl's name was Esther.

"When I returned to camp a few hours later, I found my young squad exterminated to the last man. The fallout was horrendous. I became the object of scorn and ridicule; everyone condemned me for the catastrophe. Their kith and kin want my head on a platter even today."

"What about Puri? Didn't she try to come back for... the baby?"

By the time Puri was well enough to start making inquiries, Kian and his family had settled in London. While Puri took the rumors circulating at the time that Kian and the baby had died on the Swazi border with a pinch of salt, there was no other rumor to counter them. For his part, Kian made a point of disappearing from the face of the earth. Georgi feels dizzy. She walks out of the hotel but returns the following day. She finds Kian relaxing near the hotel pool, reading 'Barefoot over the Serengeti'.

"I thought you'd left for good," he says.

"Is that what you wanted me to do, leave for good?"

"No, but I'd understand you needed some fresh air, given what I told you."

"You don't understand the half of it, Dad."

Kian's mind no longer stays in the 21st century. Instead, it drifts back to adventurous times: "For us in the liberation struggle in Angola, Tanzania, Kenya, Mozambique, Libya, and other African countries felt like our home away from home. You are a big girl now, and I can disclose that you were conceived in a tent near Lake Manyara in Tarangire National Park. It was a hot but a little breezy afternoon."

"'Busy' sounds more like it, Papa."

"Don't push it, child."

"Dad, I was conceived in a tent on the desert lake shoreline? That sure set the tone for my turbulent life, right?"

"Blame the turbulence on your mother's genes."

"And my name is Georgi? I know you've always been economical with the truth. Why Georgi?"

"Yes, Georgi. I named you for a middle-aged Indian lady who owned a cleaning outfit there and personally cleaned our room in the park. They called her Georgina..."

"You named me after what? A cleaner? Couldn't you find a suitable name from your ancestors?"

"I believe the cleaning lady had good ancestors in Kerala, and they must have been happy with her because she had a good heart."

"And Odessa? Is that an African name?"

"Let's stick to Georgi for now."

"Okay. I suppose you were disappointed that the baby who came out and was delivered to you in that Angolan terrorist camp was a girl. A cleaner, indeed!"

"Terrorist camp? Stop playing wise-guy on me..."

"Never a dull moment with you, Papa."

"And you told Ellen I was Georgi? But now Puri says I am Esther!"

"We don't have anyone by that name in our clan," he retorts with irritation. "And you are telling nobody about my conversation with you regarding Puri, least of all about Esther. You are Georgi. That's your name."

"Dad, I am a big girl, as you said. You're not going to order me around. I'll talk about our conversation anytime and with whomever."

"I know you can, but it's not wise. You must take seriously what I told you and Odessa about our Rosedale Garden when you were small. Family-unit secrets are sacrosanct. If a member falls on hard times… into a pit of shame, keep that within the unit's walls. Protect secrets because they are like family silver. Your Mofokeng clan comes first."

"Oh, Dad, you're beginning to sound like an African chief."

"Of course, I am your African chief. Don't put your life and family members in harm's way."

"Okay, Dad, being an indigenous African yourself, how do you feel about people like me?"

"You are an African…"

"But once I landed here, I discovered I'm no African. There are lots of us in the Western Cape. I am colored, and my biological mother is white. I ask you again. How do you feel about people like me?"

Kian's lips are twitching. He wants to respond to his daughter's challenge, but seems confused. He finally says, "I feel about you as I feel about Odessa."

Even though she thinks her father's long explanation is a clattering chain of excuses, Georgi is pleased to have heard from the horse's mouth that he and Puri used the magnificence of Tarangire's location to bring her and her twin brother into this world. While she knows her father well enough to read sincerity in his eyes and voice, distinguishing reality from fiction will take some doing. She decides to stick to fiction, which sounds more romantic than her parents' life story.

Kian orders drinks. When the waiter comes in, he takes advantage, sneakily removing the stuff Georgi found him reading the previous day and pacing toward the window and back to his seat like a magician. However, Georgi can figure out the sleight of hand a mile away.

"Back here, I found Belle's place, the home of the guy who picked you up from Puri and saved your life?"

"Where is he? I want to meet him."

"Shot dead the very night, a few minutes after he handed you to me."

"I guess they suspected him of carrying weapons of mass destruction – Me."

"They suspected him of something because he would not tell them anything. His stalling tactic allowed us to sneak out of the camp into the swamps and hills. His parents live in squalor in White City, two miles from my previous Soweto home. The new government is struggling to bring back whatever remains of its dignity. I expected them to be in a better situation than that…"

"Yeah, Odessa says the only blacks who seem to be hitting the big time since liberation are those who went into exile and came back alive."

"Yes, I heard her. Didn't she add, '…and those so-called heroes who were stupid enough to get detained on Robben Island'? I heard her."

"And Belle Aire's parents must have been happy to see you."

"I told Belle Aire's parents I was a journalist from The Star. His elderly father kept saying, 'Your face looks familiar.' I cut short my fake interview and slipped out. I should have told them I had traced the man who killed their son. He is in Parliament now, so one has to be careful."

"About the picture, you suddenly hid under your bed when that woman brought us drinks; was that Puri... in her prime?"

"You saw nothing," he says.

"Do you sometimes slob around together with her in this suite?"

Kian evades the question. He cautions Georgi that the country is a pressure cooker. However, he concedes they will get his support if Georgi and Odessa are serious about returning to South Africa permanently.

"What's changed? Aren't we on our own anymore?"

"I had a long, uncomfortable talk with Puri, your real mother. After all her threats to get me and Ellen locked up for kidnapping, she relented when I pointed out how severely that might affect you; after all, I am your father."

"What do you mean she relented?"

"She wished me a nice trip to hell for causing her daily stress for two decades."

He remains coy about 'Uhuru,' but instead, says, "I was expecting some good news about the Taung boy. What happened?"

"Ryan, you mean? I'm certain you loved Puri, but you married someone else. Don't you think of Puri every night?'

"Listen, Georgi. If you love two people simultaneously with equal intensity, it's called a love triangle. Throw a coin and give yourself a break."

"Talk about failure to walk the talk. Did you throw a coin before sliding into the tent with Puri?'

"I was involved in the struggle. My generation did all that for you."

"I'll remember you in my memoirs, Daddy. You do know, though, that each generation faces its struggle. Yours is no loftier than mine."

"Memoirs are a collection of ghostly voices, sounds, and thoughts kept by people with impostor syndrome."

"Say what!?"

"Yes, you compose memoirs to get back at your family or ex-work colleagues. Avoid memoirs. As you said, leave everything be."

"Yeah?"

CHAPTER 21

Off to the Free State

Georgi is absorbed in her thoughts about Barend, Ryan, and her father, the three men she regards with some trepidation. She accepts that she must live with the duplicity inherent in her family. Marcia's exciting story about Codi saturates her memory like a classic movie. She laughs aloud, claps her hands, and composes a song. 'Liars surround me, the Codis of this world, and all upstanding citizens of this rainbow nation. They supply Meals on Wheels to the destitute while stocking up on secrets to feed their children. My fate! My destiny! What a long and winding road!'

She repeats the sounds, refines them, and shouts her song even louder. She then switches to Vivaldi's sounds, which fill the velvety night.

"When the Bottom Drops Out," she murmurs. "Yes! That's my next title."

A shadowy figure on the lawn shatters Georgi's reverie. Fear paralyzes her, and she holds her breath. She opens her mouth to scream and then stifles it as she hears Barend's voice. "Don't panic. It's only me."

Her heart is hammering against her breast. The two remain silent, gazing into each other's eyes. She takes a shaky breath of relief, smiles, and says softly, "What are you doing here, Van der Watt? I nearly had a heart attack! How did you get in? Where have you been all these days?"

She leans into him and tries to put her arms around his neck, but he steps away. Fresh from a long, hot shower and now touched by Barend, her body seems to be on the verge of spontaneous combustion. He hands her a rosebud. She can't tell its color, but she thinks it looks pale. It is cool, slightly moist, and plucked from Marcia's Garden.

"How can I trust you, disappearing like that for over a week without a phone call?"

"You don't want to know."

"Says who? And don't take cover behind your imaginary intelligence duties."

"Where do I come from? Let's find a quiet spot under that tree—confession time. I come from a distraught family. When I was young, a landmine killed my little sister. I haven't mentioned her name in years because of a family vow. When Mimi-Koo died, a wave of anger fell over my family, and it nearly consumed our reality for generations. Thanks to Retief, I've been able to see things more clearly lately. Lenin has always been a suspect. The top apartheid secret police refused to comment on it. The truth still lies buried somewhere among the ruins of our untouchable apartheid past. That murder was an act of brutality. Our families need healing, but it's a difficult process."

"Our families?"

"Yes, my family, your family."

"Tell me about Mimi-Koo."

"We should not be afraid of releasing pent-up anger. I told my sister Sofia to stop spreading her insecurity virus around."

"What kind of virus is that she's been spreading?"

"All I can tell you is nothing in this lifetime will stop me from loving you."

"And why, in the name of God, would you fall for a girl from a family responsible for murdering your kid sister, as I gather from your insinuation?"

"Love has a pull. That's the main point. Still, honest self-reflection shows that Europeans in Africa aren't always angels. Honestly, I spent the past few days examining the situation and realized that no one should make life-changing decisions based on a single moment in history. There's more to the story than what's visible."

"Meaning what?"

"I met your father, Lenin, over the past few days and formed my conclusions. There should be no more excuses between us. I see the celestial bodies, the moon, and the stars in your eyes, watching and listening. Looking at your face, I can hear the waves breaking on the surf zone of the shore. I love the waves and their mysterious ways. Over time, waves come from somewhere very far, but they never tell because, perhaps, they don't know either. I want you and me to behave similarly, overlook the shores we've crashed into, but move on to one shoreline after another, as long as we are together."

The next day, Barend and Georgi drive to the Free State. Georgi has arranged with Sanna to help with her errands while she is away.

Georgi's mother, Ellen, had many unflattering stories about what they used to call the Orange Free State. In the minds of black people, the Free State is still notorious for its ridiculous apartheid laws. There was a law in the 19th Century that aimed to stop the influx of Asians and the removal of White criminals entering the state. Laws that prohibited Indians from staying more than a day in the province still stick in the minds of Indian communities, as Apartheid treated them with the utmost disrespect by White people there.

It is dark when Georgi and Barend arrive at a remote smallholding outside Bloemfontein. As they navigate the shadowy, tree-lined driveway, Georgi's apprehension quickly increases. A thought crosses her mind that she might be a target of Barend's 'final retribution.' She has not seen Barend show any emotion about Mimi-Koo. Instead, he has always been mechanical, factual, and dry. Odessa's vivid image of Barend as a 'white mamba seducing you with his smooth tongue' suddenly feels real.

When the car stops opposite a majestic farmhouse, Barend says, "We are both tired. Let's go inside and sleep. We'll enjoy our sightseeing in the morning."

Georgi remembers that she never told anyone where she was going. Right now, she is in the middle of nowhere with a mysterious man who has strange stories. She sends Nathaniel an 'SOS,' then recites Psalm 23 until she finally falls asleep.

In the dim light of dawn, Barend's loud whistling wakes Georgi.

"This place, spooky after dark but paradise at daybreak," remarks Georgi, relieved that she is still alive.

"I know what you're thinking. This used to be my uncle's little farm."

Georgi says, "Farm, now abandoned?"

"The family went to Australia. They gave me many keys to watch the property, and I come here now and then to think. My uncle is a Professor of Theology and Philosophy, a dangerous mix, enough to drive anyone crazy. He called this place 'verligte.'"

"Aha? Isn't that… political?"

"Yes, 'enlightened' in English. In the past, when Apartheid was legal, political tendencies by Afrikaners were either 'Verligte' or 'verkrampte.'"

"Yeah? And which side of the fence were you on?"

He directs her to a large balcony where the table is overflowing with a buffet. Georgi thinks Barend makes an excellent meal for two. She relishes snoek fish and freshly baked bread. She then enjoys her favorite cappuccino, mixed with fresh orange juice to help neutralize the caffeine. Barend seems to get great satisfaction from his Castle Lager.

"My father enjoys angling to save money, she says. There's a lake in Rosedale with plenty of rainbow trout."

"I hope to join your father one day. We'll leave you home and bring the largest baby you have ever seen."

"They all say that. One guy said that men are as fascinated with fishing as they are with women's breasts, but they can't seem to decide which gives them more kicks. Do you agree?"

"What counts is the idea of casting a line and waiting for something to happen."

"Why would you leave me home, then?"

"Well, you can come along… help carry our spin-casting outfit. I'd have to buy you a pair of hip boots, though, unless you own one."

"If you do come, do so during the fall fishing season. That's my father's prime time."

Later, Georgi stands alone near the edge of a large timber porch on the other side of the mansion, marveling at the solitary mountain view. She gasps with delight as the soft wind whistles against the sweet thorn, fading away and then gusting and whistling again. Her eyes slowly move across the lilies. She spots an army of frogs in the pond and marvels at the long weaverbird nests hanging precariously from a twig. The derelict garden is lined with flowerbeds filled with tulips, daisies, colorful little daffodils, and other flowers she cannot identify.

She falls in love with the flowering shrubs and mutters, 'How I adore this place.''

Barend's voice startles her, "Yes, it's Verligte. I see you are smitten. The flowering vegetation that you see extending over the hills is called Fynbos. Here we have Protea, Rose, Erica… you name it. My folk spent their days here doing their part to contribute to ecological conservation. Of course, they made mint-producing seeds."

"*Greeny-beeny* couple? Very sharp of them to abandon their ecological passion and fly off to Australia, don't you think?"

"Forced out by circumstances. My aunt, Jessica. Felt betrayed by the present crop of leaders…"

"Black leaders, you mean?"

"She wasted her university days peddling liberal ideas, making a fool of herself."

"Wow, that's heavy. I learned whites left the country in droves before Mandela became president. Odessa has been studying South African expats in Toronto. She thought most of them made fools of themselves because they now want to return. And do you know what they miss most...?"

"Sunshine?"

"No, swimming pools and maids."

"Your sister's research sounds like a bit of a thumb suck. My aunt feared for her life, living here at Verligte. White farmers had become easy prey. The elderly couple left this estate and walked out on South Africa with heavy hearts; that much I know."

"What a shame."

As they relocate back inside, Georgi notices a large row of mud buildings with a well-constructed fence, separated from the main house."

"Are those your neighbors over there? She asks.

"No, that's our native compounds, where our black workers live."

"Native compounds? Are you sure you told your aunt and uncle about me?"

"Yes, they know we are here, and nothing makes them happier."

"What did you tell them about me?"

"I called them. My aunt laughed and quipped, 'Today salvation has come to the Van der Wats' house.'"

"Yeah? What's that supposed to mean?"

"That was exactly my question to her. She replied, 'Zacchaeus had to fall from a tree, while Saul of Tarsus went on a journey to Damascus before they discovered the light. That was her response."

"I see. What about Sofia? Has she gone to Damascus or fallen off any tree yet?"

"Forget about her. My aunt encouraged us to enjoy ourselves here and experience the tall grass waving to the wind."

"As a matter of interest, any relations with Niel Van der Watt, the music composer?"

"All the Van der Watts are related," he laughs.

"Yeah? He wrote 'I Am the Voice of Africa'. My father appreciates it. I tried to read an Afrikaans poem framed nicely. I've never encountered Ockert Kruger before. I blame it all on the walls between cultures and languages. I wish I could read Spanish, Japanese, or other languages. They must be saying something profound, hidden from us, and making us poorer! Please read the poem and explain it to me. It must have been special to your uncle."

Barend downloads the frame from the antique mantelpiece over the fireplace. "It's called `Golwe op die Strand`' – 'Waves on the beach' for you. After listening to him read and translate, she says, "Delightful. Do you think I'll ever learn your language?"

"Language? Afrikaans is not just a language, dear child, but an experience, a spiritual journey we embarked upon two centuries ago."

"But a spiritual journey is about seeking truth. How far have you gone? And in your spiritual journey, do you include people of a darker hue, *les gens qui me ressemblent*?"

"Well, it's been a hazardous journey full of risks in Africa. If only we had figured it out long ago, that color would have nothing to do with it. I agree; the poem is special. How do you feel when you step out into the fresh air and soak up the sun's gentle rays?"

"Oh, I like that a lot. Walking barefoot across the wild park is like watching eagles, bee-eaters, weavers, and starlings marvel at the wondrous landscape and the blue skies."

"Have you been to the Kruger?" Barend asks.

"I am a prisoner of hope. But, listen, I have two nice ones on our mantelpiece at home. One is by Miriam Makeba."

"Of the *Pata Pata* fame? I didn't know she was a poet."

"Music is poetry, Barry. Besides, Makeba was not just about *Pata Pata* and ethnic clicks; she was a serious political activist. I'm amazed at how little people know about her in this country. At thirty, she delivered a significant speech at the United Nations. It's been in our living room since I was five years old. Part of it says:

Would you not resist if you were allowed no rights in your own country because the color of your skin is different from that of the rulers, and if you were punished for even asking for equality? I appeal to you and all the countries of the world to do everything possible to prevent the impending tragedy. I appeal to you to save the lives of our leaders, empty the prisons...

For her pain, the South African government revoked her citizenship. Georgi tells Barend that she visited a Soweto suburb called Mofolo, where Makeba had lived with her mother before they were banished. When her elderly mother passed away, the regime refused her permission to enter South Africa to bury her. Stepping inside that small house, the surreal scene made Georgi's head spin. She imagined seeing Miriam walking out, bucket in hand, to fetch water from the tap outside. The kitchen was tiny; from her seat, she could see the doorframes leading to the two small bedrooms and an additional room that served as a dining area or living room.

"How could Miriam Makeba survive in such an environment? The new tenants, an elderly couple, must have thought, 'This girl is round the bend.''

"Later, under the wilting peach tree, I recited Makeba's speech to them. The man said, 'Many knew little about Makeba because of the system. The media told little about her. But we secretly bought her records in Swaziland."

"Yes," says Barend, "a prophet is never known in his hometown. At school, they taught us that people like Makeba were communist terrorists."

"And at home? How did you all feel after your sister's death?"

Barend's silence speaks volumes. Georgi says, "I have another great poem on our mantelpiece. When I turned eleven, my father framed it himself and gave it to me as a birthday present. It's called 'Childhood' by Margaret Walker. It sounds simple, yet so deep and mysterious. I wonder what she had in mind. When I recite it, I think of the people around me: neighbors, friends, and people I love. What do you think?"

Lost for words, Barend brings wine, and they chink their glasses, drink to each other's health, and embrace.

"Stay with me forever, and we'll decipher Walker together here on this land."

"Tell me about your Afrikaans poem."

"Ockert Kruger?"

"Yes, I could feel its meaning through the sounds, like a collision between the flood of the Mississippi downstream and the tidal wave upstream surging like a Tsunami. I think Kruger was inspired, which is more than I can say about you. One moment, you are a number 007, a licensed-to-kill agent, and the very next, your name is Robert Frost?"

"Ah, Mrs De Bruyn's favorite; 'What gets lost in translation'! I'm sure my high school teacher would be proud of me today. The truth is, before I met you, I was never into poetry. I now realize that perhaps something has been missing. Are you thinking of publishing?"

"Oh, Yeah. I'm almost there with my anthology. It's called 'Sharpeville'."

"Sharpeville?"

"Why, you don't like it?"

"No, no. I like it. Sharpeville is nice."

"Nice? That's not good enough. When are you planning on translating Kruger for me?"

"Save that for later."

"May I challenge my knight in shining armor to take me to Manenberg for a visit with Saartjie Baartman? In my dreams, she is still alive, and I want to be inside her galaxy, making her cry and laugh because she must have done all of that during her troubled episode in Europe."

"Her story is upsetting. I am more upset with our education here because we knew nothing about her story growing up in the Cape."

"I wish to meet Diana Ferrus while at it."

"Consider it done. Meantime, can my damsel keep a secret?"

"I chose my parents wisely. Of course, I can keep your secret."

Barend holds Georgi's hand, and she closes her eyes. He places a frayed pouch in her hand and says, "Now you can look."

"What is this? Oh my gosh! It's a... Is this genuine?"

"Never mind 'genuine,' try rare."

"This is a diamond, Barry!"

"It's graded slightly below 'Hope of Africa.' This stone is from the belly of the land of Kuito, and it is worth millions of dollars."

"What!"

"It was christened 'Uhuru' by the survivors of that ill-fated camp before you were weaned from the warm arms of your mother."

"Uhuru! No kidding! What must I do with it?"

"It's yours, but remember you're now like a caged bird being freed to fly alone."

Georgi examines the stone and hurls it like a hot squash ball. She sings and chants widely, "Rough-cut, square-cut, pear-shaped, whatever... diamonds are a girl's best friend. I don't know what hit me, but I feel like Elizabeth Taylor."

Georgi remains unsettled. As late afternoon approaches, Barend helps her to the stoep while he goes inside for a nap. She remains dazed, seriously weighing up her options. She misses her mother, her hare-brained brother, and her quiet, wintry suburb of Rosedale. Tears start rolling down her face, and she can now identify with Ellen's loneliness. She misses Odessa's company. More than anything, she realizes she has lived in symbiosis with her sister since the day they were born. Without Odessa, a vast space threatens to drive her to the edge. She wonders if her life would be worth anything without Odessa, the only person on whom she can blurt out her every emotion. Odessa's every reaction to all her feelings is like oxygen to her soul, and right now, she is suffocating.

After the sun disappears, she has her moments of cooling off. She carefully strolls to watch the flickering stars and the distant moon.

Her long walk takes her across a stream to the native compounds. She becomes uncomfortable observing the muddy surroundings, the poorly dressed children, boys, and girls playing or walking around. There is a sprinkling of young women doing chores while their men are in the fields. The poorly constructed row of houses is made of logs coated with mud plaster. She wonders if the structures are durable enough to withstand strong winds and heavy rains.

An African man emerges from one of the houses, wearing short pants, black gum boots, and a broad smile.

"Can I help you?"

"No, I'm just looking around."

"Your colored people don't stay here. They have their place on that side of the hill. I know all of them by name. Who are you looking for?"

"I am a visitor here. I came with Barend?"

"Yes? Baas Barend? I know him. His relatives went overseas. Are you here to make the Baas happy?" he puts it, flashing a wicked wink. "My name is Teulo. You are free to spend the night here with me if the Baas throws you out," he laughs and walks back inside.

When she returns, she finds Barend relaxing on the balcony. She immediately asks him if his uncle and aunt plan to build decent structures for their African workers. Barend deflects the question by pointing out that without the farm, the Africans and their many children would be starving in their Native Reserves.

"I don't appreciate your answer."

"Well, what should I say?" he retorts, "Ask the people who deserted this farm?"

"Your aunt and uncle, you mean? I find it astonishing that you gifted me a magnificent diamond, yet there are mud huts with poorly dressed women and children just across the stream you don't seem to care about."

Barend rises and walks out. At midnight, Georgi steps out of the bedroom dressed in an unusually bright, see-through dress, with a white doek on her head. Barend can see her belly button through her fancy-looking outfit, and when he looks into her eyes, he thinks she resembles an angel about to fall. After he apologizes for his snappy response earlier, she asks, "Barry, where did this stone come from?"

"Do you remember those days I disappeared? I met someone who said, "Give this stone to Georgi and tell her I love her..."

"That someone wouldn't be Lenin, my father, by any chance?"

"No name, please. These walls have ears. I suggest you dig a hole that only you will remember its location."

The moon's brightness is intense and hangs low over the distant maples. Barend says, 'This is the happiest moment of my life.' Georgi wraps her arms around him and spins him around as if she's mad.

"Now, regarding the Afrikaner secrets, come clean tonight as promised."

"Promised? So I did."

Barend fiddles with his laptop, and Nat King Cole's 'Stardust' sounds set the farmhouse ablaze. He slowly folds Georgi's hand, wincing slightly, "Yes, let me tell you something about this Afrikaner called Barend Van der Watt. Pardon the lack of real waves crashing on the shoreline, but we can gaze at the tall grass waves in the wind and pay homage to the full moon watching over us. If you stick to your promise to be good to me tonight, I'll do the translation of Ockert's poem someday."

"Someday won't do. What about Mimi-Koo? 'Someday' can't give me sleep and peace. I think about her endlessly. I even suffer constant dreams about her; sometimes, she smiles and sings like an angel."

"Mimi-Koo? Brittle bones, a powerful voice like Mimi Coertse. That was Mimi. She is here now, enjoying 'Stardust,' singing along and rooting for me."

Barend takes a cherry-shaped, heart-shaped ring container out of his pocket. As he opens it, he drops to his knees and says, "Georgi Moffet-King, you know I love you. Let us spend the rest of our lives together. Will you marry me...?"

Georgi screeches clumsily, "Wow! If I must..."

Barend holds Georgi's hand, slips his diamond ring onto her finger, and whispers, "Let's try it for size."

She feels dizzy and says, "This ring! I feel beautiful."

"You're special to me. This ring belonged to my grandma from Chantilly, France."

"Oh, it's priceless! Divine! Now that I'm wearing her ring, tell me more about her."

"There's nothing more to tell, Georgi."

Barend's ambivalence concerns her. Is there a hidden skeleton behind her story?

CHAPTER 22

Money to buy ARVs

Georgi and Odessa exchange emails:

'Dearest Odessa,

How I wish you could respond to my emails! Anyway, the latest news here is concerning. Barend told me a beauty therapist named Jardine came forward with information about Luca. Finian has been embarrassing himself at the Provincial Prosecutor's office, claiming he knows who killed him. According to Barend, the Luca case was solved long ago, but national interest had to take precedence over everything else. Dad said he wants me to keep quiet. In short, the Luca dossier is stone-cold dead. But knowing you, I'd rather keep my advice to myself on this.

Second, there's Nikita. Remember her? The girl known for 'Kaffirs' and 'Hotnots'? A month ago, she called from Langa and invited me to her aunt's place. After avoiding her invitation for several days, I finally gave in. As I walked through the shelters in the scorching heat, brushing past malnourished children, it became clear that while the term 'apartheid' may have originated with the Afrikaners, the British were the ones behind this bizarre concept in the first place. Nowadays, the 'Boers' are the ones taking the blame. Did you know that a chief named Langalibalele from the Drakensberg was imprisoned on Robben Island in the 19th century for opposing British colonial rule? They named Nikita's area 'Langa Township' in his honor, making it the oldest Black settlement in Cape Town. How impressive! Anyway, Nikita was shocking, showing no trace of her famed Coco Chanel flair, except for the odd mascara and her usual afternoon delight. She told me all about her plight. When Finian, whom she referred to as a shameless narcissist, fired her, she fell on hard times. But her nightmare came when she discovered her HIV condition. Her folks in Pinelands, just a stone's throw away, rejected her and made life a living hell. However, her aunt, who barely has two beans to rub together, was happy to accommodate her in her shack, provided she kept mum about her HIV status. Nikita needed money to buy ARVs. The hospital could not supply her with Nevirapine until her CD4 count dropped below 200. Poor Nikita couldn't wait. She said, 'Please, Odessa's sister, I am afraid to die. There's no such thing as protected sex,' she said.

I had a major mascara crisis, I assure you! The girl needs all the help she can get. Marcia was more than generous. Fifteen minutes after charging, Nikita was walking away from the hospital registrar's office, carrying a sachet of medication and a bowl of rations.

Finally, I hope you have dropped the Pedro case because you are on your own.

All the best to Mom and the two young lions (and to Dad, if he's there with you)

An hour later: 'Dear Georgi,
Did you ask your two-timing, AIDS-infected phony why she circulated lies about me?
Dear Odessa,
No.
And why not?
-Odessa.
Nikita has post-traumatic stress disorder. I'm not planning on ruining her life any further.
Georgi, you don't seem to care at all that your Nikita has ruined MY life. I guess it makes you feel good to align yourself with my light-skinned African enemies while I struggle alone on the creek. 'Mascara crisis'! You always have your mascara tubes and applicators handy in your purse—they should have been useful. I appreciate you keeping your thoughts about Luca to yourself. Right now, I need your opinion as much as I need a hole in my head. Your father may deny it, but he knows what happened to Luca. I've moved on from this.
From Odessa Mofokeng of Rosedale.
P/S. I wonder why I'm not surprised I was the last to know you've been scheming all along to marry the white man. I guess he's one of those who now claim they had nothing to do with apartheid. Pity the nice chap, Ryan. But you'll never get Ryan out of your mind; I know you. As for Pedro, I'm conducting my inquiry to determine a 'critical mass' of victims. Your name is at the top of that list, I assure you.
Love you, Odessa. Fix yourself Quix soup. As for Pedro? Forget about him.
A few days later, Georgi receives a call. Sounding excited, Odessa says, "Hi, Georgi. You'll never believe this... about Pedro? The courts will now believe us because I'm not the only one. Three other girls, plus you, of course. That makes five of us."
"Odessa, you miss the point. I won't get involved in this..."
"You're scared of what your white boyfriend will think of you, knowing you were once raped? Of course, your white boyfriend will reject you because a colored girl who gets raped is a whore in their books..."
"Please, Odessa, I beg you, my Dear Sister. Drop this whole case."
"Georgi, does it occur to you that Pedro may have raped many girls and that he continues to use his high office to refine his skill?"
"You're on your own, Odessa. I won't be going along with you."
"Well, in that case, you'll have to stand before a judge and deny what Pedro did to you."
"Please, Odessa, don't."

CHAPTER 23

Ashley Kriel of Bonteheuwel

Away from Verligte, Georgi is completely 'strung up' as she contemplates the day's activities. She makes a point to remind some of her relatives and friends that the planned get-together is not an engagement party, but a solemn occasion to honor Mtunzi Radebe.

She takes a call from Lieutenant Morrison, "This is Morrison. I am outside your gate. Get your skates on; I'm waiting."

"Waiting for whom? I'm expecting the Taungs to pick me up."

"Please, Miss King, make it snappy. Mrs Taung is not coming. Hurry up, we are late already."

Georgi feels insignificant after losing her willpower to stand up to Lieutenant Morrison earlier. She feels uncomfortable with Morrison's insistence on treating her like a brain-dead celebrity.

"Thank God I'm in the suicide seat today," Georgi jokes. "Last time, you made me feel like Miss Daisy. Are you alone for a change? Where's Morgan Freeman?"

"Inspector Mbatha, you mean? I'm never alone, Miss King. You're not going to give me trouble, I hope."

"Do people give you trouble?"

"Sometimes, even my male colleagues often see me as a woman and assume I have a high level of estrogen and need their help."

"You pack a punch, don't you?"

"I tell the truth."

"You seem concerned about me. Why?"

"Why would anyone turn their backs on the comfort of Toronto and boost the numbers of maids on this sweltering Continent?"

"I'm not a maid; I'm an au pair."

"Perhaps one day, when I'm mature enough to retire, you'll take me slowly through the difference."

The car speeds along quietly. Georgi's cell phone rings, showing an unfamiliar number. She pauses briefly before answering.

"I'm glad I found you, Georgi. Ryan here."

"Hi, Ryan. How did you get my number?"

Can we meet this weekend, Saturday, at Midrand Estate? A couple of friends are eager to meet you.

"Ryan, I'll get back to you later. I'm in a bit of a pickle right now."

"Aren't we all," whispers Morrison as Georgi hangs up. "I don't suppose you have a satisfied customer on the other side of the line."

Georgi does not answer. After a while, she says, "Does Marcia know you're taking me to Soweto?"

"Yes. And so does the president of the country. Your father is a powerful man, Miss King, a cloak-and-dagger type, pulling strings here, tweaking cords there... to get his way! Mind-blowing."

"You don't like him?"

"Since he returned to the country, our NIA offices have been busy. This new group of politicians and top officials is using state facilities to hide their tracks. Freedom fighters from all over Africa have returned to settle old scores. I see trouble brewing among politicians, and if you include the threat of exiles, this country will be like Krakatoa's eye."

"What's that got to do with my father?"

"How much do you know about him?"

"Between you and me? I discovered things about him that made me lose faith in Homo sapiens."

"The struggle has casualties. Let's judge our ancestors with empathy. Your father is a good man. Honestly, he's one of the most attractive guys in town right now. I'm sorry, I shouldn't have spoken about your father that way. I really wouldn't mind having dinner with him."

"Yeah? Where? Inside a tent near some salty African lake...?"

"Inside anywhere.' He is an enigma; he received his early training at an exclusive private school and didn't stop using his brain when he entered the murky world of political struggle. He shuns attention, and I admire that in a man. The corridors of power are in absolute awe of him, and his sudden arrival – incognito, I must add – has unsettled his former allies. I'm sure you're proud of him."

"Yes, he protects his daughters like an endangered rhino assembly. He has been sticking his nose in my business since I arrived here. Why shouldn't I be bloody proud of him?"

"What kind of business?"

"He seems to have this thing about the guy I fancy."

"Yes, I know. He has spent the past few weeks smoothing out some long-standing issues. Be patient with him. I understand you're officially introducing the guy to the rest of your folks."

"Serious stuff because the guy, as you call him, is rushing to get us matched. I just hope I'm not making a fool of myself."

"Once you've recited those vows, you've entered a dark, one-way tunnel; the only exit is a risky U-turn. Sometimes, the vows turn into a curse. I can tell you a thing or two. I've been there. Women are suckers for sparkles and bells..."

"But so are men."

"No, men are only fixated on their conjugal rights, that's all."

"Yes, the tunnel of love. You split up with your man? You don't look old enough,

Lieutenant."

"Please call me Zola. I am twenty-seven, and I am a 'returned soldier.' Age has nothing to do with it," Morrison pants as she puts her foot hard on the gas. "It was doomed from the beginning. For a girl, if you feel those teeny-weeny niggling qualms, it's time to disengage. Don't tie that knot. In my case, I know we shouldn't have set sail, as I could feel at the outset our yacht listing to starboard. It all began with spats over ridiculous things, such as wearing a miniskirt. Do you know he even accused me of flirting with my work colleagues? It drove me to the absolute edge. My coach once said, 'Nothing is as potent as jealousy except sex.'"

"Oh, my nerves! Why should women go through the mill...?"

"I wanted it to work. So, I avoided confrontation, but that only emboldened him and drove him crazy."

"Walking on eggshells allows them to take full control of your life."

"Then we got into our Desert Storm; I was now earning a higher salary. Our job is specialized and risky, you see."

"And lucrative..."

"Most men feel emasculated, and that's the beginning of the U-turn of your blind subway."

"I sometimes open my eyes in the heat of darkness, sweating, all in fear over what I am getting myself into."

"My family and friends had a field day. You see, my ex was an indigenous African. When we first hooked up, some members of my community abandoned me. The rest gave a lukewarm response. No one said it out loud when things went wrong, but I could tell from their cynical eyes that they were thinking, 'We told you so'."

"Indigenous? Aren't you indigenous, Zola?"

"Search me. To be considered Indigenous in this country, you have to qualify at birth. Having prominent melanization plays a major role. It's not easy being a young person of color in South Africa. What are your thoughts, Georgi?"

"Colored? I don't know, Zola. This colored thing..."

"Stop being PC," squeals Morrison. "It's our reality. You and I are a reality, and we are hurting."

"Phooey! Now I'm terrified. Time-bomb stuff this! It's gonna take me forever to navigate my way through our democratic minefield, I see."

Join the club. But before we part ways, tell me now—this Afrikaner, do you want to marry an Afrikaner? They told me about his family background. Don't you think he's doing everything to make himself seem authentic in the new political order?

"You mean...?"

"Hooking up with a colored girl, I mean."

"A black girl, you mean?"

"Okay, a black girl."

"Maybe. I can't read his mind."

"Just brace yourself for a rough ride. If you let his white clan poke their noses into your affair, you can kiss everything goodbye..."

"You got that right. Anyway, Zola – between you and me – I've got this little thing poking its nose into the works. I am in love with another man."

The car skidded to a perilous halt, and they narrowly avoided an accident.

"Go on."

"He's what you call an indigenous African, although his mother is Indian."

"Oh! Now I understand why you are in a pickle. You are in deep waters, Girl. Men of such mixed blood are dangerously sexy; I know them."

"I've suffered nightmares all my life, but this is the mother of them all."

"Is he in love with you, too?"

"I've never heard him say the word love, but all his actions suggest it, and I can't help but lead him on.

"Does Van der Watt Know?"

"Maybe. He's a spy, isn't he? You spies seem everywhere, unlike that little rat Anna Sage, who snitched on Nat Dillinger. I don't know what to do. My existence seems to be on autopilot right now."

The car moves forward smoothly, but the long silence makes Georgi a bit uneasy. Morrison breaks the uncomfortable pause by saying, "I learn you are a powerful woman. A left-handed black woman who writes angry poems can never be on autopilot."

"Aha!"

"Yes, my bosses gave me all sorts of trivia about you... to prepare me for what I'd be dealing with. I know you don't care for daffodils in your poetry, but heavy tanks and missiles."

"Oh, please! When did you first find out that my sister and I were in the country?"

"Long before you left Toronto. Luca's death alerted us to strange movements in our party politics. I've been shadowing you since you arrived; it's a burden I must bear until you return to Canada."

"But why? What's the big deal?"

"Your father, that's what it is. It's about the post-apartheid fallout. Only God knows: secret shallow graves, bleak relics, footprints of the struggle scattered across the Continent. Yesterday's events are catching up with us today, and there's a sense of paranoia at the highest levels. Don't worry; I borrowed the lines from somewhere... Maybe Archbishop Tutu's words? But get this: I'm repeating all of this because you are part of the clan..."

"The clan being a collection of spies, I suppose."

"Yes."

"You do like your job, don't you?"

Morrison sighs, "Yes, it's not a job for me. My mother died in a police van when I was seven."

"I'm sorry."

The vehicle slows down, allowing Morrison to relate the Bonteheuwel sob story of Ashley Kriel, killed by the police in the 1980s.

"We lived in a colored township called Eldorado Park, not far from here. We celebrate Ashley's life yearly and pay tribute to his struggle for liberation. After one of these celebrations, the apartheid police and soldiers swooped on the township, arresting many young people and shooting dead those who tried to flee. The following day, they came looking for certain people and then arrested my mother. They later told us she had died without explaining how that had happened. The people remain angry. Eldorado is now a crime-ridden part of South Africa, one of the many hideous blots on our social landscape. Some of us believe that Eldorado should be part of Soweto and that Coloreds and Africans should start waging their struggle together. Otherwise, they'll continue fighting shadows, being exploited as voting cattle by crafty politicians. Soweto is a seductive place nestling on top of a hidden political volcano. Someone created a monster we romanticize or lie about! My father still lives in Eldos with his third wife. For me, it's Aluta Continua. I want to get into the head of the apartheid policeman responsible for my mom's death. And the day I find him, I'll ask him if he has his daughter and what he was thinking when he killed my innocent mother..."

"How did you get this job? Did you apply to be a spy?"

"I studied psychology and majored in intelligence. From there, I was summoned to the Union Building and offered my new career without applying."

"Really? Summoned by the President? It's called nepotism where I come from..."

The vehicle suddenly jerks as Morrison retorts with a dash of anger, "Where you come from, there aren't stockpiles of armaments stashed in remote farms by faceless militia; the old regime has foot soldiers that will never rest until they return this country to apartheid or turn it into an endless bloodbath. Our recruits include émigrés or expats who masquerade as enemies of the state. We gather a whole heap of dirt that way because certain elements here and abroad think African governments are stupid."

"No kidding! I sense a real moral vacuum in this Rainbow Nation. African governments throughout their history have not covered themselves in glory, to be honest. Puri, my new mother, says while she expects better from the ANC, she won't be holding her breath."

"The ANC is already colonized by Multinationals and hollowed out through factions. Unless its leaders handle things creatively, I see trouble brewing."

"What trouble?"

"What trouble! There's big trouble in Africa. Don't you know?"

"This is Mandela's party you are talking about."

"Georgi, this is politics. Mandela is a figurehead, no different from Reagan or Trudeau. Unless you're a strong leader like Margaret Thatcher, you can't run a democracy."

"Yes, she who emasculated the unions and closed the mines. That's no power but tyranny."

"Why didn't Tony Blair overturn Thatcher's excesses, then? I'll tell you: men want to please everybody. And women, we don't care about people's rantings during the day as long as we can go back to feed our children and read them bedtime stories. I think I've said too much. Please keep your mouth shut about these things, okay? I'm not ready to join the dole queue."

"So, everyone keeps telling me, Keep your mouth shut."

They slow down and stop outside Orlando Hall. Several Metro police vehicles are around the perimeter, and a few more are inside the parking enclosure. Smatterings of coniferous and deciduous trees shelter the newly refurbished and imposing structure. Morrison parks the car under a pine tree, and as Georgi steps out, she stares admiringly at her. She notices Georgi glowing in her prim and powder blue trouser suit.

Morrison looks Georgi in the eye and says, "And think about this, Miss King; I don't like giving advice, but as a returned soldier, my words might be worth something to your stubborn self. When the time comes, go ahead and marry your Afrikaans Prince Van der Watt, but keep your indigenous man hidden somewhere in your heart. You can take him wherever you want, any day or night. All women have their indigenous men, their true desires, the men of their dreams, tucked away secretly in one dark corner. In moments of passion, the indigenous man lurks in the shadows, watching, building up heat and fury. Go ahead, marry Van der Watt. Otherwise, you'll hesitate forever and lose what you have…"

They walk toward a crowd that is slowly gathering around.

"A crowd indeed! What is Lunga, the homme célèbre, doing here?" Georgi asks rhetorically.

"Glitzy Lunga! Paternity has become the trendy cliché these days. I can't stand the kinky hair, though! I last saw him at the Beesfontein wedding. We were there, babysitting you and your sister. You couldn't see us because we are professionals…" Morrison brags as she walks away."

"What are you doing here, Lunga?"

"Aren't you happy to see me, Georgi? I am family. In Africa, we don't invite people to weddings."

"Oh, yeah? And whose wedding is this?"

"I'm told it's a prelude to your wedding with that white man. Where is your sister, and how is my baby? I learn he looks just like me," he screeches loudly. "You are responsible, Georgi. You talked her into running away back to Canada with my child."

"How sad."

Family members, friends, and a few officials are inside the basement conference room. Cecilia and Reeva – her unreadable permanent smile intact – are holding hands warmly. They are having an amusing chat with Puri and Caleb. Finian and Doreen look bored but smile politely when they see Georgi. Barend approaches from the east side, accompanied by his friends, minus his family. He cuts a dashing figure in his light Khalique suit and pink shirt. Georgi catches Retief, who tells her that Sofia is absent;

without further comment. Puri's 1950s wiggle dress, with its notably accentuated bust and high waist, makes Georgi pause for a second, thinking, 'She looks youthful and pretty.'

Following the pleasantries, people mingle around, waiting to drive to the 'Heroes Acre,' a shrine dedicated to the heroes of the struggle located at Soweto's Avalon Cemetery.

Georgi walks to a man in a black corduroy suit who cuts a lonely figure at the edge of the parking lot under a maple tree.

"Why am I not surprised to see you here, Mr April?"

"Your smile tells me you finally cracked your 'Globetrot' and 'Uhuru puzzles," he giggles.

"You lied to me. I wanted Barend's secret contact, and you sent me on a merry chase."

"The man was retired and given a job as Director-General in KwaZulu-Natal. How was I supposed to know that?"

"You're a spy. Were you lying when you said you knew everything?"

"That's true. And do you remember the two Kuito gentlemen, Tom and Gerry? They recently joined the army as Lieutenants. Your father, Lenin, claims he knows nothing about their sudden rise. Do you believe that? Since he arrived here from Toronto, we've only had hurricanes and tornadoes. He's been rubbing elbows with the high and mighty of the rainbow nation..."

"And it makes your blood boil. Anyway, have a good day." Georgi starts to walk away.

"Before you go, congratulations on the generous gift from Barend's aunt and uncle. Jessica is a good person. I'm unsure about the uncle with his habit of raising mountain tortoises and always chasing butterflies and all..."

Georgi walks back, her heart pounding a bit. She has a sinking feeling that Barend may be hiding secrets from her. She whispers, "What are you talking about, April?"

Out of his depth, the secret service man mumbles, "I'm talking about the estate, Georgi. Verligte. Don't pretend now. Barend was his favorite. The farms are being returned to us because we are the genuine owners..."

"Us?"

"The indigenous children. Many whites are leaving the country. I'm happy for you, getting that farm on a platter. Your mother's contacts will help with the export markets in Europe for your daisies."

This is news to Georgi. All she knows about the farm is that Barend's relatives emigrated, leaving him to care for it. Failing to conceal her bewilderment and rage, she whispers, 'How could Barend hide this crucial part of the story from me?'

"Are you certain they gifted him that whole property, Mr April?"

"Of course, I'm sure. Not just him, but you as well. It's yours, Darling."

"How did that rumor get to you?"

For a moment, April is speechless. He finally replies, "Call me Ganon, Georgina. You and I are one nation, an indigenous nation. And there's no rumor between us, Georgina. It's the grapevine. Maybe your white boyfriend is keeping it for a Valentine's surprise. Don't mention my name, right?"

Georgi gasps for air. After a moment, she stops gasping but braces herself for a confrontation with Barend. She says, "Everyone I trust tells lies straight-faced, Mr. April. And that includes my father. I'm no longer anybody's adolescent little girl."

"What? Please, Darling." April murmurs.

Georgi walks away but quickly comes back, daring April to swear on his uncle's grave that what he just told her is true—that Barend is the beneficiary of Verligte.

April hesitates and then says, "Two different people concurred... How come you don't know?"

Georgi reaches into her handbag and pulls out a leather pouch. There is something inside. She says quietly, "Mr April, about 'Uhuru'; here, I want you to have 'Uhuru.'"

"Georgina!" April blurts out, completely stunned, as his arm swiftly snaps out like a chameleon's tongue. He tucks the pouch securely inside his corduroy jacket without checking what's inside. His whole body begins to tremble. He whispers, "Are you serious? This is 'Uhuru' from Angola."

"Three people concurred, ye of little faith! You once mentioned wanting to run an NGO in your neighborhood, right? You said it was your mission to save humanity, including all those young unemployed people who have HIV."

"Yeah?"

"I have faith in you, Ganon."

"Georgina! 'Uhuru' ' And how do you expect me to launder the damn stone?"

"You're with the National Intelligence. I'm sure you mingle with what my sister calls the new rainbow upper crust. I learn you shared a vegetable patch with Mr Nelson Mandela on Robben Island. Child's play, laundering 'Uhuru'... "

"Damn, Girl. You make my life difficult," he whispers still. "I know Lenin gave you this thing from Kuito. Did you discuss it with your boyfriend? He might even have had you bugged. He scares me too much, that white man. Does he know?"

"I'm keeping it a surprise for Valentine's Day. Mum is the word," Georgi smiles and walks away.

Duly freed from her usual spectacles, Kora happily heads toward Georgi and invites her to visit the Northwest someday.

"You mean it?"

"If you can, your cousins will be glad to have you there. I am your blood aunt because Kian is my brother. When I met him at the Holiday Inn, I thought I was seeing a ghost. He told me everything. At first, I was angry with him for keeping such a secret even from me. I blamed him for making me speak out of turn to you. My priest cleared me and accused my sister-in-law of treachery. Now that I know we are family, we need to come together and pay our respects to Daniel, your uncle. You and Odessa should see his grave and help me properly engrave the headstone."

Georgi gazes at Kora and realizes that without her sunglasses, something reassuring about her eyes is revealed. She steps closer, takes her hand, and they embrace warmly.

"Have you changed your mind about my plans, Aunt Kora?"

"Your plans? I guess you're talking about the white man you're planning to marry. Since you're asking me, I'll tell you. We all, including your father and Odessa, agree that this is wrong. It's an awkward situation you're putting yourself in. You are a Mofokeng. Is there no Black man who fits into your family profile? Since you asked me, no, I won't change my mind until those who oppressed us and broke up African families apologize and pay reparations. But your uncle and I will be expecting you at the Northwest."

"Thanks, Aunt Kora. I'll spend time with you and my cousins."

CHAPTER 24

And Voila! I'm Jewish?!

Before the procession to Avalon Cemetery, Puri, who looks like a lost tourist in an African jungle, signals Georgi to come closer to her under a pine.

Puri says, "Now that you have met me, you know that I am the one who gave life to you, don't you, Esther? I am delighted."

"Puri, can we agree on one thing? I'm just as happy as you are. I know I am your daughter, but my name is Georgi."

Puri is quiet for a while. A tear slips down her cheek. She says dejectedly, "That is the name Kian gave you, based on a lie. It hurts me to say it. No matter. Hearing you say you are my daughter fills me with satisfaction. Please do understand that I have been praying every morning for over twenty years, loudly and fervently, since your father disappeared with you. I pleaded with the God of Abraham and Nehemiah to keep you safe, to bring you back to me. I mentioned your name each time I spoke to God and reminded Him I am the daughter of His glorious Covenant. Now that we are together, I know I have a daughter who will gently close my eyes with her fingers when I am about to sail away."

"Put out to sea? When you die, you mean?"

"Please, Esther, don't use such disturbing words. I have read some of your poetry; even poetic license has some limits."

"Okay, you have my word, Puri. I'll be with you before you put out to sea. But call me Georgi."

"Now that God has delivered you to me, I do not have my little daughter but a person with a strange name. Is that fair?"

"That's me, Puri. That's who I am. I hoped you could stop forcing me to be what I am not. I'm no stranger..."

"I'm sorry. I'll have to start using that strange name with no history. But tell me, what do you want to call me?"

"Purely, I guess, if that's okay with you. Last time you said to call yourself 'Puri,' didn't you? I like your name."

A scowl visits Puri's face, and she puts it firmly, "Puri? I am your mother. Please, I am old-fashioned. You can't call me by my name."

"It's hard for me too, Puri. Look, let's tread softly on this whole thing. I'm not ready. You can't expect me to flip over and become someone else just like that. My mother is Ellen..."

Puri's scowl breaks into a flood of tears as she sobs, "Ellen is a phony and a thief. She stole twenty years of my time with you," she whispers angrily. "I carried you here," she says firmly, sticking her angry thumb into her stomach, "you and Nathaniel, for nine grueling months in the bush fighting a system worse than that of the Amalekites."

Georgi's mind races. It slows down again when considering DNA testing prospects, but it quickly screeches to a halt at the sight of Puri's rosy cheeks. When she focuses, it feels like looking in a mirror. Georgi instinctively traces Puri's face down her cheeks with her fingers.

Puri speaks softly, "Please, my child..."

Georgi smiles. And a dazzling set of teeth glows like daybreak sunbeams across the Golden Gate. Puri reciprocates to Georgi's touch.

"Okay, Mother. I guess I'll have to get used to this," she says.

"God's timing is always perfect. You may not realize this, but I need to tell you something right now. It's crucial. I once told you I'm Jewish, right? We sang Hava Nagila together and danced in the driveway. You should know that because I am a Jew, you are Jewish in equal measure..."

"Me, a Jew?"

"It's an incontrovertible bloodline..."

"Dad is Black. How can I be a Jew? Jews are white people, as far as I know. Only Odessa, who hates whites, thinks Jesus was a Black man."

"Color has nothing to do with it. Have you not heard of the Ethiopian Jews, the Falashas, the black Jewish community airlifted from Africa to Israel in early 1980?"

"Yes, we did discuss the Ethiopian Jews back home... with Odessa and Father. Those black Jews are systematically victimized in Israel because of their color. Father even said the Israeli regime brought Africans to Israel because they needed to do menial jobs the white Jews found demeaning."

"It doesn't matter. All you must know is that you are a Jewish woman. It's up to you to do the right thing."

"Odessa thinks the white Jesus is a fake. What do you think, Puri?"

"A fake! That's a nasty thing to say, Esther. What does your sister know? Those blinded by color have a blind spot in their hearts."

"Just like the Europeans who came preaching a Christian religion to the indigenous people of the planet while they ravaged and stole their wealth?"

"Please don't listen to your sister. I know she does lots of outlandish research and reads tons of history from large volumes."

"You know?"

"No, I'm just speculating."

"Yes, she has been reading 'A Short History of Everything'... something, or other...by Bill Bryson. She even reads the bible when she thinks no one is looking."

"History is a mysterious universe worth exploring. Come with me sometime soon so we can learn more together. I want us, you and I, to touch and kiss the ground of Israel. I can't let Auschwitz be. It's personal. And you, Esther, you are part of it. We can even visit a church where Jacob's well is located, where Yeshua had a dialogue with a Samaritan woman."

"Let me get this straight: you're Jewish, and you go to church?"

"Yes, there are Messianic Jews worldwide," Puri responds impatiently. "We believe in Jesus... Yeshua"

"And where do you stand, for or against the Palestinians? Odessa had a French girlfriend who told her Jesus was a Palestinian."

"Yahushua ha Messhiach was born in Bethlehem, and his parents lived in Nazareth in Galilee."

"Is that not the area populated mostly by Palestinians today?"

"Does it matter? God created Jews and Palestinians, and one day, he will judge both. The Torah says a star will come out of Jacob, and a scepter shall rise out of Israel. No army will prevail upon Israel."

"Yeah? I think the siege they impose on Gaza has already judged and sentenced poor Palestinians to hell..."

"You and your brother are alike. I expected you, as a woman, to be more understanding. Let's put politics aside; you'll have plenty of time for that with Nathaniel and your father. Still, it must fill you with pride to be part of the Jewish Diaspora. How do you feel?"

"How do you feel?" Georgi smiles derisively and says, "I feel disoriented, Puri. First, Papa says I am an African, but now you say I am not an African, right?"

"You are Jewish..."

"You know, Puri, growing up on Cluny Drive back home, fooling around with other kids at Ramsden Park, people called us, our family, 'coloreds.' I always knew, even then, that I was African, despite being Canadian. But something about elementary school made me start questioning my *mon amour-propre*. I argued with a black girl one day about something or other. And she went back to her mother the next morning, and right in front of my teacher, the mother shouted, 'Just because you're a fair-skinned nigger, you act all stuck up!' When we arrived in Cape Town, I heard people refer to me as a 'colored with an accent,' but then to Odessa as a coconut 'with a 'model 'C' accent,' whatever that means. But I discovered, in a funny way, that it softened all the gritty parts for me, being a colored at the Waterfront, Cape Point, and down the Table Mountain Basin. I felt at home there because many people looked like me. The opportunity cost is lower for me living there than anywhere else in the country. Next, we moved to Johannesburg. Odessa became black, and the people I always thought were black, like me, called me 'Boesman.' Then came you, Puri, and Voila! I'm Jewish?! How do you think all of that makes me feel?"

Puri sniffles, heaves awkwardly, and softly says, "Yes, you are Jewish, Esther. There's something much deeper in you, and it's up to us, the three of us, with Nathaniel, I mean, up to all of us, to resolve it."

"Aren't you whistling in the dark, Puri? What color is my skin?"

"You're no *Sikas*'. That's what Aunt Pnina often said. You are no *Sikas*."

"Yeah? And what is that?"

"Skin color has nothing to do with being Jewish."

"No, Puri, skin color is tied to our existence. Odessa once said, 'If you are black, you exist in the plantations wherever you may be.' Yes. In North America, what might happen to you if the police stop you on the highway is often predetermined. Here in this country, it affects who gets called for a job interview. I saw how Odessa felt hurt when Leslie Silko, HR at Reeva's company, invited her for an interview because they needed someone to serve their black clientele, a black body, to attract the Black market. I know how damaging that experience has been to her mental health. She is my sister, and that incident broke her heart. She is tired of this rainbow nation right now. "

"But admit it, Odessa is an angry black woman. Let's put all of that behind us now."

"No, listen to the story of my introduction to the Taung household. Can you believe they preferred your angry black woman to me? When I got introduced, Marcia couldn't hide her disappointment. 'We were expecting a black person,' she said."

"Black person?"

"So, you see, Puri, 'everywhere we go, we pop up as pigmented bodies first and human beings last'; Odessa's words, not mine."

"I know. I was in the trenches fighting racism."

"Racism is felt mostly in lived experience. You have no idea how debilitating life can be for a black woman in the Western Cape because black skin is a swear word. I know because, over there, I am treated differently with some sense of humanity. I am privy to offensive private chats by whites and coloreds that float like fresh air against black South Africans."

The police sirens sound off as the convoy lines up. Georgi slips into Puri's car, and they follow behind. A procession of Metro police and unmarked vehicles, with sirens blaring and lights flashing, leads the convoy as it slowly makes its way along Chris-Hani Road, past Regina Mundi, to the cemetery. Puri tries to dodge Georgi's question about Nathaniel's location. She finally reveals that he has gone to Cuba. From what she knows, the Castro government has loosened its restrictions somewhat, and the South African government has sent Nathaniel there to gauge the workers' reaction.

"I see. Our cynical lecturer once said African governments love Cuba, Russia, and Libya don't they?"

"Responding to the cynical view, Samuel, a fellow student from Jamaica, pointed out to the same teacher that Western governments do love Israel. In the ensuing argument, Samuel asked if the teacher acknowledged the kindness of Cuba for having given refuge to Assata Shakur, the black woman wrongly accused of murder by the Americans. Samuel lost his scholarship before he was deported. I almost traveled to Cuba once for my essay research on nursery schooling, which I learned is among the best in the world. I couldn't get funding because everyone linked Cuba with the devil incarnate..."

"And bigoted at times.

"A Palestinian professor once came to 'Varsity to give a lecture on the Balfour

Declaration, but she was driven off campus by a crowd of Jewish supporters."

"Nathaniel says he has been trying to differentiate between the Israeli and Apartheid regimes. Talking about Nathaniel... now that we all know he is a secret civil servant, can you tell me what work you do apart from masquerading as a photographer?"

"Masquerading? Me?"

"Yes, Puri. I want to write about these things. You let slip; you knew what Odessa reads behind closed doors. How could you know unless your line of work is the same as Lieutenant Zola's? Is it?"

"I told you I was guessing. Reading is good, and so is writing. Yes, you must write about your experiences and what you've done. I love your poetry, but try adding dandelions and Valentines to your despondency, lest you slide down Ingrid Jonker's slippery slope. All of us are vulnerable, but she was too young to die. There was winsomeness about her that moved me. What drives a young woman to suicide?"

"How eager I am to visit Three Anchor Bay, to confront the beach, the waves, and the deep, to ask why their splendor faded when Jonker needed it most. I want to question the sea lions, seabirds, and seals. Where was the Hallowed penguin community waddling when they placed a false navigational beacon in her path? I sometimes long for the touch of the rainbow when all else seems lost. Father told me you habitually put your writings through a shredder. Have you ever felt you could end the nightmare and fade away like Jonker?"

"No. I've had someone to live for. I never felt like disappearing like Jonker did."

At Avalon Cemetery, a large crowd is being watched by a line of male and female police officers, most of whom have recently missed a few dinners and beers. As the convoy approaches, spectators begin to shuffle toward the marquee.

Cecilia Trent edges closer to Georgi, hugs her, and says, "Thanks for opening my eyes, Georgi."

"Yeah?"

"Reeva? We are friends again," she crows.

Georgi notices that Cecilia's expression lines and dark circles around her eyes, which greeted her when they first met at Robertson, are fading.

"It's such a blessed thing for mother and daughter to bond..." says Puri.

Kian, the Patriarch, is nowhere to be seen.

CHAPTER 25

Fly your kite with Ryan.

The Hallowed diplomatic immunity shields Pedro from facing charges in South Africa. However, he returns to Canada as a disgraced envoy, thankfully. Three other women have come forward with claims that Pedro abused them at various locations during their upbringing. One is an Indigenous American medical doctor in Toronto, originally from California. Her name is Tracy, but her real name, as translated, is 'John-Augustus-Sutter-we-shall-get-our-gold-and-our-land-back.' The women, with the predictable exception of Georgi, file charges of rape, grievous bodily harm, and attempted murder against Pedro. Odessa is furious with Georgi.

Tracy took advantage of the rape case, turning it into a significant platform to call for reparations for the Californian genocide that occurred in the 17th century, which negatively affected 20,000 indigenous Americans. The Mail publishes a supportive piece on her demands, stressing that the 'Red Indians' deserve restitution. She threatens to sue the Mail for referring to her as a Red Indian, pointing out that the label is comparable to 'Hotnots' used by racists to undermine the dignity of Indigenous people of Africa. The newspaper challenges her to sue.

After the celebrations in Soweto, Georgi refuses to stay alone on the Verligte farm while Barend is in Holland, supposedly fearing for her safety. Tension is building, and Georgi becomes depressed. She later moves into a flat in the Kenilworth suburb of Cape Town. Upon learning of her activities, Barend is so upset that he calls her, demanding she return to the farm. She responds to his threat by challenging him to resign from his mysterious job and come back home.

The haunting feeling of boredom drives Georgi to madness. One morning, she stands bare in front of her life-sized mirror, examining her feminine form in detail. She gently touches her nipples and clumsily presses her fingers into her belly. Georgi believes she appears unattractive, which deepens her misery. She retrieves the bathroom scale, steps onto it, and winces at the weight displayed on it. Overcome with nausea, she turns to a vase in an attempt to vomit. Suddenly, she hears the sound of a car slowly approaching her driveway. Carefully, she draws back the curtain and is startled to see who has visited her.

Ryan is casually dressed in his usual jogging attire. Georgi rushes to the bathroom to freshen up her appearance. He turns the doorknob and steps into the lounge. Georgi emerges wearing a towel and a mortified expression. Ryan puts on a cheerful façade to conceal his resentment at seeing Georgi's sparkling engagement ring on her finger. She remains speechless in response to his overwhelming smile.

"Don't inquire about how I located you. A few of your well-connected relatives are friends of mine," he chuckles.

"What are you doing here, Ryan?" she says, twisting the ring on her finger in an attempt to conceal it from view.

"I thought you'd ask what took me so long. Last time we spoke, you said you'd get back to me. Are you still in a bit of a pickle? I have been waiting for your call, Georgi. Remember your promise to take me to the Kruger National Park?"

"I made no such promise, Ryan. Besides, I don't feel well right now. Please go."

"Odessa contacted me, noting that you might feel lonely since your boyfriend is busy training in Amsterdam with the intelligence police."

"Odessa is crazy. I'm not lonely. Get that out of your mind."

"Are you upset with her for proposing that I come here to help you and alleviate your loneliness?"

"She's overreaching, that woman. I hate her."

"I came because I miss you and know you miss me too."

Georgi begins to feel strange tremors in her belly, and she swiftly runs to the bathroom to throw up. Ryan waits and then calls out, but Georgi shouts that she is okay.

Ryan moves to fix himself a drink while Georgi takes a shower. She wears an oversized 'Winnie Mandela' T-shirt when she walks back. Ryan is seated comfortably on the couch, drinking. He appears amused at the sight of Georgi.

"Are you a fan of Winnie Mandela? The ANC doesn't like her very much..."

"Men resent independent women."

"What about the Women's League? What kind of women do they support? Do you know?"

"I don't care, Ryan. Please go before my snooping neighbors start making unsolicited calls..."

"Calls to your white boyfriend, you mean?"

"Yes."

"Does his presence make you feel uneasy?"

Georgi remains silent.

"You were throwing up just now."

"You heard that? It's nothing. I'm clean now."

"Tell me about yourself."

"Why?"

"I've seen your sister, Odessa. You do look alike, but then again, you don't. You remind me of Esau and Jacob, the notorious bible twins. Esau was a hairy white man, while Jacob was black as night. Can you explain that?"

"Where do you get that about the color of bodies in the Bible?"

"I think you're hiding something from me. I hope you're not sweeping things under the carpet like our present crop of politicians from exile."

Georgi's mind is in disarray. She says, "Ryan, you'd better leave."

"The other day, I challenged some white Christians to tell me if they would worship Jesus if they knew he was a black man from Congo. They got so irritated that one of them said That's blasphemy…"

"Please, Ryan…"

Ryan changes the subject. He asks Georgi to accompany him to a quiet place near the Streenbras Dam to fly kites. Georgi paces and says, "Ryan, I don't have time for jokes. I can't go with you. You know I'm engaged to be married."

"Well, I brought two kites, one for you and one for me. Let's have a good time flying our kites on the banks of Streenbras Dam, and then you can come back to marry your white man."

"That's not fair. How can I go with you?"

Georgi wants to puke. Ryan walks out to his car. Georgi feels queasy. She opens the refrigerator and gulps a mouthful of Coke. Ryan pops his trunk. Georgi glides toward the window and stays behind a slightly drawn curtain, peering out. She quickly pulls back when he looks in her direction. Georgi's eyes are fixed on her childhood mantle clock ticking away on the mantelpiece. She runs her hand over her stomach.

Ryan is back to show off two large kites, his broad smile spreading more and more across his face. He strides back and says, "I made these kites especially for us. Have you ever made a kite?"

"No."

"We used to build them as tots. It's not easy to make a kite fly away into the sky. Life is like that; not easy, Georgi. You have to choose the spot and wind speed. But you must take advantage of the slightest breeze to launch your kite. Don't you want to see how that happens?"

"Make a kite, you mean?"

"No, fly your kite and see how far you can soar to the clouds. When you think you have maneuvered and reached your limit, you surprise yourself because an unexpected blast of air puffs across the tail, redirecting your kite."

"What?"

Ryan puts it seriously, "I want to go out with you. Don't you care for my feelings, Georgi?" He slumps on the couch and continues, "I see you look unhappy. Hope deferred makes the heart sick. That's what the bible says. There's nothing better than fun to make your heart as cheerful as I have known you to be. Kite flying is fun. Once your kite gets up into the heavens, you close your eyes and feel the sensation of tugs and jerks touching your heart. When that happens, you empathize because your kite is battling the wind all alone among the clouds, and all you can do is relax and reminisce about your childhood in Canada. By the time it's over, you'll wonder why you did not go out kiting with me before," Ryan chuckles.

Georgi sits on the coffee table and says, "Please, Ryan. It's not right; you know my situation now."

Ryan pulls a long face and counters seriously, "I've been thinking about you since we nearly kissed after I gate-crashed Marcia's party that night. My high school teacher used to say, 'Rule one: always finish a chapter once you've started reading it.' Do you remember the night you barely touched my lips in that dimly lit space before someone barged in?"

Georgi's gaze drifts away, and she awkwardly responds, "There are many girls at UCT. As a lecturer, you hold influence over your female students, right? I know how male lecturers behave. You can finish your chapter with your girl students there."

Ignoring her digression, Ryan parks himself intimately by Georgi's side, and his fingers caress her neck, and they gradually embrace and kiss.

Georgi steps back. She quickly goes inside, closes her bedroom door, and calls Marcia.

"Hi, Little bride."

"Marcia, please help me. Ryan is here with me in the flat, waiting for me to do kites with him..."

"Yes? I guess you're having fun."

"Fun? What must I do, Marcia?"

"You invited Ryan to do your kite in Barend's flat? Have you forgotten about Barend already?"

"No, I'm talking kites, real kites."

"Oh, real kites. I thought you were reciting some homographic pun."

"He just came uninvited. I don't know how to get rid of him..."

"Do you want to get rid of him?"

"I don't know, Marcia... He brought two kites with him..."

"Have you ever done kite-flying before? Real kites, I mean?"

"Why did he come? I'm so confused."

"Go fly your kite with Ryan. It's exciting once you get the hang of it, pardon the pun. Ryan used to make kites like you have never seen. They didn't call him Tako Kichi for nothing. He's so much fun! Did he tell you he is a trained bomb disposal official? He enjoys flying kites and hides in dark corners, tinkering with explosives. That's between us, girls. But I know you want to learn some Tako Kichi tricks. Ryan is a good teacher."

"Oh, Marcia. I feel like a trapped mouse. What would you do? I can't get rid of him."

At the Streenbras

Georgi puts on her long shirt, red tights, and maroon scarf, and they are on their way. When they arrive at the enormous Streenbras Dam, they move a distance, far away into the shoreline brush, and create an obstructed sightline against snooping eyes. Georgi spreads her beach towel on a well-manicured embankment under the Weeping willow tree. Ryan serves ginger ale and sets a bottle of sparkling apple juice on the grass. There are a few couples scattered around, minding their private business. When a thirty-something black couple in swimming gear walks past, Ryan's eyes follow the well-endowed woman.

"I see you like her."

"No, not particularly."

"No? There's a lot of her in that pair of swimming see-through garb. Isn't that what men's eyes always like to feast their eyes on?"

"Why are women always jealous of other women? I'm here with you..."

"Anyways, thanks for Ginger-ale. The nausea is waning a bit."

"What's your problem, Georgi? Are you sick?"

"Forget about my problem. Let's fly the damn kites and get it over with; I want to go back to my flat."

"Right, the two kites; this one with a blue line, the Blue Diamond, that one is yours. This one of mine is the Monster kite."

Ryan expounds at great length on the parts of the kite, from nose to spine to tail. But Georgi is bored to death.

"No sweat; you'll grow into it if you stay with me long enough. I know that's what we both want. A kite is like a human being. It's got feelings and ambitions. That's why you must always fly as high as you can. No limits."

They release their kites to the airstream. Georgi's radiant smile returns as her kite swerves sharply, curving and soaring through the windy Cape skies.

"My Blue Diamond can fly higher... I must be careful. Can you see that? Higher and further... it goes. But it shouldn't disappear into the sunset," calls Georgi excitedly.

"As long as you can feel the tug, you haven't lost it. The higher the altitude, the thinner the air and the lower the wind resistance."

"I can barely see it now," shouts Georgi. "There! I see my Diamond fade away, and there... she's returning. What fun! I love you, Ryan!"

Ryan ties the twines of their kites to the twig of the Willow crown and unpacks the snacks and drinks. The two are seated close to each other while their kites hover like two tiny cobras among peppered clouds high above the Streenbras.

"Thanks for that, I'm starving."

"You must be. What about all the throwing up?"

The lovers snuggle up, lazily scanning the cloud-spattered heavens and stealing a passionate peek at each other. Ryan pulls Georgi's left hand and hums, "First, there was a ring on her finger, and then there was no ring..."

Georgi swears awkwardly, "Oh, I forgot to wear it after showering."

"Do you remember Lee Greenwood's tune, 'Ring on Her Finger and Time on Her Hands'?"

"No."

Ryan continues chanting, rubbing it in: 'She stood before God, her family, and her friends and vowed...'

"Please, stop the sarcasm, Ryan," Georgi stresses with irritation.

"The next Diamond on that finger should be from me, Georgi. From Me." Ryan repeats before he lies on his back, whistling and chanting, 'Ring on Her Finger and Time on Her Hands.'

Georgi dozes off. In a short while, the string of her Blue Diamond snaps from the willow anchor, and the sky swallows the kite out of sight. Ryan rushes to hold the cord of the remaining kite, but when he feels the turbulence pull it away, he lets go and lies down next to Georgi again. She flaps her eyelids and falls asleep.

When Georgi opens her eyes again, the sun has shifted a bit. She sits up to study the skies, but no kite is visible.

"You let the kites fly off?"

"The diamond snapped first, and that's ominous, don't you think, Georgi?"

"Why ominous?"

"I had to unleash the monster to pursue the diamond."

Georgi shrugs and lies on her back.

"I saw you in Soweto... Orlando Community Hall, that big day. You didn't see me because you were basking in the coterie of celebrities, all those gloomy-looking politicians with pretentious struggle diplomas. Didn't you feel suffocated in that small space?"

"What are you talking about?'

"Your face over there in Orlando was... I said to myself, 'Look at her being sucked into their rainbow nation farce.' Surely, you can't be thrilled, being mollycoddled by hypocrites who call themselves freedom fighters. Do you know who the genuine freedom fighters are? Those single mothers parked themselves on street corners selling snoek-fish and fat cakes to make a few cents for their families."

"You know what, Ryan? I'm yet to meet a South African man who is not angry, black or white, or colored. I see Indian men always smiling because they are working and making money. I expected better from the likes of you..."

"I confess to being gatvol. The new black elites don't feel a twinge of guilt, forcing their children into arranged marriages to keep the jewels in the family. Do you see yourself in this picture, Georgi?"

"No one can force me into a marriage. You're talking nonsense."

Deliberately stirring the pot further, Ryan says, "Marcia tells me your entire clan has been swimming in the struggle all their lives. Did you know that?"

"C'est la guerre, Ryan."

"So, why let them negotiate your entire future instead of you asserting your individuality as a black woman? Do you have to be pulled by the nose just because your folk and their erstwhile white enemies have become buddies? You're entering a world of wolves masquerading as sheep, claiming to know all that? They are setting you up as a child bride to atone for their sins in Mozambique, Angola, Tanzania, and other countries..."

"My folk have nothing to atone for."

"I heard through the grapevine your father recently held top-secret talks with an exclusive Afrikaner crew, including your boyfriend's people..."

"Please, Ryan..."

"Am I crossing the line? I see you're sleeping through a revolution. The big narrative of black-elite forgiveness and white arrogance has replaced apartheid. Your father is a trusted member of the neo-elite."

Georgi rises and says bleakly, "My father is a good man. I love him."

After a long silence, Ryan persuades Georgi, and they roll up together again.

"Okay, Georgi, after this, I want us to spend time backpacking up the Drakensberg where the full moon is as bright as your heavenly eyes and where you taste fresh water from the springs of Lesotho. Just the two of us; no blue-light motorcades, no gratuitous extravagance, no hypocrisy. Do we have a date? You know we need each other."

"That won't happen, Ryan. I came today because I spoke to Marcia, who advised me to make my own choices. Here I am, then..."

He gently removes her scarf, after which an unrehearsed theatre unfolds. They slowly part with one item after another, tossing each wardrobe piece on the overhanging willow branch as if planning to stay hidden backstage forever. She glides her arm over his shoulders, and he cradles wildly inside her breasts. Memories of their world's troubles melt away as they both finally move to satisfy their voracious craving for each other. He feels the humidity of her breathing as her inaudible murmuring raises the warming weather inside their Streenbras grassy space. They remain cuddled firmly, floating inside their private cloud. Georgi dreams of freezing the moment forever as nothing else seems to matter. The impromptu excursion that commenced with two kites aloft the Streenbras waters has culminated in the two lovers losing control.

Clouds paint the western sky orange. To the far Eastern shore, darkening waters refract and crinkle the setting sun. Georgi and Ryan partly reinstate their gear and lie down facing the heavens. They are both in silent reflection over their desperate desire to remain in eternal embrace. However, reality begins to frustrate the electric current as Georgi's searing conscience pounds hard upon her chest. For his part, Ryan fantasizes about taking Georgi on his yearly pilgrimage to the Drakensberg. However, Georgi recalls Marcia's wisecrack about her confused state of mind: 'betwixt and between is an awkward place for a girl to be in.' Georgi knows only too well that by connecting with Ryan and keeping him deep in her heart, she has lit a fuse attached to gunpowder.

Georgi returns to her long Winnie Mandela T-shirt and struts around firmly. Ryan can smell mischief.

"It's not my fault you lost your diamond."

"Forget about the Diamond, Ryan. Do you love me?"

"You are the first girl I've ever invited to fly kites with me. That should count for something, shouldn't it?"

"I asked you a question."

"I know you're in a bind right now. Let's struggle together to get you out of the political maze you got yourself into."

Ryan and Georgi are now sitting side by side, like a couple having a serious discussion about their future.

Georgi begins, "Ryan, in the future, please find a girl to fly your kites with. There won't be any kite-flying rendezvous with me ever again. I'll have to negotiate my way through the maze, as you say... my way."

"A fine time to say such things. What's your game plan, Georgi?"

"No games. Listen, Ryan. I'll cherish the moments I spent with you today for the rest of my life. I enjoyed flying my Diamond until she reached the sky, even though you tricked me by letting her break away. But please, Ryan, stay away from me from now on, and I'll stay away from you..."

"I know why you are hurting. Marcia whispered something into my ear the other day. It's not easy to discover you have been lied to all your life by people close to you, especially your parents."

Jolted, Georgi sits up and says, "What did Marcia say?"

"Your real mother... a Jewish lady...? Imagine that!"

"I see."

"Don't be fooled by the snare of cults and casino religions. Stay away from that trap."

Georgi adjusts her tallit to ensure she appears appropriately dressed. She says, "What do you know about these cults, Ryan?"

"I know. My parents were always fighting about religion; a Muslim on one side and a cynic on the other."

"And what about you?"

"I'm agnostic if you wish to know."

"Hedging your bets?"

"Say what?"

"Ellen, my mother, says agnostics are people who contribute nothing to society except copious philosophical hot air."

"I was not born to peddle religion to unsuspecting members of society."

"You intend to peddle cynicism to your children. I have been an atheist all my life, which, admittedly, is worse than being agnostic. One of these days, I want to link up with a bat mitzvah. I don't suppose you've ever heard of a bat mitzvah. Have you...?"

Georgi stands up and starts dancing passionately, just like she did with Puri in the Taung's courtyard. Her husky voice crackles but stays firm, and she looks as proud as a Prom Diva in front of Ryan, barely touching the ground with her feet.

Mesmerized by her beauty, Ryan gets close to hug her. In his rough voice, he says, "I love you beyond measure, Georgi."

"I'll sing Gunter Kallman's 'Daydream' in my heart for the rest of my life."

"Daydream? Sing Daydream for me, Georgi."

"I don't feel okay right now. I'll hum quietly and whistle when I think of you." She smiles and continues, "Tell me about your sister. Do you feel like sharing personal family secrets?"

Ryan pulls a face. He puts it on awkwardly, "What do you know?" Georgi feels sorry for him because she can't reach the depth of his heart about what Sesi means to him.

"I'm hearing too many versions. When people tell too many mysterious tales about a person, there is often much more hidden about her and her immediate relations. Tell me and unchain my soul. No, tell me and unchain your soul, Ryan. Her name is Sesi, right?"

"You don't look well. What's the matter, Georgi?"

Georgi suddenly loses her balance and tumbles over. It's too late for Ryan to answer questions about Sesi or protect Georgi's head from hitting the sunscald patches of the tree bark. Ryan calls for an ambulance.

Georgi is in the Intensive Care Unit at the Southern Tip Clinic, while Ryan is seated on the bench along the corridor.

Late at night, Doctor Sibeko, an obstetrician, approaches a drowsy-looking Ryan. She directs him to go home, as Georgi will be in the clinic for observation. The doctor adds, "I am sorry to tell you, Mr Taung, your wife had a miscarriage..."

Ryan returns in the late afternoon on two successive days. On the third day, he looks fresh in his casual blue jeans and multi-colored shirt. Georgi now occupies a bed in a general ward, and she smiles and moves cheerfully when Ryan walks toward her bed. The ward is half-empty, and the three white female patients on their beds raise their eyebrows with interest. A folding screen covers one bed, and the nurses conduct medical activities there. Ryan puts two bottles of juice and a plastic bag containing new clothing on Georgi's dining table. A young white patient takes a keen interest in the conversation that follows.

"Did you call your boyfriend?"

"No! And nobody knows I'm here."

"Not even Marcia or your mother?"

"Listen to me, Ryan. I appreciate your help, but don't you dare speak about my being admitted to the clinic?"

"Fair enough. Odessa called to inquire about my movements since the day she encouraged me to contact you."

"Don't tell me you continue gossiping about me with that woman."

"That woman? I just told her I visited you. I mentioned to her that we drove together to Streenbras to fly kites. She was so thrilled she promised to pop the champagne and make the cork fly to the sky like our kites."

"You lie, Ryan."

"I told her my kite is still chasing after yours up there. She laughed until she coughed and nearly choked. Does she smoke?"

"Yeah, her pantyhose."

"And she said, 'Way to go, Ryan'. But I said nothing about Dr Sibeko."

"What about Dr Sibeko?"

"Sibeko told me everything, like the whys and wherefores of fatigue and nausea... on the part of feminine physiology, I mean."

"Oh, My Dear God. Please do not say anything about this, my Dear Ryan."

"The doctor referred to me as 'your husband'... or did she say 'you are my wife'? Has a nice ring to it, don't you think?"

"Oh, go away."

"Have you confided in him... about your miscarriage, I mean, your white boyfriend?"

Two days later, Georgi emerges into Ryan's warm arms, dressed to tease in her Scottish kilt, Tartan shawl, and beret tam he had brought earlier. They are driving to her flat when Barend calls. He is fuming over Georgi's failure to answer his calls or contact him for days.

"Where are you? What's going on?"

"I've been with girlfriends...a baby shower."

"Georgi. I'll be in your flat in a few minutes."

"What?"

"See you."

Ryan's car slows down in the middle of a leafy, white suburb and parks under Cape Grassbirds and Morton's big fig trees.

"This is your moment to choose, Georgi; go back to your desolate flat or come with me right away for good."

Georgi is silent. She looks distraught, and when she puts her head on his shoulder, he backs away and says, "Well, Georgi? Are you coming with me?"

Georgi removes her beret, puts on her scarf, and answers, "No."

"You just lied to your boyfriend."

"What's that to you?"

"It says you're a liar, and people don't trust liars."

"So, you were lying when you said I'm a woman of integrity? You come to my flat with your kite-flying charade and disrupt my schedule. Look at the soup I'm in now."

"My kite flew higher than your kite. Any silly idea why?"

"Who cares about your stupid kite, Ryan?"

"Your diamond kite snapped and disappeared. Do you know what happens to kites that snap from their anchor? They are difficult to guide, so they fly away anywhere and everywhere. My kite soared higher than yours because I don't lie. I'm not afraid of anyone. A woman who lies to a man she plans to marry is a loser, a battered woman terrified of her partner. So, she lies. Why? Because such a woman can't be trusted to protect her ass against an abusive partner who makes her take shortcuts by lying to him. She goes to work with purple bruises on her face and lies to colleagues, 'I fell on the stove... I tripped, and my forehead collided with a staircase. After spending the most enjoyable time with the man of her dreams, she lies, 'I was with my girlfriends having a baby shower...'. You're such a weakling, you can't stand shoulder-to-shoulder with Odessa. Your sister is a real African woman, proud of her heritage. Besides, your unilateral rejection of their principled stance to testify against a rapist who abused many girls, including you, is most pathetic. Odessa told me all about it."

"Shut up; you shut up," Georgi cries before she jumps out into the footpath, banging the door with explosive ferocity. The window drops to the bottom and remains there. Ryan throws her duffel bag through the door that has just lost a window and settles on the ground next to her foot. Undeterred,

Georgi leans and shouts, "Since you know so much about principles, when were you planning on telling me about your bipolar sister you have been hiding? Your sister! Are bipolar genes in your family? Guess who is pathetic."

"You're so devious, you delete your engagement ring from your finger when you go out on your cheating spree. And you even lie to me about it...." Ryan retorts.

"Go away. I never want to see you again," she cries.

Ryan's car screams away, leaving Georgi to weigh her options under the Moreton Bay fig tree. The traffic wheezes past at high speed as tears roll down her face. She is suddenly overcome by the memory of her youth when she stabbed Odessa with a pair of scissors. The incident has been erased from her troubled mind until now. Georgi wipes tears from her face when a memory jolts her to the reality that she can be dangerous without knowing it. She is shaken to realize that her mind can reenact with clarity the stabbing incident, something she swore never happened. She turns around, away from the rough traffic, and begins to justify to herself that Odessa had it coming, what with all her poking fun at her over her sleepwalking.

Georgi begins to pray, "Lord Jesus, look after the baby I just lost, but please don't disclose the name of the father. Amen."

She dips her hand into her handbag and begins to clown and sing as she retrieves her engagement diamond, 'Ring on her finger and time on her hands.'

"Oh, Ryan."

After casually examining the ring, she slides it onto her finger. Her thoughts drift back to her teenage years in Canada. She then leans against a tree and falls asleep. Georgi is quickly jolted awake by the squeals of a minibus taxi pulling up beside the tree. She feels relieved that the taxi driver has light skin, but her relief quickly fades when she realizes that all the taxi passengers are Black Africans. She tells the driver she wants a taxi to take her to her apartment. The cab erupts in laughter while the driver, who is a person of color, remains stoic and asks, "Askies?" Not only does Georgi not understand how the taxi system works in the country, but she also doesn't realize that her apartment is only a short walk from where Ryan dropped her off.

Barend is sound asleep when Georgi enters. She wonders how he managed to get in without her keys, but quickly remembers that Barend works for National Intelligence. He opens his eyes and catches Georgi tiptoeing inside. Georgi stays in the bathroom for a while, and Barend remains on the couch. Knowing how upset he must be, Georgi considers her responses. The words of Lieutenant Morrison are now echoing in her mind, 'For a girl, if you feel those teeny-weeny qualms, it's time to disengage. Don't tie that knot...'

When Georgi comes out, she has changed into a striking red miniskirt and a large plain T-shirt. Barend is not moved. The kiss is mechanical, a preamble to the imminent storm.

"How are you, Barend?"

"You must explain where you have been and what has held you incommunicado for so long. And don't lie to me."

"Don't you ever say that to me? I'm not your child. I am not your wife."

"Stop dodging my question as if you have lied to me."

"I am not a liar. I hate it when people talk down on me."

"Answer my question, then."

"I was in a hospital..."

"What were you doing in the hospital?"

"I had a miscarriage."

Barend retorts, "Earlier, you told me you were having a party with your girlfriends."

"I am telling you now; I was in a clinic, Southern Tip Clinic, sorting out a miscarriage."

Barend walks out to make a call. Georgi is a bundle of nerves as she stands up to snoop behind Barend. She parks herself close to the window and strains her ears, eavesdropping. She prepares a quick meal when she misses Barend's top-secret conversation. Barend walks back.

"Do you have to walk out to make a call? Who were you calling?"

"Southern Tip Clinic. I called to get the details about your miscarriage story."

"Story? They confirmed my story, then."

"No. When I'm away, working my ass off for you, you're busy hanging out with Ryan? What is that man to you?

Although dazed, Georgi counters, "Calm down, Barend. I had a miscarriage. Doesn't that mean anything to you?"

"Did you sleep with that man?"

"What kind of a question is that?"

"A straightforward question. We are in a relationship. I have the right to ask."

"And what right is that?"

"Who made the payment at the clinic?

"Ryan offered. I'll repay him. It was an emergency."

Barend steps to the door, whispering indignantly, "This explains why you moved to this flat behind my back..."

"Where are you going? Let's talk."

"Okay. Pack your stuff, and let's go to the Free State Farm immediately..."

"I told you I can't stay there alone. That place gives me the creeps."

"We've got workers and security..."

"And do you know what your workers and security call me? 'Khoisan'. One of the girls kept referring to me as 'Patricia de Lille.' And when were you planning on telling me your aunt and uncle gave you the farm gratis?"

"In good time."

"And you call me a liar? Do you remember 'Uhuru,' the stone from Kuito? I gave it to him, the guy who told me secrets about the farm, because I am fed up with your surprises."

"You did what? Did you give the stone back to your father?"

"Yes? Now I know my father gave it to you in the first place. Did you and my father make deep political deals behind my back?"

Barend steps out onto the balcony.

"Never mind your private political deals. I want the truth, Barend. Tell me about Avigail."

Stopping dead in his tracks, Barend walks back and says, "What do you want to know?"

"Avigail. What was she doing, escaping the Nazis?"

Barend heaves with frustration and sits back on the couch. Georgi lounges seductively on the coffee table.

"What are you talking about, Georgi?"

"You just accused me of being a liar. Maybe you're a bigger liar than I am. Remember how you sterilized the storyline, telling me Avigail was from Chantilly, a pleasant and exotic rural town in Northern France? Tell me now, who is Avigail? When she got married, why did the families fail to come to dinner together to celebrate?"

Barend slowly lifts himself and says, "I have a plane to catch."

Georgi stands tall on the coffee table and shouts, "Fine, you go catch your plane, but Georgi here has Avigail's stainless ring on her finger."

CHAPTER 26

Woman-to-woman

Georgi develops postpartum insomnia, which goes on for several days. She calls her father, who snubs the call, claiming to be in Australia. Georgi calls again, "Australia, Dad? Please come to Cape Town immediately. I want to talk."

"About your future? Have you finally decided what to do with Van der Watt?"

"Yes, Papa. We're getting married…"

Kian shuts his phone. Georgi calls Nathaniel, "Where are you, Nathaniel?"

"I'm in Australia. What is it?"

"You are in Australia with Dad?"

"No. Are you sure he's in Australia?"

"Please call him. I need to talk to him."

"He's not thrilled with your Barend. What do you want to talk to him about?'

"He slammed the bloody phone on me…"

"The Last time we spoke, he told me you've become a prodigal daughter, and he'll welcome you back the day you change your mind about Van der Watt."

"Prodigal? Do you know how insulting that is? Please, Nathaniel. You are my brother. Speak to Father and convince him that Barend is no enemy. Tell him he is a prodigal father if he refuses to talk to me."

"Some history your Van der Watt dynasty has!"

"What do you mean?"

Nathaniel cuts off.

Two days later, Georgi gets an early call from Puri. She has just touched down from Germany.

"I should be at your flat in an hour."

Georgi makes the most of the hour, ensuring her finicky mother finds the place spotless.

"This had better be good," Puri greets Georgi as she alights from an Uber taxi. "You ordered my instant call. What's the problem?"

The two women walk in, and Puri sits on the couch. Georgi takes her seat on the coffee table, facing her mother.

"I ordered your instant call? I did no such thing. It must have been your son, Nathaniel."

"I keep reminding you, Nathaniel is your brother. Are you pregnant?"

"No, Puri, I'm not pregnant…"

"But your eyes! A face mirrors the heart, and your enlarged lips tell everything. When did you decide to lease this apartment?"

"You know Marcia does not need my services. What's the use of hanging around with everyone stabbing you in the back?"

Georgi is speechless over what Puri reveals: that Marcia and Moroka have separated.

"Why?"

"Let's talk about you. What do you want to say to me?"

"How did Father convince you to come here?"

"Nathaniel called from Australia. You need me urgently, he says. Imagine!"

"What about Papa?"

"The last I heard from him was when he called from a government helicopter from Soweto. This must be serious."

"Mama, you are my mother, right?"

"Of course."

"Have you spent nights with Father at the Holiday Inn recently?"

"No, of course not."

"You told me once that you and Dr Caleb have not been intimate for ions."

"I should not have ventilated such private matters to my daughter."

"So, you've not been intimate with Father Kian while you visited him several times at the Holiday Inn...?"

"What did your father say to you?"

"I didn't ask him. He told me during the struggle that you two had to spend some time away at the Tarangire Resort, and that's where you did your family planning to make a set of twins."

"Esther! You and Nathaniel have such unbridled tongues. You said you wanted to talk."

"Was he playing your favorite Abdullah Ibrahim tune, 'The Call'? You still enjoy each other's tastes, don't you? Never mind, I'll ask Papa about it next time he shows up."

"Okay, please don't ask your father about such things. I was with him for just one night; I'm ashamed to say..."

"Yeah?"

"A woman ought to be on her guard; you can't entrust your conscience to a man and hope to get it back intact."

"Papa once said that if you love two people equally, that's a dangerous love triangle. Are you two guys still crazy about each other?"

"I've said enough. But for your sake, I must tell you that after that night with your father, I reflected on the Samaritan woman who confronted Yeshua at Jacob's Well. I know Yeshua understands."

"You met with Father months after threatening to kill him?"

"I wanted him to apologize for what he did."

"Anyway, I'm happy you're here, Puri. I want to talk to you woman-to-woman. You asked if I was pregnant. Yes, until recently, I was. I had a miscarriage..."

"Esther! And how are you doing?"

"Surviving?"

"Barend must be devastated."

"Fuming. He treats the whole thing like I'd had a little blackhead that just popped. He accuses me of cheating on him, all because Ryan helped me to the clinic."

"Ryan? Are you sure that was all he helped you with?"

Georgi makes tea. Puri smiles lazily, saying, "Good idea. Let's have tea, and feel free to share everything about you and Ryan. Where was Barend when Ryan unexpectedly showed up at your flat?"

"Barend works in the Netherlands. I'm sure you and your son know more."

"Nathaniel is your brother! Are you saying when Barend is in Europe, Ryan helps you along, including ferrying you to the gynecology clinic?"

"It's much more complicated than that."

"I see. What did you tell Barend?"

"That I lost consciousness, and Ryan helped me..."

"My child, learn to keep your mouth shut. You had no business announcing that the man you've been having a tête-à-tête with behind closed doors helped carry you to the clinic for an abortion."

"Oh, Puri! Abortion? Barend wanted to know the ins and outs of my schedules while he was away."

"You're not planning on reneging on your pledge to Barend. Right? My heart has stabilized since your engagement, and I have cut smoking to one per day or less. I know your father has been unenthusiastic about Barend. Just do what's right..."

"What is right, Mother?"

"I'm happy you say 'Mother'. If you love me, you will do as I say and stop massaging your father's ego. Do you love me, Esther?"

"I love you... But I love Father, too. And please call me by my name. I prefer it that way."

"By your name? Please keep my heart in good shape. I am your mother, and I gave you a Jewish name because I am the only one with the right to do so. Please understand my feelings."

"Remember, I have feelings too, Mother."

"Right. I saw Barend's demeanor that day in Orlando Hall and knew he was the right man for you. Promise your mother you'll stop your philandering..."

"Move on, Puri."

"Right. I'm getting details from you about what I heard. I learn that some women have lodged a case against one Pedro. What can you tell me?"

"I'll tell you because you claim to be my mother."

"That's a nasty thing to say. I AM your mother."

"Okay, sorry. I once attended an in-camera case of a girl raped by her teacher. The court portrayed her as an unreliable witness, and even a female judge insinuated that she was fabricating the entire scene. I'm not subjecting myself to any of that."

"So, you are telling me, your mother, the man did rape you?"

"The man stuck the nozzle of his gun inside of me and threatened to fire if I did not give him what he wanted…"

Puri screams, and Georgi tries in vain to calm her down. Finally, she leads her to her bedroom to lie down.

Georgi calls Ryan soon after, and the two have a long conversation about this, that, and nothing more. The following morning, Puri warns Georgi that she will not take what Pedro did to her lying down. Georgi responds that whatever Puri wants to do, she must never drag her name into it.

"I understand now how a mother feels inside after losing her daughter through rape. My soul has been violated. The apartheid regime was evil beyond words," says Puri, "but rape was a serious crime then, not a misdemeanor as we see it today. Such people must hang," Puri stresses. "The majority think capital punishment targets black people, but the majority is not always right. Look at the majority that voted, thinking they were putting Mandela into power. I know many of those comrades. I lived with them in African countries. As a voter today, I wouldn't touch the party with a barge pole."

"Life is so complex…"

"You bet! Mother's instinct tells me all is not well with your plans."

"All is not well with choices, Mother."

"I know you've got problems with Barend's family, particularly Sofia. But tell me the truth; do you love Barend?"

"First, tell me the truth about Barend's family history. I know you are privy to secrets because you are a spy, although you refuse to confirm it. You once said history is a mysterious, dark universe worth exploring. How far did you go exploring Barend's family?"

Puri heaves an answer, "Let Barend tell you about his family history. That will build trust between the two of you."

"This ring on my finger belonged to Barend's Great-grandmother. How much do you know about her?"

"I found out by chance about Avigail, but when I told Nathaniel that Jewishness is matrilineal, he sniggered and said, 'Count me out.' As for you, I am glad to see you will be in Avigail's warm hands."

"You knew all along about Avigail, yet you never bothered to whisper a word to me."

"To everything, there's a season and a reason why God made such an unlikely connection between you and Barend."

"Unlikely, why?"

"I suppose Kian divulged the Mimi incident to you?"

"Circuitous comes to mind."

"As circuitous as your game with Ryan? I hope it's a short-lived infatuation.

"I don't know, Mother."

"A woman will always reflect with nostalgia on her awe-inspiring ecstasy with her previous flames…"

"Like her Indigenous man who prowls around the shadows of her mind…?"

"Nicely put and quite to the point. But a woman will avoid hopping from one set of sheets to the next on an adventure with no exit plan. Your mother's counsel brings you blessings; a perfect man is a mirage. Marriage is a struggle, but stick to Barend. You both come with serious emotional baggage. So does Nathaniel and his Sofia. Any woman worth her salt takes personal risks and."

"Why 'his Sofia'?"

"A rumor has been circulating about your brother and Sofia…"

"Mother! With Sofia? What rumor?"

Sofia's Folder

The pendulum has moved back and forth in an irregular fashion for Georgi. She can hardly decide which way to turn. Fortunately, she got accommodation at the quiet Taung's Houghton Estate in Johannesburg. Something has been nagging her ever since she met Sofia. The more she wonders about her behavior, the deeper she drifts into restless nights. This time, flashes of Sofia's face search empty spaces in her mind, and in her waking hours, she can see her image in Sofia's sunken eyes.

She recalls that Sofia had always snooped around when she was having a quiet time with Barend. She even accompanied Barend when he fetched her from the Airport on the day of Willem's funeral. What was Sofia doing there? Then Sofia became as gracious as Mother Teresa, offering to take Georgi to colorful scenic nature reserves in the Cape. Georgi further wonders about Sofia's incongruous utterances: 'Jan van Riebeeck landed at the Cape 352 years ago today'. She further recalls how, in lamenting Mimi-Koo's death, Sofia hardly said a word about her brother, who was about to be buried.

While Georgi deliberates on Sofia's pastimes, Odessa suddenly drops in unannounced, carrying two heavy suitcases.

"What a heavenly place! Marcia must be desperately fond of you…"

"She likes me, alright. And You? What a surprise. I would have fetched you from the Airport if someone had told me…"

"I used a taxi… a white female taxi driver in the middle of Africa!"

"It could have been the ghost of Lilias Drummond of Scotland. Ever heard of her?"

"Your scary tales about blonde female ghosts give me the creeps."

"I was told dark clouds and heavy rains are a predictable feature of Beesfontein. In my dream the other night, I saw you dancing inside a violent Beesfontein storm. Then, in the next scene, I observe that the storm is your born-again aunt, Phantom Kora …"

"She's your aunt, too, Georgi. Don't tell me about dreams. I hate dreams, especially your bloody hallucinations. I don't like the mention of the word Beesfontein any better."

"I wonder why."

"Fine, you can rub it in..."

"I knew you would come thundering in uninvited—all praises to Marcia. You should have alerted me instead of behaving like Puri, flying here and there and everywhere, looking for who knows what! Where is Baby Danie...?"

"Home with Mother. I spoke to Marcia today to ensure she approves of my turning this into a halfway house. Why didn't you tell me she plans to give you this property after firing you?"

"She never told me that. What did she mean?"

"Sorry, I rushed to open my mouth on private matters."

"Marcia mentioned it once, but I turned her down."

"The Bible says those who have will have more, and some of us will end up sleeping in the Rosedale subway. You turned her offer down?"

"Any reason why you are here?"

"Last time I heard you were getting married. Didn't you beg me to act as your Matron of Honor? And now you call me an uninvited guest? I'm here because of an invite from April. I believe the name rings a bell?"

Georgi's throat dries up instantly, and she shouts, "Ganon April? What would that man possibly invite you for?"

"I don't know, Georgi. Remember what Papa used to say about men? They invite women for one thing."

"One thing? And you're ready to oblige, of course, gladly."

"Perhaps that's why he invited me. The guy sponsors my entire trip."

"April?"

"Yes, Sister, April Ganon. Are you jealous?"

"Yes."

"Look, Georgi, he told me about 'Uhuru'..."

"What?"

"Yes, 'Uhuru'. He wants assistance running large projects in Cape Town, Johannesburg, and maybe Durban. I'll help him set up the operation. But you'll be pleased to hear I'm not planning on sleeping with him. I need the money, and that diamond has also come in handy for my projects."

"Did he say who gave him 'Uhuru'?"

"You won't believe this, Georgi. The man risked his life at Kuito Cuanavale to get the stone. You learn to ask no questions with these ex-freedom fighters."

"Yeah? I don't suppose you asked your freedom fighter to share with you what he knows about your murdered boyfriend."

"No, Georgi. I have moved on. Try doing the same and connect with the one you love: a handsome African hunk called Ryan?"

"Odessa, you don't seem to have gained much insight from your experience with your kinky-haired man."

"Spare me your pity, Georgi, and start planning your exit strategy from Barend's racist community. You're not exactly white; just accept it. Colorism affects you just as much as everyone else. Reeva tells me Sofia has been ostracized for years by her family. Do you know why?"

"I don't know. When I'm with her, she says pretty little."

"I'll reveal the secret to you. Once upon a time, Sofia allowed a black man to stick his tongue inside her mouth. Whites resent that, especially white women, unless they are the recipients of the black tongue. These women hook up with their white men for status and wealth, but deep down, there's always space for emotional engagement with black men."

"You know what Father said about you? He said your research and philosophy are driving you crazy."

"Listen to me, Georgi Girl; jealousy is multifaceted. You say Sofia says little to you? Silence speaks louder than a thousand words. I suspect this whole grapevine hoo-ha with Barend is a ruse aimed at avenging their dead sister. One day, we'll discover you and your twin brother stuck at the bottom of a slimy swamp. Make sure you take up life insurance in time and make me a beneficiary."

Georgi's entire demeanor changes. Her face wrinkles, and she impulsively clenches her fist and shouts, "You disgust me, Odessa. I rue the day I ever met you."

"Stop blaming me for your failures. A black nanny about to marry into a white family with racist credentials must question her amour propre. Get on with it, Georgi; marry the white man, and if you were clever like me, you would milk the multi-millionaire dry until you get our land back. Ryan is the only man who can save you from yourself. I know where you go when you're alone in your bed; your dreams saturate your face with floods of tears you cannot wipe out until your body melts into that of the black man."

Georgi has come out worse for wear, and she cries. Odessa moves to wipe tears from Georgi's face. She holds her by the hand and begins to sing. Georgi reluctantly joins Odessa, and they crackle, wheeze, laugh, and chant, 'We can work it out.'

"Something else we have to work out, please, Georgi. Each time I say something awkward, like mention Pedro's name, you want to eat me alive."

"I have no interest in Pedro. Please spare me."

"You'll be happy to hear the Red Indian girl with a long name..."

"Tracy?"

"Yea, 'John-Augustus-Sutter-we-shall-get-our-land-back.' She won the case against Pedro despite the all-white jury. But Pedro has appealed the verdict."

"What a nerve!"

"I am glad you are here. You'll help look after the place, my Dear Sister, because I have to fly out for a few days."

"Yeah? Before you go, Georgi, let me say sorry. I should not have said you're an underachiever. I admire you so much, but I'm jealous, that's why."

Georgi gives Odessa a little fist bump on the shoulder and says, "I missed you,

Odessa. Thanks for coming. I love you. But I'm disturbed to hear my parents have cut off all communication between them."

Georgi is on her way to Berlin. At the Central Station, a female ticket examiner is making her rounds.

"Fahrkarten bitte"

Georgi notices passengers pulling out their tickets and presenting them to the examiner. She does likewise. She further notices that the ticket examiner looks much like a woman of color she once met at Mitchells Plain. The examiner then moves on to the next passenger.

Georgi calls Puri and says, "I'm here in the Berlin Main Station."

"Berlin? What are you doing here? Is Barend there with you?"

"Calm down, Puri. I'm alone. Aren't you happy to hear my voice?"

"Not from a Berlin Station, I'm not."

"Nathaniel gave me your location and assured me you're home. So, I'll be with you shortly. Please don't go out."

The two-level residence is breathtakingly spacious. Caleb Lieber is in his scotch Bermuda, which he tops with a frayed khaki shirt. He is tending their attractive country garden and whistling weakly. On seeing Georgi, he leaps forward and escorts her to their inviting open-plan dining space. Puri is in tears as she throws her arms around Georgi. The two women sit on the cream Persian carpet facing each other. Caleb is on hand with iced tea and a wad of comfort tissues before disappearing to the vegetable garden.

"Please, Puri, don't ask why I am here. I've grown tired of that salutation."

"So, why are you here?"

"You do remember your promise, right? You said you wanted me by your side to do camera and magazine work with you."

"So...?"

"Well, here I am."

"You flew from Africa to do camera work with me? Did Barend subsidize your futile flight?"

"Futile? No. He doesn't have to know I'm here. Nathaniel subsidized my trip."

"Nathaniel is a nut-head. What do you mean, Barend does not have to know your movements? Is that the way to treat your prospective husband?"

"Look, Puri, there won't be a wedding, let alone a husband."

Puri cannot hide her dismay. Tears begin to form again in her eyes, and she struggles, "Are you postponing it?"

"No, I've changed my mind."

"Barend is a gentleman. Where do you hope to find another man like him?"

"I'm not desperate for a man right now."

After Georgi freshens up and changes to her light dress, Puri says, "I am disappointed, Esther. What about the ring he put on your finger when he propositioned?"

"It's my ring. He gave it to me. And I am Georgi."

"It won't be appropriate. You must reconsider, not about the ring but the wedding."

"You know very little about him, Puri. But I'm here to tell you about the documents I stole from a property owned by Barend's family. Before we discuss that, I want to know why you cut off communication with my father."

"Who told you that? Did he tell you?"

"No, a lady from the Holiday Inn witnessed a skirmish between you two, and she nearly called law enforcement? You had no right to order him to cut me off, too."

"The man messed up our lives. You should be supporting me…"

"No, Puri. He is my father."

"You said something about stolen documents…"

"I can't make head or tail of the stuff in the folder, but I also found this picture," Georgi hands over the folder and the photo to Puri.

Puri takes a cursory look at the documents, puts the folder and the photo on the floor, and says, "What do you want me to do?"

"What do you make of them?"

"Look, Esther, I have no interest in this sort of thing. I was expecting you to come tell me all is well with your wedding plans…"

Georgi rises from the floor, sits on the side of the couch, and shouts, "My name is Georgi. I am no bloody Esther. I'm not here to talk about any wedding. You claim to be my mother, but all you care about is selling me off to the highest bidder. Don't you want to see the seriousness of the contents of these folders? If you want us to keep in touch, use my proper name. Please!"

Thoroughly embarrassed, Puri returns the folder to her lap and pages through with some purpose. Tears stream down her face.

"And the photo? Who is this child?"

"Puri, are you not in Intelligence? Just open up with me…"

"What Intelligence?"

"The National Intelligence Agency of South Africa."

"Whatever gave you that idea?"

"Zola Morrison gave me some hints. She said the NIA has ex-pats who gather a whole heap of dirt everywhere because people think African governments are stupid. How much do you know about Zola Morrison?"

"Promise you will go with me to Home Affairs to get your date of birth and your name corrected on your documents. Then I'll tell you everything because you are my child, and you have the right to know."

"Okay, let me tell you about Sofia. She is harboring family secrets, and it seems she is being kept on a tight leash. The poor girl is isolated and afraid, and until I know why, I will jump into quicksand if I get married to Barend. Call it a gut feeling. When we were at Robertson, she kept making curious, flitting eyes at me as if warning me against the 'Hounds of the moors of Dartmoor' in that large farm. At the time, I didn't think it made sense. I never got to be alone with her, and now I know someone made sure that never happened…"

"What do you want me to do?"

"Now that we've all established you are in the National Intelligence…"

"No…"

"I know investigating this woman will be a breeze. There's more to the Van der Watts than meets the eye."

"There's nothing I can do from here. I'll speak to Nathaniel."

"Please, Puri. Don't mention this to that man."

"That man is your twin brother."

"Yes, and my twin brother called me on my way here and whispered like a ghost, asking if I had ever heard of an apartheid policeman named Van der Spuy."

"Well? What did you say to him?"

Poem on a Bottle

Because of her botched visit to Puri, Georgi flies to Canada, where she finds Ellen unwell. Ellen tells Georgi that her health is failing and that she looks forward to the day her daughters will be back home. Georgi is touched, and she promises Mother Ellen she will be back.

"Odessa went to Johannesburg to help you with your wedding arrangements. I was mad with her because she said I could not look after her baby."

"What? That's what she said to you, Mama? Where is Baby Daniel?"

"She left him with Jean Mackenzie, where you did your summer job."

"Is Odessa Stark staring mad?

"She told me she wants to surround her baby with love, not infections…"

"Infections? You, Mother? She makes me sick, this girl."

"She told me you are still dating Ryan. I got worried because I knew that a girl ought to build a wall around herself and make the right choices. What are your plans?"

"Odessa has no right meddling in my affairs."

"Your affairs are her affairs… unless you reject her as your sister."

"No, I can't reject her. She is doing a good job of it without my help. Fancy ascribing infections to our mother who raised us with such love…!"

Ellen discloses to Georgi that a young man has been coming and going from the home several times, looking for Odessa. He finally left his contact number and said he was through with his studies and going back to Ghana.

"That must be Okobi. Let me get his number."

"Yes, he seems to be a decent young man from Africa. Oh, Georgi, I wish I could fly with you back to my village, where I could think more clearly. I want to go back to Africa to be buried with my blood relatives."

"I'll fetch you, Mother. We'll go together to your village for a visit."

"One day, you gave me a poem to read. It made me cry because I knew you were honoring your mother for the pain she endured for twenty years, when she did not know what happened to you. She deserves praise, and I know I'm destined for hell."

"No, Mama. What choices did you have as a woman? None."

"Please engrave your poem on a bottle and give it to Puri. Do you promise?"

"On a bottle?"

"All my tears of sin and penitence will be in that bottle."

Both women shed ominous tears. Georgi promises to engrave the bottle and fill it with water from Ellen's village before presenting it to Puri. As Georgi checks in at the Airport, she yearns for the two kites that beat the winds on the Streenbras theatre. Although her concern over Ellen's health keeps distracting her reverie, she finally calls Ryan. Georgi can hear a muffled female voice in the background.

"You've removed my name from your cell already?"

"You changed your name, Georgi. I can't spell your new Jewish one."

"I see. Where are you?"

"Up the Drakensberg. Where are you?"

"I'm boarding a plane from home…"

"Home? Meaning Canada?"

"I'll be in Johannesburg by 9 am. I won't stay long because I left Mother badly."

"You turned down my invitation. You should be here with me."

"There's a cute girl there with you. So, stop moaning."

"I'm still expecting my invitation. When is the big day?"

"The girl with you over there; what is her name?"

"Call me when you touch down, will you? What's your new name again?"

"Read the Book of Esther. You'll find it in your bible."

On boarding the plane, Georgi notices that someone has switched her seat location and that the one allocated to her is too awkward for her long-haul flight. She tells one of the aircraft crew members that she prefers a window seat near the front, rather than one on the aisle near the back. When she fails to swap, she blames herself for ignoring the 'pick my seat' option for her connecting flight. Then, from the corner of her eye, she notices that one of the passengers is Inspector Mbatha, Zola Morrison's partner, who suddenly turns away and pretends to be reading a newspaper. Georgi is not amused. She sees Mbatha's hand in the swapped seats. She reluctantly takes the seat and struggles for some hours to let go of the memory of Ryan.

Somewhere during the flight, Georgi notices that Mbatha has a magazine on his lap but is asleep. She quietly lifts the magazine and presses it against her bosom before saying, "Sorry for waking you. Where is Miss Daisy today? Not with you?"

"Go back to your seat."

She ambles triumphantly with her steal back to her seat.

CHAPTER 27

Vanessa van der Spuy

Odessa is still in bed when Georgi walks in. It is mid-morning. "You told me you were off to Germany. I hope you have not joined your brother as a spy. You are beginning to exhibit strange habits."

"Like what, you lazy woman?"

"Like duplicity. Didn't you say you were off to Germany? Mother calls and says you went home. Don't ever practice your brother's secret service habits on me."

"You should have told me Mother is ill. She cried when I left."

"Why did she cry?"

"She is lonely. Have you no sympathy for Mother?"

"Funny, she never cried over me when I was there and when I left."

"You obviously looked her in the eye... and saw she never cried?"

"Parents dote over their blue-eyed daughters..."

"You are pathetic, with your constant gaslighting. Go back home and take care of Mother. What are you doing in Africa? Mother needs you back home, and so does your child."

"She needs only you, Georgi, not me."

Georgi sits on Odessa's bed and says, "Call Mother and apologize for what you said to her before you relocated your child to Jean Mackenzie. Your attitude stinks."

"I was feeling sorry for her... I didn't want to burden her with a baby."

"You lie, you evil woman! Call her now and apologize for inferring she has an infectious disease; otherwise, pack your bloody stuff right now and find your accommodation."

"This is not your property. I spoke to Marcia..."

Georgi attacks Odessa and chokes her. Odessa tries to fight back, but is no match against Georgi. Leaving Odessa to cough out of the awkward situation.

"Listen, Odessa, I'll shoot you dead if you don't apologize right now, and I mean it. Marcia lost her gun, and I am keeping it to protect myself."

"You stole Marcia's weapon?"

"She won't miss the lone 48, what with her large military-style armory in her main bedroom."

"Georgi, you've become a criminal, just like Father..."

"I won't serve a day in jail because my entire family is a band of government secret agents."

"You are evil, Georgi. You are a dangerous psychopath. One day, you will murder someone."

"And you will be my first victim if you don't call Mama right now."

Later in the afternoon, Odessa is still recovering in bed, lazily wiggling to 'Zabalaza,' the music of popular Thandiswa Mazwai. She has somehow recovered from the earlier trauma. Georgi gazes at her sister and shakes her head in disapproval. Georgi is unhappy with Odessa's apology to Mother Ellen. She insists that Odessa call their mother every night so she can update them on her health.

"You can't order me around. I'm leaving this place tomorrow."

"Where will you go?"

"Anywhere I won't be facing Mrs Hitler."

"Don't go, silly. No more hassling you. I can't live without you."

"Go to hell, Georgi."

"We should be preparing something to eat... I crave anything cooked by you, Odessa."

"Pregnancy encourages some women to lie through their teeth. But word on the street is that you had an abortion. So, you can't be pregnant..."

"Street?" "Why did you do it? Now I know you were for real when you kept directing me to abort..."

"Go tell your rumor mongers to stop lying. No abortion happened."

"I suspect you did it because you were unsure who the father was. Your blue-eyed blonde boyfriend would get a shock to see Ryan's dark piccaninny pop out. Unless, of course... Look, Georgi, girls do change their minds. Just because you're engaged and have this guy's exclusive engagement ring doesn't mean a thing. Tell me. I'm your sister, even though you nearly murdered me today; should we buy select outfits for your wedding, or will it be a waste of money?"

"I'm considering that marriage."

Odessa sits up, smirks, "Stage fright... or you've come to your senses?"

"I know you're gloating."

"No, I can't even raise a crocodile tear. Are you serious? You've changed your mind?"

"I didn't say that. I'm considering options."

"Ryan is your only option, Sister Girl."

Georgi forces a deep breath, and after rising, she says, "Guess who's coming to dinner tonight."

A surge of adrenaline is released through Odessa's entire body, like the tingling she felt the first time Luca grazed her neck under the streetlight.

She rises and shouts, "Ryan, of course!"

"Wrong! It's Sofia."

"Sofia? Barend's sister? You've hooked up with a white woman?"

Puri has located a man named Dieter van der Spuy. He was a colonel with the previous apartheid regime's police. Van der Spuy has agreed to meet with Puri along the edge of the Westdene Dam in Johannesburg. In March 1985, Westdene became the site of a serious accident in which a bus carrying 78 white students from a nearby Vorentoe

High School crashed into the local dam, resulting in the deaths of 42 students. Van der Spuy is now over 80 years old. Westdene is a previously whites-only leafy suburb nestled snugly between Melville and Sophiatown. Nearby is a university, formerly known as Rand Afrikaans University, which was established exclusively for the white Afrikaans-speaking community. The area has faced hard times due to the 'Rainbow government's failure to address the new demands of an increasingly diverse population. Van der Spuy finds Puri waiting in a nearby Libyan restaurant, a short distance from the 'Westdene Disaster Memorial stone.' Aside from a slight limp and a bemused expression, the larger-than-life khaki-clad ex-policeman appears fit and eager to engage. After they shake hands, he sits and speaks softly, his tone deep and resonant. He feels comfortable with Puri because she has a perfect command of Afrikaans. Puri asks him for his views on the political situation. Van der Spuy laments the advent of democracy and is particularly scathing about the takeover of his country by 'communists like Nelson Mandela.' He said he agreed to meet with Puri near the dam for sentimental reasons. In 1985, his 15-year-old daughter was one of the casualties when the bus plunged into the dam. Puri is eager to learn about another case in the Cape Province. The car in which the girl was traveling with her family had detonated a landmine.

"I remember the case because it was my only investigation in the Cape. I found it odd at the time, but during those days, we took orders without question; that's why there was law and order then. With this new lot of police with big tummies, what can you expect?"

"Yes, that's why I needed to speak to you," says Puri. "What was special about the case that necessitated dispatching you from the Transvaal?"

"Well, they wanted someone objective..."

"Do you remember the name of the child concerned?"

"Mimi Van der Watt. That was her name. She did not die instantly. Although she was in a bad state, she appeared to recover and even sang when I spoke to her. She told me they were on their way to church when the incident occurred. Her brother, whose name escapes me now, had encouraged her to drive his car as part of her driving lessons."

"So, she was alone in the car when the explosion occurred?"

"That's what she said."

Van der Spuy tells Puri that after some time, he and his partner discovered several inconsistencies. First, when the family learned that Spuy and his partner were talking to the girl, they sent their lawyers, who halted further interviews with her. Second, the police report indicated that her brother was the driver and had escaped unharmed. However, by the time Spuy and his partner tried to resolve the discrepancies, the child had died.

"We were never privy to the autopsy. The family took the body and buried her a day or two later."

"What do you think happened?"

"Well, the local and international media coverage painted a picture of terrorists beginning to invade the Cape. My partner and I saw the device that killed the child. That's another anomaly. At the time, terrorists used anti-vehicle mines where they operated, from Angola to Mozambique to Rhodesia. Suspicion began to swirl among a few of us as we looked into this matter. We found the use of anti-personnel mines to attack Robertson, a small farming village in the middle of nowhere, quite odd. The whole thing did not add up."

"Did you express your reservations...?"

"At the time, I kept my reservations to myself. However, several years later, I learned that one of the family members suspected foul play of a different kind from the outset, although the inquest had pointed to a certain MK terrorist cell led by a man with a curious name of Lenin."

"Did you buy that?"

"When you serve under PW Botha, you buy whatever goods they sell," he laughs, coughs, and laughs again. "When I snooped around later, much later, doing my sleuthing, I found little things about the family that I could not confirm. I couldn't buy the rumor that the brother was responsible either..."

"Was that Willem?"

"Yes, now I remember the name."

"In the first place, there was no apparent motive. The person who used the mine was intent on wiping out the entire family."

"Do you know that Willem is dead?"

"Don't tell me. He was murdered, right?"

"A couple of months ago."

"Yeah. I hope a young prosecutor re-examines the cold case. There's no statute of limitations on murder. I can tell you now that the murders are connected. There's no statute of limitations on revenge either. One of my colleagues said the case was as complicated as solving the real causes of Hitler's industrial genocide."

"That's family for you. Do you know the name of the dissenting voice in the family and whether the terrorists were ever apprehended?"

"I know the name, but I can't divulge that to you."

"You can tell me if it was a man or a woman."

"No, let's not go there, Miss Puri. They traced the Lenin fellow to his grave somewhere in Northern Transvaal. I know he served time on the Island, but I have no idea what happened after."

"Are you concerned that the case left many loose ends..."

"This has troubled my conscience because I should have spoken to my superiors about my concerns. But in those days, orders were orders. The case has languished ever since, and time has stood still for me. I can't erase the sweet voice of that child from my head. She sang as if she thought she would be discharged in days..."

I'm sorry. Let's revisit the accident that took your child's life; I learned the driver was a person of color, and many white witnesses viewed it as a terrorist act against whites. Did you feel the same way?

Yes, he was colored. Remember, racial tensions were very high back then. As for my wife and me, after losing our only child, we still believe that it was no accident. I hope I'm wrong. I want to leave now, but please tell me again how you came across my name and your interest in all of this.

"As I told you, I am a researcher. I am compiling material on historical incidents of a similar nature for our German audience."

"My mother, Vanessa, she was German... from Chemnitz..."

"Yes, I know Chemnitz. It was almost destroyed during World War II. Have you kept links with your mother's family?"

"I'm afraid not. People die, and links are severed. But one thing I have learned since the Mimi incident is how wrong it is to sever links with the truth. I've told you all I know for the sake of my daughter, who died at the same age as Mimi Van der Watt."

"What was her name?"

"Vanessa, named after my mother. On the memorial plaque. Please take a picture of her portrayal there... Vanessa Van der Spuy. I miss her."

CHAPTER 28

Black Like Us

Georgi is on tiptoe with anticipation all day. However, when the sun sets, she gives up on Sofia. Odessa continues to irritate her with her frivolous comments:

So, your white girlfriend is a no-show for your dinner. But hiring a temp to look after your white girlfriend? Wasn't that a bit much? What are we going to do with the poor black woman?"

"Chiurai? I'll see to her salary. She can't be a temp for the rest of her life. Marcia pays me for doing pretty little. It's high time she stopped playing games, making me feel like an appendage in her household machinery."

"I could smell her duplicity from day one, and I tried to warn you, Georgi."

Ignoring her sister, Georgi goes to bed, and as she dozes off, she receives a call from Puri.

"I'm here in Johannesburg. I've just chatted with an ex-policeman who knows something about Barend's family."

"When were you planning on telling me you were in the country?"

"Everything happened quickly because the man specified the date and time for the interview."

"You know, Puri, the only time I expect the truth from you is when your lips are not moving. I was with you barely a week ago, and you didn't mention anything about flying to the country. Do you remember the day you denied you had been to Soweto?"

"Calm down..."

"Forget it. Tell me about the policeman you met."

"His name is Colonel Van der Spuy. I'll tell you about it tomorrow. Let's meet at the Holiday Inn..."

"Is Father there with you?"

"No, your father is not here with me."

"I am at Marcia's Houghton Estate..."

"I know where you are, Georgi."

"You can come over if you wish. I'm not coming to the Holiday Inn where two adults make a spectacle."

Puri slams the telephone.

"What's the matter with this woman?"

Much later, Georgi gets out of bed and says, "Odessa, I can't sleep. Please use your phone to call Sofia. Tell her we have been expecting her for over twenty-four hours."

"Georgi, don't ever ask me again to talk to your white girlfriend. You know very well I don't like white people."

"So, you're a racist."

"I'm no bloody racist. How many slaves have I shipped from Africa? Do you know enslaved Africans worked hard on plantations and railway quarries?"

"Please call Sofia, will you?"

"And enslaved Black people were shot on sight if they tried to escape? Jim Crow invented nothing but studied the script to mimic his racist ancestors."

"Go to hell, Odessa."

"My throat is hurting like I swallowed sand from the seashore because you choked me and tried to murder me, and now you want me to call your lesbian friend? You can choke me again and save me the trouble of hanging myself. But I'm not calling your mate."

At an intrusive hour of three, at dawn, Odessa rushes into Georgi's bedroom, whispering anxiously, "Georgi, there's a strange-looking car on the driveway with its headlights off. I can't see its occupants."

They both rush to draw the blinds carefully to investigate. Odessa wants Georgi to call the police. After reading the car's plate numbers, Georgi says, "I think Sofia is here."

"At this bloody hour?"

Georgi walks out to the car. Sofia greets her in her distinctively staid manner. Odessa quietly helps Sofia carry her small luggage inside. She quickly returns to her bedroom, leaving her door slightly ajar to eavesdrop—Georgi and Sofia sit in the breakfast bar.

"I am sorry to get here this late. I got arrested at Sasolburg yesterday for speeding. They released me at midnight after paying a fine."

"Thanks, you came. Can I make you something?"

"Rooibos will do, thanks."

"Then I'll show you to your room..."

"This is a lovely place."

"Thanks, it's owned by the Taungs."

"You wanted to speak to me, right?"

"Can't it wait till after breakfast? You must be tired."

Sofia smiles clumsily and says, "Yes, I'm exhausted but eager to hear what you say. Dolly said I can trust you. We can talk now."

Georgi serves tea and gets back to her seat.

Sofia continues, "Tell me what you saw when you went to Willem's place."

"I saw something, Sofia. When was the last time you were there?"

"Long ago. It's our family property, but Willem forbade me from entering it. We fought over this, but everybody stood against me. I went there one night, unaware that Willem had installed a burglar alarm, and I got arrested."

"Did you have to break in?"

"I was looking for something there. Please, I am tired of the suspense; let me know."

"Okay, Sofia. I'll show you something, and I want you to tell me about it."

Georgi walks away, and Odessa emerges in her pajamas to speak to Sofia, whose eyes are oozing with tears, and says, "Are you spying on us? I know all about your tricks, you white people. Your flood of tears doesn't fool me at all. Why are you here?"

Sofia says, "The black woman who arrested me for speeding looks like you."

Odessa catches Georgi's footsteps and dashes back to her room to eavesdrop. When she comes back, Georgi sticks a photo on the table in front of Sofia, who takes a quick look before she shrieks like a red fox. Odessa emerges and holds Sofia's hand, trying to figure out how to deal with the confusing situation.

"What is it, Georgi? What's the matter with her?"

"You should go to bed, Sofia," pleads Georgi. Let me show you to your room."

"No, I want you to tell me more…"

"Sofia, Georgi is telling you nothing until you are well rested. Let's go."

Odessa leads Sofia to her bedroom; "Here. You need a shower first. It's not nice for a woman to be in a police cage like an Amazon worker. I didn't know they detain white girls for speeding. Isn't that treatment reserved for black males?"

Sofia ignores Odessa's remarks and repeats, "Thanks, I'll shower. I hope the water is warm…"

"Of course, they have a geyser here. This is not just a lovely place," counters Odessa.

"Sorry, I didn't mean to be rude…"

"What speed were you making when they arrested you?" Interjects Georgi.

"Just over 280."

"Over 200 Kilometers per hour? Oh, that was something, Girl!" shouts Odessa.

It is a bright garden-fresh morning in Houghton. Odessa, Sofia, and Georgi are seated comfortably on the air-flooded porch, having breakfast. Chiurai, a strikingly pretty young woman with adorable dark skin, is on hand to serve.

As Puri joins them, Odessa introduces Chiurai to her. Odessa makes a point of presenting Chiurai as a pretty black girl from Alexandra.

"No, I am a pretty girl from Bela-Bela, not Alexandra… Most of us live in the Alexandra backrooms to look for work in Sandton."

"You are so pretty, Chiurai. I want to take a portrait of you before I return to Germany. Do you mind?" says Puri.

"Yes, I mind. We can talk about the business in private. Tea, Coffee…?"

Puri goes on to summarize her meeting with Van der Spuy. She asks Sofia, "What do you think happened to Mimi, your sister?"

"The police told us terrorists planted the bomb that killed her. Look, I don't want to talk about Mimi until you tell me about the child in that picture you showed me, Georgi."

"Do you know the child?" asks Georgi.

Sofia's lips quiver as she says, "Yes, I know her. She is the baby I lost. Where is she?"

Silence descends on the porch. Puri rises and walks to the corner to cry. Finally, Puri asks, "You lost your child? When last did you see her?"

What Sofia says next makes one's hair stand on end. Throughout her pregnancy, the family keeps her confined to a house she cannot identify. During that time, Dolly, an illegal immigrant from Malawi, takes care of all her needs. They threaten Dolly with deportation should she ever open her mouth about the matter. Sofia's father, a church deacon, having condemned Sofia to hell for bringing the family into disrepute, menaces Sofia with his God-given entitlement to curse her if she fails to follow his instructions. Dolly contacts the eldest son, Lyndon, on the day she feels labor starting, as ordered. Lyndon is in the strange house for three days, awaiting labor. On the third day, two midwives arrive, and after Sofia gives birth to a baby girl, she names her Skylar. One of the midwives takes pictures of what she can see around. However, as they busily cook up a scheme to cover up their deed, one of the women puts her cellphone on the chair in plain view of Dolly, who quickly snatches and disables it in the toilet. Sofia is administered midazolam, which induces a deep sleep. When she wakes a few hours later, the only other person in the house is Dolly, who tells her that the nurses took the baby and left. Sofia has no clue where they took the baby. Dolly decides to use the phone as a bargaining tool should their threats to deport her materialize. Unfortunately, a raid is conducted by a team of eight white men at Dolly's mud quarters a day later, and the cellphone disappears.

Georgi produces the file with copies of the adoption papers. Sofia is shocked to see her name and signature.

"Who are these people? I did not sign to get Skylar adopted."

"How much does Barend know about all this?"

"He should have supported me instead of making me look like a dumb Boer girl. My family has no concept of justice."

"Did you open a case with the police?" asks Odessa. "They are quick to respond if white people report a crime."

"My Ouma advises me against it, but I still go ahead and report it. The police do not take me seriously because they say I am mad. Lyndon shows the police a document with my name from Stikland Mental Hospital. Nobody believes me. They say they can't proceed because of a lack of evidence."

"Thanks, Sofia. You are a brave girl. Puri and Nathaniel will help."

"Yes, Georgi, I'll go with them wherever they go."

"If you don't mind telling us, where is the father?" asks Puri.

"We went our separate ways after he accused me of murdering the child on account of... she was colored, like you, Georgi."

The porch falls into another pause of uneasy silence. Chiurai walks back to offer more 'waitron' services.

"Your boyfriend was black?" Odessa asks with a naughty whisper.

"Oh, no! No!" Sofia says with pounding emphasis, "He was a colored lecturer in animal husbandry."

"So, he was not black?" Odessa takes Sofia on.

"Certainly not," Sofia pummels more deeply.

Chiurai and Odessa instantly march out in a huff. When they reach the corridor, Odessa asks Chiurai, "Do you know Ryan?"

"No. Who is that?"

"Look, Chiurai, Ryan is a handsome man who teaches at UCT."

"Your boyfriend?"

"I want him to be your boyfriend."

"Why do you want a lecturer to be my boyfriend?"

"You are a very pretty black girl, and I like you. Ryan must meet you. You'll be happy to meet him. He is black like us."

Odessa says to herself, 'Chiurai must do it. Once my green-eyed sister hears this black beauty is dating her Ryan, she will jump back into his passionate embrace like a springbok.

Marcia brings her children to Houghton for a day. They are en route to Victoria Falls. Taylor wants Georgi to join them, but his mother offers excuses. Georgi is aware of Marcia's inexplicable veto, and she concludes that there is more to the rejection than meets the eye. When it is time to leave, Marcia motions for Georgi to the poolside, and they sit there admiring the miniature blue waves playing in the pool.

Marcia says, "I have been worried about you. How are you getting on?"

"I'm getting on fine. Why are you worried about me?"

"You're like a daughter to me. Mothers will always be curious about their daughters' daily activities and interests. A mother wonders about the dangers lurking in her daughter's space as night falls. When I call you in the morning, I only want to hear your voice..."

"You wonder what I do at night?"

"I wonder who you are with when you do what you do at night. You're a fragile girl in a strange country."

"No need to worry, Marcia. I'm always here with Odessa."

"Yes, but what are you up to? I get the feeling your marital plans are on hold. Am I correct?"

"Everything is on hold right now. There's time to keep and throw away, says the bible."

"Should I take it you are throwing someone away?"

Georgi has lost all trust in human nature, and that includes Marcia. She recalls the day she and Odessa introduced themselves to Moroka and Marcia. She cannot shake the feeling that, in truth, the couple preferred Odessa to her. Marcia had put it plainly: 'We particularly asked for a black person.' The more she thinks about the episode, the deeper she sinks into depression.

Marcia tries to smooth the rough relationship: "I've been walking a tightrope,

Georgi. But as promised, I'll make it worthwhile financially for you. We have to leave now. Moroka and I have decided to give you this property. I hope you'll enjoy it with Ryan because you deserve a home as beautiful as you are."

Georgi is silent for a second, and then she says, "I am hearing rumors about you and Moroka. Please, Marcia, tell me."

Marcia says, "Couples do break up when there are disagreements, Georgi."

"Disagreements are like colds or flu. You don't kill off a family just because one member has the flu. That's what Mother Ellen used to say. Sorry for nose-diving into your territory. What do you mean you want to 'give' me the property?"

"It's a gift to you, lock, stock, and barrel."

After she collects herself, Georgi says, "You threw in Ryan's name. Do you want me to enjoy the house with Ryan? Is that part of your terms and conditions for the gift?"

Marcia reflects on the question before she says, "You know how we feel about you and Ryan, but you make your own choice."

"Look, Marcia, I appreciate your generosity. I love this home, but I'm unable to accept the gift. Please extend my sincere gratitude to Mr Moroka…"

Nathaniel calls Georgi. After ignoring the call several times, she finally answers, "Nathaniel, please stop calling me for sweet nothing. When are you coming to meet with me about Sofia's case?"

"Listen, Georgi… by the way, I understand you've finally decided to change your name following your miraculous conversion to Judaism… you see, Puri, our mother, she is a bit mental. Don't get yourself sucked into her New Age thing or whatever she calls it…"

"Nathaniel, what do you want?"

"Right. This girl is called Sofia. I don't know her from Eve. She calls to say she wants to talk to me and says, "You know the story?"

"Puri once told me rumors have been circulating about you and Sofia. Is she your girlfriend? I tend to believe her because I suspect she is a spy for this government."

"I just told you I've never met the girl."

"Didn't Puri ever brief you about Sofia?"

"I don't take calls from Mother anymore. She yells and constantly tells me to go with her to Israel. I think she's developing dementia. She needs our help, Georgi. Why would she name you Hadassah? I told her I prefer the sexy name, 'Bathsheba,'" he giggles.

"Hadassah? Is that what she said to you?"

"She said Esther is the synonym of Hadassah."

"Yes, seriously now; please be gentle with her. Convince her she'll never get me to be Esther or Hadassah."

"She wants you and I to go to Jerusalem. I once toured Gaza and the West Bank. What I saw there made me wonder if the Israeli regime have ever read a simple history book. Puri gets mad when I ask her to explain. This latest craze about being Jewish…?"

"What did you see in the West Bank?"

"Ask your Mother to help you tour the Palestinian territories. You will see for yourself what I saw."

Georgi heaves and says, "Alright, please come to Marcia's Houghton Estate. You know the location because you're always snooping around like a restless Chihuahua wherever I am. I'll explain everything about Sofia when you get here. When can I expect you?"

"I'm just across the street, visiting friends. I'll be there in five minutes."

"What friends, Nathaniel? You don't have a single friend in this world..."

When Nathaniel steps in, Chiurai is on hand to welcome him.

"Please call Georgi. Have we met before?"

"No, I'm sure you would remember my face."

"Yeah, you're pretty."

"I know. Even my mother thinks so. Can I get you a drink?"

"Ginger-ale if I'm lucky? I'd love that."

Chiurai helps Nathaniel with drinks, and just before she disappears, Nathaniel asks her if she has a name.

"Yes, that's an old Bill Cosby joke. My name is Chiurai."

"Yes? What does it mean?"

"What's your name?"

"I'm Nathaniel."

"Does it have a meaning?"

"If you read your bible, you'll know who I am," he put it, giving a harsh, derisive laugh.

Chiurai winces and walks out. Nathaniel wanders around the bar, inspecting pictures and paintings on the walls before he shuffles out toward the poolside. Georgi emerges, and the twins relax on the easy chairs.

"Nice set-up you've got here. Who's that nice black girl inside?"

"Why didn't you ask her?"

"I'm asking you."

"Do you like her?"

"Of course, I like her. I have no doubt you like her just as much; otherwise, what is she doing here? No need to apologize if you're attracted to another woman..."

"Oh, please, Nathaniel! Her name is Chiurai."

"She told me."

"That's a start. I know of your social anxiety, while putting on airs to impress. Just smile and make eye contact with her. Tell her you like her body. You might be lucky...."

"I'd rather not. She looks like an African Princess in those third-grade South American movies, pretty and pretentious."

"She's a strong black woman, you mean? That's why I find her attractive."

"No doubt Puri knows you've come out of the closet."

"I learn Odessa is linking up with Ganon April. Is that a death wish? That man is psycho."

"Perhaps I should ask you again, Nathaniel. The truth. What's your story with Sofia? Puri talks of the telltale signs of a romantic affair between you two. Do you rendezvous with her in secret?

CHAPTER 29

An Angry Boer Girl

There is something suspicious about Sofia. While she seems shy and innocent, a closer look shows her acting like a skilled performer. Nobody knows where she went after leaving Georgi and her group. However, one day, Dolly answers Georgi's call and says Sofia has been hiding in the African servant's quarters inside her room. Dolly explains that Sofia escaped from police custody after being rearrested in Sasolburg.

A few weeks later, Puri and Nathaniel secretly trace an address and find a couple living there with several children, all of whom are white. Someone must have tipped off the pair because when police pounce on the property, they find five abandoned children. Police have cordoned off the premises as a crime scene, with the unknown adults nowhere to be seen.

According to Nathaniel, they have moved the children to a safe location at Saint Helena Bay. Given that three years have passed since Sofia lost her child, she will need to take a DNA test for identification. Due to the haste with which white, blue-eyed children are trafficked across Europe, finding such children is often impossible. However, there is a chance with Sofia's lost baby because she is not white.

Nathaniel calls Puri to inform her about the developments in Sofia's escape from her holding cell.

"Is this your new number, Nathaniel?"

"No, it's one of those I use to get you to answer my calls."

"Tell me about Sofia."

Nathaniel tells Puri that he has just picked up Sofia from her hiding place and found a safe place to hide from her family. He tells her that Sofia gave him a new version of what happened to Mimi-Koo. He wants to talk to her father about the incident.

"And about the safe place? Are you having an affair with that girl?"

"I want to clear our family name, Mother."

"What for? You leave that matter alone. Your father has dealt with it, and that's it. I asked you to tell me about the safe place you are keeping Sofia. I am concerned about you because you are always hasty and tactless. How much time do you spend with her in that safe place?"

"Okay, not your business; I must tell you about Sofia. It was love at first sight…"

"Sofia?"

"I feel like we have great chemistry, but I haven't said anything to her yet."

"What are you waiting for?"

"We must clear the air with her folk on her sister's matter."

"Nat, when last did you take your medication?"

"Medication! I've had it up to here with you harping on about medication. Do you still think I am crazy?"

"Calm down. Nobody said you are crazy. You are my only boy. You know I'm always concerned about you..."

"Stop belittling me. I'm not your little boy anymore."

"You are. And Esther is my little girl. Love at first sight with Sofia, you say? What makes you think that's normal for an intelligent young man like you? I learn that the girl has spent half her life in mental institutions around the Cape. What are you doing?"

Nathaniel has tried to convince Sofia of the need to meet her father. He warns her that otherwise, they won't proceed with her case. Because Sofia is desperate to find her child, she has no choice but to direct Nathaniel to her family's farmhouse. As they steer along the driveway, he repeats his intention of clearing things up with her father as she begs him to avoid talking to him. They stop in front of the mansion under an avocado tree. Sofia is shaking and in tears. She pleads, "Please, Nathaniel, help me get my child first. We can talk about Mimi afterward."

"Sofia, I promise. We are on top of your situation now, but I must clarify something with your family patriarch."

"My father is a Deacon or elder or something. He possesses spiritual powers to curse, and I am aware that he has cast several curses on me. He will do more if we appear together, because he dislikes people of color. Please, Nathaniel. I am terrified of looking into his eyes. I can't deal with this. If we don't leave, there'll be trouble."

Dolly comes out of the veranda to meet them. She informs Gert, Sofia's father, about their presence.

Gert, a tall man with a colossal presence, descends from the veranda like a cyclone. His lips are as tight as a cowhide drum. Skipping the niceties of greetings, he demands from Sofia, "What is this about?"

"Nice to meet you, Mr Watt," Nathaniel says. May I speak with you in private for a moment?"

Gert motions Nathaniel to the large, shiny table on the veranda. Sofia tags along and takes her seat on a bench a distance away. Shaking and feeling nauseous, she signals for water from Dolly.

"I am Nathaniel Lieber, Georgi's brother and son of a man you know as Lenin or Bekker..."

Gert nearly falls off his chair. Sofia's trembling gets worse, and her eyes focus on her father. She deeply regrets having met Nathaniel.

"What do you want?" Gert roars.

"Your family, or some members of it, have accused my father of something he never did, and I would like Sofia to tell you what she knows."

"Sofia? We don't discuss such matters in this house, and Sofia is the last to enter such discussions. She will tell you nothing we don't know already. Barend dealt with the matter at a level I am not interested in. But Barend is his own man."

Sofia is quiet for a little while. Her face is wet. Finally, she stands up and says, "Pa, I am tired of being oppressed by this family just because I tell the truth about Willem abusing Leandra. But I want you to tell me today: what happened to my baby? The last thing I remember was hearing someone shout 'push, push, push.'"

"How dare you? What makes you think that child is any concern of mine?"

"Only Barend matters in this house; it's Barend this, Barend that…"

"Please, Sir, tell me what you know about Willem's criminal activities," Nathaniel says boldly.

Sofia juts her chin and blasts, "I'll tell you, Nathaniel. Willem came here on a Sunday after church while we were having lunch, and he said he wanted to say something to the family. Then he told everyone he had proof I was pregnant, and my Khoi boyfriend did not even attend church. He said all these coloreds were Muslims who wanted to destroy the white Volk. Father forced me to put my hand on the bible and swear I was not pregnant. I refused to answer. Then you, Papa, you forced me to put my hand on the cover of your bible and swear I would terminate the pregnancy."

Gert rises and says, "You have disgraced our name, Sofia. And as for you, Lieber, I resent your audacity to come here to meddle in my family affairs…"

Gert lurches out in the direction of the cornfields.

The Saint Helena trip yields little regarding Sofia's child. However, an unexpected moment with a white older woman offers some promising hints. On their way back, Nathaniel and Sofia stay at the Blueberry Hill Hotel in Vredenburg.

"Separate rooms?"

"Of course," retorts Sofia. "What else could it be?"

Late into Nathaniel's deep sleep, a panic-stricken Sofia bangs on the door, shouting for Nathaniel to wake up.

Opening the door, he chides Sofia, "You said you wanted separate rooms."

"Yes, that was before a crazy woman came into my room, claiming to be a prophet."

"What did she prophesy?"

"First, she wants Fifty Rand, and then she says she knows why we are in the area. She says many people come here looking for their lost children or girlfriends. When she hears I am traveling with you, she ups the demand to Two Hundred Rand for information…"

"Why?"

"I ask her why, and she says I am traveling with an Arab."

"What has she got against Arabs?"

"I don't know. But even Barend says all Arab men carry bundles of Dollars in their travels. The prophet says that Sandy Point has a villa where they hoard a monthly children's consignment before they make them disappear. The Arab man will give you One Thousand Rand if you give me the Villa's address."

Nathaniel takes Sofia's ranting with a pinch of salt. However, he insists on meeting the prophet. It is too late, though, because Sofia has already given away the money in exchange for the address to the Villa.

"What are we going to do? I can't go back to that room. That woman could be a spook. She did look like one."

"Yeah? Why did you give her the money, then?"

"I want my Skylar. Do you know what it means to lose a child? Let's fetch my stuff from my room. I'll sacrifice and put up here with you; I don't mind. She gave me the address. We'll have to drive there first thing in the morning."

After relocating, Sofia says, "There's only one bed, Nathaniel. How am I going to sleep?"

"It's a double bed, Sofia. What do you suggest?"

"Okay, we can share. I hope you don't snore."

"Yeah, but no nightmares about prophets. I need my sleep."

"But we can chat a bit before we sleep."

"Chat about the prophet?"

"No, about me. About Sofia."

You're on your own

Five days later, a state helicopter lands at a Durban Airstrip. Sofia feels nervous as she walks across the barracks' tarmac. Nathaniel is waiting to take her to the Clarion Hotel, a few kilometers away. The sight of Sofia in her black denim skirt leaves little to the imagination and makes him salivate. He thinks it matches her striped arm sweater perfectly, although he finds her pink baseball cap a bit too much. He can't help but admire her fresh new look. Nathaniel has already booked a suit.

"We have our room already. I hope you don't mind sharing the double bed with me. After all, we have already gone through a dress rehearsal after your prophet spooked you to death."

Sofia smiles and rolls her eyes.

"Dress rehearsal? I wanted us to chat before you started snoring."

"We can start our chat right now. It's difficult to have a nice chat when one is tired."

Sofia is pleased with the hotel amenities. After she unpacks, she freshens up and changes into a white T-shirt and blue jeans—no cap this time. She goes to the restaurant, where Nathaniel is already perusing the menu.

"I'm happy to be here, but don't keep me in the dark. I don't like mysteries and surprises. Anxiety is killing me."

"Yes, you do look happier than I've seen you before. And when you're happy, you look pretty."

"Wait till I get my daughter back; then you'll see pretty."

"It looks like you have been hiding your beauty behind the shadows of white anger or feminine agony. That's what Georgi says about you."

"About me?"

"Are there any shadows of agony in your heart?"

"Yes, of course. My shadows of agony are called Skylar. I suppose you and Georgi, being twins, discuss matters of the heart?"

A young African waiter stands next to the table, seemingly more interested in the conversation about matters of the heart than the menu and the orders.

"Matters of the heart with Georgi? No. I don't." Nathaniel continues after the waiter takes orders, "I treat Georgi as a distant relative, and I have to suffer. She has an oblique rejoinder for everything I say. Would you like me to talk about heart matters with you?"

"About Georgi?"

"About you, Sofia."

"I don't have any interesting matters to talk about... Last time, you forced me to share a double bed with you for nothing because I wanted us to talk about me."

"For nothing? So, why didn't you talk about you?"

"I was waiting for you to ask interesting questions. Don't you have interesting questions to ask a girl?"

"You can tell me about your baby."

"You know she is missing. I thought you would tell me something about her."

"Before she went missing, you undoubtedly had exciting exploits to share about men. I want to know how things happen among the Volk... the Afrikaners."

"Apart from circling ox-wagons, much the same as any nation, I guess," she grimaces. "You want to know about the father of my baby? Everyone wants to know, as if a mother's life is incomplete without answers about her child's father. I'll tell you because you are trying to help me. He moved on after the child disappeared, accusing us, me, and my entire Boer nation of causing his child's disappearance."

After enjoying their snacks, they move to the pool area and order more drinks.

"I wish I'd met you when I first landed in South Africa."

"Yes? Why?"

"We would have solved your problem long ago."

"I thought you were South African. When did you first land on these shores?"

"A year or so ago. I am what South Africans call an exile, although I have no clue what that means. Only my mother got herself into the struggle. But the education she gave me helped me get a job in government, even before I set foot here."

"What job do you do, if I may ask?"

"We can park that one for now, but would I be correct to say you own a wine farm?"

"How do you know that?"

"That's part of my job."

"It's a family thing. I'm out of it for now because of some family issues."

"We all have family issues. May I join you as a junior partner the day you decide to return to it? I like winemaking, and I can put up with family issues."

"Not my family, you can't. You saw some snippets when you invaded my home and met my father last time. Besides, winemaking is a full-time occupation. One day, I'll own my brand of wine, which is produced straight from my vineyard. I know more about the business than most men. I'm not allowed to share my brand with anyone. *Een keer gebyt twee keer skaam.*"

"Think about it. We can call it *'Sofia L'amour de Ma Vie'*. Wine Connoisseurs, worth their salt worship anything French."

Sofia laughs out loud and screams, "Yes, they do. I like that." Sofia appears to reflect seriously and repeats in a chant, "'*Sofia L'amour de Ma Vie.*' Oh gosh, Nathaniel! Do you remember the homeland of Bapetikosweti?"

"And where is that?"

"I guess you do remember Evita Bezuidenhout…"

"Oh yes, Pieter Dirk Uys?"

"Only Ouma in my family circles found him hilarious. One day, she took me to see 'Skating on Thin Ice', and the audience laughed their lungs out. What about him?"

"His wine is ingeniously branded *'Jeau Moer.'* You need to use a French accent when placing the order. It's popular in France and Germany.

"Ahhh!"

Nathaniel takes a moment to admire Sofia's cheerful expression.

"I remember; Dirk Uys used satire to poke fun at his own Afrikaners."

"Can an Afrikaner ever be a hero of the struggle, Nathaniel? I know something about Bram Fischer and Molly Krige, his wife. How can I forget them when my family used their names as swear words or ogres to scare children? Perhaps one day you'll teach me about the struggle. When will it finally end? Every black man I come across seems angry, and it appears that everyone is in a struggle. Black women are worse. My Afrikaans accent seems to get on their nerves."

"Yeah?"

"We own big chunks of land with the specter of expropriation hanging above our heads like the Sword of Damocles. They say we stole the land, and the Afrikaner Boers must return it to the Africans. As a young Afrikaner girl, whose land did I steal, and where is this struggle taking me?"

"Talk to your people, Sofi, to have a serious dialogue with the Africans about land. You sound like an angry Afrikaner girl. When a girl is angry, she can't feel other people's distress. Are you an angry girl?"

"No. I am an angry Boer girl. That's what this country has turned me into. Please, please, let's not talk politics. We're not here for that. You didn't tell me you'd be coming to Durban too. Why did you lie? You said someone else would be helping me?"

"Well, I'm here, Sofia. Are you disappointed?"

"Funny! I'm delighted you're here with me. Did you manage to arrest the woman from Blueberry Hill?"

"Surveillance cameras. They didn't arrest her. She's not a black woman."

"But they handcuffed me for speeding… and I am a white woman. Please, Nathaniel, stop your racist card and tell me about the Blueberry woman."

"The Blueberry woman? They asked her questions and then let her go. When the police raided the Villa, they met with a 'house to let' sign. Fortunately, they discovered enough leads. That's why we are here."

"I've never used a helicopter. That's how you move around here?"

Nathaniel nudges closer to Sofia and begins to probe her about the stories she has told him about her missing child and her family. Sofia's face turns red, and her voice shakes like a primary school child in trouble. He apologizes for her and assumes a serious tone, "At dawn, before I flew here, I saw the five children that the law had earlier discovered, thanks to the leads supplied by your Blueberry Hill prophet..."

Sofia begins to hyperventilate and falls sick. She rushes to the bathroom and stays there for a long time. When she comes back, she appears drained but smiles awkwardly. Nathaniel hands her his camera along with a photo album filled with pictures of children of different ages. She examines the images and grimaces before shaking her head, feeling a sense of disappointment. She composes herself, and they finish their drinks in silence.

"These images show me nothing, Nathaniel. Did you see a child with a birthmark behind her ear?"

Nathaniel holds Sofia's hand and rubs it before he throws her a curveball. A couple from Namibia claims the child with darker pigmentation is theirs, which means Sofia would have to take a mitochondrial DNA test before they proceed. Sofia might still face difficulties even if Nathaniel finds the child. Society is often unkind to women who have been previously labeled mentally unwell.

"What dark pigmentation?" Sofia challenges irritably. "I am talking about a birthmark, Nathaniel!"

"That child has brown skin. She might be your Skylar."

"My baby has no bloody dark pigmentation."

"With that kind of attitude, you're on your own."

Nathaniel angrily slams his drink on the table and storms off. Sofia rushes after him, pleading for forgiveness for the hurtful things she said, but she can't stop him from leaving her. Following the disagreement, Sofia suffers another intense mental breakdown.

CHAPTER 30

Skylar

Meanwhile, Odessa and Georgi are in the Houghton kitchen, cooking and chatting.

"What did you say to Marcia when she offered you this house?"

I asked for the terms and conditions, but she wasn't forthcoming with anything that made sense.

Georgi, a stranger, offers you property beyond your wildest nanny dreams, and you're insisting on terms and conditions?

"Yes."

"Did you ask her to be forthcoming with those terms?"

"She mentioned something about squatting with Ryan..."

"Look, Sweetie Georgi, go on your knees and beg Ryan to marry you. With your dubious credentials as a colored nanny, you won't survive in South Africa. I've read a lot about the coloreds of this country. They are not facing the same challenges as the coloreds of Canada and America, as you well know. You need Ryan, unless, of course... let me put it this way," Odessa carries on. "One day, my friend said..."

"I know what Okobi said. You've rehashed your line ad nauseam..."

"You remind me of one of my white respondents who said people are tired of talking about apartheid, that we must move on. Do you agree with that? I'll repeat my ad nauseam story. One day, Okobi said, 'The blacker the berry, the sweeter the juice'."

"Odessa, let's talk about something of grave concern. I learned from Silvia with two 'i's. Remember her? She tells me the police helped locate Sofia's child. I once promised to find a school for that girl in Canada. Please help me help her."

"Speak to your father. He's swimming in connections, that man."

"Okay, I think they found Sofia's baby..."

"Yeah, they will always find a child if a mother is white. And did you know your brother has been on a fancy jaunt to exotic destinations with Sofia? Marcia told me."

"Nathaniel is a big boy, Odessa..."

"Yeah, Nathaniel is a big boy who wanted to sleep with you, remember? Aren't you jealous? Sofia beat you to it."

"Nathaniel is my brother."

"Ryan is not your brother. I can imagine what he would have done if he had laid his eyes on Chiurai before your airport encounter with him. Don't you think the Bela-Bela girl has classic African curves to die for?"

My father is difficult.

For several weeks, Sofia has been under observation in a mental institution. Georgi drives late one night to talk to Dolly in secret. Dolly is uneasy about the call, and she warns her to stay away. Following Nathaniel's stopover with Sofia, Gert, the Patriarch, had become so agitated that it took three days before he paid his workers their wages.

"Dolly, please tell me what happened after Sofia gave birth to her baby."

"I am not allowed to say anything about that."

"Nathaniel tells me you are from Malawi. Is that true?"

Dolly begins to talk. Gert had been threatening to get her deported for misdemeanors. During the three days of the wage drought, he warned Dolly to stop discussing his family matters with strangers. He even demanded that she hand over her illegal identity documents to him. So, she had no choice but to go along with the silent treatment. Her role was to nurse Sofia and attend to all her needs until labor began. She was there when they offered the baby to a couple under the illegal adoption scheme.

"You can tell me what happened. Nobody else will know what you told me. Who took that child after Sofia delivered her?"

"A man and a woman. They were young but looked rich because they drove a new car."

"Did you get their names?"

"No, but the woman called the man Eric."

"Eric?"

Georgi pulls the images of the papers and pictures she had stolen from Willem's flat and checks the names of the signatories to the adoption papers. There is no Eric.

"Can you describe the couple and the car they were driving?"

"It was a white couple. The lady was shorter than I, and she had red hair. The man was tall with a sharp nose."

"His hair?"

"I don't remember."

"Did you take the registration number by chance?"

"No, but it was a navy blue Volvo. I don't know the number."

"What else can you tell me, Dolly?"

"I stole a cellphone owned by the woman who took Sofia's baby. But the following day, some men ransacked my room, and after they had caned me on my bare bottom, they left."

"Were those men white?"

"Yes. I think Barend's father sent them."

Georgi returns angrily, suspecting an elaborate hoax about the papers she'd found. The next day, she drives to the farm owned by Lyndon, Sofia's elder brother. She arrives late afternoon, anxious to leave the lonely farming area before dark.

"I don't know if you remember me..."

"I remember you, alright," he snaps. "What are you doing here?

Sofia is in the hospital. Did you hear?"

"Sofia is not my responsibility."

"So, you could not have heard she suffered a mental breakdown? She was almost certain she had gotten her baby girl back. But alas, it was not to be, I learned. Does that concern you at all?"

"You have five minutes. I'll get security to drive you out."

Nathaniel finally succeeds in his mission to rescue Sofia from the mental clinic, prompting the local police to reopen the case of the Italian doctors through Interpol. In Sofia's case, it appears the issue is only the tip of the iceberg. The action by the police raises some hope among a lot of white parents who have lost their children over a long time. Nathaniel flies to Italy to investigate the matter, and Morrison joins him soon after. Following three weeks of investigation, a theatre choreographer comes forward with information about twelve children living on the southern tip of Italy in an estate. They conduct a sting operation with Morrison as the potential 'buyer' from Saudi Arabia. The police detain a woman who fits the description of the fugitive doctor. Originally from Albania, the doctors had taken advantage of porous South African borders as well as racial profiling that often advantages Europeans. They immediately place ten children with social workers.

After an intensive police investigation that includes DNA analyses, they isolate one child as having a significant amount of DNA matching that of Sofia's. After a month, Sofia, Nathaniel, and Skylar fly to Cape Town. Sofia looks executive yet relaxed in her dark blue sports jacket, plain white blouse, short light grey denim skirt, and white sneakers. Nathaniel is comfortable wearing blue jeans and a white Bob Dylan T-shirt. Nonchalant Skylar is in her khaki trucker jacket and unicorn sequin denim jeans. She is playful and talkative most of the time.

"Are you sure you want to take this child back home?"

"I'm sure. Why shouldn't I be?"

"What will you say to your father and your people?"

"I'll tell them everything. I brought my daughter back home, and I am thrilled."

"Did you warn them you're on your way home with your black child?"

"She's not a black child," Sofia screams.

"Yeah? You don't think those who abducted her from you think she is black?"

"I don't care what they think."

"What will you say about me?'

"I'll tell them you are my friend. Isn't that what you want, to be friends?"

"I said I would be happy for you to be my mate. And what did you say before you gave me your first kiss?"

"I know what I said, Nathaniel, but we'll have to ease the whole thing gradually…"

"How do you plan to do that?"

"Please understand. My father is difficult, and my brothers are always spoiling for a fight. I leave when Father enters a room because we have nothing in common. My aunt, his sister, who lived in the Free State and left the country because of him, said of him that he is a control freak. Imagine that! I have to be careful. He is a high-profile preacher under strange, toxic spells of our church: purity of white blood, excommunication for premarital pregnancy, no matric dance, and all of that. This oppressive theme permeated the entire place as I grew up. Lyndon, my brother, called me a whore once."

"What do you think of black people?"

"Africans? They hate the Afrikaners; that's all I know."

"Why did your brother refer to you as a whore? Do you know?"

"Because of my colored boyfriend, Skylar's father. That's when I stopped working with him on the wine farm, which, by the way, belongs to me."

"Georgi went to your brother, Lyndon, to talk about the day you delivered…"

"She shouldn't have done that. That man is vindictive and has connections with the apartheid remnants in government."

"You don't think Lyndon will try to harm you and your child?"

"If they try again, I'll fight like a molly queen. I want all of them to know I got my child back without any help from anyone."

"What about Zola Morrison? She found your daughter…"

"I appreciate your help, Nathaniel, and I will tell Zola when I meet her one day. But as for my people! According to them, I am useless; there is nothing positive that I can do, all because my grade was always D or C, and then I got pregnant by a colored man."

"What about Barend? He is a nice guy. Georgi seems to like him."

"Well, Barend upset the apple cart when he brought Georgi home. After Willem's funeral, an all-male meeting took place behind closed doors. They spent over two hours in the main bedroom. What the topic was in there, your guess is as good as mine."

"What did you think?"

"Of course, they were debating a colored girl in a white funeral… a colored girl dating a Van der Watt. What else? It was all about Georgi. Nobody listened to the preaching or the speech during that holy funeral or church service. Georgi dominated the entire service, and the minister was not himself that day, choking and all the pretense. I could feel the mourners squirm, and Lyndon wanted to leave soon after the burial, but they were all dragged into the secret meeting. Dolly gave me hints, but I left it at that. Everyone is scared of Barend as he does no wrong in the eyes of the dynasty. That's what happens when you get distinctions all your life. I was amazed when he was hauled into Father's bedroom, of all places, so that they could grill him about Georgi. For me, it's been like walking on eggshells, and the way things have turned up, I am scared senseless that we are heading for a volcanic eruption."

"You are scared of Barend?"

"I'm scared of the situation. Barend is creepy. When Mother died, he became something of a recluse. I heard through the grapevine that he was honored as Employee of the Year. No one knew about it except Dolly. Oh, Barend! But he can't hide my deep secrets because I can read his mind. My family is like a pressure cooker with no release valve. How can I expose my affair with you without setting off an explosion?"

"Did you have an affair with Skylar's father?"

"It was difficult. We often hid in the vineyard until my abduction. When I came back with no pregnancy and no baby, he couldn't take the insults anymore. He went on his merry way and married someone else."

"What if he comes back to claim his paternity rights?"

"I don't mind that, but Skylar is mine. Are you going to tell me about your affairs?"

"Well, I hope you won't be scared of me, given that I have been getting distinctions all my life. My affairs? The only other woman I have ever found attractive is Georgi…"

"Sies! Your sister?"

"We got separated at birth and only got reunited recently. I craved her body the very first time I saw her. Weeks later, I reluctantly took the advice to see a shrink who told me relationships between twins are fraught with psychological abnormalities. She said when it's a girl and a boy, the magnetism becomes intensely sexual…"

"That's awkward to hear. Is the feeling mutual…? I mean, sexual attraction?"

"When I asked her to talk about her sex drive, Georgi got mad, accusing me of being a pervert…"

"And what did you think of what she said?"

"Every angry outburst reveals hidden discomfort. We all hide secret feelings behind the noise and tend to roar like hungry lions. I grew up in a place where we discussed real issues openly with my parents, not about Cinderella. How open were you about sex with your family?"

"What family? No. My brother Lyndon! He lectured me against 'making a Hotnot child' and dishonoring his Christian family tree. Can you have an intelligent argument with people like that?"

"I want to have an intelligent talk with you, Sofia. Do you mind?"

"Not wishy-washy stuff about my body."

"How do you feel about me?"

"Infatuation comes to mind. Over there in the restaurant, you said something pleasant. You said my backstory inspires you. No one has ever said something like that to me. I wonder about your secret backstory. After you said mine is inspiring, we spent time till the morning hours together, but you left me burning without touching me."

"Why? Did you want us to make love?"

"The thought crossed my mind… so far away from my two-faced family? The further from home one treks, the deeper the desire; there's no better space for a deep connection between two lost souls…"

"Tell me about it."

"That doesn't happen to you? Even as teenagers, a school outing filled our brains with naughty thoughts to experiment with. I ended up sniffing dagga, which helped me feel good and relieved me of family hypocrisy. Yes, not even a touch from you! Then I thought maybe my backstory isn't that inspiring after all. As for you, your backstory troubles me. I am battling to reconcile the man next to me to the deep-rooted image I have of a terrorist."

"The man next to you has his own story. Let's go to St Helena again so you get that story. Don't you think St Helena is the most attractive Bay to tell each other tales and fairy tales about terrorists?"

A cabin crew member who overhears Nathaniel's remarks snaps a smirk. "It's more complicated. You leave me in a hotel for days without telling me what's happening? How do you connect with people... females in particular?"

"Let me tell you about my connection with females. I often argue with my mother, and I find her to be boring at the best of times. But we love each other to bits. My mother and newly discovered sister are the two females closest to me. Communicating with them is like deciphering Lord Byron's 'She Walks in Beauty.' Georgi gave me a copy to pique my interest. I think that poem is about you."

"Oh, please. I don't even know the poem. Have you told Georgi you want me to be your mate? She and Barend are totally in love."

"How do you know they are totally in love...?"

"A couple gets up early, drinks strong coffee, and then makes love?"

"You were shadowing them and taking notes for your fantasies, I see. Look, Sofia, Georgi, and Barend do not amount to my universe. From the day I first looked into your eyes, I knew you were the total of my fantasies."

Skylar happily rests on Nathaniel's shoulder when the Airbus touches down at the Cape. They walk past the 'pickup-and-go' area into the covered parking lot.

CHAPTER 31

Sofia on her Knees

The tension on the farm gets thick again, perhaps even worse than the last time around, as Nathaniel's BMW pulls into the driveway. An excited group of black and colored workers greets Sofia and Skylar. Nathaniel parks himself under the umbrella of avocado trees, where he waits and dozes off.

Dolly greets Nathaniel, saying, "Georgi called and told me you found Sofia's child. I have never seen Sofia so happy. Can I offer you something...?"

"Ginger ale, please. Where is Mr Van der Watt?"

"In the lounge or his veranda..."

Sofia and Skylar take a few steps toward the stairs leading to Gert's section of the veranda, where he watches rugby on television. He turns his head slowly in their direction but remains poker-faced, his eyes focused intensely on the child.

"Hi, Pa."

"Yes, Sofia."

"I brought Skylar back."

There is a long silence, more simmering tension below the surface. Skylar walks out to play with Dolly.

"We found her in Italy. Georgi's brother and Zola Morrison helped trace her."

"What are you hoping to achieve by bringing this child here?"

Sofia grabs the remote control and defiantly clicks the television button off. She shouts, "Please stop watching rugby when I am talking about family matters with you. I thought you would be happy to see your grandchild. I want to raise her myself because she is my child..."

"You'll have to find another place. You can't stay here or in your ouma's flat."

Sofia slumps onto the couch with dejection.

"Grandma gave me that property because she loves me. That flat is mine."

Father and daughter remain in total silence. However, amidst the tension, she can smell the incongruous sweet scent of the family vineyard, and reminiscences of her sins with Skylar's biological father play out in her mind.

She says, "You told me you would disinherit me last time. What have you done, Pa? What will happen to the vineyard and this estate?"

"It's not for you to know my Will before I die..."

"I know you removed my name. Lyndon told me that after you discussed the Will with him and your other son, Barend. Never mind, whatever you do, you can't take away my winery. I left because Lyndon and Willem were intolerable. That land and businesses are mine. No one can run the estate as well as I. Even Mother said it in front of everyone before she died."

"Your mother died before her time because of your pig-headed behavior that started long before you even turned eleven..."

"Mother died of pneumonia. What did that have to do with me?"

"I educated you. You hold a degree..."

"That's your degree, Pa. I don't hold any degree. I wanted to be a winemaker, and what did you say? That's too difficult for a woman to handle. So don't talk to me about that linguistics degree."

"Do what big girls do; look for a job and get your own house."

"That's not going to happen. No one in this family will treat me like a second cousin anymore. You will do three things for me. Number One, forget about the Will. Number Two: transfer the Northgate property into my name. There's no one occupying it since Willem died. That's all I want from you because I want my child to inherit a decent environment. As for my wine farm, I'll fight you in court if you dare to take it away from me. Tell your son to start moving house because I am returning there."

"You had a decent Christian upbringing, but chose to go on your wayward ways. This family has been through a lot of pain. Don't burden us with grief by continuing to treat my advice scornfully. What is that black man outside doing here?"

Sofia stands up and walks out quickly. Gert also gets up, looking dismayed at seeing Sofia turn her back on him. Ouma, in her wheelchair, is being helped to the scene by Toto. Sofia rushes over to hug Ouma, who seems happy to see Skylar. She then signals for Nathaniel to follow her to the tractor shed. He sits on the large John Deere tractor, admiring Sofia's figure as she strolls into another nearby flat. When he tampers with the ignition, the tractor suddenly goes into reverse, nearly causing a crash and an accident. Everyone steps out to watch from a distance. Gert, not pleased, rushes over to check his tractor and shouts, "What are you doing?"

"Sorry, Sir. I didn't notice I'd set it on reverse."

As Gert returns, Nathaniel treads on his heels to catch up and walks beside him. Gert stops.

"As I said before, there are serious issues I would like you and my father to thrash out."

"I have no interest in meeting your father. And you must leave my property right now."

Dolly approaches from the kitchen, holding Skylar aloft. Gert marches away and parks himself safely on the veranda. Dolly and Skylar tag along playfully. Skylar makes her childish moves and settles on Gert's lap. Dolly walks back to the kitchen.

I don't have a Ring, but...

When Sofia returns, she stops in front of Nathaniel, and they study each other awkwardly before she invites him to take a ride with her. The rugged John Deere groans away slowly until it disappears into the endless vineyard. Once they reach a silent spot where they can only see the blue sky beyond the tall vines, she alights and says, "Do you remember what you said to me the other day and repeated earlier today?"

"Remind me."

"You said I am the total of your fantasies, and you said you want me to be your mate. What did you mean?"

"If you don't get a joke the first time, don't expect a repeat to make you laugh."

"So, you were joking? Why don't you tell me what you meant?"

Nathaniel descends, wraps his arm around her shoulder, and says, "Okay, Sofia, tell me what you think I meant."

"I am an Afrikaner girl, hated by everyone in Africa. Nobody thinks I am a woman, let alone one with my thoughts. Do you have an idea how racial profiling affects a Boer girl? They arrest me and start calling me names after they get a whiff of my Boer accent, 'Just because you are a white bitch you think you can do 280 in a 120 zone!' And those are black women saying those things to me."

There is silence as the two size each other up once more.

"It feels good to be a girl of one's fantasies. I want to do something. I know no one in this goddam wide world can see us here except God."

"What do you want to do?"

Sofia kneels before Nathaniel and says, "I don't have a ring, but will you marry me, Nathaniel? We don't do our things this way as Afrikaners... culture, I mean, but I feel spiritually drawn to you in a way I cannot explain."

Thoroughly stunned, Nathaniel says, "That night in the hotel... I said something else. I said your large blue eyes are *an objet d'art*. Is there anything you want to tell me about yourself?"

She squirms a bit, and her face flushes with unease before slowly rising from her awkward position and responding, "About my blue eyes? I like the great outdoors."

Nathaniel gives Sofia a blank stare.

"It's a joke, Nathaniel. Gee! You want secrets?"

"Yes. Tell me anything you're afraid of disclosing, even to your closest friend. Just one shocking family story you don't mind trusting me with."

"I'll tell you my family story, even though I suspect you know more than I do. How you worked with Morrison to find Skylar makes me think you are well-connected, and I can't hide anything from you."

Sofia discloses something about the murder of Mimi Koo to Nathaniel. Just before the explosion that killed her, Willem got out of his car and hitched a ride with the rest of the family. Mimi drove Willem's car on her own as a learner driver. Soon after, an explosion ripped Willem's car apart."

"Was it a mine or a car bomb?"

"I don't know. The army police were there briefly, and they removed everything."

"And you suspect Willem?"

Sofia stresses it must have been Willem. He and Barend were familiar with explosives from their youth. When Sofia told the family what Mimi said to her before she died, they accused her of being possessed by demons, and they loaded her into a police van and sent her to a psychiatric hospital. The police refused to speak with her when she returned. Mimi had told her a week before she died that she had threatened to expose Willem for habitually forcing African girls to sleep with him in the goods shed. When one of the girls disappeared, it was the last straw for her. She immediately threatened to inform the church pastor and to ask him to investigate Willem. Mimi died before they reached church that day.

"So, you think Willem and Barend did it?"

"Not together. Those two were enemies. Let me tell you a secret. I suspect you already know it because you are a spy with German connections. Germany is most developed in high-tech agriculture. South African farmers are the world's most sophisticated because we learn all the finer points from the Germans. Connect the dots, Nathaniel."

"Get to the point, Sofi."

"About Barend and Willem? One of our family farms was commandeered by the government for military use. My father sold it to them and gave the income to Willem. Barend was upset with both my father and Willem. One day, I overheard them argue so heatedly that Barend threatened to kill Willem. Ouma came to speak to Father about this, but he said Barend had made his own choice by abandoning hard work on the family farms to earn a meager income as a civil servant."

"Was Willem not killed by black men avenging the disappearance of their girl?"

"There's no such thing. What about Barend? After Willem was shot dead, no investigation was conducted at the crime scene. They just arrested some black men on suspicion. And another thing, even now, they have not found the black teenage girl who skipped the wall from Willem's house when the police arrived after the Willem shooting."

"So, the girl must have been the killer."

"No, I think she was one of Willem's drugged sex pets that didn't know what was going on."

"You think Barend killed his brother? I don't think he is capable of doing such a thing."

Barend is cunning. He could get away with anything. I know he could kill Willem, given how much he hated him. Still waters run deep, Nathaniel. I blame Father for the way he treated Willem like royalty among us all. And I must tell you this: look after your twin sister, the one you say you love. Hear me out on this. Take it from me: I don't believe Georgi is safe living with Barend because even now, he thinks the Bantus are responsible for Mimi's death. The boomslang venom takes a significant amount of time to have its fatal effect. He uses the K word when talking about the Africans he believes killed Mimi. The love affair Georgi is entering into is a trap. Barend vowed he would someday avenge Mimi's death.

"I think Barend and Georgi are in love…"

"You must warn her, all the same. I don't think she is safe, living alone on that deserted Vrystaat farm. She is a sitting duck, and if you love your sister, you will force her to return to Canada. "

"Okay, tell me the truth about yourself."

"I knew you would ask me that after discovering I am crazy. I am ashamed, but I must tell you the truth. I have been to psychiatric clinics all my life. Thank you for rescuing me from those shrinks where you found me a few weeks ago. I have continued to see a shrink since I was small. When I was eighteen, I was forced into a mental clinic with bipolar disorder. Things get worse after Mimi dies because it is the first time for me to see a corpse up close."

Sofia's eyes get misty. Nathaniel dabs her face.

"I visit Mimi in the hospital, and she sings her favorite song by Mimi Coertse, and then she says, 'Be strong even if they discourage you.' She knows how everybody runs me down. I go to visit her the following day, and I collapse when I hear that I can't see her because she is dead."

"Do you continue getting medication?"

"If I stop, I am on a rollercoaster that triggers something in my brain, and I lose control."

"How do you feel right now? Does your family prefer to hide you like a family secret, like a blight in your family tree, because of your mental condition?"

Sofia leans on the tractor's large rear steel wheel. She replies defensively, "Are you trying to trip me up? Mental condition? People like me are an embarrassment to our folk, so we get stuck in dark tunnel holes like moles, neither to be seen nor heard."

Sofia gets down on her knees, facing Nathaniel. Who starts relating what he calls a secret to Sofia about something Puri told him when he entered University.

Sofia appears confused and raises herself, leaning on the large wheel.

Nathaniel was utterly shocked to discover from her that he is Jewish. As an emerging militant at a German university, this revelation profoundly affected his mental health. While grappling with denial, Puri firmly stated that Jewish identity is inherited from the mother. After concealing his Jewish identity for a year, he found out about 'Jewish Voice for Peace,' a Jewish organization that strongly opposes Zionism. Then, Reeva quietly mentions something about his family, adding, 'Where a complex web of lies begins to unravel, everything else rushes down like a mudslide.'

"What are you talking about?"

"How do you feel about the Jews or Israel?" persists Nathaniel.

"I don't know much about them to feel anything."

"I resent what they are doing to the Palestinians."

"I know Reeva. What gossip did she whisper about my family?"

"Something about your people, that your great-grandmother was Jewish?"

Sofia begins to breathe heavily, her stomach churning. She shouts angrily, "She was

French; that much I know, and we are true Afrikaners. Where do they get their Jewish story from? Reeva has been much too much for my liking."

"Her name was Avigail, right? I learned that Avigail's ancestry tore your Afrikaner kinks apart. Nobody shared that history with you?"

Sofia frowns as Nathaniel continues, "My mother is Jewish, and she has convinced Georgi to convert to the Messianic sect."

"I'm sure you will tell me what they do."

"They tell Jews that the messiah they expect has touched down in Bethlehem incognito. The bad news is that the same messiah has flown back to heaven without establishing their long-awaited kingdom."

Ignoring what she perceives as Nathaniel's red herring, Sofia kneels again and says, "Please, Nathaniel, no more irrelevant stuff? As I was saying, I don't have a ring..."

Nathaniel interrupts, saying, "I'm glad you mentioned your mental state. It means a great deal to me. I started seeing therapists at age seven after my mother told me I was born in a guerrilla camp in Angola, which explains the turmoil..."

"What turmoil?"

"Let's forget about our turmoil, Sofi. You'll make a remarkable partner. I don't have a ring right now either... will you marry me, Sofi?"

Sofia soars into the sky, and the lovers collide and embrace passionately. She rushes to the edge of the small cornfield, away from the vines, and plunges her lower body into the concrete canal, shouting so loudly that her voice echoes across the vineyard. The workers appear in greater numbers, watching in bewilderment as Sofia splashes water from the Vaal onto her face and hair.

A tentative drone of applause welcomes Sofia's animated announcement. Then, excitement swirls like a whirlpool across the farm. An upsurge of clamor and anticipation occurs as Sofi's father emerges from his sanctuary, unintentionally elevating the performance. Sofi's bemused Grandma joins the applause, clapping while covering her teary face with her scarf, and Skylar bobs up and down excitedly.

CHAPTER 32

Ellen back Home

Barend is back from Europe on a month's sabbatical. He tells Georgi he will take her to the secluded Pride Mount Grace Country House in Magaliesberg. Not impressed, Georgi says, "No. Come next week, Barend. You should have alerted me in time to prepare."

"The venue has been booked already."

"You can't make bookings and expect me to fit your schedules. I work, Barend. I am a part-time au pair. You know all of that because of your line of work. Reschedule the bookings. I'll be available next month."

After two weeks, Kian calls Odessa and delivers the news that Ellen has died. She was alone in the house when she passed away. Her friends got concerned when she failed to attend their weekly soup kitchen chores. The family repatriates Ellen's remains after a week, and the burial takes place in Beesfontein. It was the first time since someone revealed Kian's true identity. Many other family members, including Georgi, Kian, Odessa, and Nathaniel, were in one place simultaneously. Marcia is dressed in her grey business suit, complete with pants, and her distinctively large black funeral hat. She stands next to Georgi, who sticks out like a sore thumb in her black skirt and a white 'Winnie Mandela' T-shirt. Kora is sandwiched between Kian and Sabelo, and they all look morose in their black outfits. Barend paints a solitary figure under a tree. To Odessa, the countryside is a surreal panorama as she recalls Kian reminiscing about the 'hillside on the contested terrain not far from the valley where my ancestors buried my mother's umbilical cord.' The angle offers Odessa a vantage spot to view breathtaking landscapes embracing silent streams flowing into far-flung, hazy clouds. She confirms in her mind that apartheid was no mistake but an evil scheme calculated not only to rip off African hearts but to disconnect them from every rich African space for the benefit of white children and their descendants. The 'C5' Funeral workers quickly removed the old wooden cross and re-engraved the inscription to 'Daniel Mofokeng, RIP.' Georgi notices a droplet roll down her father's cheek.

The pastor reads Revelation 21:4 to a small, silent group of mourners:

'He will wipe away every tear from their eyes. There will be no more death or mourning or crying or pain, for the old order of things has passed away.

The North-Wester intensifies, and the midday sun gradually disappears behind dark clouds. As the staff lowers the casket, Odessa screams like a siren. Beneath her pain, she mourns not only her biological mother, who died alone in a distant land, but her biological father, murdered without justice by apartheid security police many years earlier. Georgi wipesg her face.

The pastor calls on Odessa and Georgi to repeat their mother's daily prayer. Odessa says: 'Out of the depths have I cried unto thee; O Lord, hear my voice. Let Thine ears be attentive to the voice of my supplications.

Georgi says, 'God makes our feet like the feet of a deer. Forgive us, Mother, for sticking our fingers into our ears when you guided us through the most difficult alleyways, yet you persisted and shed tears for us.

Georgi and Odessa stay close to each other.

The pastor concludes with a poignant line, "Ellen has finally come back home and been laid to rest next to her husband, whom she loved."

Barend's Charm Offensive

When the mourners begin to disperse, Georgi walks toward a tree where Barend is trying to hide from view.

"I didn't expect to see you here, Barend."

"When there's a funeral, expect anyone. That's what my mother used to say. And by the way, when I attended Luca's funeral, someone said the same thing, 'I didn't expect you here.'"

"You went to Luca's funeral?"

"Guess who I saw there? Your father. He didn't expect me there. Funny, the feeling was mutual. But ask me no question about Luca."

"And you'll tell me no lie, right? Don't you think this government is trying to build the country on the sand, with all the lies and secrets from the so-called struggle?"

"All countries are built on lies. Ask Americans about the Boston Tea Party."

"Oh! Anyway, thanks for coming to my mother's funeral."

"I'm sorry about your mother."

"I should not have left her to die alone."

"She was a victim."

"Yeah, just one victim. Many died at the Vlakplaas Farm while the culprits enjoyed a barbecue. To think that many more apartheid victims died a gruesome death at sea, in the streets, and in their homes, and nobody will know their names!"

"I heard you helped Sofia trace her daughter."

"Her daughter? That wouldn't be your niece, by some chance? When did you first hear about this child?"

"Dolly, one of the workers, told me."

"And what did you ask Sofia?"

"I had no clue about this child. So, I asked Sofia nothing."

"I don't believe you. Your family and church elders shove Sofia into a cave away from civilization during her pregnancy, and when she gives birth, someone steals her baby, and all you can say is you had no clue?"

"What do you want me to say?"

Georgi sighs gently, then puts it forcefully, "Did you know about Willem's raping spree... black girl part-timers? Tell me about his habit of abusing black girls on the family farms."

"Yes, I heard about it."

"From Dolly?"

"Our family discussed it. Get your Dolly out of it."

"Are you for real, Barend? Sofia tells me Willem is responsible for the death of your sister. Does that surprise you?"

"Willem loved Mimi-Koo. Sofia has a serious jealousy streak that drives her nuts. You saw how she followed you around after Willem's funeral. There is no proof Willem killed anyone…"

"Did you ask her to provide proof?"

"I have better things to do than to listen to Sofia's delusions."

"Does it occur to you that your family is directly responsible for her so-called delusions?"

"My people paid her university fees in full, and she spent half the time squatting with colored boyfriends on campus."

"You know that for sure, of course. Look, Barend, my father was accused of your sister's murder, I discovered when I got here with my sister. Yet, you couldn't lift a finger to follow up on Sofia's truth. What have you got against her?"

"Sofia has never quite clothed herself with honor since she was a tot. Nobody believes anything she says. By the time she was thirteen, she was jumping out windows by night to have sex with boyfriends…"

"Colored boyfriends, I presume. So, you've always been snooping around, spying on her. Let me tell you something you don't know despite your spying profession. Nathaniel is with your sister… somewhere in exotic places as we speak. My biological mother and Caleb Lieber are hosting them. Skylar is great fun. Does the name ring a bell?"

"How much does Nathaniel know about that girl?"

"That girl? I don't think her tendency to jump out of windows keeps Nathaniel awake at night. He loves Sofia and told me he would help create a nurturing environment for Skylar."

After considering what he believes is a mismatch between Sofia and Nathaniel, Barend asks, "Are you saying he is planning to marry Sofia?"

"No one mentioned Sofia getting married. You can show some emotion and be happy for your sister for once. There are fireworks in Germany because she sounded bubbly… a cheerful Sofia for a change."

"It will be too late when your brother opens his eyes. I know Sofia. Today, she's Sofia; tomorrow, she's shouting about her belongings in church."

"No, you don't know Sofia. What makes you think a girl needs someone to control her choices? Sofia is a vulnerable girl neglected by your family and ostracized by your church for kissing boys of color. But Sofia is also a resourceful girl who carefully charts her own course.

"Cornered, Barend says, "Great T-shirt. I think about you every day. Can we continue with our plan—the Magaliesberg meeting, I mean? Mount Grace Country House is a lovely spot for a private event, for just the two of us. I want to keep my promise of reading you that poem, 'Waves on the Beach' by Ockert Kruger—remember it?"

Georgi's face beams a little. Then she says, "Ockert Kruger?"

"Yes, Kruger, because I am an Afrikaner."

"And Avigail? What about Avigail?"

"I can't deny Avigail, but my Boer ancestry precedes everything else. I know Cecilia Trent has been speaking softly as if my family has something to hide. Avigail's experiences during the Holocaust should not be used to shame communities with Jewish heritage."

"Your mother, Puri, wrote an essay in the late 1970s while she was an activist in Tanzania, in which she warned her Christian allies in the ANC to treat Israel like a 'cancerous state' because it threatens freedom in South Africa. I found that piece in a Russian journal."

"I'm really exhausted, Barend, from all the divisive South African discourse, yet people could focus on nature and everything we share, without spending a dime. Or about the poor living in squalor…"

I promised to take you to the *Festival d'été de Quebec*, right? Let's discuss the country club before the storm catches us here. Nothing's perfect. But for now, we can settle for 'The Grace' in Magaliesberg, a perfect setting for peace of mind and poetry inspiration.

"Okay, 'The Grace' it shall be. Call off all your false Intelligence engagements, including your phony trips to Namibia. Esther Hadassah is all yours."

CHAPTER 33

Twin Weddings

Nathaniel and Sofia plan their private wedding to take place in the Bafokeng scenic valley. Sofia demonstrates her independence by managing every detail, including the guest list and the number of tables. She emphasizes that her wedding shouldn't resemble a township political rally. Among the people she swears never to invite are her father and Lyndon. On this 'casual wedding' day, the bride and groom are surrounded by surprises: friends and family, including Ouma, Kora, Gert… and Jessica, from Australia. Sofia looks relaxed in her pink dress, while Nathaniel has opted for Italian-style attire: blue jeans, a pink shirt, and a light-brown blazer. But Sofia's father makes his loud, unexpected appearance.

Sofia speaks privately with Jessica, who looks elegant in her Basotho patchwork outfit. "Aunt Jess, how did you convince Papa to come?"

"I am his sister. Little sisters know every secret their big brothers would rather die than divulge."

"Yeah? Would you like to share just one?"

"Don't push it, Sofie. You want to get me into trouble?"

"And Lyndon…"

"I don't know any of his secrets. He's my nephew, not my brother."

"You're right, Aunt Jess. Lyndon is here after Ouma's persuasion. Ouma is a vault of family secrets."

Georgi and Barend, dressed as wedding guests, walk around the rotunda, happily greeting guests, shaking hands, and hugging. Two female security guards, brought from Robertson, are present to verify credentials and prevent the 'undesirables' from nearby villages from approaching. The ceremony proceeds quietly with little fanfare. Odessa is not present. Marcia is seated beside Sanna, who smiles broadly at the sight of Georgi.

"I am happy for Sofia and Nathaniel," says Marcia to Georgi.

"Yes, Marcia. Is there any reason why you never mentioned Sesi to me?"

Squashing like a concertina, Marcia says, "Please, let's not talk about her; not a hint to Ryan…"

Dolly responds to Gert's prodding. She gently hands Skylar over to him, and Gert cuddles the snoozing child close to his heart.

At the appointed time, the officiant asks Questions Before the Consent: "Who gives this woman to be married to this man?"

After a few tense seconds of silence, Gert hands Sofia's child to Puri, who looks bemused. He stops a foot from Nathaniel and says, "I do."

Then, Sofia hugs her father as Kian walks in, accompanied by echoing murmurs of delight rippling through the rotunda. Lieutenant Zola Morrison also accompanies Kian.

Taking advantage of the noise, a group of uninvited youths evades the docile security and slides into the scene. Sofia's planned private wedding has suddenly become a community spectacle. The sight of Morrison, nestled comfortably against Kian's shoulder, sends Georgi's suspicious mind racing in all directions. Georgi can read wicked contentment in the Lieutenant's glistening eyes while Kian appears detached from the wedding excitement.

Nathaniel and Gert shake hands, and the patriarch gently guides Sofia's hand to Nathaniel's. Morrison quietly sneaks toward Georgi and whispers, "Georgi, your father says he will support you in whichever path you choose."

"What does he mean, Zola?"

"Follow your heart, he says."

Georgi whispers something to Barend as Sofia and Nathaniel recite their vows. In an instant, Georgi starts walking the aisle with Barend in tow. Kora and Puri hold hands, teary with emotion. The officiant reacts to the impromptu development, asking, 'Who gives this woman to be married to this man?' The tense moment is answered by Odessa, who turns up unexpectedly, fully dressed in her traditional Tswana attire with a sizeable matching doek. Odessa has brought along Teddy, her little brother. She has also successfully lured Ryan and Chiurai to the occasion, intending to arouse ultimate jealousy and pain in Georgi. The shocking entrance of Chiurai, who saunters expressively, hand in hand with Ryan, is bound to fracture Georgi's fragile emotions irreparably. Odessa's entourage enters the scene with fever and excitement, all heads whirling in unison in their direction. Chiurai and her newly discovered lover show off their African attire and are quite demonstrative in their affection. Her elaborate 'Bantu' hairstyle, purple lipstick, and matching eyelids enhance her peacock personality. Odessa's grand entry causes stabbing pains through Georgi's belly button. The officiant repeats, "Who gives this woman to be married to this man?"

Kian steps forward. Georgi bursts into tears. Yet, the vows are exchanged amid fierce turmoil in Georgi's heart. She barely keeps her eyes off Chiurai, the striking black beauty whose head rests comfortably on the shoulder of her 'Tako Kichi' lover. Deep inside, Georgi swears never to talk to Odessa ever again.

A wistful smile flits across Kora's face, and she whispers to Puri, "Today, you and I are sisters…"

"Yes, Kora, only through divine providence."

A week after their whirlwind honeymoon, Sofia and Nathaniel travel to Germany for a visit, and Puri and Caleb host them. Meanwhile, Georgi and Barend enjoy theirs at the Sun City Resort. However, they face difficult marital issues even after they settle among the greenery of their farm. Barend spends most of his time away as an Intelligence officer. The wound Odessa caused Georgi by inviting Chiurai to the wedding digs so deeply that it persists without relief. In her confused mind, she misses Ellen, the mother who took her on long walks to a psychiatrist, even though she had resented what she saw as a nuisance back then.

CHAPTER 34

Let's take a Ride, Ryan

Georgi has started to enjoy nurturing and showing off her rainbow of garden flowers to her neighbors. She is becoming a serious international exporter. However, she has other distractions besides having enough time to relax and explore her romantic and radical poetry. Occasionally, Rachab, a 'colored' student of Palestinian descent, uses her free time from her college studies to run errands for Georgi, helping her pay her tuition fees. Georgi knows she needs to be discreet about her activities, including her naughty calls. Rachab's habit of snooping around and eavesdropping makes Georgi suspicious and irritable. Her mood has become unstable lately due to her feelings of loneliness. Her lonely spell has triggered a strong urge to make call after call. But what could satisfy her longing for true companionship if not for the voice of Ryan?

Late one night, Ryan answered a soft voice on his phone, "Where are you, Ryan?"

"Georgi, you promised to delete my number from your gadgets."

However, once they launch their clandestine chat, the whole thing degenerates into long-winded fantasies until dawn.

"You must be thrilled I failed to remove your ugly face from my gadgets. How is Chiurai?"

"You shouldn't be asking me about Chiurai..."

"You must treat her well. She's a smart girl."

"Yeah, I think she's cool."

"Rough around the edges, my dearly departed mother would say."

"Where are you? At Verligte?"

"Where else, Ryan? Look, I am all by myself here. Please come, let's take a ride."

"You want to be my diamond kite again?"

"When can I expect you?"

Puri is overjoyed to hear that Georgi might be expecting a baby, but Georgi pleads with her to keep it a secret between them for now.

"Nathaniel must know. Have you told him?"

"Why should Nathaniel know?"

"He is your brother. When last did you speak to him?"

"Long ago. Why?"

"Look after yourself. I'll call to congratulate Barend on the sweet news..."

"Puri, you will do no such thing..."

"Why not? He is your husband."

"Exactly. I'll tell him myself. I want to see his face when I deliver the 'sweet news' as you call it."

"Fine. I am taking some medical tests, but nothing to worry about... suspected lung cancer…"

"I'll come over to see you, Mother! You look after yourself, too."

One cloudy evening, Georgi puts on her jogging gear and sneaks out of her farm to meet Ryan. His new C-Class blends in with a thick brush at the driveway's edge. The rising moon paints the scattering clouds with wine-red colors, enabling Georgi to see Ryan's silhouette as he leans on the bumper. She rustles the dry grass and ducks the tree branches until she reaches Ryan, who silently extends his arms in impassioned welcome. Georgi and Ryan melt into each other's embrace forever.

Georgi withdraws. She sighs awkwardly, "So, you came?"

"Well, you ordered a drive. What Kind of silly drive do you have in mind?"

"I don't know, Ryan. You're the one with weird ideas…"

"You seriously want us to go to Streenbras again?"

"No, Silly. Just think of something more creative. Kite flying was the dumbest thing I've ever done since I came to Africa."

Ryan heaves and says, "Georgi, let's get this over with. Please marry me."

"That will never happen, Ryan," Georgi retorts, diving into the front seat and chanting, "Nice transport. Let's get going before someone spots you here. Did you pay cash for this Merc?"

"Some of us have to work, Georgi. Only your privileged elites with struggle credentials pay cash for planes and yachts…"

"I'm sure Marcia's sponsorship came in handy. After all, she is your Aunt with struggle credentials, too."

Ryan slides into his seat and retorts, "The only contact I have with the crème de la crème is tolerating the smiling faces they parade on television. And that includes Marcia."

"Seriously, now, just give me your account particulars. I'll get the crème de la crème to pitch in. Your bank balance must be bone dry after this indulgence…"

"Being a senior lecturer in archaeology and history has benefits, Georgi.

"Archaeology? Is that right? Now I know. Let's go. I hope you'll give me a shout the day your bank account turns red. Back home, my dad once had his car towed away by two men who claimed to be debt collectors working for banks. My father later summoned all of us into the kitchen to apologize for his 'lapse of focus.' But Mother Ellen got to rein him in over his gaming activities. The whole affair was embarrassing. I can talk to Marcia without mentioning your name, and you'll never hear from any bouncers. Imagine Chiurai seeing you drop from your Million Dollar Merc to a fifteen-seater taxi. Start the car, and let's go."

"You said you were all by yourself, Georgi. Aren't we going to your mansion? I need some rest. After my long drive, I don't feel like going anywhere."

"You want us to spend the night together at my house? This entire mansion is flooded with hidden cameras. Let's drive somewhere straight away; we'll take a break. You can see I only brought my duffel bag. My workers must not know I left the house."

The car starts moving slowly along the tarred farm's periphery.

"Georgi, I see a string of outbuildings. You own all of this?"

"We have 'native quarters' for workers."

The car stops, and Ryan asks, "Mud houses for natives? What about that large outfit below the hill? Native compound, too?"

"That one has been vacant since the previous owners, Jessica and her husband, emigrated."

"I take it it's your property now."

"Yes."

"Now tell me, Georgi. Do you have native compounds on your large property, which you proudly call Verligte?"

"Look, Ryan, I have discussed the incongruity of the situation with Barend, and we are addressing it," she says awkwardly.

"Classic oxymoron, don't you think; native compounds and Verligte in one sentence?"

Somewhat embarrassed, Georgi says, "Please, let's move on, Ryan."

"Right. We shall drive to the Granny cottage vacated by your Aunt Jessica…"

"Please, Ryan. We can't do that. I don't even have keys to that flat."

"In that case, get out of my car."

"Picky, are we? You want to dump me like you did after your kite-flying prank?"

"You can walk back to your mansion now. Don't leave your bag behind."

"Fine," Georgi shouts as she drops out, banging the door behind her.

Ryan rolls the window and shouts, "Don't ever call me again."

Pitching Ryan a curveball, Georgi challenges, "Tell me about Sesi. Do you know where she is?"

The atmosphere seems to freeze.

"Sesi?" Ryan heaves and says, "Sesi has nothing to do with you." He rolls the window closed, and the car screeches away.

Georgi begins a doleful walk back to her farmhouse and immediately calls Moroka to ask about Sesi.

"Listen, Georgi, that matter has nothing to do with you."

"I see. Ryan said the same thing. You once presented a puzzle about Sesi to me. What did you mean, 'it's a no-go area'?"

"Did Ryan say something about Sesi?"

"Yes. He said Sesi has nothing to do with me."

"Quite! Listen to me carefully, Georgi Girl from Canada; focus on your tulips and lilies, and forget about Sesi."

"What is she doing in Finetown, Sesi, I mean?"

"You should have asked her when you visited her. I hear you've been in Finetown more than half a dozen times. What is Sesi to you?"

"So, you're also a spy, Mr Moroka?"

Moroka cuts off.

Georgi gently throws herself on the bed, holding her tummy as if protecting the developing bundle. But she continues to wallow in longing and more tears. She calls Sanna.

"Hi, Miss Georgi. Please, they said, I must not talk to you…"

"Who said that? Marcia?"

"No, Mr Moroka. But I know why?"

"Because of Sesi?"

"No, it's because of Chiurai. Moroka wanted that girl to take your place after you got engaged to the white man. He likes her because she is black."

"Chiurai? Where is she right now?"

"She flew to Europe with the children."

"Did Marcia go with them?"

"No, Marcia and Moroka… they are separated."

"Divorced?"

"No. They get separated sometimes, but get together again. They got separated because of Chiurai. They were cheating on Marcia, and Mr Moroka took Chiurai and the children to Europe."

"I don't care if they are cheating, but they must not use my children as a cover for their cheating. I'm the only nanny for those children."

"But you have your farm now…"

"I don't bloody care for the farm. I'll kill that girl. When are they coming back?"

When Georgi finally watches TV, she hears the sound of shuffling feet outside. After opening the door, Ryan walks in slowly.

"Nice castle…"

"What are you up to, coming in here, Ryan? Where are you parked?"

"Don't worry. No one saw me, and I hid my car in the bush somewhere."

Georgi gets into a terrible panic. She rushes to her wardrobe, picks up her duffel bag, throws it in Ryan's direction, and whisks him out of the farm. He relocated the car to the yard of a native compound unit owned by Teulo.

"You want to get me into trouble, Ryan?"

"I spoke to your sympathetic native in one of the mud castles there, gave him R50, and asked him to keep mum about our secret."

"Secret? Oh, my gosh! You told that man Teulo about us?"

"He seems like a street-wise man-about-town sort of guy. He mentioned a few things about you. Do you drop by Teulo's pondokkie to have a good time with him when Barend is overseas?"

"Don't be silly.

At last, Ryan gets the car moving. Georgi heaves a sigh of relief and asks, "Where are we going?"

"What do you have in mind?" he snaps.

"I'm sorry, Ryan; I had to call someone. Are you mad I called you?"

"Mad doesn't quite cover it…"

"Let's drive to the Granny flat up there then. You'll hide the car in the garage. No one will see you when you take off tomorrow night."

"You said you don't have the keys to that place."

"I do have the bloody keys; just drive."

The car moves again. Georgi discloses that she once went to Finetown to meet Sesi. She tells the incredulous Ryan she gathered a treasure trove of family secrets from Sesi.

The car screeches to a halt, and following a long silence, Ryan angrily puts it, "We're not going to your bloody granny castle."

"And why not? Just because of Finetown? Please, let's go. No more Finetown or Sesi."

Following their long, silent drive, they wander in the obscure wilderness, and Georgi asks where they are going. Ryan answers like crazy, exerting more pressure on the throttle. Georgi's appeal for him to slow down falls on deaf ears. She shuts her eyes, and her stomach rumbles like distant thunder when her mind's eye focuses on the native compound on her Verligte farm. She reflects on Ryan's bitter reaction to the compound, exposing her hypocrisy. She recalls her father's ranting about her lack of respect for poor people. For the first time, she feels proud of her father's decision to name her after a poor Indian woman who worked as a cleaner. Georgi knows what she must do once she gets back to her farm. Apart from demolishing the compound and creating new suitable homes for the workers, she thinks she will pressure the government to eradicate informal settlements in the country. She carries on listening to her lofty musings until she dozes off.

Georgi is jolted out of sleep two hours into their drive when the car seems to be struggling, swerving, and almost veering off the muddy dirt road, before it comes to an abrupt stop. She notices a heavy downpour, and the world around her is shrouded in darkness. The droning wipers are dancing to the heavy clatter of the shower. Looking through the left window, Georgi spots a prickle of porcupines prancing around a ravine. In front of them is a motionless zebra accompanied by her suckling foal. But Ryan's furious hooting does nothing to intimidate the two animals. Georgi digs into her bag, rummaging for her cell phone.

"I know you yanked my cell out of my handbag while I was napping. I want to make a call. Bring back my phone."

"You're crazy."

"Where are we?"

"You said you wanted a ride, didn't you?"

"I didn't have a muddy side alley in a wild animal park in mind. Where are you taking me?"

Ryan answers by steering the wheels slowly out of the muddy patch until the wipers hypnotize Georgi back to sleep. In her dream, she is Mother Zebra, lying down her young one in a manger. However, her scene is catapulted into her juvenile nativity drama, in which she portrays young Mary, the mother of Jesus. Georgi slowly opens her eyes and smiles with nostalgia, "Ryan, did you know Jesus was from a poor family?"

"No, Georgi. And I don't want to know such things."

"Later, his mother could not afford a lamb. During those days, people experiencing poverty were allowed to offer two turtledoves instead of a lamb. I want to help the poor in this country."

"Several more noble women tried rescuing the poor but ended up in caskets."

"Don't you ever have motivating words to share?"

Another hour passes. The car stops next to a disused farmhouse buried behind a tall thatch, inside what Georgi thinks is a jungle. Georgi begins to shake with fear. The situation stirs up further suspicion in her mind, given that she knows little about Ryan, apart from his link with Marcia or his supposed job as an archaeology lecturer. She knows how easy it is for people doing archaeology to bury bodies so carefully that they cannot be discovered.

"We'll put up right here," he says with little emotion.

"I don't think so. The house is dark. Does anyone live here?"

"We have the house to ourselves; aren't you pleased?"

"Please, Ryan. I can't get into this rundown, spooky house."

"I've got your cellphone. If you refuse to go in, I'll call your husband. Imagine what he will say when he hears you galloping with me through the wilds."

As they get out of the car into a chilly breeze and a clearing sky, Georgi begins to imagine her body submerged inside a slimy ravine, never to be found again. Marcia's haunting words, 'Betwixt and between is an awkward place for any girl to be in,' are ringing ever more loudly. She regrets ever meeting Ryan.

When they were young, her father taught them various tricks to distract their debating opponents. The military teaches people many ways of deception.

She instinctively points at a hill a distance away and says, "Can you see the owl?"

"What owl?"

"Look in the direction of the moon; you'll see the owl nestled on the crest of the hill."

"I see nothing."

"Is your eyesight that poor? I want to recite the poem I wrote for my mother, Puri. You'll be the first to hear me recite it. I want you to hear my rehearsal, so tell me what you think before I stand before my mother next week and make a fool of myself."

Ryan is bewildered. Georgi ambles away from the mud-spattered car and treads carefully until she lies her body spread-eagled on the wet grass, facing the murky sky. There, she starts reciting, her voice echoing across the silent night: 'Mother Owl…'.

The thought of dashing it flits through her mind with every word and stanza. Her voice rises in a crescendo, and it becomes clearer that the rough country poses more danger than the two eyes trained ominously on her.

She goes on: 'Spotted Eagle Mother Owl...'

Once she is through, she says, "What do you think, Ryan?"

"Think? Why is my opinion important to you?"

"I value my audience. Are your archaeology students not important to you?"

Ryan remains silent.

In her restless state, Georgi walks back and accidentally makes a faux pas, saying, "How I wish people could show some emotion... like Barend. I wrote 'Mother Owl' for Puri, my biological mother, when I was far away in North America, because she searched everywhere for me until she found me two decades later, right here in Africa. Mothers do care for their children even when they are wild. I engraved the words on a glass bottle for Puri's birthday, knowing she would appreciate the thoughts behind them. I'll ask again: what do you think of my poem?"

"I don't know, Georgi. I'm not in the mood for poetry right now."

Oblivious of her earlier blooper, Georgi continues, "I have not shown it to Barend either, but he often kisses the page on which I write my poems, and each time I recite in front of him, he pops champagne, and we enjoy ourselves under candle lights,... those charming trinkets whose glow never flickers. And then our navels kiss."

Ryan, who had seemed out of it, responds indignantly, "Stop being such a chatterbox."

Georgi feels threatened by Ryan's belligerent voice. Her mouth is dry as she wonders if her high school self-defense coaching might be helpful, but she quickly thinks better. Turning to the house up close, Georgi observes rusty chains hanging around a collapsing steel gate. She goes to give the gate a little tap, and it crashes with a heavy thud on the paved entryway. Navigating further, she tiptoes towards the porch. The yellow paint that once brightened the walls peels off under extreme weather conditions One of the windows is shattered, with glass fragments still visible on the floor.

He switches Georgi's cell phone on before attempting to open the large door in front of them. They notice that the door is slightly ajar. Following his prodding, she pushes the door slightly and opens it into a large, empty lounge with a dingy aroma. The dense cobwebs brushing against their faces tell the story of the property's extended abandonment. Most of the electricity trappings are gone, and all that remains are fragments of a large chandelier covered in a forbidding collection of dead spiders and a more tangled mess of cobwebs. Neither curtain nor railing is in sight. The elite wooden floor looks intact, and so does the fireplace mantel, which is etched with a wooden springbok head. A fire iron, mysteriously left on the floor near the fireplace, gives her much-needed courage to stand up against any danger.

"You're not planning on murdering me, Ryan? Whose rundown house is this?"

"One of Aunt Marcia's bed-and-breakfast secrets," he puts it. "Moroka knows nothing about it, and you're not reciting this to him. I know you won't open your big mouth to your Mama Marcia either; otherwise, you'll have to explain to her and your Boer husband."

"Listen, you, Ryan; if you brought me here to kill me, you may as well do it. No one talks to me as if I were an idiot. Tell me about this place. Where are we?"

"You want to know? This is Boshoff. It's the rural back of beyond, hidden from black folks for centuries. While Mandela was on his New York ticker tape Parade, being feted by African Americans, your struggle comrades back home were splashing out on estates from your white Pack-for-Perth racists who could not countenance black rule."

"Marcia bought this property?"

"She's not as dumb as she looks... she owns this bed-and-breakfast, which she bought for a song."

"Does she know what's happened to her bed-and-breakfast... that there's no bed and no breakfast anymore?"

"We'll make do with what we have. I have a sleeping bag and a blanket. Sorry, no sheets; you won't need them tonight as we'll be cuddled together."

"That's not what I asked. When will you tell your loving auntie her property has become a rundown chicken shack?"

When Ryan walks to the car, Georgi takes advantage, removing her cell phone from his jacket. She calls Nathaniel.

"What, Georgi?"

"Please, Nathaniel, I am trapped here in the middle of nowhere with Ryan. I am scared; I think he wants to kill me..."

"Relax. Morrison asked about your strange movements tonight."

"Morrison? Is that woman still shadowing me?"

"She's doing her job."

"What did she say to you?"

"Something I can't tell Mother about you and your boyfriend."

"Oh, my Gosh! Please keep your mouth shut, Nathaniel. No word to Puri."

Ryan quietly approaches and eavesdrops on Georgi's call with Nathaniel. He hears everything, including Georgi's secret about Pedro.

"I know about it, Georgi, and Pedro won't get away with it," vows Nathaniel.

"What are you planning to do?"

"I'll do what I know you want me to do..."

Georgi sighs in unease when she realizes Ryan overheard Nathaniel's voice.

The Pony Stable

In the morning, Georgi takes a tour of Marcia's smallholding. She had earlier imagined a thick forest with only a lush grove of apple and orange trees. As she explores it, she becomes increasingly proud of Marcia's courage for 'stashing' such pretty lodgings, even though it's in a one-street town she can hardly locate on the map. Back home, her mother often advised them that when they get married, they must save up some significant cash or property in exotic places without their spouses' knowledge.

Georgi cannot help but lament the neglect visited on the pony stable, though. The image of its ramshackle wooden columns and rusted troughs supports the stereotype that blacks emerged from the dark dungeons of oppression to pillage and destroy what exists, what they could otherwise use as a building block to their advantage. She walks away from the pony barn with a heavy heart and looks far into the distance. Someone once said, 'When you are tense, evening becomes night, and you cannot see the flowers all around you. ' At night, while she delivered her poem under the overcast sky, she could hardly see the empty pool or the murmuring canal conveying irrigation water from the Vaal River to the Boshoff countryside. Only now does she notice that the outer building has electricity and a fully functioning shower.

Ryan suddenly appears.

"Where did you sleep?"

Ryan winces and says, "Georgi, you refuse to marry me, and you expect me to behave like a bloody husband to you?"

He walks away, and Georgi clears her way into the shower. She is enjoying the hot water when Ryan walks in and asks if he should join her. She hesitates, but he steps inside. Afterwards, they are seated on the porch, having coffee and cross-buns, when Ryan insists that Georgi confess how she found out about Sesi. He suspects Sanna and Gibson of betraying their trust.

"Guess who betrayed Sesi's trust: your cultured family circle. Now I know that mine is not the only clan in which dysfunctional relations are normal."

"So, you admit Sanna fed you all the stories?"

"Finetown; that's where I got fed the stories."

"That girl can't be trusted. Did she tell you she is a dangerous fugitive?"

No, she didn't, because she's not a fugitive. She served time and is a free woman now."

Georgi relates her Finetown trip to Ryan. One day, she and Rachab went to Finetown in search of Sesi. When they finally caught up with the twinkle-eyed, 'disabled' young woman in a wheelchair, she initially denied being Sesi until Georgi confronted her by asking if she knew Sanna. Sesi said, 'Sanna is an angel sent to this earth to save my life'. She told them how Sanna worked tirelessly to get her out of jail.

"I ask her about her family, to which she responds, 'Why would anyone bother about a crippled girl who murdered her mother?' before she laughs wildly."

"Crippled girl?"

"Her words, not mine."

"Yes? What did she say happened?"

"She confirmed everything Sanna had told me, but she was hesitant about her mother's murder, only repeating that they released her 'from the stinker' five years later. Any reason why you, Marcia, and Moroka have stayed guarded about Sesi's case?"

"Search me."

"Most high-flying elites find their disabled kith and kin an embarrassing inconvenience."

Sesi is Ryan's half-sister, his father's love-child. Some families disown relatives who are charged and convicted by law. To crown it all, Finetown is hardly a fine place for a quadriplegic girl trying to make ends meet in a wheelchair. Ryan's family gets hot under the collar whenever Sesi's name is mentioned.

Changing the subject, Ryan says, "You promised to go backpacking in the Drakensberg with me, right? Please wait until we're up there inside the hot springs of the Giant Castle. Over there, we'll talk about Sesi and then whisper to each other about you and me. Don't renege on your promise. After the Drakensberg, you'll be Mrs Taung because there's no other man for you."

"Qué será. Barend and I are partners, and I made no such backpacking promise to you. Odessa warned me against you long ago, and it's embarrassing to admit she was right; I can't get you out of my heart, and I think that's a curse. As for Mrs Taung? Perish the thought."

"Why would a married woman invite a stranger on a nighttime joyride unless she's admitting she made a mistake getting involved? Thousands of couples regret their foolish actions barely a few hours after their honeymoon."

"Let me tell you why I called you. I was shaking because of what I had just read and seen. Loneliness causes depression, and it can push a woman to the brink. I can't cope with being alone for too long because of nightmares and doing something I can't explain afterwards."

"Such as calling a man you love to take a night ride with you?"

"The truth? I had to call you, Ryan, because whenever I dream of you, I get up with a damp pillow."

"It's called love... You wanted a drive with me. I came because I am in love with you and find you irresistible. I know you feel the same because that's what you said to me over there in our passionate, warm shower an hour ago. Don't you think it was beautiful when your sizzling body melted with mine?"

Zola Morrison's words come rolling back to Georgi: 'All women have their indigenous men, their real desires stashed privately in one dark corner...'

But she says, "We all fantasize and cross lines when we soak in a shower. Don't you fantasize about being in a steamy shower with Chiurai?"

"Are you jealous of Chiurai, the way you go on?"

"That girl has no right to take my place, gallivanting the globe with my children."

"So, you're envious of her triumph over you."

"Stop seeing Chiurai if you love me. You just said you're in love with me, but you know you're lying. Do you know where Chiurai is right now?"

"Who cares about her when I am with you?"

"You should care because you and that girl have been cheating on me. Do you know

Chiurai has been cheating on you? Sanna tells me Chiurai has gone overseas, consorting with Moroka, your uncle. She tells me this has been going on since the elderly couple separated."

"Forget about her. Marry me, Georgi."

"If you promise Chiurai is history, you can have me... forever."

"Yes, and I'll do anything for you. But I want you to be honest about the stories I have heard about your rape experience. Are you prepared to open up about that?"

"Where have you been hearing such lies?"

"You must be hiding it even from your man because you're scared of rejection by your white man. Odessa is unhappy about your cowardly stance..."

"A woman's profile is her secret and not on public display. Cowardly stance...?"

"That man who molested girls in Canada... I'll find him and incinerate him. No one will get away with causing you harm, Georgi."

"How much do you know about incinerating people? You're not incinerating anyone. Forget about my cowardly stance, and stop your secret rendezvous with Chiurai. I am serious."

Feeding you lies

Ryan drops Georgi along the tree-lined driveway of her farm, a safe distance from the residence. It is early evening, and in the sky beyond the hill that surrounds her granny flat, the sunset's yellow glow fills her heart with a troubling longing for her school days. She gulps tears and yawns from lack of sleep. Lumbering up the paved walkway, she can hardly appreciate the blooming tulips and roses spread around her. Instead, she yearns for good company all over again, anything to relieve her from her constant anxiety over her stress-filled marriage. Piercing phrases like 'divorce' and 'separation' and Ryan dance in her head like an apparition from Penrose Strawbridge House. When she steps onto her porch, she is surprised by the sight of Teulo seated there in the attitude of a security guard. He offers to help carry her duffel bag inside.

"No, Teulo. I'm fine. What are you doing here? And where is Rachab?"

"She said she was going to the library, but I know she lied because her boyfriend picked her up. I'm glad you're safe, Georgi. I need some money. I told you once about my daughter back home."

"You have a daughter?"

"Yes, she needs school fees and clothing."

"I gave you R500 last time for your son. Now he is a daughter? I don't have money right now."

"The R500 was for disconnecting the surveillance, remember? Please, Georgi, I don't want Barend to know about the man who came driving a Mercedes. He asked me to tell him if I see anything..."

"If you see anything like what, Teulo?"

"You know, things he does not like to see happening when he is overseas."

"Barend told you to spy on me?"

"No, he said he does not trust women. Please help me."

"How much?"

"Maybe... about two thousand..."

"Teulo, please let's start here; reconnect all the cameras. Can you do that right now?"

Once inside, Georgi calls Marcia.

"Hi, Little Bride."

"Please, Marcia, can we talk... woman-to-woman?"

"You're in trouble, right?"

"Just a little pickle. Say, do you know a town called Boshoff?"

Marcia is silent. After an extended minute, she says, "Why?"

"Marcia, I went to your bed-and-breakfast outfit in Boshoff. What happened to the ponies?"

"It must be Ryan. Did Ryan take you to my place?"

"Please, let's not mention the name 'Ryan'. If Barend calls you, tell him you sent a young man to fetch me in your Mercedes because you want me to help with the ponies. Can you do that for me, please, Marcia?"

"And what is the name of your fictional young man?"

"Name? Marcia, what did you call your friend who loved it when you did Reed's 'Naming of Parts'?"

"Codi?"

"Yes, if Barend calls to confirm my story, tell him the young man you sent to fetch me to attend to your ponies in Boshoff was Codi."

Marcia's breathing is heavy. She says, "I don't like this whole thing, Georgi. Where is Ryan?"

"I was with him for two nights, and he just dropped me off an hour ago."

"Two nights? Georgi, last time we were together, you got married to Barend. Have you given your man his conjugal marching orders? What are you doing playing Russian roulette?"

"Sorry, Marcia. I couldn't help myself. But trust me. I told Ryan we shouldn't do it ever again. How are the kids? I miss them."

"I'll make sure they don't use you as their role model."

"Oh, Marcia! So, that's why you've been holding me at bay like a broken-down trawler!"

"Georgi, I'm facing serious family challenges right now. I'll explain everything someday. In the meantime, keep the Boshoff secret to yourself, right? Moroka knows nothing about it."

"Okay, let's talk about the guts of your Boshoff property. I saw corroded troughs in the kraal hanging by rusty wires and two stacks of decomposing hay near the kraal. What happened?"

"It's not a good idea to run two husbands. That property became my second husband. Besides, I had my job and children to look after…"

"I'm sorry about the ponies. How many were they to start with, and where are they now?"

"First, there were six, and then only one filly was left when I last went there. I asked the neighbors to rescue her."

"You say the children are where?"

"Moroka took them for an outing in Sweden."

"And you let that girl Chiurai take my place? I trusted you, Marcia."

"What could I do, Little Bride? You got married."

"Those children of mine will have another nanny over my dead body. I'm the only one."

"Shall we talk later when your sister gets here? I know you two are close, and you share deep secrets."

"When she gets here? Odessa is not coming back to Africa anytime this century."

"No? I suppose it is a secret. Or a surprise, maybe? She is on a Cape-bound plane as we speak."

Georgi snaps shut the line and calls Barend.

"How are you doing, Georgi? I've been calling…"

"Why did you get someone here to spy on me?"

"What makes you think I need someone to spy on you?"

"There must be mutual trust in any relation. Isn't that what you rave about every day, Barend?"

"What are you talking about?"

"Did you promise to pay Teulo two thousand for snooping around and feeding you lies about me?"

"Let's talk when I get back. I'm busy right now. When last did you speak to your mother, Puri?"

"Why?"

"Call your father. It might be urgent."

CHAPTER 35

A Bundle in her Arms

Georgi struggles to reach Kian, Nathaniel, or Puri. The next morning, she picks up a call from Odessa, who sounds cheerful, "Hi, Sister! I've been hearing whispers about the upcoming baby or the fetus, as you once called mine! You've stayed away since you ended your first pregnancy, selling daisies and lilies to the new bourgeoisie...

"Odessa, Marcia says you're in Africa. Would it be expecting too much for you to call me before you break secrets with strangers about your African safari?"

Odessa has touched down in Cape Town to interview potential partners for her company, which is based in Toronto. While in South Africa, she will meet with Marcia to discuss Marcia's offer to transfer the Houghton Estate to her.

"To you?"

"You turned down Marcia's generous offer. So, you're out of this picture. It's been rumored that Marcia is giving the mansion to Chiurai and Ryan. I support that wholeheartedly, given your rejection of your black people.

"To Chiurai and Ryan? Are they getting married?"

"Why is their affair any of your concern?"

"Why? Because that will never happen. The only woman for Ryan is me."

"Where's your white man...?"

"Odessa, your snide remarks about Barend must stop."

"Leave Ryan alone and stop sending him on a futile wild goose chase. But let's leave all that, Georgi; I'll talk to you about Daniel, my baby, when we meet..."

Three days later, two unmarked black vehicles with multiple aerials make their way slowly into Georgi's farm. She rushes up to the balcony, from where she is stunned by what she sees. Lieutenant Zola Morrison climbs out of the back seat of the second car, carrying a bundle in her arms. The driver, a tall, bulky white female official with a genuine smile, quickly jumps out and attends to the second passenger.

Odessa is beaming as she calls out, "Hi Negro! Come down."

The driver of the first car is unfamiliar to Georgi, but the passenger is the ubiquitous Inspector Mbatha. Georgi walks out to meet them. Morrison generously places Odessa's bundle into her arms. After exchanging pleasantries, Georgi invites the guests inside the rotunda, where Rachab prepares them refreshments.

Later, Georgi and Odessa are seated at the water's edge, overlooking one of the colorful flower beds. Rachab gently places Daniel Junior on Georgi's lap and serves finger lunch while Miriam Makeba's classical tunes, featuring 'Suliram' and 'Olilili', fill the air. Rachab keeps sliding close by to eavesdrop.

"I wonder what it takes to get a job one fancies in South Africa."

"And what job would that be?"

"An official… in Intelligence, like Zola Morrison."

"Oh! Have you tried?"

"Yes, and Zola told me circuitously that I don't measure up."

"We all have dreams, Georgi. In your case, your dreams are circumvented by your choice of partner, which means your Afrikaner friend. Nobody trusts these people."

"Oh God, Almighty. What am I going to do? Anyway, forget about that. "I should have been the first to know you were coming to Africa."

"Marcia arranged everything. She told me I had to come over incognito…"

"Incognito? What's the matter with these people? They start by being coy about Sesi and the Boshoff property falling apart, like the Palace of Westminster. Next, they fly people incognito!"

"So, it's true what Zola said; you went flying kites again with Ryan?"

"Not quite. I needed a conversation. As you said, all women crave a good tête-à-tête with a man."

"But don't tell me you spent the whole week with Ryan in Boshoff talking sweet nothing together. I'm certain you were keeping each other posted on your wedding arrangements. But remember, you need divorce papers even in Africa."

"Well…!"

"You stop raising hopes over nothing. Tell Ryan the truth, that you have seen the light and you want to marry him."

When Fats Domino's ' Jambalaya' takes over from 'Olilili,' the sisters jump up and do a tango, with Rachab their solitary audience, joining them with her Palestinian belly dance.

"Tell me about your real secret: your Jewish roots. Are you happy to be Jewish now and have come to terms with your new name, 'Esther'? I'm being serious."

"Puri invited me into her world, and I feel drawn to its history and universe. It is rich with symbols, imagery, and poetry. There is a wealth of stories by such Jewish female authors as Marion Moss Hartog, whose prose I am seriously sinking my teeth into."

"Have you been to a psychiatrist since we left Canada?"

"Oh, shut up, Odessa."

When Miriam Makeba's 'One More Dance' starts, Odessa smiles and says, "Come, Georgi, it's time we shared your juicy surprises about the good news."

"You want juicy surprises?"

"We can't let nice secrets about the baby you're carrying go to waste. Tell all, and I'll be proud of you."

After a short while, Georgi says, "You'll be proud of me?"

"Yes, Georgi. Whose daughter are you carrying?"

"Time will tell. You will have to stay with me, right here at Verligte, until you help me deliver the goods. Then you will be the first to know whose daughter she is."

"Fair enough. In the meantime, let me know your plans about the Houghton Estate. I know you. Knowing that Ryan is out there flying kites and having fun with a pretty black girl who seems to drive him wild must drive you green with envy. Tell me you are not jealous."

"Me, jealous!? Oh, what madness, Odessa! Always bringing Ryan and Chiurai into every chat."

"I want my sister to be free. Only Ryan can make you free. Call Ryan and beg him to get back to you instead of tempting him with your kite flying and Boshoff tricks. Tell him you have seen the light."

Georgi slowly rises, wheezing her Pedro lullaby for Daniel Junior while toddling to the middle of the freshly mowed lawn to lie spread-eagled, hugging the baby to her bosom.

Odessa follows her slowly and lies spread-eagled next to her. After a while, she says, "Georgi, you know how I feel about staying in South Africa. I want you to know that if this whole thing between you and Ryan doesn't work out, I shall have no choice but to fly back home. If I make such a decision, I shall hand over the Houghton House to Ryan and Chiurai with a clear conscience."

Georgi sits up but says nothing.

Odessa continues, "Father named you Georgi because he wanted you to care for the poor. He explained it to me after I asked him how you got your Russian name, the day you became the school's official goalkeeper. Everyone was shouting your name, and I just wondered. I even figured you could be an adopted mixed-race Russian girl. When I asked Mother Ellen whether you were adopted, she accidentally dropped and broke her cup of tea. That girl from Bela-Bela might be pretty, but she is destitute. Be true to your name. Ryan has been playing big to impress, but he also needs a wind beneath his wings. There would be no better couple than Ryan and Chiurai to inherit the Houghton Estate. But I'll need your blessings for that."

Georgi lies down on her spot again. The sisters fall asleep.

An Explosion kills Pedro

Much later, Rachab and Odessa serve their early evening dinner. Georgi seems to have forgotten about Odessa's earlier invasion, as the goings-on in her head are taking precedence. Then, two strange luxury cars with tinted windows slide into the driveway. There are two occupants in one, and Georgi can make out when the headlights go off. The man who gets out of the car is Kian, which brings some unsettled relief to the sisters' unease. He is in a dark suit, blending with a striped maroon tie, which reminds the girls of his suffocating official bank uniform back home. Kian does nothing to remove the frown on his face. At the motion of his hand, the two sisters walk inside the house. Rachab remains on the veranda with Daniel. Looking exhausted, Kian sinks into a couch. The furrowing of his brow tells of intense stress.

"What brings you here, Dad? Has anyone died?" asks Odessa callously.

Rachab sneaks closer to the open window to listen in. Directing his response to

Georgi, Kian says, "It is not just anyone that has died, but the man alleged to have raped you."

After a moment of awkward silence, Odessa sighs and says, "He stuck his gun between her legs, Dad. Did you know that? Georgi is in stupid denial."

Kian rises from his seat and faces his two daughters awkwardly.

"The man was a sociopath. How could I know if nobody told me the seriousness of the whole thing? I would have protected you. I should have protected you from Pedro. What a pity we spoke openly about everything but rape. It never occurred to me; it could have happened to my daughters."

Kian sinks back into the sofa. He tells them that he received a call about an explosion that killed Pedro."

"Explosion?" Cries Georgi.

Are you sure, Dad?" Screams Odessa.

"That's not the question. What was Pedro doing in Africa when he was facing charges of rape in Canada? He skipped bail. That we know. But Interpol informed law enforcement here that they were closing in on him. I did not know he settled here in Cape Town after he jumped bail."

"Porous borders, this South Africa is a haven for white fugitives," sneers Odessa.

"Our sources say the police are keeping a hawkish eye on Ryan."

"Ryan! Why Ryan?" Georgi shouts

"Ryan could never do such a thing," Odessa protests.

Georgi murmurs as she recalls Marcia's banter about Ryan, 'Did he tell you he is a trained bomb disposal official?'

"I went to see Ryan, but he is not talking," says Kian.

"Good for him," chants Odessa.

"Now, you girls, before things get out of hand, tell me straight: what do you know about all of this?"

"About what, Dad?" retorts Odessa. "Are they trying to tag us with his murder?"

"Well, if you have anything to do with it, you can tell me. I am your father. According to sources, 'one of the girls flew from Canada just before the murder.' The Intelligence is swirling with suspicion."

"They suspect me?" challenges Odessa. I am here to build my business. We know nothing, Dad. But if Ryan did it, all praise to him. He saved humanity from the predator."

"We received information that Interpol, both here and in Canada, has placed you on the list of persons of interest regarding the killing. All his accusers are potential suspects. So, you, Georgi, you'd better lie low and avoid sharing information with Ryan. He is under 24-hour surveillance.

"Yeah, avoid flying kites near that dam…"

"Oh, shut up, Odessa."

"When we see vultures circling in the sky, we know they've detected a carcass," Kian says, as he gets to his feet. and says, "As for you, Odessa, how many times have you flown between Canada and South Africa over the past three months?"

"Me?"

"Yes, you."

"Once or twice."

"I'll tell you because I know. Not once, but five times. And you used an alias four times. I won't ask you what all the flights were for because you lie. Please take my advice, girls. South Africa might be a third-world country, but we know what's going on in the first, second, and fourth worlds. In case security comes here asking questions about Pedro, invoke the Fifth, as they say in the USA. Avoid being too clever by half."

"Oh, Daddy..."

Georgi tries to make a call, but there is no response.

"Who were you calling?"

"Marcia. She can tell us something, but her phone is off. Marcia knows everything, and this separation with Moroka is a hoax."

"You know what? I think you're right. I never liked that woman from the day we came here. It's like I have been riding into a storm with my eyes shut. How I wish we had never set foot in Africa! Our parents were right to talk us out of it, even though self-preservation was their motive. We should have listened."

"Et tu, Sister Girl?"

"C'est la vie," Georgi says, gulping back her tears; "You are very perceptive, Odessa, and the things you scoop out of my soul have left me restless. I made bad choices, and now the dark hole is swallowing me up. What can I do?"

"Instead of regretting why you set your crooked foot on Africa's shores, you tell me with some emotion how much you love Barend."

"I love him a lot. There... I've said it."

"'A lot' does not mean that much. Fly to the Netherlands to tell him you're in love, or else call and say 'that's it'. There's no use keeping up the façade; life's too short. One expects to see passion and feel a hurricane in your voice when you mention his name. I know it's there when you talk about Ryan. Where's the passion, Georgi?"

"I don't know, Odessa. We often lose touch with each other. With Ryan, I can blurt out anything without thinking. I feel like I can really be myself around him. But I collect myself like a set of cards when I'm with Barend..."

"Here's good advice from your big sister: avoid self-isolation. You don't need a man to raise your child, even if he puts her in your tummy. All you need is your Dandelions, Blue Moon Roses, Lilies, and African Daisies. Think, Georgi."

"You're a real master of mixed messages. Do you want me to fly to the Netherlands or attend my African Daisies?"

"I want you to act like the strong African woman that you are."

"Let's drown our peccadilloes inside the lyrics of our tune, 'We can work it out.'"

But Odessa, *parlons de toi.* You are my sister, so let's be open to each other. It seems you have resigned yourself to the life of a hunter and food gatherer, a rolling stone that gathers no moss. You mentioned earlier that you are in Africa to develop your business. What happened to your company with Mr April?"

"Oh, Georgi. You are the perceptive one. I'll let you know about Ganon April in a good time."

"Did he finally disclose to you where his diamond came from?"

'I suspected he lied before I cornered him."

"Now, talk about your half-dozen flights and stop fudging your answer."

"Are you accusing me of something?"

"No, I want to drink a toast to my sister, a prey that accomplished a quintuple glide under the radar, setting an ingenious trap for the predator."

"Oh, Georgi."

"We all know you are not dumb, Odessa. Tell me like you used to when we were alone in our home bedroom. Did you help Ryan bump Pedro off? He swore to incinerate him. Please tell."

"There's nothing to tell."

"Not even a wee bit?"

"Maybe just a wee bit. If you love your sister, you would do anything for her."

"Yeah? Tell me more."

"More? Never underestimate your twin brother's love for you, either."

"No kidding!"

Georgi cuddles Daniel Junior and recites another craftily improvised lullaby for the benefit of Odessa, who takes a second look at the surreal imagery, her baby warmly ensconced in her sister's bosom. She senses a tingle in her body as the picture evokes memories of their days of innocence, when they performed their modern-day Nativity for their nursery school audiences. She cannot help but smile wistfully as she recalls their heady days as teenagers, fighting their suspension from school after they referred to their Headmistress as Mrs Hitler. Her recollections take her to the day they donned their track joggers and sneakers before receiving honors as top debaters from the same principal.

"Georgi, do you know what happened to your goalie of the year cup?"

"You know it disappeared."

"Your goalie of the year thing? I threw it in the trash can."

"Odessa! Why? And don't lie, now."

"Okay, I was jealous, I'm sorry."

"No need. I retrieved it."

CHAPTER 36

Mother Owl

Georgi takes a call from Puri. Odessa listens in. Puri discloses that she has resumed her rounds of radiation therapy for lung cancer. Georgi feels a quake in the pit of her stomach. Puri is in a Munich Cancer clinic, with Caleb and Nathaniel by her side. By the time the specialists had diagnosed Puri's stage four condition, it was too late to save her life.

She can barely speak but manages a few words to Georgi, "They say I have not got long to live… chain-smoking," she chuckles incongruously and continues, "Is it a girl you are carrying; do you know?"

"It's a girl, Mother."

"A baby girl? What will you name our girl when I am gone?"

"You're not going anywhere, Mommy. Esther will be with you shortly. I'll fly over in a day or two."

"Your baby's name is Pnina. Pnina was my aunt from the Cape Province."

"I have not given it much thought, Puri, but Pnina, she will be."

"There is joy in my heart because God kept me alive until I touched the face of my Esther. Please keep Avigail's ring firmly on your finger; in that case, my blessings will follow you wherever you go."

"Blessings? I wrote a poem for your birthday and engraved the verses on a ginger beer bottle. I'll bring it with…"

Her life hanging by a thread, Puri whispers, "You can recite it right now."

"Okay, I'll do it for you. Mother," Georgi starts reciting her 'Mother Owl' poem:

> Baby spotted eagle owl Tumbles to the ground.
> Pregnant giant Mother-fly lays eggs on owl's eye.
> Spotted Eagle Mother Owl Plummets to the ditch.
> Keeping Baby Owl alive, Classic mother's hunch.
> Mother Owl abandons all up there in the nest.
> She's on edge with the kid off track; one eye in distress.
> Spotted Eagle Mother cares, just one gone AWOL.
> She'll surrender all her tots till she's done with one.

Following Georgi's performance, Nathaniel continues with the call: "Do you have any idea what happened to Chiurai? She went missing."

"I don't know. Isn't she supposed to be looking after Marcia's Houghton Estate?"

"She disappeared under Zola's nose. Mbatha, Zola's partner, went over there and found the girl gone. The police are investigating. Something looks fishy."

"Please tell Puri I'll be with her in a day or so."

"The only clue the police have," responds Nathaniel, "is a 48-bullet casing they found lodged in a swimming pool wall. Its origin has not been tracked."

"I'll get Rachab to book flights for me asap to fly over."

Odessa finds Georgi's nonchalant attitude towards the news of Chiurai's disappearance disturbing. Georgi refuses to discuss the matter. Instead, she snaps, telling Odessa to keep her nose out of Chiurai's private life.

"This is no private life! You got that girl to temp at Marcia's house…"

"She must be squatting with Moroka. Have you considered that? Or maybe Marcia got so green with jealousy that she caused her disappearance, hiding her body in one of the mine dumps. Did you know Moroka has been cheating on Marcia with your pretty black angel?"

"Where is Moroka?"

"Leave me alone, Odessa."

In the morning, Georgi notices an ominous call from Caleb. She hesitates, answering it, hoping he will hang up. Deep down, she knows that she is evading the inevitable. She slowly grabs the phone, rushes to Odessa's bedroom, and roughly shakes her up. After she hands the phone to her, she steps out into the large field that charms a kaleidoscope of the Free State blue. Georgi talks to her flower stems and kisses dew-draped white rose petals.

Bewildered by what she considers another routine performance by Georgi, Odessa answers the call. When Caleb starts to speak, Odessa thinks the call is an update on Chiurai's disappearance. However, after listening to Caleb's entire message, she sits on the porch to watch Georgi's wild performance. Odessa waits and heaves helplessly.

Georgi limps back and slumps on Odessa's shoulder; her tears, so close to the surface from the moment of her recital, will soon flood her sister's bosom. The call is about Puri, who has passed away.

Georgi takes two paces and shuffles across the mantelpiece. Whirling around with a dry smile, she delivers an impromptu eulogy to Puri:

> 'My queenly mother Puri, when we first spoke – over a generation after you released me into this world – you charmed me with your silky voice and disarmed me with the most wicked smile. Father Kian, let slip your moonlit trysts down Tarangire Lake, where you broke open your H.Q. so you could hide two riotous beings in your womb. Trapped inside guerrilla trenches, you delivered us in a cold birthing puddle filled with grimy waters before severing our umbilical cords with an Angolan nugget. Mother Puri, you hugged us with your quivering hands amidst enemy shelling and smothered our mucky bodies with generous kisses. All through the ticking moments, your recollection of Aunt Pnina's memories – being rescued from the Auschwitz gas chambers – made you whisper courageously as the apartheid enemy offensive forced you to let go of us finally; me with unresolved names, yet I should have known you loved me so much you blessed me with Queen Esther's crown. Mother Puri, you once hinted at the narrow thoroughfares of your life and the debilitating 'no thoroughfare' signs you scaled with courage, but you only whispered and kept the full horror of your backstory inside your big heart. Your

rollercoaster ride – in and out of the dark caves along the equator, searching for Esther – did not extinguish your burning passion for the concerns of the real women's liberation movement. I marvel at your composure as a Jewish white girl in love with a black African 'Gentile' in a world mired in racism and chauvinism. Help me navigate my reality as a black woman struggling with my unresolved skin color. I should have been with you, Mother, when you put out to sea. I was raring to grow with you so you could see me mature and look more like you. I was hoping you would raise all five of your Jewish grandchildren, whom I have yet to bring forth. Puri, Mother Owl, every rose blooms and withers, but an interminable star has sashayed to the Milky Way. Very soon, you'll look down at poor me with Pnina, your granddaughter, sporting our tallit wear and amusing you with our attempt at Hava Nagila. But when all is said and done, you will see us, year after year, celebrating our black Purim Carnival in Style.' Georgi plans to fly to Germany the following day.*

"Go, Georgi. You'll find us right here on your return," says Odessa, "then, when the time comes, I'll hold your baby in my arms, regardless of her color. And I'll be the first to know when the heavens reveal the secret," she cackles. "But go well, my little sister. I know what it feels like to bury a mother. In your situation, you lost two mothers you loved deeply. You'll be in my thoughts."

CHAPTER 37

A Whirlwind

This is a fine autumn month and a lovely day to enjoy Mangaung (Bloemfontein to the European colonizers). Mangaung abounds with written history, with the Anglo-Boer War deliberately raised to a status that holds neither merit nor truth. Lacking in that discourse are genuine stories of struggles waged by the indigenous people against the colonial land bandits from Europe. The only history that has flooded private and public education has been one that extolled the virtues of European conquests on the one hand and African savagery on the other. As Easter approaches, the skies in Mangaung, this semi-arid region, become turbulent, leading at times to fierce thunderstorms that transform dirt roads into streams. In May, the sky becomes a teasing torment, with drifting clouds adorned in pastel hues, occasionally parting to reveal a bright blue as nature bids farewell to the departing sun.

Georgi is relieved to find Odessa faithfully stuck at Verligte when she returns. However, she is disturbed by her sister's eternal fixation with Chiurai's disappearance.

"Let's talk about the Houghton Estate," harps Odessa. "Chiurai adores the Houghton Estate. I wonder what happened to her. Do you know, Georgi?"

"We know nothing about that girl. She might be married to a chief in Bela-Bela," Georgi counters callously.

"So, let's settle the Houghton Estate issue once and for all. You're well aware of my passion for our lovely home in Rosedale. Since we can't trace Chiurai's whereabouts, what do we do? I must go back home, but before I leave, I shall invite a few friends for a farewell blast at Marcia's Estate, where Rachab can do her hootchie-kootchie belly-dancing, and you can get Sofia to come display her Boer Great Trek Sokkie dance. And perchance, as they say, Chiurai might turn up to show us how they rhumba in Bela Bela as she flaunts her astonishing Afro-body movements."

Odessa has just triggered a whirlwind. Georgi is now freaking out, leaping to her feet, her back stuck to the door, and her face twisted clumsily with exasperation. Odessa should have known that the whole situation, her mention of Chiurai in that light, would push her sister over the edge. The split personality she sees has happened a few times as they grew up in Rosedale. Odessa knows that each time Georgi got into such a state, another complex bipolar episode was already playing out. However, this time around, she faces the worst form of disturbance attacking Georgi she has ever experienced. Mother Ellen would take Georgi for a mental evaluation with less severe warning signs. But their mother is no longer around to shield her from Georgia's eerie outbursts. However, Georgi's over-the-top hostility toward the idea of a farewell bash takes Odessa by surprise. While she had noticed long ago that the mere mention of 'Chiurai' often hit a raw nerve with her sister, Odessa remained unaware of how her allusion to Chiurai's

Afro-body might trigger such deep-seated ill feelings in her.

"What nonsense! Let me tell you this, you," Georgi yells, pointing a finger offensively at Odessa's face, "you are not leaving that Estate to Ryan and any of his girlfriends. There won't be any belly dancing or rhumba there; you are good for nothing, woman. I won't cry anymore. Puri warned me against smiling enemies at the door. She wanted to visit Israel with me, but that never happened. I'll go there with Rachab, Sesi, and Pnina. Everybody hates us. I shall tour Auschwitz."

Rachab is overwhelmed by the spectacle but remains silent.

"What are you on about?"

"I hate you, Odessa. I want to be strong like Sesi... like Winnie Mandela. We shall go to the Hill of Megiddo, where Deborah the poet proved that no army can ever defeat Israel. Ryan and I enjoyed a warm shower together in Boshoff, and I will visit Jacob's Well in Shechem with Ryan."

"You want to go to Israel with Ryan? What about Barend?"

"Forget Barend..."

"And Nathaniel?"

"Nathaniel? He promised to fly me to Gaza at his expense because he was itching to sleep with me. The itch was mutual if you asked me. Go away. I told Nathaniel about the horrendous slums in Harlem, worse than Gaza, where people are living in the subways. Even in your Rainbow country, half the population lives in slums. Mother Puri, who has visited Jesus, says Nathaniel has a jaundiced view of the world. Oh, how I know; I am sent to this world by Jesus to feed poor children..."

Rachab interjects inaptly, unaware of the challenge sparked by Georgi's outbursts, saying, "Okay, guys, I'll go see for myself what is happening at Gaza. My father says no country is worse than Gaza. He fled Palestine after an Israeli attack that killed my mother, and he sought refuge here in South Africa when I was three. Nothing will make me happier than to touch my roots and to pay my last respects at Mother's gravesite."

"Do that, Rachab. Odessa's belly dancing in Houghton is nonsense," adds Georgi.

Unexpectedly, Georgi answers a call from Ryan. Odessa motions to Rachab to leave the room, and she listens in with heightened curiosity to her sister's call, her nerves fraying as the chat between the secret lovers continues.

"I saw your message," says Ryan. "You want us to meet? I am busy."

"You must fetch me. I am afraid. Fetch me today without fail?"

"You are joking, right?"

"I am not bloody joking! What time should I expect you? We must go together to one of Marcia's mansions..."

"Where is Marcia?"

Stop harping on about Marcia. Her house is empty right now, and I still have keys to every room. I'll see you later this evening. Please, Ryan.

"I have a faculty meeting tomorrow morning. I can't come to you."

"I've known all along you've fancied finding my body stuck at the bottom of a slimy swamp. That's what you wanted to do at Boshoff. What does your bloody faculty meeting have to do with me?"

"I can't deal with your mood swings anymore…"

Georgi's voice softens, and she says, "Ryan, I miss you. You know I'm all yours. I'll make it easy for you. Meet me at Marcia's place after your meeting. I'll get myself there. Don't you dare leave me to put up alone in that castle? What if they come me when I'm alone? And remember your right to remain silent in case they start asking you questions…"

Odessa immediately snatches Georgi's phone and shouts, "What are you doing, Georgi? Hey, you, Ryan; where is Chiurai?"

"Chiurai?"

"Yes, the pretty black girl you have been fraternizing with. Where is she?"

Ryan cuts off. Georgi shouts, "Bring back my cell, you meddling bully."

Odessa's chest heaves with frustration, and she tries to march out of the room, but Georgi continues to block her way. Lowering her voice, Odessa demands to know why Georgi accepted a call from Ryan after their father's explicit warning against it. "Did you put your hallucinations into practice? You have a long conversation with Ryan and have not spoken to him about Chiurai. Why didn't you ask him about her? Is it because you were so full of jealousy and spite that you attacked the poor black girl and buried her body in a mine dump? Does Ryan know what you did?"

Georgi cries so loudly that Odessa smacks her in the face. Her screams echo disturbingly across the length of the farm.

"I should have listened to Mama Ellen," she sniffs. "Jesus is telling her he forgives the Samaritan girl of her sins. When he comes back again, he will tell me how he forgives and forgets because he knows women are suffering in this crooked world. Ellen cautioned us against our stupid expedition. Look what we see now: a dreary, miserable third world. I want Ryan. I know Ryan wants me. That's why he called. We shall hide in that mansion until no enemies can get us. We'll be together until we know for sure. Only Ryan makes me happy in this world."

Odessa tries to pull Georgi away from the door, to no avail. She shouts that Georgi stop being melodramatic, "I know you're crazy over Ryan. I regret encouraging it. I should have known it would come to this foolishness. You are a crazy girl."

Georgi turns and raps hard on the door with her knuckles, "Who is crazy? I'll kill you like they killed Luca."

This turns Odessa crazy. She angrily bangs on the door, "What! You are mad. Mother warned me. Why get Luca's name in your foolishness? Let me tell you this, you silly Jezebel; before you kill me, I'll kill you first like you murdered that black girl!" Odessa pulls Georgi away with such force that the door suddenly swings open, letting Rachab, who has Daniel in her arms, tumble inside like a sack of potatoes, almost injuring the baby. Odessa marches out in a huff, away from Georgi's volatile spectacle.

CHAPTER 38

Epilogue - Quid Pro Quo

As she struggles through a little swamp, Odessa's mind flashes back to the quality time she spent with Chiurai at the Houghton house. She remembers Sofia's moment of bigotry that so angered her and Chiurai that they marched out of the pool patio, sparking a passionate affair between Ryan and Chiurai. Tears begin to well up in Odessa's eyes as her mood sinks with despondency over the missing poor black girl.

A deluge of tears falls to the ground when her own words ring like peals of church bells in her heart:

'You are a very pretty black girl, and I like you. Ryan must meet you.

You'll be happy to meet him. He is black like us.'

Odessa rests her body on a moldy rock. She says a little prayer for Chiurai's safety while trying to atone for her depravity of using the Bela-Bela beauty as a decoy beacon. Her mind quickly disengages from her prayer when she recalls Georgi's conversation with Ryan, that is, before she snatched her cell phone from her. Georgi had spoken softly to Ryan, '...remember your right to remain silent in case they come asking questions.' Odessa confirms to herself that Georgi's concern, far from being about Pedro, is, in fact, a coded reference to the mystery of the missing girl. However, deep down, she recalls that her instincts had been screaming at her when someone broke the news of Chiurai's disappearance. But Odessa knows that, however she may feel about Chiurai, she must remain faithful to an unwritten pledge to protect her family.

When she casts her eyes upon a moss-covered rock near a shrub, she observes three fledglings struggling out of their nest without their mother around to help boost their weak wings. Odessa decides about her future as she stares at the defenseless nestlings struggling without their mother. She remains seated, watching for a while, until she descends into sleepy thoughts about her mother, who spent a lonely time in a snowbound North American country, only to be buried by two dozen mourners in a desolate countryside somewhere in South Africa. But today, she finds her thoughts catapulted once more into something daunting. She becomes conscious of the burden of secrets her mother had to harbor for over two decades. How much can a woman's heart endure unending sleepless nights, fruitless prayers, while taking a shower, and hours at work where she must step up her art of deception, wondering if Interpol law enforcement across the oceans is closing in on her? Odessa knows that her mother's heart started weakening the day she left South Africa with two little girls whose skin color she had to explain daily to the curious people around. And that in raising them, the day would come when the self-same girls would each start asking the obvious questions. A weakening heart is unable to sustain such heaviness. And, here they were as a family, facing something similar over secrets around Pedro and Chiurai, hoping they would evade the long arm of the law. Odessa ponders the close affinity among the suspects that one could easily implicate in Pedro's incineration. Not that she is complaining; she smiles wryly. She believes Nathaniel, Ryan, Kian, and Puri have the collective intelligence and capacity to execute the elaborate scheme that caught Pedro off guard and baffled law enforcement. Odessa partly admitted as much in her "wee bit' response.

She takes seriously their father's warning that they may be under law enforcement surveillance. Therefore, she takes little solace in Georgi's cautious confidence in the culture of impunity protecting those connected to the new government. While her troubled heart causes dampness all over her body, the cool Drakensberg breeze sweeping across her face brings some relief.

On her return to the mansion, Odessa finds Georgi all smiles, with Fats Domino's 'Blueberry Hill' floating in the air. Georgi is preparing lunch and singing along, piercingly. Rachab, wearing Daniel on her chest, has turned the kitchen into her dance floor as she multitasks with Georgi.

"I was getting worried about you, Odessa," chirps a transformed Georgi. "Where did you go? There are poisonous snakes on this farm, and one can't be too careful."

"I just took a stroll, a bit of fresh air."

"I learn from Rachab here that you visited Teulo's homestead a few days ago and saw his two children. The guy turns out to be quite a charmer. One can't help but recall another man-about-town called Lunga. Be careful, Dear Sister. I don't fancy being the bearer of one more piece of news to Aunt Kora..."

"Oh, please! What are we eating?"

"Patience, child," Georgi clowns as she hooks up with 'Blueberry Hill' again.

Rachab walks out and perches herself at the corner of the veranda, enabling her to gather more juicy gossip while hiding there. Her curiosity pays off.

Sofia wants to take Georgi on a tour of her wine farm along the Garden Route. Nathaniel will join Sofia after he completes his contract.

"Sofia's brand," Georgi crows, "is 'Sofia L'amour de Ma Vie,' she calls it."

"How sweet! Vous ne pouvez jamais vous tromper avec le français."

"No, Odessa."

Odessa says softly, "Listen, Georgi, I know you love me, right?"

"That's a trick question, right?"

"I'll stick around your farm until the day little Pnina decides to pop out, so we can admire her beautiful black coily hair, fingers crossed..."

"Coily?"

"Of course. Even the Jewish Jesus – not the one created by Europeans – was a black man with woolly hair. Wouldn't it be lovely if Pnina were as melanated as Ryan and me, her hair as woolly as our Jesus?"

"Whatever! I'm happy to hear you'll be staying with me for a while, nonetheless. Then you can fly home with little Daniel to look after Teddy."

"Georgi, please, I don't have a grain of nanny qualities in my bones. When I return home, I'll have to leave Daniel with you because God gave you good brains to be a nanny. Let's make a deal. Look after my Daniel, and I won't tell a soul about Chiurai's disappearance."

Although slightly jolted, Georgi seems to reflect momentarily and then says, "I'll have to think about it, Odessa. Do you remember how Hamlet staged 'The Mousetrap'?"

"No?"

"Good. Never try Shakespeare on me, Odessa."

"Let's talk about Daniel. We all know how your in-laws feel about dark babies. That's why you cunningly use Shakespeare to dodge the issue. Please, Georgi, help me. Besides, what else do you plan to achieve with such a huge piece of land?"

"I'll increase the number of my rose garden beds and spice up stem cutting because roses sell like donuts overseas. Sesi will be here with me with fresh ideas. I know Barend is looking forward to baby Pnina's arrival."

"That's assuming the baby will have blue eyes," Odessa chortles sarcastically.

"Let's ignore that. Barend loves me. When he returns, we shall relax on the balcony in the company of Nat King Cole's 'Stardust.' That's what we do. We mostly chill out, savoring my favorite George Wyndham red wine because he appreciates my poetry. I know that makes him happy. You'll never know how much he lifts my spirits, holding my hand and motioning me to an empty dark space to let my soul bathe in the Milky Way."

"Oh, Georgi, what empty words! You sound like a damsel drowning in quicksand. Who are you kidding? I remember the last time you, yes, you, told me that you and Barend keep losing touch with each other. Now you say you cool off with him on the balcony surrounded by 'Stardust'? And you want to make him happy? What about your happiness? Pull yourself together, Girl. Waiting for the wind to blow a lily your way? You wish! That's no way to fill empty spaces in one's heart. No, Georgi, my sweet little sister, make your own choices and don't wait for lilies to crop up out of nowhere. You can't simply flip a coin like you did before you became the best goalie at Rosedale. This is serious stuff. Take a deep breath and start leading the lilies where your heart tells you to. What have your gut feelings told you since you cried inside the airport restroom? Take a bold step and liberate yourself from your low self-esteem. You don't need a man to appreciate your art before feeling valued as a woman, especially if you feel ambivalent about your commitment to him. Let your poetry flow and see how the Milky Way drapes your verses under the clouds."

"Oh, Odessa," Georgi responds with teary eyes, "So you read my poem?"

"Take a plunge for the sake of Pnina, your daughter; the only plunge called Ryan."

"I am haunted and afraid, Odessa. My eyes are sore from hours of sleeplessness. Please stay with me for a while. Hell has no turbulence like fiery conflicting emotions."

Whatever happens, Odessa is determined to fly back to Canada and leave her country behind. At that moment, she feels her little sister is as vulnerable as the nestlings she saw in the veld. She has to try her luck, all the same, because Daniel needs a birth mother. Facing each other that close, Odessa is suddenly charmed by Georgi's smirk, which evokes reminiscences of their childhood mischief. What's more, something in Georgi's uneasy smile prompts Odessa to take a second look at her little sister, and she's amazed to discover that she's the spitting image of her Jewish mother.

"You loved your mother... Puri?"

"I feel sorry for her because she wasted two decades of her life in deep distress over losing me."

"I'm glad I won't lose my Daniel because he will be here with you forever."

"Odessa, let me be clear; I can't cope with Daniel."

"Why not? You hate him because he is my child... because he is black?"

With her labored breathing, Odessa lifts Daniel from Rachab's chest and angrily transfers him to Georgi's arms, reciting words laced with sarcasm and tricks to cajole her sister to agree to her desperate request.

"Daniel, my Baby, let's talk about Georgi, my sweet little sister. Listen, Daniel, here is Aunt Georgi-Esther. She will raise you well here at Verligte because you are her son. She is the one who saved the Jews from Haman's pogrom. Your new mother is beautiful, feisty, and intelligent. You'll be in the company of Pnina and other children. Esther will sing her song for you, 'Let the children come to me and do not hinder them'."

"Please, Odessa!" Georgi scoffs. I hate it when you start sounding all marshy. Control yourself. I am not Daniel's nanny, and that won't change."

"Marshy?" Odessa rants on, "That's a verse from the good book I just quoted, you atheist. Listen, Daniel Baby, your genuine Mama is a beauty queen who rescued Jews from genocide somewhere. You can take the story with a pinch of salt if you wish. I can't blame you. After all, this Esther thing is a fairytale plonked into the bible to make the Israelis create enemies and justify killing people."

"Guess who's an atheist right now?"

"I know one day Georgie and Ryan will be together for life because she often hallucinates flying kites with him. Ryan told me Georgi gossiped about me, saying I'm a terrible mother who can't even change a diaper. The self-same gossipmonger undertakes to build houses for people with low incomes, but nobody believes her because she lies like a lizard with a stomachache. You can't blame her because she was bred and buttered by phonies."

The sisters are unaware of the Palestinian Girl who has been sneaking around, eavesdropping. Odessa continues, "Georgi, the real Mama, will keep you here because the fake Mama, called Odessa, will hide her 48-caliber secret in the fish pond of Rosedale Garden. No one else will know about the bullet because I am the only one who found it after the incompetent investigators hovered over it and left it lying there. I will stay silent as long as Daniel grows up among the flowers of Verligte. It's called quid pro quo."

Georgi's eyes turn red. Directing Odessa, she puts it, "Sit down, Odessa. Here's the real quid pro quo, Sister: You remain mum about the bullet, and I say nothing about the serious case of your mother, Ellen, abducting me when I was a baby..."

Odessa's stomach begins to churn, her body quivers, and she fails to hide her face that is quickly turning wet with tears, "How can you be so callous, Georgi?"

"What are you doing, Odessa, sticking a gun in my temple, employing a ruse to force me to look after your child? I challenge you to say anything about that bullet anywhere—I dare you. Let's see what you will do when the law investigates your movements; those international flights you made between Canada and South Africa, using an alias and trying to fool Interpol. That will be in addition to the case of my abduction, poor me, by Ellen, your mother."

Georgi's words are like a knife in Odessa's guts. She feels so dizzy that she almost loses her balance.

"Please, Georgi..."

Georgi pulls a smirk and says, "You flew from your home in Canada with your Daniel, hoping you would simply dump him with a dumb colored nanny, who will fall for the feeble song and dance about how perfect she is with children..."

"Why, Georgi, my dear Sister..." Odessa exhaled softly, her knees buckling.

"Odessa, you have 24 hours to leave my property. Take your child along and go back to your home in Rosedale."

"But that's your home too, Georgi. What are you saying?"

"That's not my home because I was a hostage for twenty years in that captivity location. My real mother suffered because of your mother."

"Georgi, you loved our Mother Ellen... please, Georgi."

Rachab, the Palestinian student, suddenly appears. She walks in and slams the door behind her. Rachab is teary-eyed, with shaky lips and fluttering upper eyelids, all of which are quite a blight on the otherwise lovely face of the Palestinian. She steps slowly towards Georgi, seizes the snoozing Daniel, and straps him to her chest. The sisters gaze at her with bewilderment.

"What is it, Ray?" pleads Odessa.

Ignoring the question, Rachab positions herself combatively in front of them, occupying the space like the emotionally overwhelming 'Queen of Tears.' After a long minute, she clears her throat nervously.

"Odessa, and you, Georgi, do you remember the song your father unfairly forced you to sing when you were young?"

"Unfairly?"

That's what you said, Odessa. Never mind; I know this because I have heard you sing it and heard you laugh afterward. But you tear each other apart soon after singing the lovely song, and this makes me wonder what I would do if I had a sister from Palestine. You, Odessa, you have an adorable baby, but I have yet to hear you say something positive about him or his father. Yet you want Georgi to look after him without checking with him first. What do you want Georgi to do with a child whose father she hardly knows and whose mother treats her like a dumb-colored girl? I know because that's how everybody in this country treats me. If you want Georgi to look after your baby, you must stop your narcissistic idea that you are the center of the universe just because you are melanated and more African than the rest of us. Georgi came to my room in the middle of the night. She was saying things in her deep sleep, just like Lady Macbeth did in that drama by Shakespeare. I stood in front of her in terror, but even though I tried to wake her, she did not even see me. She slowly walked past and then back to her room. What you said that night in my shadowy bedroom, Georgi, made me realize the universe is more profound than we think. Still, I won't repeat the confusing words of remorse you uttered, mystery chants about the perfumes of Arabia. I can only repeat what my white professor said in class. If someone showers you with compliments, you must realize immediately that it is a test of your integrity. You, Odessa, have been flattering Georgi with empty words, trying to make her feel she is the most excellent nanny in South Africa. I heard when she explained what "quid pro quo' a favor for a favor, meant to her, because she did not fall for the bait. I know I'm going out on a limb here, being a non-melanated Palestinian from Little Harlem.

Rachab turns around and begins to retreat the way she came, with Daniel still strapped to her chest.

"What did Georgi say in her dream, Rachab?" Ignoring Odessa's prying, Rachab walks out and slams the door. The sisters stand frozen for a moment, feeling a wave of embarrassment wash over them. Odessa quietly limps outside and hides in the underbrush. Meanwhile, Georgi stretches out on the lawn and falls asleep. The cold evening breeze wakes her up, Odessa lying beside her.

"Are you awake, Odessa?"

"Barely. Are you?"

"It's chilly out here. Don't you think?"

"Not when I have my little sister next to me."

"Your little sister is a sucker for your sumptuous soup and dumplings. Mama Ellen taught you well."

"My little sister was too lazy to cook anything."

I haven't forgotten, Odessa. Last time, you promised to tell me about your Dozey company in good time. This is as good a time as any."

"I managed to wrest 'Uhuru' from the clutches of Mr April. Now I know the fascinating history of that stone. My company is standing, Georgi, and you will be proud of your big sister. My little sister is lazy when cooking and thrifty with the truth, making a fool out of her big sister. I know Uhuru was mined from the little quarry of my little sister's handbag."

"Okay, time for soup," Georgi jumps quickly to change the subject.

"Incurious people make poor inventors. But let me fill in the gaps. April deposited half a million American dollars into my account."

"Mattress money, I know..."

"So, my Dozey is flying high..."

Evading the subject, Georgi says, "Soup, please, Odessa."

"Give me two hours; soup and dumplings will come our way. But from now on, let's protect each other. We have purged our tainted past and have no more secrets between us; nothing should hold our relationship back. Be strong for me, Georgi, and I'll try to be strong for you. Let's help each other grow…"

"Yes, Odessa, this means keeping away from the interdependence of 'quid pro quo' because it results in an unending cycle of fear and suspicion. Mother Ellen showed us how to love and support each other unconditionally."

"We shall stay at Verligte with you as long as Pnina remains in your tummy. I want to read your poems and dive deep into your heart. I want to study your work on Sarah Baartman, 'The Hottentot Venus'."

"Barend is always in the mood for my poems. He often remarks, I am a caged bird being freed to fly alone. This has motivated me more than anything to do more. I know Barend's love for me is genuine because he quietly explores the depths of my heart as a woman. Ultimately, such tender affection can only be mutual. A man who scratches the surface, as most men do, is not truly invested. Any girl can tell. I want a man who will be eager to share my emotional connection to my leisure pursuits, a man who expresses it openly. However, I must apologize to Ryan for besmirching his kite-flying hobbies; certainly not the dumbest thing I've ever played a part in. He will always hold a place in my heart after my diamond kite soared to the heavens."

"My eyes are now wide open, Georgi. No one will hamper your deepest aspirations. As for me, not anymore. I'm sorry I pressured you and restricted your life's journey. A girl must be free to direct her future unhindered. The family's inadvertent collusion was a terrible weakness, my dear little Sister. Nothing should be held against a girl who directs her own path…"

"Yes, nothing should be held against a girl who changes her mind, not so, Odessa?"

"Only heaven and the lilies know."

"And only heaven knows the depth of a girl's heart, not so Odessa?"

The sisters hug, then step back from each other. Rachab suddenly appears, tears filling her eyes, her lips tightening oddly. Daniel remains pressed against her chest…

"What's wrong, Ray?" Odessa asks, trying to steady her trembling voice.

"There are five police near the rotunda."

"Do they say what they are looking for?" Odessa wheezes with fright.

"The female officer whispers to me… they arrested a paraplegic woman from Finetown, and they now want to speak with Georgi."

Rachab's scary words hang in the air for a bit.

"It's the vultures. The vultures have gathered…" sighs Georgi with a cryptic, wistful smile. She pecks Odessa and Rachab on the cheeks, then calmly walks away toward the rotunda. With tears streaming down her face, Odessa follows closely behind her little sister down the pale hallway.

~The End~